A CURIOUS DREAM

supports literacy
Sale of this
LIB
DI250475

Also by Kate Pullinger

The Mistress of Nothing
A Little Stranger
Weird Sister
My Life as a Girl in a Men's Prison
The Last Time I Saw Jane
Where Does Kissing End?
The Piano (*with Jane Campion*)
Tiny Lies

DIGITAL WORKS

Inanimate Alice
Branded
Flight Paths

Visit Kate Pullinger online at
katepullinger.com

A CURIOUS DREAM

Collected Works

Kate Pullinger

McArthur & Company
Toronto

First published in 2011 by
McArthur & Company
322 King Street West, Suite 402
Toronto, Ontario M5V 1J2
www.mcarthur-co.com

Copyright © 2011 Kate Pullinger

All rights reserved.
The use of any part of this publication reproduced, transmitted
in any form or by any means, electronic, mechanical, photocopying,
recording or otherwise stored in a retrieval system, without the express
written consent of the publisher, is an infringement of the copyright law.

LIBRARY AND ARCHIVES CANADA CATALOGUING IN PUBLICATION

Pullinger, Kate
A curious dream : the collected works of Kate Pullinger.

ISBN 978-1-77087-032-1

I. Title.

PR6066.U45A14 2011   823'.914   C2011-905954-1

 Canada Council   Conseil des Arts
for the Arts   du Canada

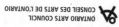 ONTARIO ARTS COUNCIL
CONSEIL DES ARTS DE L'ONTARIO

The publisher would like to acknowledge the financial support of the
Government of Canada through the Canada Book Fund and the Canada
Council for our publishing activities. The publisher further wishes to
acknowledge the financial support of the Ontario Arts Council and
the OMDC for our publishing program.

Cover design by Bill Douglas
Typesetting by Kendra Martin
Printed and bound in Canada by Solisco Printers

10 9 8 7 6 5 4 3 2 1

Contents

Stories from *My Life as a Girl in a Men's Prison*

Stories from *Tiny Lies*

Introduction

I'VE BEEN WRITING stories since I first learned to hold a pencil; I began publishing short stories in the mid-1980s, when I was in my early twenties. In 1986 my story 'The Micro-Political Party' won a magazine short story competition; around the same time I had stories published in two other magazines. This sudden flurry of publishing brought my work to the attention of an editor who wrote to me to ask if I would be interested in publishing a book of short stories. That letter arrived on Christmas Eve.

It is a cliché that in the life of a writer nothing can beat that first contract for that first book; like many cliché's, this is true, and those few months of seeing my work in print and being asked to write more were everything a young writer could ask for.

My first book, *Tiny Lies*, came out in 1988. Short stories were having a brief summer in the UK where I lived (and still live, despite the fact that summer did not last). My book did rather well; there were multiple reprints, it sold into a number of translations and territories, and was optioned for film. People invited me to fashionable parties. I was too young and too naïve to realise that this was unusual – a successful book of short stories by a total unknown – and thought that all first-time writers got to spend their days with make-up artists being photographed for glossy magazines.

My second book of stories, *My Life as a Girl in a Men's Prison*, was published in 1997. I had written a couple of novels and had my first child during that intervening decade. The stories from these two books differ in many significant ways – the writing in *My Life*, particularly in the two long stories, 'Small Town' and 'Irises', is much smoother, more polished and ambitious. I'd spent a year working as writer-in-residence in a men's prison, and the harshness of that environment influenced many of the stories in that book. But the stories in *Tiny Lies* have a kind of rackety charm; they are funny and sweary, agog at life and its possibilities. Reading them now, more than two decades on, is like entering a time-machine with a direct line to the 1980s – cassette tapes! records! newspapers! going around to someone's house because they didn't have a phone! These are a young woman's stories, full of the politics of squatting, and Marxist reading lists, and sex. Quite a lot of sex.

Many of the stories throughout this collection switch locations between Canada and London, England. The stories often use an odd and idiosyncratic mix of Canadian-English and English-English: there are at least two uses of the somewhat puzzling and very English term 'infant school' (which means the lower years of elementary school) and one instance of a Canadian character using the very English word 'fortnight'. But this dislocation – the young Canadian in London – was part of what fuelled my desire to write; indeed, it was part of what enabled me to write.

The newer stories, those that haven't been collected prior to now, were written slowly over the past decade and include two pieces of near-memoir, 'A Serious Arteriopath' and 'Our Mother's Hair', both written after my parents died. As well as these, there's a series of linked stories about a character called Richard. Most of these are comic tales, and comedy is a driving force throughout this collection.

Since 2001 I've also been writing digital fiction, short stories for digital platforms – a new kind of hybrid story that employs text, image, sound, music, animation, video and sometimes games. Although these stories can't be included in print editions of this collection – they're 'born-digital' and not reproducible in print – they can be read online. The digital fictions listed here are all collaborative works, which I've created working with web artists and developers. It's a joy for me to include these in this volume of collected works, as too often these twin aspects of my work as a fiction writer are viewed separately.

The short story is a difficult form and I won't claim to have mastered it. But putting together this collection has been a great opportunity for me to revisit these pieces and to think, yet again, about how much I love the short story, and what a great form it is for the twenty-first century.

Kate Pullinger

RICHARD STORIES

At Home with Jodie Foster and George Clooney

I WAS AT home with a sick child when the doorbell rang.

My boy was not the kind of kid who didn't want to go to school; he liked the business of rubbing shoulders with his pals and playing football on the tarmac during playtime; he liked the food the dinner ladies served at lunch. So when he said he didn't feel well enough to go to school, even though he had no temperature, no cough, no sign of any ill-health whatsoever, I had to agree. Ruthie was off at a conference, so it fell to me to stay home. Not such a bad fate really; my boy and I could watch children's telly and lie around, bored and moaning.

But, like I said, the doorbell rang, and when I went to peer out through the glass in the door (we used to have nets hanging there, but they were always filthy, and had a kind of prim but grim feeling to them that my wife and I both rebelled against – 'rebelled', I know, it is sad when your only form of rebellion left is re-moving the net curtains in order to make yourself feel less suburban, but there you go), I was faced with a small army of Mormons. Mormons are unmistakable, especially the men in their suits and short hair. British Mormons have always puzzled me, but lots of people want to be American these days. I, myself, would like to be George Clooney; we are the same age after all, as I remind Ruthie from time to time. Anyway, there they were, the Mormons, ten of them, all men. I don't know that I've ever had a Mormon lady come to my door. They're all at home, I guess, having their polygamous babies.

'We have come to share our news with you and your boy.' The tallest one spoke first.

'You have?' How did they know about the boy?

'Yes, Richard, we have heard you calling us, late at night, we have heard your voice in the blessed ether.'

'You have?' How did they know my name? And calling out, late at night, this was news to me. Or was it? Did I call out at night for a God I did not believe in? The idea felt uncomfortably familiar. What was Ruthie not telling me? There'd been stuff in the papers recently about a man who, late at night, gets up and cooks in his sleep. Maybe at night I become a Mormon preacher without realising it. But the sleep-cooker was actually a chef during the daytime whereas I, well, I'm practically a professional atheist. I work as an orderly in the secure psychiatric wing of a hospital. God abandoned those people a long time ago.

'You know,' I said – I wasn't going to be rude, how could you be rude to the most polite people in the world, no matter how deluded they might be? – 'the boy's not well. We're having a quiet day. You'll have to come back another time.'

'We don't have long here on this earth,' it was the

shortest one speaking this time, and he actually was an American. 'Things are happening.'

'Well, nothing is happening in my house. Thank you.'

I closed the door and wished I had some net curtains to peer through. They turned away, and as they turned, a couple of them gave each other stiff masculine hugs. They shook their heads and mumbled to each other, as though expressing the depth of their disappointment in me.

I went back into the sitting room where my boy was watching a bunch of kids sing karaoke. I lay down on the sofa, and my boy came over and got on top of me. I put my arms around him and we turned our full attention to the telly.

Late that evening, I was still lying on the sofa and watching TV when Ruthie got home. The boy had been tucked into his bed hours ago. I heard her key in the lock, then I heard her put her bag down. Without leaving the sofa, I could picture her every movement. She took off her coat and hung it in the closet. She took off her shoes and put on her slippers (we both wear slippers, a true sign of middle age; I know, it's not good, but who in their right mind can resist a nice comfy pair of slippers of an evening?) and then she called out 'Hello,' to me. She walked through to the kitchen without entering the sitting room, and I heard her put on the kettle.

'How did it go?' I said, raising my voice above the volume of the TV.

'It was fine,' she called back to me, her voice even louder as the kettle began to boil, 'they seemed happy enough with the presentation. Train was late though.'

'The boy's okay,' I shouted back at her. 'His cold is a little better.'

Ruthie came into the room now; she had made camomile tea for us both. I've never felt able to tell her that I can't stand camomile tea. It tastes like brewed compost heap (and yes, I have one of those as well, to add to my list of suburban accomplishments). 'What did you do all day?' she asked.

I shook my head. 'Nothing.' I didn't have the heart to tell her that we'd watched TV, and then we'd watched TV. 'Oh,' I said, 'some Mormons came by.'

She sat down and put her feet up on the pouf. Here's a sad but true fact: I gave her that pouf for her birthday. She's the same age as Jodie Foster. 'Did you tell them to go to Hell?' she asked.

'Yes.' I looked at my wife. She works hard; she's the reason we can afford slippers and poufs and compost heaps. 'Do I turn into a Mormon preacher late at night?'

She laughed. 'Not as far as I'm aware of, honey.'

We drank our tea and watched yet more telly. Then we went to bed, happy.

In Lieu of Parenting

MY THERAPIST WAS following me.

I'd been seeing her for so long I'd almost forgotten I was seeing a therapist. I thought of her as part of my routine, like taking a bath or going to the barber. I'm not actually interested in therapy; I don't have much faith in it. But my father pays for me to go in lieu of parenting. So I go. I don't say much – what is there to say after all these years? She knows almost everything there is to know about my childhood and, frankly, my childhood is not that interesting: I was born, I grew, my parents made me miserable. After that I left home, met my wife, had my son, and discovered how to be happy. But still, I went along and I sat on her couch. It felt like too much of a cliché to lie down, so I remained upright. I spent quite a lot of the time – time I imagine she thought I was mulling over what to say next – trying to figure out how to get the money my father paid her for myself, but as he sent a monthly cheque, and I didn't even know what her hourly rate was, I didn't make much headway.

At the time, my therapist was undergoing some kind of training. She told me about it – now that was a surprise, my therapist telling *me* things. I'd never really got used to it, even though it happened frequently. Although I wasn't interested in therapy, nor in therapists, I'd watched enough TV to have an idea of what it should be like and I had always imagined she would remain largely silent, just asking the odd question to get me started on the fascinating story of my own life (or not, but you see what I mean) or making a pithy but thought-provoking comment once every couple of years. But, in fact, she was talkative. Some days I'd pretend that I was the therapist and she was my patient and while she talked, I'd nod sagely. Other days I'd pretend that I was Tony Soprano and she was Dr Amalfi but I couldn't dwell on that particular scenario for too long because, truth be told, like Tony Soprano, I fancy Dr Amalfi. And from time to time I'd imagine that I was John Cusack in *Grosse Point Blank*, a hit man wracked with neurosis, and that my therapist was, in fact, very very frightened of me. But mostly I just sat there with a kind of stupid blank look on my face and we alternated between silence and the therapist telling me stories about her latest bout of training.

She was always training! It was as though herself-as-therapist was in a state of continual evolution, continual revolution; she was always learning new things. I suppose if I'd been interested in therapy, my own or anyone else's for that matter, this could have been fascinating. But, I'm sad to admit, I did not pay much attention to the things my therapist had to say to me.

But a few things filtered through anyway. For example, I knew that recently she'd been studying someone called Hillman or Hillsman and that Hillman had some kind of theory of psychotherapy that involved getting to know the patient beyond the confines of the therapy room, moving with the patient out in the world once the session had finished, getting on the tube train with them. I remember thinking at the time that this bit, the getting-on-the-tube-train-with-your-patient bit, must have been a metaphor for a particularly patient-centred approach to therapy, but it seems not, or at least not as far as my therapist was concerned; this was something to interpret literally. I don't know. All I do know for sure is that my therapist started following me.

The first time it happened I thought it was a co-incidence. I'd never run into my therapist in London before, but in a way that wasn't surprising; I don't live anywhere near her practice and London is a very big city. I was in the West End, doing a bit of shopping in John Lewis. I like to look in on the kitchen department from time to time; I'm interested in coffee grinders and colanders and Le Creuset. These are the things that make me feel real in life, they make me feel I can say, look, here I am, I am a grown-up person, I'm buying tongs, I'm a married man with a kitchen and a wife and a child.

I caught sight of her across the shop floor. She was looking straight at me. She blanched – I saw her blanche, it was unmistakable, I probably blanched right back at her – and then she ducked down behind the row of KitchenAid blenders, one of which I would be able to afford if I could ever figure out how to get my hands on the money my father forked out every week for my therapy. I wasn't surprised that she didn't want me to see her, so I paid for the toaster prongs and went on my merry way.

During the next session I thought about asking her about our chance meeting – you could hardly call our chance passing a meeting – but I didn't want to embarrass her, and I didn't want to remind her that we'd breached the etiquette of the therapy session in this tiny but potentially damaging way. Imagine if I had been interested in therapy; imagine if I'd been experiencing a bit of transference or something like that, that well-documented (in the movies and on TV at least) phenomenon when the patient falls a little bit in love with the therapist. Or maybe a lot in love. Obsessed. Wants to actually possess the therapist, have sex with the therapist, spend the rest of his or her life with the therapist. This happens, apparently. Not to me, of course, as I wasn't interested in therapy and, consequently, wasn't interested in my therapist either. So I didn't say anything.

But then it happened again. On Monday of the following week I was in HMV browsing the CD racks, thinking about how in another minute or two CDS might become entirely obsolete, and wondering if anyone would mourn the passing of the CD in the way that many people mourned, and continue to mourn, the passing of the vinyl LP. I was in Americana and there she was, over in R&B. She was standing there, and she was staring at me. I saw her, she saw me see her, she blanched, as usual, and then, believe it or not, she ducked down behind the row of CD racks. This time I couldn't help myself and I went after her, but she was gone. She was nowhere to be seen. She must have remained bent over double and walked as quickly as possible straight out the front doors of HMV.

Two days later, in the ladies' scarf department on the ground floor of Liberty, where I was thinking about a birthday present for my wife, there she was. My therapist. Staring at me.

I go into the West End all the time. I pass through on the way home from work and I often get off the bus and go for a wander in the shops, though I hardly ever buy anything; even if I linger over the saucepans I can still get home in time to be there when my boy gets back from school. I have no idea what draws me there, it's not as though the West End of London is all that wonderful – it's very crowded for one thing, and the shops are mainly enormous versions of the same shops you find in every other high street – but there is something about it that I like, something that comforts me. It's a widely known fact that the centre of London has more CCTV cameras than anywhere else on earth, that as you move from shop to shop you are under surveillance every step of the way. I've heard it said that the only place you aren't filmed is in the John Lewis toilets.

But now, every time I got off the bus, no matter where I went, no matter how zigzaggy or nonsensical a route I took to get there – the chemist, the sock department of a big department store, the expensive shops off in the side streets – my therapist would somehow find me. Two, maybe three times, each week. I kept going to see her and, because I hadn't mentioned it the first time, it felt silly to mention it the second time, and then it would have seemed odd to mention it when it had happened three times and was clearly not some kind of weird and wonderful coincidence, fate throwing me and my therapist together with unnerving determination. I sat opposite my therapist, and I looked around the cosy room with its proliferation of cushions and books and lamps that threw out a warm orange light, and I looked at her – neither of us were talking at that point, she was writing in her notebook – and I suddenly realised that my therapist was stalking me.

What could I do? I couldn't stop going to see her, that was out of the question. Firstly, if I stopped going to see her, I'd never have the chance to figure out how to get the money my father paid her every month diverted into my own pocket. Secondly, I didn't want to tell my father that I'd stopped seeing the therapist, mainly because that would mean I'd actually have to ring him up and speak to him, something we'd both been avoiding for a very long time indeed. Thirdly, I'd no longer be pretending that my therapist wasn't following me, so she'd definitely know that I knew she was following me, and God knows what she'd do then – she'd probably have to kill me.

But, I reasoned as I sat there opposite my therapist who had started to follow me several weeks previously, if she tracked me down in the West End and tried to kill me, at least it would be on CCTV. There'd be plenty of witnesses because it's always so crowded and that would make it easy for the police to track down the tape that contained footage of the murder – blurry, pixellated, but sufficiently detailed to be used in court. From that day onward I made sure never to go to the loo on my way home, never to end up alone in the men's toilets in John Lewis. Which meant that most nights I walked in the front door of the house bursting for a wee.

I was going to have to tell my wife what was happening.

My wife and I are very happily married. We've been married for a long time and we live together in a state of permanent tranquillity. She's the main breadwinner, and I'm the main parent, and these roles suit us both perfectly. That's not to say we haven't had our ups and downs, because we have. There was that problem I had with the Mormons the year before. She knew all about that. They kept coming to my door and trying to make me their leader. They said I was calling to them through the ether. Each time they knocked I opened the door and remained polite, as did they. After a few months of unflagging politeness, they stopped coming. I knew they were disappointed in me – a leader refusing to lead – but there was nothing I could do about it; I'm an atheist, for heaven's sake. I was relieved when they stopped, but, to tell the truth, I also missed them a little. My wife was understanding throughout the whole episode – though, of course, she was never home when the Mormons came by – and she said she hoped I would talk about it with my therapist. I didn't, of course, but I didn't tell my wife that either; it is these small untruths that perpetuate tranquillity.

But I felt compelled to tell her that my therapist was following me. We were sitting together, watching the telly.

'She's what?'

'I know it sounds strange, but a couple of times a week . . .'

She cut me off. 'How many times exactly?'

'Well,' I said, reluctant to admit it, 'I've spotted her

a dozen times now, spread over the past five or six weeks.'

'A dozen times?!'

'I know. Weird, isn't it?'

'Are you sure it's her?'

I crossed my arms and gave my wife a look. The boy was in bed, fast asleep; he was very good at falling asleep, it was one of the many things I admired about him and the way he lived his life.

My wife continued to speak. 'I don't know what to say.'

'She must be in love with me, don't you think?' My tone was conspiratorial; I thought my wife and I could have a little laugh about this strange situation.

'In love with you?'

'Reverse transference, or something.'

My wife did laugh then. 'You should report her.'

'To whom?'

'I don't know.'

We both fell silent, contemplating.

'I'm thinking about stopping,' I said.

'Stopping what?'

'Going to see her.'

'Really?'

'It seems like madness to continue – I mean, clearly she's the one with the problem, not me.'

'I don't know, honey.'

'What?'

'Maybe you need that therapy.'

I know that my wife doesn't believe that my therapist is following me. She didn't really believe that the Mormons were trying to make me their leader either.

But she humours me, which is sweet of her; it is what is required for perpetual tranquillity.

We kept the boy out of all of this, of course. He's just a boy, interested in football and collecting incredibly expensive trading cards and negotiating to be allowed to watch the same things his friends are allowed to watch on telly. He's not interested in therapy or my therapist; in fact, it's safe to say he's even less interested in my therapist than I am. During the day he goes to school and at night he sleeps soundly. My wife and I finished talking about it and went back to watching telly.

And then it stopped. As suddenly as she began, my therapist stopped following me. Several days went by before I realised I hadn't seen her in any of the shops for a while, then a whole week passed. I waited another week before I risked saying anything to her and then, of course, I didn't want to say anything too direct or incriminating. So what I said was this:

'I'm thinking about getting in touch with my father.'

Her response was gratifying: her eyes went very wide with surprise and amazement, although, for once, she didn't actually say anything.

'I'm thinking about giving him a ring.'

Heaven Knows I'm Miserable Now

I DIDN'T MEAN to become a laughingstock. I made a woman I work with a virtual birthday card, nothing more than that. Not because I fancy her or anything, I'm a happily married man! Though I do fancy her, to tell you the truth. It's a work-thing, you know how it goes, she is kind and clever and when I'm with her I'm funnier and sharper and a little bit more alive. And it was a simple enough gesture, really – give your colleague at work a birthday card, nothing sinister about that. But things got out of hand. Things always seem to get out of hand. 'A laughingstock' – what in God's name does that mean? I should know, because it's what I became.

In my job I don't spend that much time on the computer but I do use it for work-related e-mail, time-keeping, logging complaints, that kind of thing. And Internet videos do the rounds, like in any office – that band dancing on the treadmills, that baby whose fart sends a mushroom cloud of talcum powder up into the air. That was where I got the idea. I had all the right technology at home; I kept our home computer up to date with all the latest bits of software and hardware because I wanted my boy to be an active user of technology, it might help him out when it comes time – perish the thought – for him to find his own way in the world. I'd never been that big of a Smiths fan – my father wouldn't let me listen to pop music when I was a kid, so my passion for the stuff came along a while after the Smiths had departed the scene, if a band like that can ever be said to have done such a thing. But there was one song I'd always liked, and I thought it would be funny to make a video of myself lip-synching to it.

For some unknown reason – unknown to me at any rate – I decided it would be a good idea to perform the song naked. I wore a skinny necktie and a pork pie hat that I had purchased especially for the video on one of my trips through the West End of London. I positioned the camera in a place where I was sure I'd only be filmed from the waist up and I planned to jump into the air a couple of times, rock-star fashion of course, as I thought that might make the video that little bit more amusing.

Downloading the track and setting everything up took longer than I expected – I wanted to be done before my boy got home from school – so when it came time to record my performance there was only long enough for one take. So I did it, and I uploaded it, and I wrote a short and, I thought, carefree and light-hearted birthday greeting e-mail to my work colleague, containing the link to her birthday treat. I pressed 'Send' and thought nothing more of it. Finished buttoning my shirt as the boy came through the front door.

That night my boy woke up with some kind of stomach bug; he came into our bedroom to tell us he was going to throw up and then did throw up, right there in the middle of the carpet. He continued to be sick for a couple of hours and I sat with him in his room and stroked his forehead until he finally went back to sleep. I called in sick the next day so that I could stay home with him; this was the arrangement my wife and I had made years before as her job is both much more lucrative and substantially more important and interesting than mine. I didn't mind, staying home with the boy was kind of like a minibreak for me.

I work in the secure psychiatric unit of a large teaching hospital here in London; I work part-time, mornings only. My job title includes the word 'administrator' but really I'm a kind of glorified orderly. I have had a certain amount of trouble in my own life with mental health, mostly when I was a teenager, and mostly because of my father, but I won't get into that now; the people in that ward put paid to any real doubts I've ever had about my own sanity. Most of them are stark raving crazy. On my first day when I went into the men's toilet the sink was missing; the night before one of the patients had accidentally torn it from the wall when he used it as a launchpad in an attempt at suicide-by-hanging; he'd almost drowned instead when his not inconsiderable weight brought down the sink and flooded the bathroom.

This craziness, and the trauma and drugs that accompany its treatment, means that here in the hospital among the staff there is a hardy camaraderie which translates into a lot of joking and a certain amount of drink-fuelled highjinks in the pub after work, at least so I am told; I tend not to socialise that much, actually not at all, with my colleagues, mainly because of my duties at home with the boy. But we get on famously, or so I thought. My favourite colleague was always very kind to me, sweet and good-natured, even though she was a Consultant and I was an orderly.

My boy took two days to recover from his night of throwing up, and then it was the weekend, and I had enough seniority by this stage to not have to work on weekends, which was just as well as my wife often had to work right through both days. So by the time I went back to work on Monday I'd forgotten all about my light-hearted and carefree birthday e-mail.

I said hello to the man who does the nightshift; ordinarily he is very cordial and he almost always asks after my wife and my child. But this time he got straight to the point: 'You're lucky she's not going to sue, mate!'

'Who?' There was no one called Sue in our unit.

'Sue you, of course, you great naked wally. Litigation. Whatever possessed you?'

Of course I remembered the video then. But how did the nightshift man know about it? It was between me and my colleague.

'The object of your affection thought it was hilarious – you are lucky she has a good sense of humour mate. She took it upon herself to spread the news. It's not the song I would have chosen, of course.'

'Nor I,' said one of the junior doctors, who came into the office then – clearly they'd been discussing it endlessly. 'But it does have a sort of poignancy to it, I'll admit.' Suddenly the room was full of other people, more of my work colleagues, laughing and talking among themselves, as if they were the audience and I was up on the stage and they were waiting for me to start my performance.

I cleared my throat, and the crowd fell silent. 'Where is she?' I asked.

'You're lucky, she's got the day off,' someone said.

'Today's her actual birthday, you pillock, not last week,' added another voice.

And then they revealed the full truth to me: I had become an overnight Internet phenomenon. My favourite colleague had forwarded my video to her colleague, who had forwarded it to the whole hospital. The NHS employs people from all over the world these days and they all forwarded my video to their friends and family who, in turn, had forwarded it to everyone they knew. My birthday greeting video had gone around the globe and back several times. Turned out the entire world, at least, millions of people with access to the Internet, was laughing at me.

What could I do? I couldn't quit my job; I love my job and it suits me and my life perfectly. I could apologise, I would apologise, but I'd probably have to keep apologising for a very long time, in fact, forever. I could front it out and claim the video had nothing to do with me, but then, perhaps, I'd look even more foolish. I could say I'd actually meant to send it to my wife, but that would remind everyone that I have a wife, and I wouldn't want anyone to have the bright idea of forwarding the video to her as well as the rest of the world. Assuming, of course, that she hadn't already seen it. Assuming that she hadn't already been forwarded my famous naked lip-synching video.

I could not think of anything to say. Luckily for me, one of the ward alarms went off, and everyone rushed away. I sat at my desk and wondered if it was possible to die from humiliation.

But no, I didn't die. I got on with the day and was almost offended to discover that my video was, in fact, pretty much old news as far as my colleagues were concerned. They were bored by it already.

After lunch I made my way home, as always, on the bus. I walked over to my boy's school in order to pick him up – these days he usually makes his way home by himself, but I wanted to see him, wanted to be distracted by him. Once we got home we played football on the PlayStation together for about twice as long as he was allowed ordinarily. Then I cooked a big tea, and ate with him, then ate again once my wife got home at nine. I had a bath and went to bed, but none of this was of much use to me.

The next day I was working at my desk when the Consultant, the birthday girl herself, came into the office. I kept typing, although what I wrote was complete monkey. I felt her stop and I could tell she was looking at me, but I could not look at her, could not take my eyes away from the computer screen. After a few very long minutes, she said, 'Hi.'

I stopped typing. It took all of the fortitude I possessed not to lower my head onto the keyboard and sob. 'Hi,' I replied. I forced myself to look at her.

She was smiling. She looked genuinely friendly.

'You don't have to be mad to work here,' I said, after a pause, and she finished the ward motto for me:

'You have to be fucking crazy.' Then she put her hand on my shoulder and gave it a squeeze. 'It's a good song,' she said.

'It is,' I replied, 'it is indeed.'

The Dig

WE LIVE IN A little house, two up, two down, no more, no less. Out back we have a tiny patch of garden where I grow stones, tin cans, broken bits of pottery and wire. Over the years I've worked hard to improve it, but the same crops come through every spring. The rain washes away most of what I've planted, and the squirrels steal the rest. We are left with a mosaic of rubbish.

When the boy was a toddler he was forever falling and gashing himself on things rusty and lethal; it got so bad he used to cry when I suggested he go outside. There is a big park nearby so we used to go there most days, before he gave up playing with his friends for real in favour of hanging out with his friends online. Now I go to the park on my own to walk Alfie, our imaginary dog. I find the nonexistent dog a useful device in my quest to engage strangers in conversation. Dog walkers always respond well when I ask them if they've seen my dog, though if the ensuing conversation goes on for too long I can tell they begin to wonder why I'm not more concerned. These days Alfie is a dachshund; given my height, most people find the idea of me and my dachshund amusing.

This past weekend, Ruth was home from work; she and the boy were on their laptops in front of the TV. Outside the French doors which we never open – did I mention the garden smells as well? swampy and sulphuric with a hint of fibreglass – I noticed yet another piece of wire sticking up out of the dirt, ready to impale the next unsuspecting passer-by.

I got out my shovel and began to dig.

I dug hard, excavating broken bricks and glass and ceramic. Every six inches or so I would pause, take a drink from the hosepipe, and then attempt to yank the wire free. But it did not budge.

I kept at it. An hour passed. Two hours. The hole was now at least three feet deep. I lowered myself into it, like a middle-aged urban miner. I wrapped an old towel that I'd just recently dug up around the wire. I pulled with all my might. The boy came out through the French doors, so I recruited him. He climbed down and gripped the wire close to where it emerged from the ground. I coiled the end of it around my hands and counted out loud, 1-2-3.

There was a very loud bang and a blue flash of light as the wire finally came away; the boy and I fell backward in a heap. All the dogs in the neighbourhood began barking, including Alfie. Once they calmed down there was a weird silence.

Ruth came outside. 'The power's gone out in the whole street,' she said.

I hid the wire behind my back. 'Oh,' I replied. 'That's strange.'

Public Image

MY WIFE RUTHIE and I have become a double-act. We have a routine. When we are with other people we have a stock of stories that we tell. We even have our own catchphrases.

Last Friday we were at friends for dinner. Jenny and Anwar have twin girls around the same age as our boy; the kids were off in another room, whacking each other over the head with the controls for the game console. There was another couple there as well, people we had never met before; they'd left their kids at home with a babysitter. The evening progressed, we had a few drinks and ate a bit, though not a lot; Anwar is one of those men who fancies himself a great cook but, in fact, everything he makes is either undercooked or just plain weird-tasting. He thinks not using salt means he's into healthy eating; he won't even put salt on the table. It tries my patience. Anyway, we had a few more drinks and got onto the subject of another friend of ours, Dave, a fellow everyone seems to think is an International Man of Mystery because he has a lot of money.

'He seems like a nice guy,' said Jenny.

'Oh he's very nice,' said Ruth, 'he is very sweet.'

'Except when he's drunk,' I added.

'Oh yeah,' said Ruth, 'then he turns into the *Daily Mail*.'

Ba-da-boom. Everyone laughed.

The truth was we'd used this line before when we'd been asked about Dave. I can't remember which of us said it first, but from then on it became part of our routine. Whenever Dave came up in conversation, which was often – people who are not rich are always curious about people who are – we'd trot that line out, reliably. Then we'd embark on our anecdote about the time Dave and Ruth had a stand-up row over democracy. Tonight was no different than any other night; Ruthie told the story while I sat back and chuckled encouragingly.

Ruth said, '"People," Dave announced, "are too stupid for democracy."'

That night, in the restaurant with Dave, Ruth and I had looked at each other across the table, amazed. Dave had made the transition from Mild-Mannered Liberal to Raging Rightwing Demagogue before our very eyes, without going into the phone booth to get into his costume first. 'What do you mean?' Ruth asked.

At the time I shook my head at her but she ignored me.

'"People don't put any thought into how they vote," Dave said. "They just pick whoever they like the look of. These days they pick whoever is more famous, whoever has the best story. We should leave voting to an educated elite."'

And so our anecdote continued. Our friends and acquaintances were always interested in this routine. I guess that's how it goes when you develop a double-act; you figure out what material works, and what doesn't. You occasionally try something brand-new, but mostly you stick to the tried and tested. The story about the row with Dave would often lead to another row with whomever we told it to; it seems that there's a lot of people who are transformed from Mild-Mannered Liberal to Raging Rightwing Demagogue once they've had a bit too much to drink.

Friday night was no different. This time Jenny took exception to my wife's ironic tone. Her voice was shrill. 'Dave's got a point, don't you think, Ruthie?'

'Ah,' said Ruth, 'no.'

'No?'

'No,' she replied.

I attempted to intervene. 'Ladies,' I said, but that was a mistake; calling certain women 'Ladies' winds them up more than calling certain men 'Gents' ever could.

'Shut up Dick,' said Jenny.

This came as a shock. Jenny had never told me to shut up before. I don't think I'd ever heard her tell anyone to shut up, no matter how much she had had to drink. And – this was the bigger shock, in fact – she had called me 'Dick.'

My father named me Richard; it's a name that is easy to dislike. It wasn't his name, nor his father's – I don't know why he gave it to me. The shortened forms of Richard are all awful: Rich, Rick, Richie, and the execrable, excruciating, gender-specific, Dick. For a while at university I tried to get my friends to call me Chard – I thought it sounded cool, like charred or maybe even Che – but that didn't go too well; Chard rapidly became Pilchard. That got shortened to Pil, which was okay because at the time we were all listening to records made by PiL, or Public Image Ltd, the band Johnny Rotten tried to make work after the Sex Pistols. But, like the band, the name Pil didn't stick. They only called me that when they were thinking about it and my friends and I weren't all that big on thinking, despite the fact that we were at university. My name is Richard; there is no escape.

I had to say something to Jenny. I had to retaliate. Now, I'm not a retaliating kind of guy. If you insult me, chances are I'll laugh, then go away to seethe in private. But Jenny couldn't tell me to shut up *and* call me Dick *and* get away with it. I sat back and listened to the ongoing conversation which had, thankfully, moved on from who should be allowed to vote. I felt tired; I yawned and stretched and closed my eyes for a moment, to gather strength. But when I opened my eyes and looked around the table once again, I realised I despised my friends. There's nothing like a dinner party to make you despise your friends. I resolved that Ruth and I would stop sharing our double-act anecdote about Dave.

Ruth doesn't like her name either, though I am fond of it. 'Ruth,' she barks, 'Ruth. It's so plain. It's so bibley.' In our house, 'bibley' is not a good thing. I escaped from my father because he's a monster; Ruth escaped from hers because he was way too bibley. 'He loved the Good Book so much,' she'd say, 'he'd use it as a weapon.' And she meant this literally – her dad used to hit her with the family bible whenever he felt she had transgressed the creed. As she got older, naturally, this became more frequent. She used to listen to PiL as well and for her the anger in those records was real, as though that band had a hotline to her mashed-up and outraged soul.

When our boy was born we gave him the perfect name. It suits him so well just saying it makes me feel happy.

I had stopped paying attention to the dinner party and the conversation; why are conversations at dinner parties always so stupid? The mix of friends and once-met acquaintances is lethal; it means you can never really talk about anything. You end up discussing celebrities.

I had another drink. Jenny's husband Anwar had got out the thirty-year-old sherry; it was like alcoholic crème caramel, smooth and burnt-tasting. You were only supposed to have one small glass of it, but I poured myself another when no one was looking; they were too busy discussing Victoria Beckham. I interrupted, 'I liked PiL,' I said. 'They were the musical equivalent to a teenager complaining about his parents – loud, irritable, ominous, and profoundly whiney.' I could hear the song in my head. 'Two sides to every story,' I quoted, looking at Jenny, 'somebody had to stop me.'

Everyone turned toward me. Ruthie gave me a look so mixed up with alarm and pleasure that I almost laughed out loud. She said, 'I remember all the words.' And it's true, Ruthie does remember all the words to all the songs; it's an alternately annoying and reassuring character trait. We could make this part of our double-act, in fact, Ruthie and her uncanny memory for lyrics.

She began to sing the song. Ruthie is a good mimic; she caught the snide nasal tone of the song perfectly. 'I'm not the same as when I began. I will not be treated as property.'

I smiled at my wife. I think Johnny Rotten meant those words for Malcolm McLaren but that didn't matter; like with all the best songs, the words are really meant for Ruthie and me. We rose from the dinner table at the same time, said our good-byes, and collected the boy from where he was watching age-inappropriate DVDs with the twins.

In the car, which Ruthie drove because I'd had too much to drink, I said, 'Being middle-aged isn't all it's made out to be.'

Ruthie laughed.

'Let's give dinner parties a rest for a while,' I continued.

My wife nodded. 'Okay.'

A Curious Dream

I DON'T DREAM much, or if I do, my dreams aren't sticky. Ruth dreams all the time, as does the boy; in fact, he talks in his sleep, he's always shouting at someone or something. I rush in to see his room, but by the time I get there he's back asleep, his breath soft and even. I had a nightmare once when I was kid, about being followed around by another boy, a wretch of a child dressed in rags, who kept grabbing at me; his teeth fell out one at a time whenever he tried to speak to me. I managed to escape his grasp, over and over again. But that's about it. No more dreams. Except last night.

The people at work are all horrible dreamers; for some of them, dreams are more dominant than everyday life. This is not something to be envied. I don't do the nightshift very often anymore, but when I do I'm grateful that I don't dream. The ward is not peaceful after dark; the night air is Largactil-heavy, punctured by the helpless yelping and yelling of our sleepers. Ruth doesn't believe me when I tell her, but during bad weather – wind or heavy rain – the patients howl and moan and weep. When the morning comes there's no point in asking anyone how they slept: you can see it on their faces.

But last night I had a curious dream, and when I woke up this morning I felt compelled to ring my father.

It's been about a year since we last spoke. I thought that cutting off all contact would mean that we didn't have to have anything to do with each other anymore, end of story, but that turned out not to be the case. If anything, we have even more to do with each other, in that I find myself dwelling on the circumstances of our estrangement much more than before, back in the good old days when we simply didn't see eye-to-eye, or didn't have much in common. Now that we're *estranged* it seems like a big honking deal, like being divorced instead of unhappily married like everyone else.

People I know tend not to ask about him, they are used to me not having parents around. I'm never the one who says 'Oh we're going to my dad's for lunch,' in *that* tone of voice, the dutiful, bored, but it's wonderful really, I'm such a good son, tone of voice. Ruth and I don't talk about the situation much, there's no point. It's all been said before.

So when I woke up wanting to call him, I didn't. I held back. I waited to see if the feeling would wear off. I waited in the hope that the feeling would wear off. Ruth rushed out the door to work and the boy and I went through our routines: 'Sandwich or soup for lunch?' 'Sandwich.' 'Ham or cheese?' 'Cheese.' 'Pick up your towel.' 'Okay.' After he left for school, I powered around the house for a while, doing my facsimile of a housewife (actually, I'm a damn good housewife, but don't tell anybody. Who am I kidding? Everybody knows. All the bleeding mums at the boy's fricking school want to marry me.) I walked to the corner shop to pick up a loaf of bread and a newspaper. I turned on the computer and thought about checking out my social media accounts for new activity and messages. But instead, I turned off the computer and turned on the TV.

The telephone is beside the TV. It's one of those wireless handsets that sit up on its base waiting to be grabbed, like an erection in happier times. I realised after a little while that I was not looking at the television but was staring at the phone instead. If I phoned him, what would I say?

MY MOTHER DIED when I was ten and I was not misguidedly shielded from her death like children in books and movies. I saw her body laid out on the sofa before they took her away; I went to her funeral and stood resolutely beside my father. In the months after her death I'd forget sometimes that she was gone and call for her or, worse, call my father 'Mummy' by mistake. He was determined to maintain his rationalist, pragmatic approach and told me in a calm voice that she was dead, she was gone, she was not coming back, that was it, it was final, there was no such thing as an afterlife. He was not cut out for single parenthood – my mother had been an excellent housewife, maybe that's where I get it from – so our dinnertime discussions moved from football to potential boarding schools and how wouldn't it be great if I could live somewhere surrounded by friends with endless playing fields and tuck shops and boys-only highjinks. This was before Harry Potter regenerated the idea of the boarding school; I was much more interested in climbing into my wardrobe and finding a whole new world when I climbed out the other side. A whole new world where my mother was waiting for me.

But boarding school turned out to be, for my father, the more realistic option, so off I went, eleven years old, with my enormous suitcase and the cricket bat given to me by my mother's father the last time I ever saw him, before she died.

I DON'T LIKE talking about this stuff, I don't like thinking about it, and I keep the details of my past close to my chest. I will admit to channelling my mother a bit when I power through the housework, though that's a little dangerous as I don't think being a housewife made her happy.

I have other ways of keeping in touch with my mum. I set up a Facebook account for her that I maintain in a way that I imagine she would if she were alive. She died before the Internet had been invented, or at least made available to people like me, but I think she would have liked it. She posts about her interests – cooking, reading, her grandchild, the current political situation – and she's fond of posting old photos of herself. She has friends, amazingly, I have no idea who any of these people are, but it is extraordinary how people like to connect online. I don't think that any of them suspect that their 'friend' is a dead person. She's got to know some of them quite well, though of course she politely turns down all social invitations.

She has a Twitter account as well – if she was alive now she'd be in her late sixties, a silver surfer, an early adopter, an avid user. She's funny on Twitter, adept with the sharp one-liner, so she has lots of followers, and her tweets get re-tweeted from time to time. Turns out there's a whole world of dead people who tweet, though of course most of them are dead celebrities. When I talk to people who tweet for real – there's a consultant at the hospital who fancies himself a bit of an online medical guru – it's apparent that they are even less likely to know the people who follow them on Twitter than they are on Facebook, so it's a perfect environment for my mother.

My father, and Ruth and the boy, don't know about any of this, of course. My father wouldn't understand, in fact he'd probably try to sue me for infringing my mother's privacy – can you infringe the privacy of a dead person? If you can, I guess I'm guilty of that, among other things. Ruth would understand, but it would make her uncomfortable, it would be one' of the many things that causes her to give me one of her strained smiles. The boy would think it was funny; he'd high-five me and slap me on the back, although he might be a little less amused if he knew that his dead grandmother is one of his 561 friends on Facebook.

THE URGE TO phone my father was not receding; if anything, as I sat there staring at the phone, it was getting stronger. I stood up and grabbed the handset. Then I realised I couldn't remember his phone number so I put the phone back down and scrabbled around in the desk looking for my old address book. Once I'd found it I turned off the TV and sat in silence for a while, staring at the handset, thinking about what I would say.

MY CURIOUS DREAM from the night before went like this: my parents were standing together in the sitting room of our old house. I was looking up at them, as though I was a small child once again. We were laughing and smiling and the room was full of sunlight. My father reached out and placed his hand on my head and his touch was warm and reassuring. He drew me close, and I put my arms around both of them, and they smelled of themselves, and I knew that they loved me.

I PICKED UP the phone and dialled my father's number.

He answered. 'Hello.' He cleared his throat which sounded scratchy.

I paused. I put on my best jaunty voice. 'Hello,' I said. 'This is a free phone call. Do you have debts? The government has sponsored—'

He put the phone down.

He was definitely still alive.

Memoir Stories

A Serious Arteriopath

AS I STOOD in my kitchen in my pyjamas, life swirled around me; my children, my husband, and our two houseguests were getting ready for school, getting ready for work, getting ready to leave. I was tired, not quite awake and I had a headache; the new Dean at the university where I worked part-time had taken a decision to shut down the successful masters programme I had spent the previous three years building and developing; my eleven-year-old son, a well-behaved and cautious boy, was in trouble at school for getting in a fistfight. My houseguests were two of my oldest and closest friends, one from Vancouver and the other from Toronto; they were both leaving that morning to go home.

My eight-year-old daughter said, 'Mummy?' She sounded annoyed. I turned to look at her; she was standing right beside me and I had not seen her. Puzzled, I looked away. Then I looked back. There was a gap in my peripheral vision – an entire region on my right side was missing. I turned my head to look at her straight on, and she appeared; I looked to one side of where she was standing and she disappeared. I held up my right hand like a pupil in class and moved it up and down, forwards and back, but I could not see it.

* * *

WHEN YOU FALL in love, you feel it in your whole being, but it is your heart that swells, that beats too fast, that makes you feel light-headed and a little faint. I fell in love with my husband at the opera when he leaned close and touched my arm lightly. My heart thumped so loudly I could no longer hear the music.

* * *

OUTPATIENT DEPARTMENT – GERIATRIC SERVICES
March 7, 2001

REASON FOR REFERRAL
Assessment of increasing functional incapacity due to multifactorial problems.

HISTORY OF PRESENT ILLNESS
This fine gentleman was accompanied by his daughter who says that he is at Saanich Peninsula Hospital for respite right now. His primary caregiver, i.e., his wife of 52 years, has gone on a vacation. She is feeling really over-burdened by his dependency which is functional and psychological. This man has poor visuospatial capacity resulting in numerous falls and increasing needs for personal care. This seems to have come on in a progressive way over the last ten years. The daughter is unable to identify any one particular time when he may have had stroke disease though he is a serious arteriopath. She has wondered about a series of strokes because of his increasing word-finding difficulty, short memory loss, urinary dysfunction and swallowing disorder. He has had

previous urinary problems with bladder neck contracture in 1992 and he is now voiding up to 20 times at night and has been recently put on a trial of antibiotics for a recurrent UTI. There has been the provisional home support working overnight every other night at the house which is helping to some degree but the burden is really growing and the question is whether there is any remediable dimension to unburden caregivers and make this fellow's quality of life a bit better.

* * *

I STOOD THERE moving my hand back and forth, in and out of the gap in my peripheral vision, with my daughter getting more and more annoyed with me as I continued to ignore her question. I turned my attention to breakfast and packed lunches for school and other such things, but I kept returning to this movement, moving my right hand up and down like a malfunctioning robot, until my husband asked me what I was doing. I kept my voice low so that the kids wouldn't hear – what could this gap in my peripheral vision mean?

Was I going blind?

The kids left for school, my husband for work, and my two houseguests and I sat down around the kitchen table for our final conversation before they left for Heathrow. I mentioned the gap. They looked at me, horrified. I explained that it was not a black hole, but rather an empty space – my brain was doing its duty and filling in what I couldn't see. The room was still there, but not really. When I waved my hand, when I turned my head, there was nothing to be seen. My mother had gone blind, and my eyesight was already poor.

'You better go see the doctor,' my friend said.

'I guess so,' I replied.

Normally when I ring my doctor for an appointment, it is several days before the staff can fit me in. This time when I rang, the response was as per usual.

'We are fully booked until next week.'

'Oh,' I said, 'okay.'

'Unless it's an emergency.'

'Well,' I said, 'I'm not sure, but I seem to have no peripheral vision on the right side.'

'Oh,' said the receptionist, and I could hear her typing. 'We can see you at ten this morning.'

I put down the phone and made coffee. Over the next hour, my peripheral vision on my right side began to return, until it had restored itself completely.

*　*　*

MY MOTHER DIED from aortic dissection. That is, the main artery that led from her heart disintegrated one day. She was with a friend when she collapsed in, of all places, a pharmacy. They took her to hospital and spent the day figuring out what was wrong with her, my sister Phyllis and her husband Clyde at her side. Because my other siblings and I had moved away, the large task of always being there as my parents grew older fell upon our sister Phyllis, and she rose to the challenge gracefully. Informed of the options, my mother decided against surgery, which would have entailed flying her to Vancouver and sawing her open and spreading her ribs apart in order to repair the aorta, a procedure with a fairly low success rate for someone of eighty-five. She was comfortable and as with-it as ever; the doctor said she could last a month, she could last a day, there was no way of telling. All her life my mother was prone to malapropisms and this day, her last, was no different. When discussing her options she said to Phyl and Clyde, 'No erotics' when what she meant was 'No heroics.' Everyone in the room fell about laughing, including her.

And then, a few hours later, she died.

She was old, her heart was old, her aorta was worn out.

She'd suffered from heart palpitations – Atrial Fibrillation, which she always called 'fibulations' like tribulations, which of course they were – for a number of years. She was blind, having lost the sight in both eyes to macular degeneration (wet: first one eye then, three years later, the other); she'd had to give up most of her favourite activities, including reading, quilting, watching hockey and playing bridge. She still lived on her own in her own place but that winter had been very hard. She'd made the decision to move into sheltered accommodation, which would have been an enormous wrench. So, as always, she had great timing, bowing out with minimal fuss, dropping dead, or near enough, which was something to which she had aspired.

But my siblings and I were not ready for her to leave us. We will never be ready.

* * *

WHEN I THINK of my mother now, three and a half years after she died, my heart aches. It really does, this is not metaphorical, my heart aches, my throat tightens, and my eyes fill with tears. A physical response to a strange and abstract, unreal but of course completely real, state: my mother's absence from my life. My heart aches.

* * *

HISTORY OF PRESENT ILLNESS CONTINUED

The wife is doing all the cooking, laundry, shopping, banking, has a homemaker once a week for heavy housekeeping. This man is on aspirin daily for stroke prevention but I fear it may be too late given his frontal lobe features today. Certainly the caregiver stress and burden and the wife's ambivalence and need for absolution in letting this man go to facility care is one of the important considerations in this man's presentation.

PAST ILLNESSES

Hypertension, smoked 40/day history, quit in 1983, long-standing peripheral vascular disease problems with aortofemoral bypass in 1983, recurrent UTIs with prostate surgery in 1988 for benign prostatic hypertrophy, fall in 1988 with fracture and recurrent fracture in 1993, both times general anesthetics which he tolerated poorly. He had a double hernia and reverse colostomy after complications from his fractured hip in 1993 (fistula) for which he was given a spinal anesthetic. He had a blocked pancreatic duct which is now diet-controlled, bladder neck contracture in 1992, benign prostatic hypertrophy in 1988 – surgery then and he now has a wound on his leg which is being attended to by home-care nursing.

MEDICATIONS
Adafat XL 30 mg once daily, ASA 160 mg daily, Sulfatrim DS for 8 days, Oxazepam 15 at hs, multivitamin, zinc, Docusate and Senokot.

ALLERGIES
Intolerant to general anesthetics, Morphine, Largactil and Codeine, all causing delirium.

* * *

ONCE I GOT to the doctor's surgery, I was seen quickly. The practice where we are registered is housed in a new building with plenty of natural light; it serves as a GP training centre as well. I've never seen the same doctor twice, but I don't mind; the GPs are always young and personable, better-looking than the cast of a hospital drama on TV. Who needs a family doctor when you can have a procession of good-looking thirty year olds all keen to prove themselves?

The doctor who saw me this time was very sweet and thorough; her entire face opened wide with excitement when I described my symptoms. She embarked on a range of simple tests – shining lights into my eyes, hitting my knee with a hammer – all of which I passed. I'd figured out by now that, whatever it was that had taken place, it was unlikely to indicate anything wrong with my eyes, but was more likely to be neurological. This was not a relief. She consulted one of her more senior colleagues and decided that I probably hadn't had a stroke, but that I should be assessed for TIA, a Transient Ischemic Attack – not a stroke but strokelike – symptoms that may act as a stroke warning. I would need to attend the TIA clinic at hospital on Friday.

That night as I sat in front of the TV, I had another little episode: flashing lights in my right eye, accompanied by bars of distortion, faces distorting on the screen. This could, of course, have been psychosomatic; by now I was gripped by the idea that there was something wrong with my brain.

My friend, safely home in Vancouver, sent me a Jewish joke: an Italian, a German and Jew go for a walk. The Italian says, 'I am so thirsty. I must have wine.' The German says, 'I am so thirsty. I must have beer.' The Jew says, 'I am so thirsty. I must have diabetes.'

* * *

MY PARENTS MARRIED during the Second World War and they were absolutely devoted to each other; they were each other's heart's content, their love for each other unswerving and not dimmed with time and age. My mother's elder sister, also called Phyllis, had made a bad marriage earlier on during the war; when her husband Duncan returned to BC from the European front, he brought with him several items of war bounty, including a huge Nazi flag he had liberated in Holland, and a Dutch girlfriend. He divorced Phyllis, and married this other woman. Phyllis was devastated. She moved in with my parents, and not long after, she died of a broken heart, or so it was said, except in this case it was true: she died of heart failure caused by cardiac valve disease, which itself was probably caused by the rheumatic fever she had as a child, both conditions that, had she lived a few years more, were to become treatable.

Her heart was broken, and she died, and I know this early death of her beloved sister caused my mother heartache for the rest of her life.

* * *

WHEN YOU LOOK at your child sometimes, you feel as though your heart will burst, with pride of course, but also with joy: look at him! you think, look at her! Miraculous, gorgeous, bigger than life, larger than the sex you had in order to conceive, greater than any other love, your giant, over-powering child. I look at my children and feel as though my heart will burst from all this love. And I cannot look away.

* * *

FUNCTIONAL INQUIRY
He requires a great deal of assistance, prompting, directing and cueing because of his visuospatial problems which are likely vascular and frontotemporal parietal in etiology. His wife is doing a lot in the way of self-care for the man and his basic activities of daily living because of incapacities. He has few pastimes, hobbies and interests now, owing to problems with vision and brain disease. He fabricates and his history is unreliable and he needs corroboration for all manner of testimony.

REVIEW OF SYSTEMS
Unreliable. He has dentures that are ill fitting. His appetite

is good. His mood can be crabby at times. Primary caregiver not here to corroborate. Vision in his left eye is poor due to macular disease. He mobilizes with a cane and walker. Says he has a scooter. He feeds himself, helps her cook which is not true. He has been at the Saanich Peninsula before for respite and says he exercises there twice a day and he exercises at home which I seriously doubt.

*   *   *

THE BABY GP referred me to the TIA clinic. I've lived in Britain for a long time now, and I'm accustomed to listening to the British complain about their health service. But, apart from having babies, this was my first serious encounter with the NHS and it performed like a well-oiled, albeit acronym-laden machine. I found myself in front of an urbane neurologist called Henry.

'You look healthy,' he said.

'I am healthy,' I replied.

He set me up for a full battery of tests that afternoon which turned out to be rather more sophisticated than hitting my knee with a rubber mallet. An ECG – an electrocardiogram, which measures the electrical activity of the heart, its rhythm and pace: a CT brain scan – a computerised tomography scan, a sophisticated x-ray that takes pictures of cross-sections, or slices, of the brain: a Carotid Artery Ultrasound – a high-frequency radio scan that creates images of the two large arteries in the neck. And finally, a series of blood tests.

They were looking at my heart to see if it was working properly, at my brain for evidence of stroke or bleeding, and at my major arteries in case they were clogged up or damaged in any way. They were looking for the things that killed my parents.

This is overly dramatic. It's not as though my parents' deaths were premature: he was eighty-four, she was eighty-five. We all have to die of something, whether it's a broken heart or furred-up arteries. The NHS was doing its bit to prevent this from happening to me anytime soon.

* * *

PHYSICAL EXAMINATION
He is a well-turned-out, bright, alert, 83-year-old man, tall, with a degree of osteoporosis clinically. Examination of the vital signs: blood pressure 140/80 with no postural drop, pulse 76 and regular. Weight 81.2 kg, height 173 cm. Examination of the head and neck – ear canals are clear. Pupils are equal and reactive though he has bilateral macular disease in the right worse than the left, I thought. Nose and mouth – mild atrophic changes only. Ill-fitting dentures. No lymphadenopathy, thyroid abnormality or carotid or vertebral bruit. Examination of the chest – air excursion normal, air entry equal bilaterally. Air excursion fair. No adventitious sounds. Examination of the cardiovascular system – peripheral pulses are diminished somewhat. No real swelling of ankles though it is hard to tell with one of the ankles wrapped because of skin disease that I did not look at today. Ulceration presumably. No signs of cardiac decompensation. Jugular venous pressure normal. Heart sounds normal. No murmurs, bruits or extra sounds. Examination of the abdomen – soft, non-tender, no guarding, rigidity, masses or

organomegaly. No suprapubic abnormalities. Genital rectal examination deferred. Neurological examination – no obvious lateralizing features. Power, tone and reflexes all about equal symmetrically. He had trouble with the left capsulitis so I couldn't test pronator drift. Plantar reflexes equivocal in the left, downgoing on the right. Tongue protrusion central. Frontal release signs positive.

MENTAL STATUS EXAMINATION
He scored 18/30. 6/10 on orientation with 3 more near misses. 3/3 on registration, 4/5 on attention and calculation for backward spelling. 3/5 with numbers. 0/3 on recall getting all 3 with simple prompting and 5/9 on language skills with real problems in following written instructions. Verbal instructions were also mildly but significantly impaired. He had true Gertmann's syndrome with left-right confusion localized to the left angular gyrus.

* * *

MY PARENTS WERE famously devoted to each other. After my father died, and I was helping my mother sort through his things, she told me that his devotion had sometimes been a little hard to bear. 'He always needs to know where I am, what I'm doing,' she said. This became more oppressive as his physical and mental health failed. 'But,' she said, switching to the past tense, 'his heart belonged to me. He loved me absolutely – he was never remotely interested in other women.' And she was glad of that. In later years, his devotion to her meant he wasn't remotely interested in anyone apart from her, including his children; he'd become such a serious arteriopath that there wasn't room in his heart for anyone else but her.

* * *

I WENT BACK to the hospital for another test: the Echocardiogram Bubble Test: an ultrasound examination of the heart, with a bubble of saline solution injected into the bloodstream, its progress visible on the ultrasound screen.

A couple of weeks had passed since my last set of hospital tests, and I'd had no further episodes of weird bits of my range of vision disappearing. So far, I had passed all the tests. I was becoming blasé, more interested in the anthropology of hospital workers and their sophisticated procedures than in my own results. I lay on my side on the gurney; the technician asked me to blow air into a paper bag in order to increase the pressure on my heart, as the saline solution moved through my bloodstream and into my heart. He asked me to blow hard again, and again.

This time I failed the test. The Echocardiogram Bubble Test revealed a hole in my heart.

* * *

DEPRESSION SCALE
3/15, not elevated.

ASSESSMENT
1. Probably frontal lobe disease likely vascular in etiology accounting for discrepancy between the dependency

functionally and psychologically.

2. Arteriopathy, widespread hypertension, smoking-related peripheral vascular disease with previous bypass surgeries twenty years ago.

3. Fractured hip 1988, refractured in 1993 affecting gait and balance. Has a shoe lift.

4. Urinary dysfunction likely local and central causes; may need to see the urologist for recurrent contracture.

5. Caregiver stress.

* * *

THE HUMAN HEART has two sides – left ventricle and right ventricle – separated by a wall. Blood should not pass through this wall. When we are in the womb, a small flap in the wall allows oxygenated blood to pass from one ventricle to the other. When we are born, this flap closes permanently as we take our first breath.

The flap does not close in about twenty percent of the population, allowing venous blood – the blood that's travelled around your body already and is now depleted of oxygen and possibly contains debris picked up along the way – to pass from one side of the heart to the other. As is the case with me.

Most people with patent foramen ovale, or PFO – at last, an acronym to call my own! – live long healthy lives entirely unaware that they have holes in their hearts.

I returned to Henry with the result.

'Okay,' he said.

'Okay,' I replied.

'I'm going to order an MRI. We'll take a good look,

in case there's any build up of debris in your brain.'

When I was a teenager I lived with my parents on a hill above a lagoon. My siblings were a fair bit older than me and by the time we moved to this house, they had long since left home, got married, and had babies. The beach that ran along the spit of land that formed the lagoon was like all beaches in the Pacific Northwest, the high-tide line cluttered with driftwood and seaweed. Debris. This was what I pictured as I talked to Henry.

The MRI did not take place at the hospital with which I had become so cosily familiar. Instead the NHS farmed me out to a private clinic in Golder's Green. I took the tube to get there, giving myself plenty of time to find it. The clinic was slick and glossy, like a place that could give you Botox along with your brain scan. To get to the examination room, I walked through a dark corridor where technicians sat in front of banks of computers; through the observation windows were the scanners – huge white machines, like undersea submersibles. The technician strapped me in and told me to expect 'loud and prolonged bursts of alarming noise.' He asked me to choose a radio station: I picked the familiar chatter of BBC Radio 4. He tightened my head straps and left the room.

'Loud and prolonged bursts of alarming noise' was an understatement. The MRI made a sound like the heaviest of heavy metal bands testing the amps at the biggest stadium gig of all time: brain scan meets 'Spinal Tap.' God only knows what an actual spinal tap sounds like. BBC Radio 4 lunchtime news didn't stand a chance.

* * *

PLAN

I am not aware of any medications that will help this man nor am I aware of any rehabilitation that could help him either. I am dubious that there is a great deal more I can offer this man beyond these comments. I don't think he needs anti-depressants. I don't think memory drugs will do much good with a story like this. I think the family and wife in particular need absolution to move this man to placement in a fairly immediate time frame.

* * *

MY FATHER WAS sick for twenty-five years, a wheel-chair-bound invalid for the last fifteen years of his life. The forty-cigarettes-a-day habit he picked up when he was a teenager had resulted in an array of symptoms and difficulties. In the early years of his deterioration, each time I went to visit I was sure I'd never see him alive again, but then I got used to it. My siblings and I all got used to it, and it felt as though he'd probably live forever in his grumpy, demanding, hard-to-be-with kind of way.

My mother cared for him, year after year, and this care took a large toll on her own health. Only occasionally could she be persuaded to take a break, coming to visit me in London, my brother in the Okanagan, or my other sister in Nova Scotia. During one of these breaks Phyllis took my father in for a neurological consultation; in his report the consultant gives my mother 'absolution.' If science is our religion, doctors are our work-a-day priests. This report enabled my mother to relinquish my father's care to other people. He did not go into sheltered accommodation, but straight into long-term extended care in hospital, such was his condition; we were told that, in caring for him on her own at home, our mother had been doing the work of five nurses.

* * *

THE MRI SCAN showed that my brain is entirely healthy. No sign of scarring or damage from debris, driftwood or seaweed.

I had a final session with Henry.

'New research is showing a link between PFO and migraine,' he said. 'It's early days. Your symptoms could have been caused by migraine – migraine aura, effectively.'

'Oh,' I said. 'Okay.' I did have a headache at the time, but I would not have described it as 'migraine' – I've never suffered from anything that I would describe as 'migraine.' I took Henry's explanation to mean the following: we don't really know what happened to you that morning. As far as we can see, you are perfectly healthy.

'So,' I said, 'PFO. Anything else I should know about it?'

Henry shook his head, almost ruefully. 'No. Most people live with it without ever knowing about it.'

'Okay,' I said. 'Well, thank you.'

'Oh,' said Henry, 'there is one thing. You're not a scuba-diver, are you?'

'No,' I said, and I pictured the MRI submersible safe in its North London clinic.

'Don't take it up. PFO hearts can't take the pressure – that hole will leak more or possibly get bigger.'

'Okay,' I said, 'thanks.'

We shook hands and I left the hospital for the final time, better informed, but none the wiser.

*   *   *

MY SIBLINGS AND I are all getting older, and our parents are both gone. But we carry them with us in our hearts as well as our genes. We carry them with us always.

*   *   *

THIS DOCUMENT HAS BEEN DICTATED AND ACCEPTED
by Dr XXX,
CONSULTATION
07/Mar/2001/ @ 1715

Our Mother's Hair

AFTER MY MOTHER died last year, my three siblings and I spent time together, something that, as adults, we had never really done before. There's a big age gap between my siblings and me; they are ten, fourteen and sixteen years older than me. My eldest sister left home when I was six months old. They were all married by the time I was nine. And the four of us live hundreds, in some cases thousands, of miles apart. British Columbia, Nova Scotia, England.

Despite the age difference, my siblings and I have a lot in common, and one of those things is our hair. We all have the same hair, and we got this hair from our mother. Wiry, coarse, very thick, both kinky and curly, but also straight, it's the kind of hair that tends to frizziness. It does not lend itself to anything resembling chic or soignée without intensive professional help and massive amounts of expensive haircare products.

My own hair started to go white when I was in my early twenties and was almost completely white by the time I was forty. This did not happen to my sisters who went grey at a more normal speed. My brother, on the other hand, is going the way of many men – including our father – losing hair off the top as he gets older.

About six weeks after my mother died, my siblings and I came together to empty her condo in preparation for its sale. My brother and I took up residence in my mother's place while my eldest sister stayed with my other sister who lived nearby. We spent long days emptying cupboards and shelves, deciding what to get rid of, dividing up what we wanted to keep.

We got on well. It was difficult but it was also cathartic, a process of examining my mother's life as represented by the stuff she left behind – not representative of her at all, of course, but nonetheless full of rich textures and memories as well as mysteries: the mysteries of our mother's life. The things about her that we never knew and now would never know.

One day I emerged from bed in the morning looking particularly gruesome with hideous jetlag compounded by six weeks of weeping and laughing hysterically – my siblings and I laughed a lot when we were together during that time, though we weren't really having fun. My brother was watching the news and eating cereal out of one of the two bowls that were now left in the almost empty kitchen.

'My hair looks awful,' I said. I didn't really expect my brother to reply, but he did.

'It does,' he said, nodding.

I sat down.

'You have that awful hair that we all have,' he said. 'It's wiry and spiky and usually looks like some kind of hedge, not like hair at all. Mum's hair.'

I was surprised by his vehemence. To tell the truth, I had expected him to say something more along the lines of 'Oh no, you look terrific, you always look terrific.'

'I was glad when I started losing my hair,' he continued. 'I didn't have to deal with it anymore. It was a relief.'

I didn't know what to say. I couldn't imagine actually losing my hair; it was bad enough having gone grey when I was twenty-five.

Not long after the house sold, my sister who lived nearby started going to my mother's hairdresser. My mother came from a generation who made regular trips to the hairdresser – a weekly wash and set and a fresh perm every couple of months. The first time my sister visited my mother's hairdresser they both spent much of the appointment crying. However, my sister has kept going to our mother's hairdresser and now, after a year, they are both almost used to it.

Last time she went, my sister told me, her hairdresser said, 'You know, as long as you keep coming to see me, your mother will never be dead to me. You have her hair.'

And so our mother lives on for all of us, sometimes in unexpected ways.

DIGITAL STORIES

Since 2001 I've been collaborating with web artists and developers to create works of digital fiction. These born-digital stories are works of multimedia, using combinations of text, music, sound, animation, video and games to tell stories. These works are not reproducible on paper. However, I see this hybrid form as part of the evolution of the short story, and the two works I'm including here reside firmly within that tradition.

For further information about my digital work go to: http://www.katepullinger.com/digital

Branded

'Branded' was a collaboration between myself and American web artist and writer Talan Memmott. 'Branded' was the first digital short story I created and, in fact, it was a precursor to 'The Breathing Wall', a large experimental project that developed the story of a dead girl communicating with her boyfriend through the wall of his prison cell.

To view 'Branded' go to:

http://tracearchive.ntu.ac.uk/frame/branded/index.html

Make sure to turn on the sound on your computer.

Inanimate Alice

'Inanimate Alice' is an ongoing series of linked short stories, a collaboration between myself and British-Canadian web artist Chris Joseph. Produced by Bradfield Ltd., 'Inanimate Alice' tells the story of a girl growing up in the twenty-first century, surrounded by technology. There are four existing stories, and six more planned. 'Inanimate Alice' has proved to be very popular with educators and there is an active pedagogical community using these stories in classrooms and seminars around the world; although we have only produced four stories to date, there are countless episode 5s online, created by young people in response to our project.

To view 'Inanimate Alice' go to:
http://www.inanimatealice.com
Make sure to turn on the sound on your computer.

OTHER NEW STORIES

Fur Coats

'WHAT ARE WE doing tomorrow?'

'Going to Emma's in the morning, school in the afternoon, then Sian is picking you up so you can play with Marcus after school.'

'What are we doing the next day?'

'Going to Emma's in the morning, school in the afternoon, then Marcus is coming over here to play.'

'What are we doing the next day after that?'

'Going to Emma's in the morning, school in the afternoon, then Tea and Cakes after school, most likely.'

'What are we doing the next day after that?'

Will she kill him? Of course not. But she contemplates it.

In spare moments, Clara thinks about the past, about the time when she was free, before she bowed down to domestic servitude. Is that what it is? She isn't at all sure how to describe her present state. There is one thing that Clara is sure about, though (whisper this, she thinks): *parenthood can be boring.*

BACK THEN, in the old days, Before Baby, Clara lived in a big dingy house with a bunch of artists; she wasn't an artist, but they didn't seem to mind. The big dingy house was one of a collection of big dingy houses around a long-neglected South London square. No one knew who owned the buildings, but they moved in anyway, jimmying the locks, climbing in through the windows, and set about renovating. Clara's house was actually two houses; once they got themselves established in the first house – electricity, gas, plumbing – they knocked through the walls at strategic places, mostly stair landings, and annexed next door. House number two was exactly like house number one, except in reverse, a mirror-image. It made for a pleasing symmetry. One of the blokes expanded his room at the top of the house to include the room next door. His space was enormous and, consequently, perfect for parties. They had lots of parties.

Her own room was small and cosy, with a tiny fireplace and enough space for a table and chair and her single bed. Clara liked the narrow bed, with its worn black-and-pink blanket; it gave the room a spartan appearance. She'd stripped the floral wallpaper off the walls when they moved in, and had left the old plaster bare; she liked the look of it as well, the meandering cracks, rough and smooth, glazed and dull like an old leather coat you might find on a skip. The artists would have made the bare walls an aesthetic choice, but Clara left them untouched out of uncertainty – what were you supposed to do next? She stuck postcards of her favourite paintings low on the wall, where she could gaze at them as she lay in bed, but these fell off within a few days, wedging themselves down between the skirting board and the wall, leaving tags of bluetack in their place.

She kept the room warm – warmish – with a paraffin heater. It sat in the corner like a pale green metal chimney pot; it was fumy and unreliable and if she had it on for long she worried it might explode. But it was better than nothing, better than the unrelenting cold.

And so Clara and the artists concerned themselves with the business of living – crappy low-paid jobs in retail and catering, signing on, eating cheese on toast late at night after the pub, endless talking. The artists were concerned with Capitalism and its Onward March through time and space; they were concerned about the World and Politics. Margaret Thatcher was in Downing Street and they felt a profound unease, casting around for a foothold against Nicaragua, apartheid, Israel. This was what occupied the artists at the kitchen table, this was what they discussed at the pub, this was what they argued about while falling in and out of each other's beds. Clara listened in; she was like a highly tuned listening device – like a spy, in fact. Except she wasn't a spy, she was just Clara. She was waiting for it all to make sense.

HE IS FOUR years old. Tall, and getting taller. Very independent, and yet dependent too, traces of babyhood lingering. Sitting on his mother's lap is still a priority at times. And his mother's opinion looms large. 'You've hurt my feelings' is his favourite complaint, along with 'I'm very cross with you,' and 'I'm very upset.'

'What are we doing tomorrow mummy?'

'Sweetie, we've been through this. You know what we're doing. You do the same things every week.'

He looks a little crestfallen.

'What are we doing the next day?'

'I don't know, sweetie. Where's your bag of dinosaurs? Have they all escaped?' At four, he remains divertible.

ONE OF THE big dingy houses on the square had its ground floor converted into a café. They took it in turns to produce big, healthy vegetarian meals – large trays of vegetable crumble, lasagna, apple bake. Any money raised went toward a cause; there were many causes, and the causes needed money. Everyone came along, to sit at the stubby old tables on the wonky chairs in the candlelight, bringing their own beer and wine, and the conversation wove itself in the air, like a rich and delicate textile one of the artists had designed.

Clara didn't know anything about the Iran/Iraq War; she didn't know anything about El Salvador; she'd barely heard of these places. They were very far away. None of her housemates ate meat and some of them took this particular tenet as far as not wearing leather. Clara had a couple of pairs of strappy leather slingbacks stuffed under her bed; sometimes when she was in town she would buy and eat a Big Mac. One of the artists had been to Nicaragua and was raising money to go back; another was dodging the South African Army draft; another had gone to prison for the ALF, the anti-fur, anti-vivisection brigade. Clara had had a teddy bear childhood in Teddington, South West London; the house she grew up in backed onto the Thames. In summer, Clara and her brothers used to swing out over the water on a rope, letting go to crash into the silky warm river, carefree dive-bombers with no known enemy. Church of England, a private girl's school, a Mummy who stayed home and baked cakes for tea: this childhood was like a basket she carried around at all times, full of good things. Because of it she would never go hungry. But it weighed her down as well, with its narrowness, its politeness, its concern with courtesy. No matter what she wore, no matter what colour she dyed her hair, it shone through: her parents' affluence, her way of speaking. She felt a barrier between herself and the rest of the world, not only far-flung places but the artists, her friends.

THIS IS WHAT he likes to eat: pasta, sauce-free, garnished only with a dab of pesto from a jar and a sprinkle of cheese. Sausages. Cheese sandwiches. Little baby tomatoes, cucumber. Mango. Bananas. Broccoli on occasion – unpredictable. Same for fish fingers. Nothing resembling grown-up food, nothing where the flavours are mixed or complicated. He eats well, providing she does not attempt to spring anything new on him. And of course he loves sweet things. Every little sweet thing.

Sometimes he can be exceptionally graceful and charming. One evening as she is getting dressed to go out he points to an item of her clothing. 'What's that?'

Clara looks. 'A skirt.' She doesn't get out much these days.

And later as she is putting him to bed: 'Mummy, you do look lovely.'

She almost cries. 'Thank you, sweetheart. Thank you.'

Their relationship has an intensity that is heartbreaking. It marginalises everything else. There he is, so little and sturdy, with his hopes, his dreams. How could he be anything other than demanding?

CLARA DIDN'T HAVE a cause of her own. She wasn't that way inclined. There was too much choice: what was it to be, the homeless in London or the disappeared in Chile? It all felt too pressing, too urgent, too desperate; and besides, she thought, perhaps the world would be destroyed in a nuclear holocaust anyway. She contemplated joining CND; she contemplated joining many things.

And sleeping around. Clara didn't do that either. No particular reason, it just wasn't what she did. The artists didn't expect it of her. 'You're too earnest,' they would say to her, as if that alone ruled out sex. 'Isn't it important to be earnest?' she'd reply. And she'd laugh and the artists would look at her as though she came from another planet.

And then the miners' strike started. Up north somewhere. Up there.

As the strike took hold, the Left mobilized ('The left what?' Clara wanted to ask but did not), and with it, the artists. In the square activity coalesced around the café; they held a meeting to discuss how to fundraise. The miners were asking for food and money.

The artists decided they needed someone to lobby the manager of the local supermarket. Heads turned. Clara swivelled in her chair to see who was sitting behind her. But there was no one. They were looking at her.

'But,' she said.

'Clara,' they replied.

And so she applied herself. She wrote a letter to the manager first, and then made an appointment by telephone. She wore a suit that one of the artists had helped her find at Brick Lane market; it was older than she was and cost fifty pence. She put on lipstick and when she looked in the mirror she thought her mother had suddenly appeared. She put on her strappy leather slingbacks and told herself it was in aid of a good cause. Then she trudged up the broad gusty road, rubbing grit out of her eyes, batting away flying crisp packets. Under the rail bridge, to the right and into the supermarket. She was so nervous she had to remind herself of her own name.

'We would like to hand out leaflets at the front entrance to the store,' she said.

The manager nodded and smiled.

'The leaflet will have a list of products that your customers can buy for the miners and their families. Food, toiletries, household items.'

He smiled again, encouragingly.

'We will be at the exit to collect the products as your customers leave.'

The manager remained pleasingly silent.

'We will be polite and discreet. Cash donations may also be given.'

At last the manager spoke: 'Sounds fine to me.' He smiled again, his benevolent, managerial smile.

When Clara got outside the supermarket she screamed.

HE CAN MAKE her angrier than she'd thought possible. How was she to know that motherhood would make her so angry?

'I won't!'

'You will.'

'I won't!'

'You will.'

They are discussing the picking up and tidying of toys.

'I won't!'

'You will.'

He throws himself on the floor and wails. She struggles to suppress her own rage, like forcing a vengeful genie back into a tiny bottle. He is four, after all, he no longer bites, kicks, or pinches, so why should she?

'I'll help you.'

He stops sobbing as abruptly as he began. 'All right then,' he sighs wearily. 'Come on Mummy.'

When he's asleep it is easy to love him. He sleeps with his arms flung out, blameless, abandoned to it, so far gone sometimes he rolls right out of bed. She lies awake in the next room and listens to him when – at 2 a.m., sometimes 3 – he gets up and, standing, drinks from the glass of milk she has left him, puts it down, goes to the loo, gets back in bed. At these moments she doubts her own perceptions; is she no longer the person she used to be? Has motherhood, with all its responsibilities, with its abrupt shifts in way of life – one minute she's party girl, all sheeny and bright, the next she's in on her own every single night – changed her as much as she thinks?

THE SUPERMARKET collection went well; the supermarket's customers responded with thoughtful generosity, supplying much more than endless tins of baked beans. And they were well organised in the square, ferrying the goods to the central collection point on time, constantly amending and updating the list of requested goods according to instructions from the NUM strike committee. Clara listened to the radio news reports with interest, wishing they had a telly. The strike had many factors against it: the power utilities had enormous reserves of coal, the Nottinghamshire union did not go out on strike, there was no secondary action. Arthur Scargill had not balloted the NUM, and the artists debated the wisdom of that night after night around the kitchen table. And there was Thatcher herself, astride the country with her pearls and her hairdo and her voice.

Delegations of miners began to arrive in London. They came down to attend rallies, to help mobilize and fundraise. There was plenty of room to put up people in the big dingy houses around the square and so they notified the strike committee. The artists began to organise a special benefit night in the café, a welcoming party for their guests. As the day approached the square was buoyant with anticipation; it was not every day that the Cause came to stay. The delegation was from a small mining town outside Manchester; none of the artists had ever been anywhere near the place. As far as Clara was concerned, they could have been coming from Namibia. She had never met a miner. She had never seen a miner, nor a mine, nor even a pit village, in fact the closest she had come was reading Zola's *Germinal*, a novel set in France during the nineteenth century.

Finally, the evening was upon them. Everyone gathered in the café. At 8:30 they put the food on the back burners. At 9:00 they started to open bottles of wine. By 10:00 dancing had broken out in the middle of the café. By 10:30 some people could wait no longer, and the kitchen was raided. By 11:00 they had forgotten why they were having a party. No one noticed the minibus arrive.

The door of the café opened. Someone shouted 'shut up' and the music was switched off and everyone stopped dancing, eating, drinking. Clara stood on a chair to get a better view of the door, and she gasped in spite of herself.

She had never seen so much fur.

They had been expecting a dozen miners. What they got was a dozen miners' wives.

They trooped into the café one by one, taking up an enormous amount of space. No one had anticipated how much space they would require; every single woman, every single wife, was wearing fur. Fur coats, brown-red and silky, silver and glossy, black and shimmering; fur hats, bulky and soviet; one woman was wearing fur gloves. The café's inhabitants took a collective gulp. And then someone shouted 'Welcome!' The miners' wives smiled. 'Come in,' someone else shouted and, with a laugh, 'can we take your coats?'

THE THING ABOUT having a small child, Clara finds, is that it forces you back into your own past, into your own childhood. It makes your parents into people – people like you, in fact. It is that negative bind that characterises so much of parenting – at Clara's worst moments, when she is too tired, too harassed, too not-herself, she thinks: I'm turning into my mother. And then she thinks: Is that such a bad thing?

'Mummy?'

'Yes, sweetie.'

'What are we doing on Wednesday?'

'Wednesday?' Today is Thursday.

He nods.

'Emma's in the morning, school in the afternoon.'

'What are we doing on Friday?'

Ah, she thinks, he has moved on a stage. Is he trying to impress me with his grasp of the days of the week?

'Friday is your swimming lesson.'

'Oh,' he says, 'that's right. I'm very good at swimming.'

She doesn't reply, she is attempting to tune the radio.

'I'm very good at swimming, Mummy.'

The damn thing has a terrible hiss.

'Mummy, I'm very good at swimming.'

She can't get it to work. It's been like this all week.

'Mummy–' he is getting louder. 'Mummy–'

She succeeds in her fiddling. At last she hears what he is saying. 'Yes, sweetheart, you are very good at swimming. You should put your face in the water next time, shouldn't you.'

He nods, pushing his train across the carpet. Now he isn't listening to her.

CLARA COULDN'T understand a thing that the miners' wives said. Their accents – specific to the village in which they had lived and worked all their lives – were unintelligible to her. The woman they had staying in their house was called Barbara; whenever Clara encountered her on the stairs or in the doorway she smiled broadly, said 'Hello Barbara,' and then scuttled away. She got on with her supermarket collecting.

In the evenings Barbara wore her fur coat and held court in the kitchen. The kitchen had no heating, but Clara and the artists had grown accustomed to it. When it got too cold to bear, they turned on the cooker and left the oven door open. While Barbara was staying, the household undertook to cook a good meal every night. The artist who grew up in Leeds – Mark – served as unofficial interpreter.

Barbara said something.

'Do we always eat together?' Mark translated. He also supplied the reply. 'Well, pretty often, I guess, maybe even most nights. We take it in turns to cook.'

Clara was sitting in the corner, hoping she wouldn't be called upon to speak.

Barbara said something.

'No, we don't have a cleaning rota as such.' Mark looked a little shamefaced.

Clara looked around the kitchen. She realised, with surprise, that it was filthy. On the floor the lino was cracked, missing in patches. The walls were festooned with ad hoc wiring and the wires were coated with oily black dust. There was no splashback behind the cooker and the area was dark with grease; the wall behind the rubbish bin was caked and streaky.

Barbara said something and then laughed warmly.

Mark smiled. 'Yes, we do have big hearts.' Everyone in the kitchen either guffawed or giggled and Clara smiled in spite of herself.

Another two days and Barbara and the artists were beginning to comprehend each other more fully. One morning, on her way to a rally at Westminster, Barbara came into the kitchen while Clara was making toast.

'Would you like a piece?' Clara offered.

'No thank you.'

Clara spread vegemite on the bread, despite not liking the taste. She thought it might be good for her.

'It is very kind of you to put us up here in the square,' Barbara said.

Clara shrugged, she didn't know how to reply.

'Things are tough in the villages now. We are running out of money.' Barbara put her handbag down and began to button her fur coat. 'No more overtime bonuses. I might even have to sell this!' She spread her arms wide and laughed, then was abruptly serious once more. 'I worry that we are running out of time. Our whole way of life – it's not nice down the pit, but–' she stopped herself. 'You know all of this already.' She smiled again. 'You people obviously have nothing.'

Clara put down her toast and looked around. And then she realised that Barbara thought they lived this way because they were poor. Nothing to do with choice.

'And yet you have been so generous. We appreciate it so much. All over England, people have been – fantastic.'

'It shouldn't be happening like this,' Clara said. She meant the strike, she meant the pit closures, she meant the violent battles on the coalfields between the miners and the police. The Plexiglas-clad police.

'Ah,' said Barbara, 'but it is. It's not the young men that I worry about; they'll be all right. It's the older ones that'll end up on the slagheap – like my Robbie.'

Clara couldn't reply.

'Okay,' said Barbara, breezy once more, 'I'm off.' And with a soft and furry flourish, she departed.

IT HAS BEEN an awful morning and it looks set to get worse. It has been raining since they got up – hard, silent rain. He has a temperature and a runny nose and she's worried he's got conjunctivitis from rubbing snot into his eyes. He won't lie down and he won't play with his toys. Instead he follows her around the flat, and whines. She has a cold too, and a hangover from the three bottles of beer she drank last night, in front of the telly. All she wants to do is lie down and be very, very quiet.

He whines.

Now she is brittle with tension, close to cracking.

On days like this he's not a little boy but a huge force, a tremendous non-stop barrage of need.

The phone rings. She leaps up and answers it.

'Hello love,' Barbara says. 'Are you up for a visit this weekend?'

It is fifteen years since the strike – fifteen years, Clara reflects, as she listens to Barbara speak. After the strike Barbara's husband Robbie took redundancy and promptly died. Their kids were grown, so Barbara went to college on the redundancy money. Now she manages an enormous supermarket in Manchester.

'I'm thinking of taking the fur coat out of storage.'

Clara laughs.

'No listen – they're back in fashion – they're all the rage.'

'They are not.'

'They are! It says so in my magazine.'

'Oh well then.'

'You're young, you look great whatever you wear.'

'I'm not young anymore.'

'No?' says Barbara. 'I suppose not. How's the lad?'

He is sitting next to Clara on the settee, his head in her lap. He takes her hand and places it on his temple, so that she'll stroke his hair. 'He's all right,' Clara says, 'he's okay.'

The Sticker King

IT WAS THE rooftops that attracted her, made her get up, move away from her desk. She could see them out the window: terra-cotta chimney pots, like massed rows of Chinese warrior-statues, and television aerials, spindly, makeshift. The big, bossy buildings of Broadgate on the left, like fat squat bankers with square heads, shabby council blocks straight ahead, down-at-heel, declaring their refugee status. It wasn't a romantic view, apart from Spitalfield's church off to the right, Hawksmoor's giant tardis of a building. She wanted to dance across the rooftops and impale herself on the spire.

That was on bad days. On good days she was content to watch the sky; if she opened the window she would smell curry. But the windows didn't open. And there were lots of bad days.

At Whitechapel she met a man who said his name was Frank. She was on her way to buy a sandwich for lunch; she'd take it back and eat in front of her computer. She stopped to speak to him because – well, she wasn't sure why, usually she never stopped for anyone or anything. 'Sticker King of East London,' he said by way of an introduction. He kept his stickers in an A4 paper box. He displayed them for her cupped in the palm of his hand, one at a time, as though they were precious, fragile things. 'Go on, make me Gay.' 'Help! I'm Happy.' Plain white rectangular stickers, slogans handwritten with black felt tip. 'Brother Man: You are Me.'

'Where do you put them?' she asked.

He looked at her as though she was stupid, then spread his arms wide to indicate: London. My domain.

And he was telling the truth, his stickers were everywhere: lampposts, walls, hoardings, railings, bus stops, curbstones, pavements. She couldn't believe she hadn't noticed before. But she was pressed at work, and pressed at home. Pressed. Squashed, in fact. She coped by keeping long lists of all the things she needed to do. But most of the things didn't get done, couldn't get done, were, in fact, impossible feats of derring-do for a woman like her, with her life. Darn holes in husband's socks. Reach project target on time. Hoover behind the furniture. Think of witty conversation to entertain younger colleagues. Tidy children's toy cupboard. Go swimming at lunchtime. Get rid of all the herbal tea that is past its sell-by date. Be more efficient. Bake a pie and take it next door to the elderly neighbour. That last one was the worst, the most difficult. Before she had a chance to go round, the neighbour died.

The day after she met Frank the Sticker King of East London, she met him again. She was on her way out of the underground, about twenty minutes late for work, when there he was. She felt compelled to stop. He hadn't noticed her. He was over by the railing, standing absolutely still, staring up into the sky, smiling hugely. His total non-movement was an event, full of drama. Instead of disappearing in the flurry of passers-by, everyone noticed him, at least, she was sure that everyone was taking note of Frank. Most people paused slightly, and looked up, as though hoping to see what he was seeing. But there was nothing up there apart from a clear blue sky which, she supposed, was unusual enough to be a kind of performance in itself, to be observed and absorbed, longingly.

She didn't speak to him then, didn't want to interrupt his roadside reverie. But as she made her way to work she read his stickers: they were multiplying. 'It was Worth It.' 'Mum, I made you Happy.' 'Beach = Pleasure.' 'Live the Day.' When she got back to the office she stood in front of the window and looked out at the chimney pots and Hawksmoor's spire until her heart stopped pounding. 'Look. It's there, Waiting.'

The week passed, uneventful enough in its time-shredding way. She got through it. She looked for Frank's stickers whenever she could, and always found them.

She worked late on Thursday, phoning home a couple of times to make sure everything was all right. Eventually she finished; she would meet the deadline after all. On the way to the underground station a young woman stepped out in front of her. 'I need help, I want to go home.' Once again, she stopped, when normally she never stopped for anyone or anything. The young woman was very thin and her clothes were cheap and fashionable – a white shag-pile gilet, white boots with pointed toes, black jeans. She had bad skin and lank hair and did not look healthy. 'I've had an argument with my fella, I can't get home, I came out without my purse.' She kept pushing an open notebook and pen forward. 'Let me take your address. I'll send you the money. I promise, I've had an argument with my fella and I just want to go home.' The girl spoke very quickly, as though she knew she had only seconds to make her plea convincing.

But she believed her. She didn't know why. She had got very used to not believing anybody, anything. She didn't believe what she read in the newspapers. She didn't believe what she saw on TV. She didn't even believe what she could see with her own eyes, there in the flesh – was that real? We live, she was fond of telling herself, in the Misinformation Age. Truth is the most elusive thing.

Not according to Frank the Sticker King. Just that morning she had seen: 'The Truth is Obvious. Believe Me.'

'Where do you live?' she asked the thin young woman in the white shag-pile gilet.

'Tunbridge Wells. The train fare is £12.50.'

She took out her wallet, more amazed at herself with each passing moment. She got out a twenty-pound note, looked at it, looked at the girl, and handed it over. When the notebook and pen were offered once more, she shook her head and walked away. What had happened? She never gave money away on the street, she didn't believe in it. The girl was probably an addict in need of a fix – but maybe not. Maybe she really did want to get home to her mum. Who cares? I don't care, she thought, I really don't care. I'm allowed to give my money away.

The next day as she walked through the market a breeze came up; the ladies' bras filled with air and flapped like wind-socks, the slips billowed like hot air balloons on the rise. The stall-holder batted his merchandise down, attempting to catch it before it flew away. She looked around for one of Frank's stickers; there it was on the wall on the far side of the street. 'Ask me, I'm Free.'

As she read, a man stepped in front of her. He was wearing a fluorescent jacket and carrying a bucket of dirty water and a scraper; he set to work on the sticker. She looked down the street and saw that all the paving slabs, the railings, the walls, had been swabbed clean. Dismayed, she turned back to the cleaner, ready to object. But he was gone.

She turned round again and, there, behind the ladies' slips, was Frank. He smiled at her, a smile of great benevolence despite his missing teeth. Then he waved good-bye, and set off down the street.

STORIES FROM
My Life as a Girl
in a Men's Prison

Small Town

PIGEON FANCY

THERE WAS PIGEON shit everywhere.

He'd had to lean hard on the door and push with his shoulder. It gave with a slow crunch and he slid through the gap. Like stepping into a ghost room, a room that was a plaster cast of itself – only not plaster, but bird shit. Oddly white at first, then grey, black and yellow. An ordinary, square, furnished room. The door he came in and a door out the opposite side, a settee, a thin-legged table, a broken chair. Net curtains on the window, a sink below, exposed pipes where the cooker once stood. Everything coated in a layer of shit one inch, two inches, some places as much as six inches thick. How many pigeons? How many years? How could such a room exist?

* * *

HE COULD SEE what she'd be like as an older woman. She'd have her own house full of odd books, the classics, anatomy, art, mostly second-hand, sheaves of music piled up around the boxed grand piano. She'd go to Greece on her holidays, drink retsina and look at the sea. She'd have serious relationships with men who'd think she was one thing, one way, until they learned that, in fact, she was not. She'd be metropolitan, wear gold-rimmed glasses on a gold chain.

And he would be old and conventional and he'd live in a small town and he wouldn't have seen her for years, but he'd love her, he'd still love her, even then he'd love her more than he'd ever loved anybody.

* * *

HE ARRIVED FROM Canada in the spring. It was part of the deal he had made with his dad – he finished his degree and worked for a year and was now having his summer of travel before heading home to start medical school. Peter was twenty-two. Twenty-two and still bargaining with his dad. He didn't know how he'd got so old – that was how he thought of it – got so old. But now he had escaped and, for a while, he was free.

London suited him. The Falklands War was on in the South Atlantic and the city steamed with fiercesome debate. He found a card pinned to a board in a radical bookshop – everything was strange in this city, even the notion of a radical bookshop was exotic to him – 'Come and Help Us Make a New City'. He took the tube under the Thames to Vauxhall. Across the wasteland next to the overhead railway line he could see a tenement building and he knew that was his destination.

Peter had checked out of the youth hostel, he was

carrying his backpack with him; once he arrived, he would be staying. The building had five floors, centred round a large internal courtyard. He walked through an archway and into the bright space, dropped his pack and sat on the ground next to it. All around the noise of hammers and saws – through open doors he glimpsed people working. After a few minutes, a young man wandered over. 'There's room,' he said, 'at the top.' He indicated a flight of stairs in one corner. 'With George.'

Peter picked up his bag and shouldered it. Everything was strange in London, this was only part of it. He went to look for George.

* * *

THEY TOOK OVER two adjacent flats on the fifth floor. There were forty flats in the building, but the entire north side was uninhabitable, even for the DIY diehards among the group. The roof had caved in and the rain had worn through, collapsing the floors and ceilings of the flats: storey after storey, right down to the ground. It reminded him of an old avalanche site in the Rocky Mountains near where he was born. In the early part of the century a ramshackle, hard-hewn mining town called Frank had been obliterated when half a mountain slid dwn onto it in the night. One person – a baby – survived, a little girl Peter had always imagined was thereafter known as Frankie. No one had seen the slide take place, there was no one to see, they were all asleep. These days the highway ran right through it, across it, the road lined with enormous ragged boulders. A small plaque on one of the rocks told the story;

Peter and his family would stop their car to read it from time to time. Now, in London, Peter wondered if anyone had witnessed the slow-motion avalanche at Vauxhall Palace Buildings. Probably not, he thought, the place had been empty for years.

On the fifth floor the flats were one-bedroom: landing and sitting room at the front, bedroom and kitchen following on in the middle, narrow bathroom and, facing into the courtyard, toilet outside on a small balcony. Everyone had their toilet outside on the balcony. In the morning the courtyard echoed with flushing. George decided right away that this wasn't enough room for them both; Peter stood and watched as he fetched up a sledgehammer and proceeded to knock a hole through the sitting room wall. 'On the other side,' he explained between bashes, 'will be another sitting room, same as ours. We'll only have to do the kitchen and bathroom on this side, but we'll have all this extra space.' Peter went back into the kitchen, to escape the dust. In the week he'd lived in Vauxhall Palace he'd been taught, after a fashion, how to weld pipes, how to run wiring. He lay back down on the floor and continued attempting to plumb the sink.

By the end of the day George had knocked a hole the shape of Frankenstein's monster through the wall. He called to Peter, who climbed through after him. The sitting room next door was identical to the one they already occupied, empty except for a large, pale, deco-style bureau that stood beneath the front windows. 'Cool,' said George, running his finger through the dust. Peter walked down the hallway towards the bedroom, which was furnished, the plain double bed neatly made as though expecting its tenant that night. At the window he pushed back the curtains, orange and blackened with age, and saw that the rear end of the flat was avalanche afflicted, collapsing into the ruin of the flats next door. It looked as though the kitchen was probably still intact, and he went to have a look. That was when he put his shoulder to the door and discovered the pigeon sanctuary. George, in his effete Australian way, was disgusted by the sight and the smell, although to Peter the room simply smelt old. When he was younger his father used to tell him he had an underdeveloped sense of smell, he was odour-blind, like some boys were colour-blind. But Peter knew his sense of smell was fine, he just happened to like tangs and aromas, a good whiff and you knew where you stood. A quick guide to intimacy. Now when his roommate shouted and rushed away from the room Peter thought he heard a stirring – wings. From the corridor George called out, 'You can have this side, Peter, you're Canadian, you're used to wildlife.'

So Peter was happy in his London flat, his bijou squatted London property. In the evenings he and George cooked together, weird and economical combinations of rice and beans, they'd both become sudden vegetarians. Afterwards they'd venture down the street to the off-licence to buy beer, which they'd carry to the ground floor flat that had been converted into a meeting place, a speakeasy. A sound system had been rigged up and the walls painted black where they weren't knocked through to create more and larger spaces. Some nights people showed slides or films; everyone living in Vauxhall Palace seemed to be an artist, or at least, at art school, Goldsmith's, Camberwell, St Martin's, Chelsea. They all did things with their hands. There was a lot of talk about world politics, about the work on the flats, the best way of finding furniture, bathtubs, cookers and sinks, about the possibilities of a money-free economy. Peter didn't say a lot, but he listened. Amanda, Simon, Katherine and Will: and then the ones with nicknames, Squeak, Ziggy, Baby. And Fancy, the girl called Fancy, Peter wasn't sure whether that was her real name or not.

* * *

HE SLEPT BETWEEN the sheets that someone had drawn up and corner-tucked years and years ago. The first night they smelt a bit musty and felt a little damp, but the double bed was luxurious compared to the youth hostel, compared to the floor of the sitting room on the other side of Frankenstein. Peter wasn't used to hardship, even though he'd been a student for four years; he was soft in his North Americanness, central heating, dishwashers, microwaves, cars. He'd lain awake for a while, mulling over the plumbing he'd done, wondering if he'd got it right. They'd find out soon enough, when they turned on the mains tomorrow. He could hear music filtering up from the speakeasy. He'd left at three a.m., and people were still drifting around, talking, dancing, George in a corner with Amanda, both giggling wildly. The music died suddenly, and Peter was held close by the night.

He woke at first light with the sound of pigeons. It took a few moments to understand what he heard – at first he thought perhaps George had been successful with Amanda – were they having sex outside his door? It was a human sound, but then its humanity fell away – cooing. That breast-full bird sound, early morning. He got up and went out into the corridor. When he opened the door to the old kitchen he was met with sudden movement, the air filled with mad fluttering. He stepped forward, the crust under his bare feet like a rough beach of drying seaweed. The birds fled through a hole in the ceiling before he could see them. He went back to bed and dreamed of flying.

Once the kitchen and bathroom were plumbed in and functional, they got on with decorating. Peter had never been one to look at walls and consider colour schemes, but George went at this task with passion. 'It's got to look good,' he said. 'It's got to be somewhere I would like to be.' George was in a band, although Peter had never met the other members, never heard a strain of their music; he planned to turn his bedroom into a recording studio and spent his days arranging the wiring. Everything was legitimate in Vauxhall Palace, at least in their flat, the electricity and gas metered up, the appropriate boards notified, and they had every intention of paying their bills. They might have looked and talked like subversives, but Peter knew their souls – his soul – had a thick layer of small town underneath. Peter's veneer of anarchy was very thin, thinner even than George's, three weeks thin, the length of time he had been in the UK.

* * *

FANCY'S FLAT WAS on the second floor of Vauxhall Palace, on the opposite side of the courtyard. Peter knew this because as he was coming out of the toilet on the balcony one day, he saw her going into hers. She was wearing a long T-shirt, and her legs were bare, as were her feet. He was relieved when she didn't look up – he didn't like the idea of her knowing he'd just been to the toilet. But he didn't mind knowing what Fancy was up to – it made her seem more normal, more real. He had spoken to her several times at the speakeasy. Once they had a conversation about Canada. She didn't know anything about Canada, except that it was part of the Commonwealth which had something to do with the Queen. She'd certainly never heard of Alberta, and she told him that her best friend in infant school had had that name. Peter wondered what infant school was – a school for tiny babies? – but he didn't ask. He thought that if he asked for explanations every time he didn't understand something in England he would become known as the Question Mark King.

Fancy had been to art school as well, she'd only recently graduated – textiles. She was a weaver. She told Peter she also did silk-screening and print-making on fabric and he noticed her thin fingers were always stained with ink. 'They don't have art schools where I come from,' he said.

She looked at him blankly. 'I wonder what happened to my friend Alberta? We lost contact.'

Peter found English people difficult to comprehend, but he liked them, with their quiet, convoluted ways, so unlike the folks back home. He got on well with George, but George was Australian and also new and confused. Peter made friends with another of their neighbours, Joseph, who was a Catholic from Belfast – Peter knew this was politically significant but didn't quite understand how or why. Joseph declared an immediate sympathy with people 'from across the water' and he told Peter they'd be mates because they both pronounced their '*r*'s' properly. 'Those English,' he said, 'they let their *r*'s evade them. Smokah,' he waved his cigarette, a roll-up, in the air 'filtah – it won't do. A sure sign of moral laxity,' and he laughed and laughed until Peter laughed as well, uncertain of what was making them so happy.

Peter got a job, which he hadn't intended. This was meant to be his summer of freedom and fun, but he found having to think of something to do every day rather taxing and thought a job would help him structure his time. And it would be easier on his savings. He worked in a take-away patisserie, a vaguely unpleasant shopfront across the Strand from Charing Cross Station. He spent his four-hour shifts down in the airless basement filling croissants from a giant vat of béchamel that a frightened Argentinian – 'Colombia, I come from Colombia,' he insisted – cooked up. Peter knew Roberto was Argentinian because when asked that's what he said every time, before growing flustered and correcting himself too emphatically. Peter did not press the point and only mentioned the Falklands once when he asked Roberto what he thought of the war.

'Nothing,' said Roberto, 'I think nothing. I come from Colombia.'

The basement was hot, made hotter by the ovens, and they worked shirtless, their backs sliding wet.

When Peter cycled home across the river after work he felt the breeze dry his underwear.

At night he and George would go to the speakeasy. Eventually George and Amanda got together and the early morning sounds of the pigeons became mingled with the sound of the lovers who seemed to feel free to make love all over the conjoined apartments, with the exceptions of Peter's bedroom and the ghost kitchen next door. At these times Peter felt lonely, and he was rather glad of the company of the birds. In the morning he would stand at his bedroom window and watch them arrive and depart from the eaves. He would draw himself up and think of the girlfriends he had had at university and tell himself he could do it again, there was no reason to think the only women who liked him were those in Alberta – and thinking of Alberta made him think of Fancy and her infant friend and he lay back down on his hundred-year-old sheets. He liked to think of them as hundred-year-old but, in fact, they were made of nylon – pink – and he knew they probably came into being during the synthetic 1970s, the last time Vauxhall Palace was inhabited.

He determined to try harder with Fancy. That night at the speakeasy he spotted her friend Katherine. 'Where's Fancy?' he asked politely.

'Off somewhere with Tony, I should think.'

'Tony?'

Katherine looked at Peter sideways, as though his interest in Fancy piqued her interest in him. 'Oh Tony, don't you know Tony? He's been in love with Fancy since she was four.'

Peter felt himself pale.

'That's what they say. Tony was mates with Fancy's older brother and when he dandled her on his knee she gurgled and that was it for him.'

'Do they go out?'

'They're practically married. But if you ask me –' Katherine leaned forward, 'Fancy's bored with him. He's so old! Nearly thirty.' She clapped her hands and laughed.

Peter shared his beer with her. Joseph stopped by for a chat, cadged a cigarette off Katherine, then wandered away. Katherine told Peter about her current project – she was painting a replica of Michelangelo's Sistine Chapel on the ceiling of her bedroom. 'Those fingers,' she said, 'they're very difficult.'

Just when Peter was beginning to wonder if he should concentrate on being nice to this girl instead of the other, Fancy came along and sat on Katherine's knee. 'Hello,' she said, leaning to one side, her arms around her friend's neck. 'Hello there,' and she winked at Peter. She hauled herself upright and nuzzled Katherine's cheek.

'Leave it out,' Katherine said, neatly sliding out and away from Fancy's grasp. 'I'm going to find Simon.'

'Hi ya,' said Peter, nodding his head, feeling as though he was coming over all cowboy.

'Hello,' said Fancy, carefully placing an elbow on the table to steady herself. She was a little drunk. 'I'd like to get to know you. Alberta.' She giggled.

Peter pushed his last can of beer towards her. He got up and moved around to her side of the table. Fancy shifted nearer and they put their heads together. 'Britain has no rightful place in the South Seas,' she declared. 'Give back the Malvinas.' Her breath smelt of apples.

'I've got a friend who's Argentinian.' Peter thought of Roberto working in the heat of the kitchen.

'You do?' she said, moving a little closer. 'I would like to meet him.'

'I'll try to arrange it.'

They talked about the speakeasy – who was there that night, who was not – Peter's job, Fancy's work. They talked about the present, immediate things. She wore a sleeveless vest that hung off her thin shoulders, he glimpsed a white cotton bra underneath. No one interrupted them and the hour got later and the black walls moved closer, the music grew softer although it still carried with it a harsh edge – the Test Department, the Velvet Underground, Crass, Lee Perry. Fancy kept her hand on Peter's thigh.

After a while he was desperate to take a piss. When he was drunk he found he couldn't bring himself to use the word 'loo', it seemed too silly, undignified. Back home they said 'john' or 'can' but those words were no good any more either. He got up and told her to wait right there and almost wished he could tie her to the seat so she wouldn't move away.

The toilet was outside in the courtyard and to get there he had to pass through a series of small rooms. He entered one that had been painted red since the last time he was through – the night before? – walls, floor, ceiling. People sat on decrepit stuffed chairs and sofas, Amanda and George in one corner. Peter stood in front of them and started to talk, but they looked at him as though he was speaking from the bottom of the sea. 'Peace man,' George said. He held up his hand, fingers in a Star Trek V. Amanda said 'Shh,' then closed her eyes and fell asleep.

He got back to their table and Fancy was gone. Peter sat down in despair. The room was full of cigarette and druggy smoke, and for a moment he longed to take a bath. A voice behind him began to sing. A song about going out to Alberta, where the weather's good in the fall.

It was Fancy and he stood up and danced a slow dance with her as she sang. He had hated that song as long as he could remember. But she knew all the words, and she led him out of the speakeasy, across the courtyard, upstairs to her flat.

* * *

NEARLY A WEEK passed before Peter bothered to look inside the bureau in the sitting room on his side of Frankenstein. He and George used the other sitting room for lounging, drinking instant coffee, reading newspapers, this one relegated to thoroughfare. A footpath led from the hole in the wall through the dust down the corridor to his bedroom. In the middle of the floor, like a snow angel, was the imprint of a human body – Peter guessed George and Amanda had made love there the night before. He strayed off the path, stepped onto the ghost bodies, and opened up the double front doors of the heavy yellowing piece of furniture. Inside sat a white china teapot with its own round and shiny chrome teacosy, and two white china cups and saucers. He took them out carefully. Both side cupboards and the drawers were empty. He carried the china through to the kitchen. After work he'd invite Fancy for tea.

George was lying in the bath. 'Make me a cup of coffee, will you, mate?' he called out.

'I'm leaving for work.'

'Oh,' said George. 'Dag,' he added half-heartedly.

It was unusual for Peter to see George without Amanda now. Since they'd got involved George had become less animated, quieter, as though the two of them added together somehow made less than one person. Peter didn't mind, although sometimes he felt as though his friend was disappearing. And he was a little envious. Fancy was proving elusive. There one minute, vanished the next, like something he had conjured. George was not a tidy roommate. Peter didn't mind, he washed the dishes and cleared the table but didn't bother with much else. George had hung a black curtain in the bright bathroom and when he was on his own, he was often in the bath soaking. Peter had never been a big bather himself, at home he had always taken showers, but showers didn't seem to be part of the landscape of the British bathroom. So when he came home after a morning at work, streaked with cream sauce and smelling of baked cheese, he learned to bathe, even though it felt to him like something one did last thing at night.

And this morning he had managed to find Fancy at home; he invited her to come round later for tea in the new teacups. He clattered up the stairs with his bicycle over his shoulder, trying not to bounce it against the wall on every landing. Inside the flat there was a peculiar smell. He leaned his bike against the wall and walked through the kitchen. George had boiled the kettle dry, there was water across the floor where he'd got out of the bath and flung the kettle from the cooker into the sink. The wall next to the cooker was blackened. Peter felt suddenly dismayed by the untidiness and, thinking he would mop the floor and clean the kitchen in preparation for Fancy, went into the bathroom to get the mop. They did possess a mop, George had found one in a skip.

The room was dark and fuggy and Peter drew back the curtain. When he turned, he almost lost his footing, there was so much water on the floor. George was still in the bath. His head rested on the rim and one arm dangled over the side and Peter thought he looked like David's painting of Marat just after he was murdered by Charlotte Corday. Strapped around his arm was a piece of rubber tubing. An empty syringe lay on the puddled floor just out of his reach.

Peter stepped forward, unsure of his footing, unsure of how to view this scene. It was beyond him, and he knew it, he felt his Albertan childhood all around and it did not include lying in the bath all morning, syringes, black curtains, speakeasies. He took another step. The water in the bath was cold. But George was warm, in fact when Peter moved closer he heard the faint sound of George snoring. Once Peter knew he was not dead, he realized his roommate looked happy, content, comfortable even. So Peter took the mop and went back into the kitchen. He concentrated on getting ready for Fancy.

They had slept together, just once, that night when

Fancy sang 'Four Strong Winds' as they danced. They'd gone into the sitting room of her flat and she turned on the radio. 'My stereo got nicked,' she said. 'I've got loads of cassettes -' she pointed to the shelves – 'but nothing to play them on.'

'I've got a stereo at home,' Peter said, and hated himself for mentioning 'home,' for even thinking of Alberta when his new home was here, for bringing up his previous life. But Fancy didn't notice. She sat on the cushions piled next to the wall. He sat down beside her.

'Would you like a cup of tea?' she asked, but he moved close to her, drawn in by her smell of apples.

In the morning Peter woke with sun on his face. He sat up and a piece of paper fell to the floor. 'Good morning! Gone to market,' it read. His arm had pins and needles. In front of him, taking up most of the room, was an enormous loom, a thick and complex piece of woven and patterned fabric emerging from it. It was as though the loom had materialized with the morning, he had not noticed it the night before. He got up and walked around it and was reminded of a piece of farm machinery, it was somehow pre- and post-industrial simultaneously.

* * *

HE FINISHED CLEANING up the kitchen in preparation for her visit and was wondering what to do about the burnt kettle when there was a knock at the door. On the way up the corridor he considered what he was wearing – he was filthy, his newest white T-shirt smudged and sticking. He suddenly realized it didn't matter, this was what everyone in Vauxhall Palace dressed like. He felt happy; Fancy was coming to tea.

He opened the front door and there she was, and behind her a tall guy Peter didn't recognize. He tried to stop himself from frowning.

'This is Tony, Tony, this is Peter,' Fancy said as she moved past. Peter stepped aside and let Tony pass as well. Tony who, according to Katherine, had been in love with Fancy since she was four.

'Glad to meet you,' Peter said; 'come on in,' but they were already in the kitchen, seated at the table. 'Would you like a cup of tea?'

Fancy nodded. 'Tony wanted to see your flat, didn't you Tony? It's always interesting to see what other people are doing to their places.'

'You live here Tony?' Peter had thought he knew everyone in the flats.

Tony nodded. 'No milk in my tea.'

Fancy was standing, moving around the kitchen, inspecting.

'Would you like a piece of cake?' On the way home from work Peter had bought a Jamaican bun loaf; they could eat it with butter. There were only two white china teacups – he tried not to worry.

Tony shook his head. He turned to Fancy and said, 'We will be late.'

'I know,' said Fancy.

Peter was boiling water in a saucepan. In Alberta, he thought, I would probably ask them to explain. Late for what? What are you doing? Who is this guy? Let's be frank. He remained silent, afraid to turn around in case he found them kissing.

'When can we meet your Argentinian?' Fancy asked.

'Roberto? I guess I could bring him to the speakeasy one night,' Peter said, uneasily. 'Yeah, he might like that.' Roberto would love the speakeasy but he would be unhappy to discover that Peter did not believe he was Colombian and had, in fact, been telling the world he was Argentinian. 'I'll ask him next week.'

He poured the tea and cut the cake. No one spoke.

After a while Fancy said, 'Where's George?' and Peter said, 'How's Katherine?' and the door to the bathroom swung open and George stood there in his towel, looking refreshed, smiling sleepily. 'Hello Tony,' he said, 'got anything on ya?'

Tony shook his head.

'I'll be off then,' said George, 'people to see.'

*   *   *

AFTER THAT, Peter felt a little low for several days. He didn't know what to say to George about the syringe, and he didn't know what to say to Fancy. He felt he had found her and lost her already. He went to work and, afterwards, hung around with Roberto. Roberto was obsessed with the British Museum; he was viewing the collection room by room. Peter accompanied him to Ming Dynasty Chinese Porcelain. They progressed from display case to display case very slowly. Roberto didn't speak, he looked from item to item, reading all the text carefully. 'What is "pigment"?' he asked Peter in the middle of the room. Peter explained as best he could, and when he felt he couldn't look at another vase, he began to examine the tourists. All the women had characteristics – an ear, a hand, a smile – that reminded him of Fancy.

He couldn't bring himself to mention the speakeasy to Roberto, and on Friday night he went along on his own. He drank a couple of beers and talked to people he suddenly felt he had grown to know rather well – Joseph, Simon, Katherine, Squeak. Around midnight Fancy emerged from the red room at the back. When she saw him, she came straight over. 'I don't know what those people see in that stuff,' she said sharply.

'What stuff?'

'You know, Smack.'

Peter took a breath. 'What people?'

'What people? Tony. George. Amanda. Amanda, for God's sake. I've known her for ages. It's like a secret club.'

Peter nodded.

'Let's go,' she said.

They emerged from the speakeasy into the night, wandering away from the tenement onto the wasteland. The large empty space was ringed with streetlamps, but it was thick black and unlit in the centre. They headed into the dark. The night air was unusually warm, like summer nights back in Alberta. 'If you close your eyes,' he said, 'and block your ears, and plug your nose, we could believe we were out on the prairie.'

'It reminds me of Leamington Spa,' she said.

Fancy turned and put her hands on his chest. He realized he was at least a foot taller than her. She pushed against him and they fell backwards slowly onto the hard ground. She lay on top of him and made small movements, adjusting their clothing. A freight train went by on the overhead tracks. The breeze blew dust into Peter's eyes, but as he raised his hand to wipe it away, she began to kiss him. She kissed him hard, with much more force than she had the night they spent together underneath her loom. She bore down on him and soon he found himself inside her. She rocked back and forth and he clutched her breasts and she moaned and later he would see with great clarity that this was the moment they conceived her pregnancy.

2

GIRL ON A MOTORBIKE

IN THE SUMMER between high school and university, Peter travelled north to work on his uncle's ranch. He left the south-west corner of the province where his own family lived in the foothills of the Rockies and drove north-east to between Red Deer and Edmonton where the land stretches out flat. That spring his father had loaned him money to buy a motorcycle. His mother had objected, but only half-heartedly, as if it was something she thought she should do but didn't really feel. The motorcycle was a surprise, it had never occurred to Peter to want a bike, he didn't think of himself as that kind of guy. When he daydreamed about forms of transport it was always aeroplanes he saw himself boarding, jumbo jets with vast, expansive wings. But of course, once he had the money and was standing in the local garage with its rich smells of oil and overalls, he fell in love with the machine before him, black, low and gleaming.

He drove it to school the next day and impressed the hell out of everyone, including his teachers – no one there had seen the Motorcycle Boy in him before either. And one month later he hit the highway on it, heading up to his Uncle William's cattle ranch. He had a room in the big house and didn't do anything as prosaic as help out with the horses and livestock, his uncle employed skilled and seasoned men for that kind of work, real cowboys. The ranch was very prosperous, mostly because of the oil rig that stood in a far-flung corner. Although his uncle owned the rig and took all the profits he liked to pretend it didn't exist and that he was still an old-fashioned down-home rancher. Peter was assigned the tasks his uncle couldn't find time for, cleaning machinery, painting the outbuildings, helping his Aunt Lisa cook for the men. The O'Briens hadn't been able to have children of their own and while they did not treat Peter like their own son, they were fond of him in his role as oddjobbing employee. The pay was good and, with his motorcycle, he had a certain amount of freedom on the long summer days, so hot he sometimes thought he could hear the skinny trees around the house crackling as though they might burst into flame.

Late afternoons he would drive the twenty miles to the nearest town and the general store where they sold cold drinks. One day while he sat on his bike drinking his coke and eating potato chips, the local youth arrived en masse in a souped-up pick-up truck with an elevated axle, flames painted down either side of the body, a clapped-out Honda hatchback, and a motorcycle. Four boys got out of the truck, four girls out of the car, and a fifth person stretched off the bike. He watched as the biker lifted off the helmet, feeling mildly superior because he didn't wear one, and saw that it was a girl. She looked his way.

'Hi,' she said, smiling. Her hair was curly and dirty blonde, her eyes brown, and when she smiled her nose crinkled. Her friends had already gone into the store. 'Nice bike. You're not from around here?'

'I'm working for the summer out at my uncle's, William O'Brien.'

'Oh, O'Brien's, yeah. What's your name?'

'Peter.'

'Helen.'

They both smiled and Peter could think of nothing further to say. He brought the coke bottle to his lips, and gave the rim a wipe when he saw that it was coated in dust raised by the vehicles.

'Maybe I'll come out and visit you –' she indicated her bike.

'Is that yours?'

'I saved up my baby-sitting money for four years,' she said, laughing.

'My dad loaned me the money for mine.' He wished he hadn't said that, it made him sound spoiled and rich. Her eyes widened.

'Boy,' she said, 'lucky.' He thought maybe she was being ironic.

As they spoke the others were beginning to reappear outside the store. Helen made a movement as though to draw him near and introduce him to her gang, but he held back. He wanted to talk to her, not all of them. 'Well,' he said, starting up his bike, 'come out to the ranch and see me. Any time.'

'All right,' she said, smiling, 'I will.'

Peter peeled off onto the highway. It was easy to be cool on a motorbike.

A couple of days later Helen did show up at the ranch. After dinner, around seven, Peter was helping his Aunt Lisa with the clearing up. Every evening she cooked a big meal for all the ranchhands and her husband; every morning, and every lunchtime as well. Peter was doing the washing up, he was wearing an apron and rubber gloves and listening to rock music on the radio. His aunt went to the door. When he turned around Helen was standing in the kitchen, watching him. 'Hi ya,' she said. He waved at her with his pink rubber hand. She sat at the kitchen table while he finished the dishes.

'And Bob and Karen are getting married in September, and that's about it for around here. I tell you, it's boring. I get so bored I could scream. What's it like where you live?'

He removed the gloves, snapping each finger off one at a time. 'The town is a little bigger, but not much. Small enough to know everyone.'

'That's the worst thing, isn't it? Knowing absolutely everyone. Never seeing anyone or anything different.'

'People come and go a bit.'

'They do? Well, count yourself lucky. No one's come or gone here for years.' She laughed and he smiled as he noticed once again how her nose crinkled.

They went outside and sat on the porch. It was still

light, and very warm. His aunt had disappeared deep into the house, and his uncle was back out working with the men. Helen had parked her bike right next to his. He thought they looked happy together.

'Hey,' she said, 'let's go for a ride.'

'Okay,' he said, 'good idea.' He followed her off the porch. She had left her helmet behind this time.

They took the rutted road out to the highway, heading east away from the town. The wind felt good, and the sky was turning pink and orange with the sunset, so he didn't mind too much that they couldn't talk. Helen pulled ahead, and a few miles down the road he noticed she was signalling to the left. He turned off the highway and stopped next to her.

'Longest and straightest and flattest stretch of packed dirt road in Alberta,' she said, indicating the way ahead. 'Goes way out, past Carter's ranch, a hundred miles at least.' She smiled at him as if she had a plan that she expected him to have guessed. 'You ready?'

'Sure,' he said, revving his bike and taking off ahead of her. He watched the needle on his speedometer rise, and was surprised when he heard and then saw Helen come up alongside, overtake him and speed on ahead. She was lying flat, her body stretched along the seat of the bike, hands gripping the bars and the accelerator, legs trailing behind like those of a bird in flight, her hair plastered back against her head. Above the noise of the bikes he was sure he could hear her whooping and shouting.

She began to drop her speed. He came to a standstill beside her as she sat up swiftly and balanced the bike. 'See?' she said. 'You get the bike going and lie down at the same time. Then you go as fast as you can. You've got to try it, it's the best, it's the best feeling.'

He watched as she took off again. He started his bike and lifted his feet from the pedals, lowering himself down onto the warm gas tank, flipping his legs out behind. He felt an odd sensation in his gut, like vertigo, like he'd stepped off the cliff for real this time, except he was unafraid. It wasn't difficult to balance, the bike was moving fast, and soon he caught up with her and they were travelling side by side lying hard against their thrumming machines and it was the longest and straightest and flattest stretch of dirt road in Alberta, and they were going faster and faster and it was more like flying than flying could ever be.

After a while he heard her lose speed, so he took his hand off the accelerator. He dropped behind and watched as she swung her legs and raised herself upright. He felt flattened by the tremendous momentum and couldn't manage to get himself upright, so when he pulled over he fell off his bike into the dirt. Helen was off her machine and laughing at him, and running out into the field of wheat. He pushed the bike away, got up and shook off the dust, like a wet dog shakes off water, and followed after her. The grain was so dry that it cut and chafed against his arms and legs as he ran. Up ahead she tripped and disappeared among the sheaves and when he came upon her he threw himself down next to her, laughing and winded, his spirit still accelerating. And Helen kissed him, and he kissed her back, and they lay there together, touching and kissing. Their pulses slowed and he felt he was swooning.

Helen sat up. 'Let's do it,' she said, 'let's just do it. I don't care that I hardly know you.' She pulled off her T-shirt and undid her bra, sudden white against her brown skin. They spread their clothes out on the ground, both keeping on their underwear, and the sky was so red it was black. They held each other close, and kissed with their eyes shut, and he wondered if she felt as shy as he did. With the sweat and the dust and the grain she smelt wonderful and eventually they took off their underwear and he was inside her and it felt even better than stretching out on the speeding motorcycle.

Later, they sat up and she rested between his legs. The night was so bright and clear he could see the little hairs on the back of her neck, soft golden hairs that made him think of goslings.

When he got back to the house his aunt was watching television and his uncle had already gone to bed. 'I'm sorry, Aunt Lisa,' he said, 'were you waiting up for me?'

She smiled benevolently. 'Did you go out with Helen Gordon?'

He nodded.

'She always seems a nice girl. I knew her mother, back in the days when Will and I used to go to church. But then we found we had better things to do than religion.' She paused. 'Where did you go?'

'For a ride on our bikes.'

'A girl with a motorcycle,' Aunt Lisa said. 'I wish I'd had a bike when I was her age. I would have driven straight down that highway away from here, I can tell you that much.'

Peter was a little shocked. 'I didn't know you wanted to get away.'

'Everybody wants to get away when they are your age,' she said, turning back to the TV.

Peter and Helen took to driving out together several evenings each week, the nights when Helen wasn't busy making her fortune baby-sitting. Sometimes they would go down to the river, and make love on the wide, slow bend. Other times they would return to their stretch of dirt road; in their passion they flattened a considerable patch of Carter's wheatfield, scattering imprints of their bodies throughout the grain. They talked a lot, about their families mostly. Peter thought it was as though Helen was biding her time, waiting for something to happen, not him, but something bigger. She had no real plans, and was unimpressed by and uninterested in Peter's future at university. On Friday nights they met up with Helen's friends from high school, the crowd of couples from the flaming pick-up and the clapped-out Honda Peter had seen that first day at the general store. They drank beer down at the river, and Peter grew to know and enjoy their jokes and their stories. After a month he felt as though he had been there with them forever.

The summer grew hotter, the mosquitoes and blackflies intensified, and the smell of their sweat and sex became mingled with insect repellent. Helen had what she thought was a brilliant idea; she bought boxes of mosquito coils and when they went out into the fields at night she would make a circle of them at twelve-inch intervals along the ground where they lay. The smouldering coils stank and stung their eyes, and Peter worried that they might set the entire field alight, but it did keep the bugs away and he could run his hand along her smooth skin and not find her back smeared with blood and wings.

At the ranch Peter had embarked on cleaning and repairing the hayloft in the big barn furthest from the house. It was a gruesome job, the unmoving air so thick with dust he thought his lungs might simply give up and stop functioning, some afternoons he couldn't even manage to cough. The loft was alive with enormous spiders and tiny mice and he banged his head on the sloping roof and shouted with fright so many times it became part of his routine. When she had time his aunt would come up to help him, bringing a jug of apple juice and ice. They'd sit on the edge of the loft and look down into the barn and she would tell him about what she might have done had she had a motorcycle and driven away down that highway.

'I've always wanted to go to London,' she said as Peter gulped his drink. 'Not because of the Queen or any of that guff, but just to see the streets. I'd like to walk around Piccadilly Circus. Piccadilly Circus!' she laughed. 'It isn't a circus, you know, with animals and things. What on earth do you think it could be?'

'Why don't you and Uncle William go? You could get away in the winter, couldn't you?'

'I know, I know, and it's not as though we can't afford it –' Lisa often made sly references to the fact that she and William had money, money that they seemed unable to spend. 'But your uncle says he doesn't like to travel – not that he's been anywhere. We went to Vancouver on our honeymoon twenty years ago.'

She began to laugh again. 'Big deal!'

'Maybe you should go without him.'

Lisa turned slowly and looked at him. 'You are a bright boy,' she said, and changed the subject.

Peter's uncle and aunt took it as given that Helen Gordon had become his girlfriend. Every so often they invited her to dinner, but after the first time when Peter saw Helen at the table surrounded by the big ranch-hands all of whom she seemed to know by name, he decided they were better off on their own with a picnic. One night, at the end of July – Peter had been on the ranch for nearly two months by then – they went down to the river to eat. Helen had been in a strange mood when they met at their appointed place out on the highway; he tried to kiss her and she moved away. Now she was sitting on the opposite side of the blanket, as far away from him as she could manage.

Peter offered her some potato salad on a plate.

'I don't want anything,' she said. 'I feel sick.'

'You do?'

'Yeah. I feel like puking. In fact I am going to puke.' And, indeed, Peter watched as Helen got up, walked behind a tree, fell onto her hands and knees, and threw up. He went over to her, reached out to touch her back, but she sheered away from him as though he'd been about to smack her. Later she returned to the blanket, curling up under one corner as if she was cold. She didn't speak, so Peter thought it best to leave her in peace. He put the food away and lay back on the blanket and looked up at the stars. They were too many, too bright, to count, but he had lived all his life under such skies. After a while, it occurred to him what was wrong with Helen. He too began to feel cold. 'Are you sure?' he asked.

'Yes, I'm always regular, every twenty-eight days, like it says in the books. It's been forty-six days now.'

'Forty-six!'

'It's a lot, isn't it?'

'Forty-six.' He moved over nearer to her, placed his hand on her back. She was very hot. Peter felt calm. 'I didn't even think about birth control.'

'Aren't we a pair then.' She smiled a little. 'Somehow I thought that, you know, doing it outside, that you couldn't get pregnant if you did it outside.'

'You mean if you weren't in a bed?'

'Yeah.' They laughed and then fell silent. 'Fat lot of good those endless sex education classes at school did us,' she said eventually.

Peter tugged at Helen's shoulder, rolling her over into his lap. Her breath was sour as he bent to kiss her face. He undid the buttons on her shirt, pulling the cups of her bra down. He moved his hands over her breasts. It was true they felt changed, and he had noticed, but put it down to the odd and lovely strangeness of the female body. He ran his hand down her stomach and into her jeans, slipping it warmly between her legs. Helen bit his other hand and they made love differently that night, Helen on her hands and knees, crying out, Peter behind her, clamped on, straining. It was as though they were older, darker, more fierce.

They didn't make any plans, there didn't seem to be anything to plan, it had happened, it was happening. Peter lived with it in his thoughts and out of his thoughts at the same time. Helen remained calm. She didn't pull away from him again, now that he knew. Sometimes in the evenings if she was baby-sitting he joined her. On the couch in front of the television he tried to imagine what it would be like if this house was their house, if the kids upstairs were their kids, if this was their life. He didn't think about it too hard when he found that he couldn't, that his imagination wouldn't travel that far. They didn't talk about it, except every once in a while Helen would look up at him and state a figure. Fifty-one. Fifty-four. Sixty. One day he took it upon himself to ask how many days there would be in total. She didn't reply, and her look was mean.

And then four days passed and Helen didn't come out to the ranch to visit, didn't call. Peter began to worry, all the vague questions that had been mumbling away in his head suddenly articulated. Should he drop out of university and marry her; can you drop out when you haven't even started? Could he pay for her to go somewhere, where? Montreal? Toronto? or could you have it done in Calgary? What would his parents say? What about Aunt Lisa? When he went round that evening to where she usually baby-sat, Kathy, one of the friends from the gang, was there in her place.

'Where's Helen?' Peter asked when Kathy came to the screen door.

She spoke through the mesh without opening the door, as though she knew something about him she didn't like. 'At home. She's sick.'

'Really?' Peter asked, his stomach tightening. 'What's wrong?'

'I don't know,' said Kathy, 'you'll have to ask her yourself.'

Peter drove across town to Helen's house. As he travelled down main street he was tempted to squeeze the accelerator and lie flat on the seat and see what the town looked like from that birdy, speedy angle, see how fast he could leave it behind. But he turned sedately up her drive instead.

Mrs Gordon came to the door. 'Hello Peter,' she said, 'Helen thought you might be round.' Her expression was placid and welcoming.

'Is she okay?' He spoke a little too quickly. He didn't want to appear nervous.

'She's been feeling a little green around the gills.'

Peter went up the carpeted stairs and knocked on Helen's bedroom door.

'Come in.'

She was lying on the unmade bed in a pair of men's pyjamas. An upright fan blew a breeze lengthways along her body and the room was strewn with bits of paper, as though the fan had been allowed to redistribute the contents of the desk and wastebin. He paused at the door, and then went forward and sat on the bottom end of the bed. She winced.

'Are you all right?'

Helen's face was blank. 'Yes.'

Peter fought to control himself, all the questions in his head. The fan whirred past him every few seconds.

After a while Helen spoke. 'My mum doesn't know. She didn't guess.'

'I haven't told anybody.'

'Good.'

Peter didn't feel he could ask if she had told her friends. He thought about Kathy behind the screen door. There was a long silence.

'Have you ever seen the Frank Slide?'

'The what?'

'The big avalanche, at Frank, near the BC border.'

She didn't reply.

'We should go there sometime. It's . . . amazing.' He fell silent again.

'I want you to do something for me,' she said.

'Okay. Anything. I'll do anything.'

'That's not necessary. Just do this one thing.' She indicated her desk. 'The brown paper bag.' Peter got up, pulled the chair away from the desk, and retrieved the bag which was stuffed full of what felt like cloth, he couldn't see in the dark room.

'I want you to get rid of them. I don't care how. Burn them. Whatever.'

Peter nodded. 'Okay,' he said. 'Anything else?'

'No. That's all. That's it, Peter. That's all. Goodbye.' She turned over and rolled towards the wall. The breeze from the fan lifted her pyjama shirt. He saw the mild furrow that her spine created along her back. Although he wasn't close enough to see it, he knew that her skin was lightly covered with soft gold hair, so fine as to almost not exist. He hated that her farewell sounded so final. He wanted to lie with her on the bed. He clutched the paper bag to his chest instead, and turned and left.

He got on his motorbike, wedging the bag between his legs. Suddenly feeling very tired, he drove out to his aunt and uncle's ranch. He put the paper bag on the chair next to his bed where he could see it, and went to sleep.

He woke at first light, picked up the bag and, without considering where he should go, found himself on his bike heading down to the wide bend in the river where he and Helen had so often been together. He left his shoes on the seat, but didn't bother to roll up his jeans. Where the river water meets the smooth mud he turned the bag upside-down and emptied it. The contents fell out in a clump. He sorted through the items one by one, pulling them apart. Two sheets, one fitted. Two bath towels. Rigid and stuck to themselves with – after a moment he realized – blood. And gristle. Peter stood stock still as he understood what he was looking at. He stepped back hard into the water as though the gang was there and someone had given him a playful shove. Losing his balance, he fell forward and grabbed for a handhold, pulling a sheet with him.

As it hit the water the sheet sank, and then rose up again, billowing. Peter hung onto a corner as the river attempted to pull the cloth away. He felt the sheet strain like an animal trying to escape from his grasp. He watched as the bright blood began to rinse out – to him this seemed miraculous. After a few moments the floral pattern re-emerged. He let go, and the sheet floated away. He scrambled up onto the bank and kicked the other sheet and the towels into the water, scraping his foot hard against the root of a tree. They too sank and then slowly rose, like great underwater birds taking flight, floral sheet and towels pastel pink, coming clean in the sun, the green and silver glinting river water washing them away.

3
GOTHIC

PETER WENT INTO work one day to find Roberto had gone.

'Deported!' shouted his boss. 'Would you credit it? Turns out he wasn't Colombian at all, but an Argie!'

'Oh,' said Peter, heading down to the basement before the man could say another thing.

The job was harder to bear without Roberto to share it, without Roberto and his tales of Great British Museums and their marvellous contents. Now it just seemed hot, and the paycheques too small, and the new cook's béchamel tasted disgusting. There wasn't any reason to stay, Peter was adding savings to his savings which was contrary to what you were supposed to do during your summer away. So he quit.

By this time George's smack habit had become fullblown, gothic. He and Amanda had grown pale and thin; they both wore black, Amanda with strategic splashes of purple that only served to show up the damaged veins in her neck and hands. When they were high they were impossible to talk to, and when they were normal they were obsessed with sorting out their next hit. Peter had read somewhere that it was feasible to be a junkie and function completely normally, to treat the habit like a small, secret and much loved pet you kept hidden in your room, but it wasn't like that with George and Amanda. They'd turned into large and swirling smackheads locked in a lurid drama of their own making, a kind of morbid sitcom that Peter found very boring. He was angry with George, and felt he'd lost yet another friend.

He and Fancy continued to spend time together; she told Peter she was well and truly rid of Tony. He spent afternoons pottering around her flat while she sat at her loom. He was working his way through her shelf of books. Sometimes they listened to the radio, which always seemed to be tuned to the farming programme 'The Archers'. Peter couldn't follow it even though Fancy was happy to explain the plot to him endlessly.

One weekend she took him home to meet her parents in Leamington Spa. It went all right, although they were made to sleep in separate beds and Peter was surprised that Fancy accepted this without arguing. He offended her parents when he referred to their garden, their lovely big garden with its hedges and roses, pergola and pond, as their 'backyard'. 'Backyard,' Fancy's father had guffawed, 'is that what you call it in the colonies?'

Fancy knew that she was pregnant after her period was only a couple of days late. She stood in front of her loom with her legs planted firmly to the floor and her arms crossed tight across her chest. 'I'm pregnant,' she announced, her expression unreadable.

Peter didn't know how to respond. It's the second time, he thought, I've made the same mistake twice. I'm only twenty-two and I've fucked it up twice. He'd assumed she was on the pill. He moved towards her and Fancy let him take her in his arms.

'I'll arrange for a termination,' she said. 'We can get it on the NHS. Hopefully I won't have to wait too long.'

A termination, he thought, I've never heard it called that before. Final sounding, and yet, euphemistic, vague. Time for your termination, darling. All trains terminate here. He felt relieved for a moment and then was overwhelmed with guilt that she would have to bear it, not he.

'I had one last year,' she said, her face hardening. 'I know all about it.'

Peter held her tight in bed that night, although he avoided touching her belly. He thought she smelt different, somehow fresher and older at the same time. She fell asleep right away but later on woke him with her crying.

'What's wrong?' he whispered.

'It will hurt,' she said. 'It did last time.'

He shivered and sweated, and rocked her to sleep.

* * *

HE ACCOMPANIED HER to the clinic for her pregnancy test, the subsequent meetings with doctors and counsellors. He was always the only man in the waiting room and the other women looked at him suspiciously. He tried to appear solicitous, good-natured, reliable, sweet, feeling as though it fell on him to redeem his reputation, the reputation of all men responsible for unwanted pregnancies. Fancy was very calm, even when they were told she would have to wait four weeks until the hospital could book her a place. She didn't exhibit any outward signs of being pregnant, and Peter watched her carefully. She stopped eating, saying she didn't feel like it any more, and after a while her ribs began to protrude a little. She wanted to keep living as though nothing had changed, nothing was altered in any way. She kept on working at her loom, listening to the radio, making and drinking endless cups of tea.

One day Peter walked into his bedroom and found George and Amanda asleep in his bed, on his pink nylon sheets, sharing his pillow, like twin Goldilocks in a bad dream. He shouted at them, and shooed them away, as though they were pigeons visiting from the next room. They gathered their things and looked at him mournfully. 'Sorry mate,' said George. 'We got a bit lost.'

'Just get out,' Peter replied, although he knew what they meant, he felt that way himself these days.

After that, George and Amanda stopped using the flat as their base. Peter assumed they were spending their time slumped in a corner round at Amanda's. When it became clear that they weren't coming back, he embarked on a cleaning campaign. He got rid of the piles of newspapers and empties, he washed the dishes, the floors, the windows, cleaned the fridge, the cooker, the bathroom. He borrowed a vacuum cleaner from Fancy and went so far as to hoover the curtains, their makeshift ones as well as the ones left behind by the flat's previous occupiers. Now he was no longer working he became increasingly houseproud. He invited Fancy round to his place in the evenings, cooked for her and tried, unsuccessfully, to make her eat.

Fancy wouldn't spend the night with him at his flat. She couldn't stand the sound of the pigeons. She hated hearing the quiet movements and soft flutters emerging from the ghost kitchen as the birds settled in for the night. 'I just can't get used to it,' she said. 'I don't see how you stand it.'

'It's not a case of getting used to it,' he tried to explain. 'I just like it, that's all. They reassure me.'

One morning he went into the toilet on the small balcony and discovered a couple of twigs on the floor. He got the broom and swept them away before heading out to do some grocery shopping. He came back, put everything away in the cupboards, went into the toilet again and found another pile of twigs, neatly arranged in a circle. He thought the wind was playing tricks and swept them away. He went over to Fancy's for the rest of the day.

They stayed up watching a movie on TV. He held her close to him on the settee, felt her deep and calm breathing. In the commercial break, she spoke quietly.

'I wonder if I ever will have a baby,' she said.

He took a breath. 'Sure you will. If you want to. When you're ready. Some day. You're only twenty-one.'

'We could go out to Alberta,' she said, 'weather's good there in the fall.'

He smiled and watched the movie.

'Do you want children?' she asked a bit later.

He had never thought about it. 'I don't know,' he said. 'At the moment getting pregnant seems like the worst thing that can happen.' He felt her stiffen. The movie came back on. 'Well, maybe not the worst thing,' he said.

When he got back to his flat late the next morning, he threw open the window and ran a bath in his clean bathroom that smelt of fresh cleanser and bleach. He got undressed and, wearing only a towel, went out onto the balcony. On the floor of the toilet was a nest. Inside the nest was an egg. A small, translucent grey pigeon egg. Peter looked at it, appalled. He went back into the kitchen and fetched a plastic bag and the dust brush. The nest was a pathetic affair, bare and thin and straggly, as if the pigeon had not realized on each of its return visits that its previous efforts had been swept away. The egg itself rested on bare concrete. Peter brushed it up and refused to think about whether or not he had broken the shell. He tied the ends of the bag together, put it in the rubbish and carried it out and down to the courtyard before getting into the bath.

That night he and Fancy went to the speakeasy. They hadn't been for a while, their news had made them anti-social, had made them want to hide away. Beforehand they walked to the off-licence and between them bought a large bottle of rum and another of coke. Then they went and sat in the room with the loudest music and proceeded to drink the night away.

Around two a.m., George appeared at their table. 'You going home?' he asked, his voice roughened, as though he'd been in a fight.

'Maybe later. We've still got this to drink.' Peter indicated the bottle. He and Fancy had been dancing and he was having a good time.

'No, I mean . . . what I mean is: are you going back to Canada?'

Fancy had never asked Peter this question. He looked at her now, she was watching him closely. 'Hello George,' she said, but neither she nor George took their eyes off Peter. He seemed to need an answer with some urgency.

'I don't know,' Peter said. 'I guess so.' He looked at Fancy again. 'I don't know. Why is it so important all of a sudden?'

'I'm going back to Oz.'

'You are?'

'Yeah.'

'But why? You seem to be . . . having a good time.'

Peter thought of George lying like a corpse in the bath. 'That's the point, isn't it,' he said, suddenly adamant. 'That's just it. Got to go home, don't I, back to Mum and Dad. Away from this place.' He passed his hand slowly through his hair.

'What about Amanda?'

George shrugged. 'God I love that girl,' he said, shaking his head. 'She'll survive. Things happen.'

'I'm going to the loo,' said Fancy suddenly, and she left.

'I hope I didn't upset her,' George said.

'She's already upset.'

'Englishwomen,' George said, 'aren't they fantastic?'

*　*　*

HE WENT WITH Fancy to the hospital for the termination. They were both frightened and they took strength in hiding their fear from each other, determinedly, cheerfully, reassuringly. It was eight a.m. and the waiting room was full of miserable women, a few sheepish men. There were posters for contraceptives everywhere. Eventually, a nurse called Fancy's name – her name really was Fancy, he knew that already. They said goodbye. Peter would come back to pick her up at five, it would be as though she'd spent the day working.

He went to the British Museum and shuffled through the endless rooms, thinking of Roberto when not worrying about Fancy. He stopped in the manuscript room for a while, and in Abyssinian statuary. He got talking to an older museum guard who told him that, contrary to public perception, Japanese tourists were very noisy. 'Canadians all wear those little flags,' he said when Peter told him where he was from. 'Americans do not,' he added. On the way out Peter bought a postcard of a da Vinci drawing that reminded him of Fancy. He had the idea that he would keep it, that he would take it back to Alberta with him and place it between the pages of a notebook and look at it from time to time. On the way out of the museum he realised he would soon be leaving.

He met Fancy at the hospital. The nurse insisted she be delivered to the door in a wheelchair and that he call a taxi. Fancy wanted to go home on the bus, but the nurse stood by, arms crossed, until the taxi arrived. Peter kept asking if she was okay, and she kept saying she was. He took her back to her flat, made her tea, and tried to cosset her, but all she wanted to do was sleep. She said it wasn't too painful; she looked very weak. Peter felt angry and useless. He knew Fancy didn't love him any more – how could she?

He sat by her bed and watched her sleeping; in the middle of the night, he went back to his own flat. He crawled under his ancient pink sheets, exhausted. But he couldn't sleep. In the next room the pigeons were already stirring. After a while, he got up. He went out to the corridor and into the ghost kitchen. When he entered the room the pigeons fled. He tried to sit on the splatter-encrusted chair but it was too broken to support him, so he sat beneath the layered table instead, leaning against the wall. The pigeons began to return slowly. He couldn't see them, it was not yet light, but he could hear them, smell them. They rustled and scrabbled. They made their pigeon noises, that throaty yearning coo. They settled all around him, and he slept.

Charlie

CHARLIE DID NOT like the Royal Family because she did not want to sleep with any of them. Not a one. Not even the little ones. What use was a Royal Family, repository of the nation's fantasies, when you couldn't fancy them? No use at all. Charlie was a republican.

Charlie's mother had named her Charlotte, after Prince Charles. It was better then Andrea, or Edwina, she supposed. Her mother thought Anne too plain. Princess Anne, the one who looks like a horse. The one who is a horse. The only one with any self-respect. A maelstrom of divorce had hit that family. Too bloody rich.

Most of the time, Charlie did not think about that family at all. Sometimes she ran into them, at film previews in Leicester Square, inaugurating hospitals and clinics. They were there, doing their stuff, and Charlie happened by. They'd wave at her in the crowd, and she'd shrug her shoulders. She didn't want any of their waves.

She had to admit it though, she had had sex with Prince Charles a couple of times. It made her bad-tempered just to think of it. It was after his wife Diana had discovered he was still in love with Camilla

Parker-Bowles, his old girlfriend. Diana had thrown a frying pan at him, and he'd agreed to stop seeing Camilla. It came out later that he'd had his fingers crossed behind his back, but decided to give Parker-Bowles a wide margin for a while anyway. During these boring, non-love-sexy times, Charles tended to frequent Irish pubs in Camden, a part of North London that smells of beer and rotting vegetables. He travelled incognito, disguised as an Irishman.

Charlie herself went to Irish pubs for the craic, for the music. That night the bar was so crowded she could hardly move. Everyone kept burning each other's hair with their fags. Charlie drank whiskey, and Prince Charles trod on her foot. At the time she didn't know who he was, but she left with him anyway.

He kept on his disguise – a black wig, sideburns, little round dark glasses, and a cool leather hat – and shagged her up against a tree. She made him use a condom, she was paranoid about condoms and carried loads around all the time, and he wasn't too pleased. His fake accent slipped as he came and that was when she realized who he was. She did not have an orgasm, never having liked the Royal Family. And she told him so.

'I've never liked you lot, you know.'

'Sorry?'

'My mum named me after you, but that doesn't mean I've sworn my allegiance or any such thing.'

Prince Charles mumbled something then, Charlie wasn't sure what. She could tell he didn't do this kind of thing often, so she gave him a friendly kick on the tush and sent him on his way. She went back to the pub for lock-up.

The next time she went down the Dog and Bone, he was there again.

'You been here every night, waiting for me?' she asked.

'What're you drinking?' he said, his Irish accent back in place.

They drank together that night, and she was unimpressed by the way he kept pace with her, not bad for a nancy-boy prince, and she told him so. Her words were garbled though, by the drink, and the music which flowed over their heads in its taps and its paces. The fiddlers were on form tonight, everyone nodding their heads to the rhythm. Sometimes London was a very Irish place.

'Bit different than Buckingham Palace,' she said.

'Too right,' he replied, sounding vaguely Australian. She didn't miss a thing.

That night they shagged up against a different tree. In fact after the musicians finished, they escaped out of the smoke into the night air and wandered up the road until they reached Hampstead Heath. The Heath whispered sex at night, and as they walked, she noticed men flit in and out of the trees.

'Don't forget your condoms,' she shouted out to them. 'It's a good life, to be a queer boy,' she said to Charles. 'Endless variety.' He didn't reply. They found a tree, and then they found a patch of grass, and they lay together passionately. Charlie liked sex, it was unproblematic. It was all the other business that went along with it that proved so trying. But she and Prince Charles were avoiding unnecessary complications. He rarely spoke, and when he did, Charlie couldn't make sense of anything he said. So she ignored him and offered her body instead.

During the day, nothing much happened. Charlie went to work. Well, she went to look for work. She had lost her job a couple of years ago now, and hadn't been able to find one since. Every day she went to the job centre. But there was never anything there. There was supposed to be a boom on, but for Charlie it was all a big bust. She rolled smaller and smaller cigarettes, and stole books for a living.

She didn't see Prince Charles for a while. In real life, that is; she did see him on the news, he was always on the news, him and that estranged wife of his. Charlie went to her usual haunts. She saw her usual friends, and spoke of usual things. She knew better than to mention shagging the Prince. Bonking the Man Who Would One Day Be King. Without the wig, and the sideburns, and the glasses, and the hat, he was truly ugly.

And then one day she sat down on a bench in St James's Park. The park was near the palace, but she was there to see the ducks. She had been evicted from her flat and couldn't think what else to do with herself. The bailiffs had taken everything, which was okay since it meant she didn't have anything to carry. She sat for a while, the sun was shining, and she raised her face to it. She felt someone sit down beside her.

She looked around. She could smell him. He smelt of greasy hair and leather hat. His black jeans were torn and faded.

'Hi ya,' she said. 'How goes royalty?'

'Fucked if l know,' Prince Charles replied.

'Good,' she said, 'good. Your grasp of the street id-iom is improving.'

They sat in companionable silence for a while. Then Prince Charles got up and wandered away, back in the direction of the palace gates. Charlie sat alone. The speeding clouds in the sky slowed their pace.

Dear All

DEAR ALL,

Another year has passed and it's time once again for my annual, up-to-the-minute letter which I send to you all out there. I know some of you feel this is a bit impersonal, but, hey, otherwise you might not hear from me at all. I don't know about you but I really appreciate the letters I get at Christmas.

Well, it's been quite a year for the Mytel family. Larry and I separated and are filing for divorce. This may seem sudden for most of you, especially if you haven't heard from me since my last Christmas letter. We didn't tell anyone until it was all sewn up. In fact, Larry didn't even tell *me* for a couple of years – he waited until just a few weeks before we put together our separation agreement and best of all, he waited until I had someone in place to fill the gap that his departure would have created. That's where Bob comes in. Larry and I had been friends years ago with Bob and his wife Donna. Bob and Donna have since divorced. At a conference in Toronto I ran into Bob. Over the years Larry often told me that he thought I should be married to Bob, not him. And, when we met again at the conference, Bob also seemed to think he was the

157

perfect man for me and went around the cocktail party telling everyone so. I was confused. Where would it all lead? But when Larry started talking 'separation' we both looked to Bob for assistance. And Bob was happy to accommodate us – me. It has worked out really well. Larry has what he wants in his life – to make his own decisions, spend his own money, do his sports, and check out the babes (all the things he wasn't able to do – or rather, wasn't *supposed* to be doing while he was with me – because he was married so young). And I have what I want in life – a home, a job, and a man who is loving, caring and protective of me. What a good Christmas this is going to be.

WARREN CONTINUES reading. He hasn't seen Debbie Barnsley – now Debbie Mytel soon to be Debbie someone else – in sixteen years, but he still gets a photocopied letter from her every year, like minutes from the annual general meeting of a university alumni association. Warren doesn't send Christmas letters. He likes Christmas, he spends it with his wife Kathy and their two kids, but he doesn't send Christmas letters. He receives them though, mostly from distant relatives, school friends, and old girlfriends like Debbie, people he hasn't seen in years. He reads them and, as he reads, he remembers things.

LET ME TELL you about Bob. He and Donna didn't have any kids, so their divorce was straightforward, just like Larry and me. He is six foot four (my mother loves that), 185 pounds, with a head full of beautiful silvery-grey hair – handsome, that's the word I'd use. And I do. Often. He owns one 1965 vintage sports jacket which he inherited from his dad, no dress pants, only jeans, Western shirts, tooled leather belts with big silver buckles, cowboy boots and cowboy hats. Otherwise his wardrobe consists of mountain gear. He has lived in town for twenty years. He's a non-smoker, has given up coffee for over four years now, and seldom drinks. He's a great cook and loves to have people over for dinner or to stay the weekend. He leaves for work at seven a.m., comes home to fix me lunch (sometimes we don't make it as far as the kitchen), and returns home after six for nice long evenings. And the sex, well, running the risk of sounding crude, let's just say Bob is a *big* improvement on Larry. We stay in a lot, listen to music, talk, things Larry and I never did.

The down side on Bob: he's poor, but of course, he's very happy as I've heard poor people tend to be. He does all the things I find scary and life-threatening but which he and his ilk think of as 'man-stuff' such as horses, guns, motorcycles and mountains. Sometimes he's so much like Grandpa I can't believe it. He loves to read which is great, but he tends to have read the entire book and remembered the facts and he corrects me when I'm making eloquent sweeping generalizations. Don't ya loathe it! But it really is love. It is wonderful to love and to be so loved. I am so grateful for the opportunity I've been given to live two terrific lives in one lifetime, my life with Larry and now, my life with Bob.

WARREN DOESN'T DO 'man-stuff'. He's surprised to hear Debbie is enjoying that aspect of Bob, she never used to go for macho types. People can change a lot though, especially over the sixteen years since university. Warren himself has changed. He's got two kids for Christ's sake, and he loves his wife, and not only at Christmas. He's happy with his job. He sells real estate on Vancouver Island. Debbie wouldn't believe it if she heard that was what he did now. Or perhaps she would. Perhaps even then, when he was a flamboyant and, he thought, Byronic youth, he had the soul of a real-estate man.

BOB AND I plan to have a family. We're not too old, lots of people have families late these days. We feel very settled together and think that we could give a child a good start in life. We just pray (yes, we *pray* – really, both of us – and it is so wonderful to be with a man with whom I can pray) that we will be able to conceive. Hopefully we will have news for you in our next Christmas letter!

My only other big news is that I've been promoted to senior manager level at work. I've been working on a gigantic project which involves data extrapolation from 2,500 files from the Chief Medical Examiner's Office, pulling approximately 1,200 suicide notes from those files for analysis. The reasons why people kill themselves are very sad indeed, but I've been down myself and I couldn't say I haven't thought about it once or twice. Haven't we all? Bob says he doesn't want me getting any ideas – and who said he didn't have a sense of humour?! If there is one thing I miss about Larry, it is the jokes and the laughter. With Bob I am extremely happy, he just doesn't make me laugh so very much. So let's pray for love *and* laughter, for us and for every one of you.

WARREN DOESN'T THINK he ever met Larry Mytel, he can't quite remember. Nor does he remember Debbie having had a particularly keen sense of humour. Warren isn't much of a joker himself but he likes a laugh. He and his wife Kathy get romantic comedies from the video store. They have a laugh.

Warren wonders what Debbie's job could possibly be. He wonders if Kathy kept Debbie's previous Christmas letters. Maybe if he reads the last decade or so he will be able to figure out where Debbie works. Twelve hundred suicide notes. Phew.

Just then, as Warren sits and stares at Debbie's photocopied letter, Kathy comes into the room.

'What you got there?' she asks.

'Debbie Mytel's Christmas letter.'

'Interesting?'

'Sort of,' says Warren, 'sort of weird. I haven't seen her for sixteen years.'

'Funny how some people like to keep in touch.'

'Yeah,' says Warren. Kathy leaves the room again. She is spending the evening cleaning up after the kids. Once a month she attempts to put everything, all their junk, from all over the house where it belongs, from where it will levitate over the next few weeks. At the same time Warren is meant to go through all the postal paper work, pay the bills, etc. This is part of their deal. Their relationship is one of many deals – Warren takes the kids to school, Kathy picks them up. Warren baby-sits while Kathy is at aerobics, Kathy baby-sits while Warren goes jogging with Al. Warren has sex with Kathy whenever Kathy wants, Warren is always careful to prevent Kathy from conceiving again. Kathy rubs Warren's back when he is tired. They are happy.

Warren would never have been happy with Debbie. Her Christmas letters reassure him of that. They had not been happy even when they were young and had had their – Warren can't bring himself to think of it as an affair even though it went on for some time and it had been nowhere near as solid as the word relationship suggests – when they were young and had had their . . . thing. It seems such a long time ago. What had they been doing together?

In those days – yes it's true, although Warren can hardly believe it himself any more – in those days, Warren had thought he might be gay. In fact, he had positively longed to be gay. It had seemed the only way of escaping certain inevitabilities. Warren shakes his head – it turned out that the inevitable wasn't so bad after all. He'd had too much Oscar Wilde too early, that must have been the explanation. He and Debbie had met during their first year at university. Everything was wild and strange and confusing. Debbie had developed an enormous crush on Warren. Warren had been bowled over by her. He'd had crushes on other people, plenty of them, all boys. None had ever shown the slightest bit of interest in returning his gaze, but

Warren preferred it that way. He kept his crushes secret. Debbie was a different proposition. She was smart, she was pretty in a boyish sort of way. She said she didn't care if he was gay, she wanted him anyway. Debbie believed that this made sense and her logic took his breath away. 'Okay,' he said, finally, 'okay.'

They began doing stuff together – movies, nights in the student union bar drinking with their friends. They went for long walks in the park on frosty mornings. They talked about their families. Warren found himself telling her things he had thought he would never tell anyone. Debbie talked about her friends from high school, how she could never get a date.

They didn't sleep together. Warren avoided that. They kissed several times, on the way home from the bar, when they'd had too much to drink. Warren would drop her off at the door of her residence building, offering up the excuse that he had to get to the library early the next day. She would sigh and turn away. They parted like this over and over again.

But then it seemed he had to decide – he could tell Debbie was getting fed up with him. She didn't say as much, but he saw it in her shoulders, in her face. He realized he didn't want to lose her, not really; he didn't want to be left on his own. He resolved to do the right thing.

They began their evening – that fateful night was how Warren had thought about it even before it happened – in the smoky, beer-soaked student union bar. They got rapidly and thickly drunk. They pretended to discuss Immanuel Kant and then they kissed briefly when the time seemed right. Warren thinks he can still remember the taste of Debbie's mouth from that night – beery, he thinks, wet, female. He almost froze then and there, was almost unable to continue. But something pushed him on, led him back to the halls of residence, that something, of course, being Debbie.

Kathy comes back into the room; she is carrying a small bicycle that belongs to their four-year-old son Teddy. 'What are you doing, Warren?' she asks, slightly suspicious.

'Paying the bills,' says Warren, 'they pile up.' Kathy leaves again. Warren looks back down at Debbie's letter.

AND SO ANOTHER year has come to an end. I hope all of you out there have a wonderful Christmas, and that you feel as warmed by happiness as Bob and I do. For those of you I haven't seen for a while, well, I've got a few grey hairs now, but nothing a little dye won't cover up!

Happy New Year!

LOVE DEBBIE, reads Warren. Warren never did love Debbie. He never had the opportunity after that fateful night. They went back to her room. Debbie lit all her candles. She loved candles, they were everywhere. Warren had never had sex with anyone before, he didn't know if Debbie had. He hoped she knew what she was doing. They sat on the bed, there was only one chair and it was attached to the desk. Debbie put on a record. Abba. Warren asked her to put on something more serious instead, King Crimson or something like that. He felt a bit woozy from the alcohol. Debbie lay down on the bed and closed her eyes. He lay down too, thinking great, we'll just go to sleep, but he quickly realized that wasn't what she meant him to do.

Debbie looked romantic in the candlelight, even more like a boy than usual, a long-haired Edwardian boy. She was giving instructions. One hand here, the other there. Lips. Teeth. Tongues. Even now Warren can remember his fumbling with embarrassing clarity. They began removing different bits of their clothing, sweaters, shoes. He was surprised by her bra, it looked so . . . architectural. They pushed their bodies together awkwardly, rubbing this, pressing that. They took off their jeans. Underwear. Everything seemed damp, slippery. Debbie wanted Warren to lie on top of her, so he did, feeling heavy, unwieldy, trying not to burp. Debbie had stopped wiggling and was lying very still. She looked up at him, her young face full of expectation, desire and fear. In her eyes he saw the future kids, cars, summer holidays. He knew what he was supposed to do next.

'I can't,' he said, rearing back, elbowing Debbie in the stomach, bashing his own head against the wall. 'I don't know why, I just can't.' Warren is speaking out loud now, in his own sitting room.

'Why not?' says Kathy who has returned with an armful of books. Warren looks up.

'Nothing hon,' he says, embarrassed again. She smiles as she crosses the room.

Later, when he and Debbie had their clothes back on and were drinking cups of tea, Warren still apologizing and Debbie still on the edge of tears, Debbie had said, 'They have clubs for people like you.'

'What?' said Warren.

'You know, the gay students' club, things like that.'

'Oh?' said Warren.

'You don't always have to feel outcast and disgusting.'

'Oh,' says Warren. 'Thanks.'

KATHY COMES BACK into the room. This time her arms are empty. She walks right up to Warren, plucks Debbie's Christmas letter out of his hands and pushes the dining room table back a couple of feet. She places herself unceremoniously on Warren's lap. The weight of her body brings Warren swiftly through the years. He puts his arms around her waist. He remembers that Kathy used to look like a boy, before she had the kids. He says to himself it's not my fault about Debbie and Larry and Bob. Kathy leans back against his chest.

'Maybe we should do a Christmas letter next year,' she says.

'Oh yeah, what would we say?' asks Warren. 'Dear All. Everything is exactly the same this year as it was last year except we're all one year older. We divorced and remarried in the spring. The children share the psychological profile of a serial killer. For those of you who haven't seen me in sixteen years, I've aged well, I now look exactly like Marlon Brando. For those of you that Kathy and I never slept with, well, you don't know what you're missing. Merry Christmas. Love Warren and Kathy.' Warren stops.

'Debbie Mytel,' said Kathy, picking up the letter. 'Did you sleep together?'

'Not really,' says Warren. 'Hardly at all.'

The Visits Room

EVERY TIME I visit James in prison he tries to have sex with me. The visits room is crowded, overheated in winter, airless in summer. We are allowed to sit on the same side of the table. We start by holding hands, we progress to kissing, he places one hand on my breast. It makes him die, I can feel it, he would give everything away if he could just have me. Before I come to visit I get a letter from him; he tells me not to wear any knickers, to wear a big, long skirt. To sit on his lap, my skirt covering us, and then to move in a slow way that will let him get inside me.

We never quite make it. An officer always walks by just when I think it's about to happen, and they always make a joke about us trying to have sex and James always denies it and gets angry and I slide off his lap and back onto the chair next to his. Once the officer goes past James always, always, looks as though he is going to cry. But he never does. And neither do I.

JAMES KILLED HIS brother-in-law. It is an unalterable fact. Bobby was a violent man. We knew he used to hurt James's sister Maria. It wasn't straightforward slapping around, we knew he tortured her, the marks on her body showed us. Finally, after years of it, Maria threw Bobby out. James was relieved, we all were. We thought a happy ending had arrived.

But then Maria came round one Sunday. She looked terrible, her hair a wild mess, her face bruised and scratched. Weeping, she told us that Bobby had broken into the house and raped her, and gone off with their two kids. As she spoke I felt James's body grow tense. He had an idea of where Bobby had gone, I don't know how. So James went round to try and get the kids back, and they got into a fight, and James killed Bobby. He crushed his skull with a heavy old mirror that Bobby's new girlfriend had hanging on the wall. He drove Maria's kids to our place. Maria was happy to see her children, but I could tell something had gone wrong. James turned towards the front door again. I asked him where he was going. 'To the police,' he said, and I knew what had happened.

James was in prison on remand for a long time. When his trial finally took place we realized he would lose. We hoped for a verdict of manslaughter. He had no previous convictions, he had never been in trouble before. But they said he had gone round intending to kill Bobby, and I guess he had. He was convicted of murder and got life. He was given a life sentence.

THE VISITS ROOM is very bare. The tables and chairs are battered and old, the walls are grey, the barred Perspex windows are filthy. An officer sits at a table on a raised platform. We are watched. Other prisoners have noisy, sociable visits but James and I often sit in silence. It is difficult to talk; I feel that James has himself only barely held in. When I'm there he will sit and clutch my hand and stare into my eyes for the whole two hours we are allowed together. He would never have done that outside.

I brought my sister Maureen to see James one day. At the next table another lifer, a young, good-looking lad, was being visited by his family. I saw him looking at Maureen, and she noticed too. They got to talking, we pushed our tables closer. James and I held hands while Maureen had a laugh with Ian. Now Maureen goes to visit Ian on her own. She says thirteen to sixteen years seems like a long time to wait for a man. She laughs and says how can you know you love someone without being able to fuck them? And then she blushes and looks at me and says she is sorry. I don't care. It's good to have someone to make the journey to visits with.

James tells me that Ian is a nice lad. He killed a woman during the course of a burglary. He was sixteen and he was not expecting anyone to be home. He graduated from young offenders' prison to adult prison a few years back. James says Ian was just a burglar and never meant anyone any harm. James is changing; before, he would have rattled his newspaper and said he thought boys like Ian should be strung up.

THE VISITS ROOM is not a good place to conduct a marriage. It is not a good place for anything except smoking and drinking cups of tea. James and I got married when we were both twenty-four, old enough and not that young any more. We were happy to be married, we felt we belonged together. We used to have a good time with flying diaphragms, mucking up with spermicide, condoms that refused to unroll. Then we decided to have a child and we binned all the birth control. But no luck. I thought we should go to the doctor and get some help, see where the problem lay, but James didn't want to. He said we should just keep on having sex, and if I got pregnant that was good, but otherwise it was not meant to be. He said he didn't want to find out if it was his fault, or mine, something gone wrong inside one of us, something sour, barren, unfit. This way we are in it together, it is no one else's business, and I suppose, in a way, he is right.

Now that James is in prison I'm glad we don't have children. It would have made it all much worse. In the visits room the children often cry, and their upsets make it harder for the adults, I can see that. There is a little roped-off area where volunteers play with the kids while their mothers spend some time with the dads. Someone has tried to make it cheery, but they haven't succeeded. The wall murals look gruesome, the plastic toys dirty.

I brought James's sister Maria to the prison once. It wasn't a good visit. Maria cried the whole time, she went on and on about her fatherless children, about being on her own, about how much she misses Bobby. I was stunned. James is her brother. I would not have brought her if I knew she would say that. James sat pushed back in his chair with a completely blank expression on his face while Maria's despair rolled over him in waves. You killed my husband, she said, plain as day, everyone sipping their tea and laughing together in the crowded, smoky, hot, visits room. James said nothing, but I could see him harden, I could see him drying out and stiffening in his chair. Maria's voice got louder and louder. You murdered my husband, she said again and again. I couldn't listen to any more: I hit her, I slapped her across the face. She stopped talking, stopped sobbing, and just sat there on the filthy, lop-sided metal chair. I looked up and saw the officer watching us, a look of contempt and disgust on his face. Two bitches and a murderer and their sordid argument. At that moment I wished we all three were dead.

LAST MONTH I was invited to go to the prison for a Lifer Family Day. I received a leaflet in the post, inviting me. There would be speakers talking about life sentences and the system for lifers, there would be time for both inmates and their families to ask questions. There would be an opportunity to have lunch with James. A whole day together, an entire day spent sitting in the visits room. The leaflet said it was a hard-won opportunity and not to be missed.

We are allowed two visits per month if I go on the weekend, four if I can get there on weekdays although that's difficult. The Lifer Family Day would not be counted against our visits. I saw James a few weeks before and I asked him if he thought I should bring his parents, perhaps his brother William who still talks about trying to mount an appeal. James said no, he was looking upon it as a chance to spend time with me. I could not help it, but part of me was filled with dread. A whole day in that room, a whole day of being next to James but no chance to be with him. Of course I agreed to go, I sent in my name, and I travelled up to the prison first thing that day.

When I arrived the visits room was already crowded. The tables we usually sat at had been pushed to one side and rows of seats were arranged in a large semi-circle. There was an overhead projector and a lectern and a number of men in suits. I found a chair in the back row. We heard the keys and keychains rattling and the prisoners' door opened and James and the other men came through. When he saw me he smiled and I felt the same searing pain that I always do. Sometimes I dream that when I leave the visits room James comes with me. We are outside in the fresh air, and the flowers, and the breeze.

James sat down beside me. The speakers started speaking, putting diagrams up on the overhead projector, explaining how a life sentence is served. The basic principle is that everything takes a very long time. The average length currently served is 15.4 years, but some men are in for much longer. Years in one institution are followed by years in another institution. In between there are one or two meetings. The speakers used words like sentence planning, sentence review, even probation once or twice. It was very absorbing for the first hour. James kept one hand on my knee and the other around my waist and when I looked at him his face seemed younger, more serene. We had a tea break. Maureen was there along with Ian's family, so we got together and had a chat. James was talkative, relaxed, nearly effusive. He told one or two stories. The speakers started up again, and then it was time for lunch.

It was wonderful to eat with James again. I had not seen him eat for such a long time; we had not eaten a meal together since he had left for the police station that day. Someone had gone to a lot of trouble over the food, there were sandwiches, bits of pie, pastries and cake. The mood in the visits room was slightly euphoric, everyone piled their plates high. Ian's brother fetched us pitchers of water, pots of tea. It was like being at a banquet, it was like our wedding all over again. James smiled and ate, and then smiled with food in his teeth. He kept one arm around me. I fed him triangles of sandwiches. We toasted the table with our mugs.

In the afternoon, the speakers started up again. The overhead projector went on, and one of the deputy governors began to talk. The room had become warmer still. People had urgent questions, lots of hands were waving, prisoners argued their side passionately. But in the back row where James and I were sitting it was a different story. In the back row couples were kissing. We had eaten together and now we wanted more.

I got onto James's lap, like I had done countless other times. He buried his face in my shirt, opening one or two buttons with his teeth. I could smell him and beneath his prison smell of tobacco and staleness; there was the smell of James. I couldn't believe what was happening. There were no officers strolling up and down the aisles, we were as far away from an officer as we had ever been. I smoothed my skirt and kept my face turned forward so I at least looked as though I was listening. James fumbled, and it was awkward, I had to lift my weight from one leg to another. But then – I had to turn, I had to bend slightly, it was a bit painful – it happened. I could hear James trying to control his breathing. A few heads turned, and quickly faced away again. I felt him, I felt it all, it was piercing and complete. James buried his face in my back and bit me hard instead of crying out.

I slid off his lap. Our smell was drowned by cigarettes, food and sweat. There were disapproving glances, but I didn't care. This was all we had to hope for, this was all we would get. The afternoon ended, James held me tight in his arms, and I left.

I KNOW THAT it is wrong to kill. I know that Bobby should not have died. James is in prison now, we are paying for Bobby's death. It is a huge debt, and his sentence is very long. But James is just James and I am his wife and the visits room is our asylum.

Black Taxis

SHELAGH SLEEPS IN the place where black taxis park for the night. Side by side in long, straight rows, the taxis wait for ignition, for their engines to lurch, diesel-filled, into action. They perch like blackbirds on a telephone wire, anticipating, silent. Shelagh waits with them. She is hungry.

Late at night in London when King's Cross Station has become too inhospitable Shelagh creeps into the old security box, unmanned and abandoned now there are video cameras. She clutches her breasts under her thick, dirty coat and sleeps like a child. Shelagh never used to be good at sleeping just anywhere but now she could sleep in the middle of Oxford Street if she had to, calmed by the sound of moving taxis.

In London the pavements are crowded with people trying to get a decent night's sleep. A blanket and a doorway, basic human rights. Walking down Kingsway is like being an intruder in a giant dormitory. The Strand – a beach along the Thames before landfill, concrete and shops – is dotted with people lying out, fishing for food and money. Shelagh sees them when she goes walking.

The security box behind King's Cross Station is as

good as any to spend the night. A drunken taxi driver might wander by hoping to grab a few hours' rest on the passenger seat of his vehicle. Shelagh might catch him off guard, she might creep up on him, surprise him. Or he might invite her into the cab himself. This is Shelagh's ambition. She wants to spend the night inside one of the dark taxis. She longs to stretch her body out along the black leather seat once again, she wants that luxury, that space, that engine power. If she had the money she would pay to be driven through the night streets of London while she slept on the passenger seat. If she had the money Shelagh would live in the back of a cab while an impersonal stranger drove her from bridge to bridge, station to station.

No one sees Shelagh come or go from her hiding place; no one looks for her. She went missing from her life six months ago. She is presumed not living. Her friends divided up her possessions; there was only one minor argument over who would get the stereo. Shelagh does not wonder what happened to her stuff, in fact, she does not care. She is not interested in stuff any more.

At night there is no better sight than a black cab in the dark, slick streets of London. Black taxis are not simply cars, not just wheels and seats, but strong and purring creatures. As they slide by under the yellow streetlights it's as though they actually breathe London's diesel air, full lungs under their metal shells, like a new breed of nuclear-age insect, parasites within a city-host. Shelagh thinks taxis can take her places where she has never been, she thinks they might show her new ways. Black taxis know the streets of London

like underground trains know the tunnels that lie below. They slip through the streams of traffic like water
through mud, tide across sand. Shelagh believes the
soul of London hides beneath the bonnet of a rain-
wet, shining taxi. She crouches in the car park and
looks out across the slumbering rows.

King's Cross sits, smoky and steamy, festering
malevolently beneath its spruced-up façade. Its mean
heart still throbs, people still sleep unprotected on
its platforms, in the sidings, the places where disused
trains wait. Shelagh used to think that nothing could
be more dangerous than sleeping on the hard ground
in a public place, each breath an act of faith, I trust I'll
be alive in the morning. Shelagh does not think about
trust any more. She thinks about keeping warm.

In the station crowds of passengers queue for taxis
under the shelter of an overhang. They come off their
trains and wait patiently, bags and parcels piled beside them. The cabs swoop down, their yellow signs
beckoning. Shelagh wanders by not noticing the rubbish, the food packaging, the discarded newspapers,
the smashed bottles and pools of sick. She gazes up
into the filthy glass vaulting of the roof of the station
and watches the pigeons fly to and fro. Trains pull in,
people run for trains just pulling out, but Shelagh is
not interested in trains. They stick to the rails, they
don't weave, they don't flow down Pall Mall like lava.
Shelagh pays no heed, she is staring upwards, a ray
of grey light illuminating her face. She is listening for
something. She is listening for something to rise over
and above the noise of London. She is waiting for ignition, like a taxi itself.

When Shelagh sleeps in the abandoned security box she dreams she arrives by taxi. She dreams of being driven. She arrives and arrives and arrives. The taxi door opens and she gets out. The taxi door closes and she is driven away. The taxi takes a steep corner. The taxi pulls away from the curb. She turns and waves. In her dreams Shelagh always travels by taxi. A black cab is always waiting for her.

Sometimes Shelagh dreams of his arrival. He comes by taxi. The cab pulls into the car park and stops next to the security box. The door swings open. Shelagh stands, pulling her coat around herself. She steps forward and climbs in.

Inside it is dark. It is warm and smells fetid, like an unaired bedroom. She can hear him breathing. He pulls her close as the cab moves away. He pushes her down onto the black leather seat. Shelagh feels his lips on her cheek, his teeth on her neck, his hands on her body. His fingers are cool like leather. The cab circles around King's Cross Station, circling and circling, Pancras Road, York Way, Pancras Road, York Way. She can hear her own heart pounding.

Later, he takes her back to the security box. The door swings open and Shelagh slowly climbs out of the cab.

She closes the door and he is driven away. She feels tired. She settles down inside the security box after looking to see how many taxis she has for company. The cabs remind her of him; they make her wait easier. He might take her away with him forever next time. It is a kind of lie, the life Shelagh lives, a prostitution or addiction, a junkie's life. But this agony is what she is after, it is what she left everything for, it is what she wants. Only when he comes in his taxi does she feel truly happy. Only in that dark, decaying dimness does she feel strong and whole.

The first time she saw him he arrived by taxi. She still had a job then, a flat, an ordinary life. She began to dream of being out on the streets late at night, in the rain, alone. In these dreams she was waiting for something. She ached for it to come. One night, after having been at a party, she found herself standing on a street corner in the rain, alone. While she shivered a taxi pulled up in front of her. Its yellow light was on. She climbed in but was not by herself He was there, she could smell his somehow familiar scent. She felt the black leather seat under her palms as she allowed herself to be taken.

The second time was several months later. She had almost forgotten, but not quite. It was early evening, windy, a bit wet. She was standing on Piccadilly waiting for the light to change. The pavement and street were crowded. Buses and cars formed a honking queue. She was tired, her back ached from sitting at her desk. She carried a bag full of shopping.

A taxi pulled up in front of her very close to the curb. The door swung open and for a moment she felt cross, thinking someone was going to get out and block her way just as the lights changed. But then the smell drifted out from inside. She bent down to take a closer look. The smell grew stronger, drawing her in. The door closed behind her and the cab moved forward through the pedestrians, cyclists, and other taxis. He was with her, she could sense, if not see, him.

The third time was several weeks later, the fourth time only one or two weeks after that. Soon she was being picked up every day. Always after work, in the dark, off the pavement. Shelagh did not alter her work day in any way – she left for the office in the morning and left for home in the evening. But somewhere between A and B, B and C, the taxi would come, the door would swing open, and she would climb in.

Inside the cab was always the same. He was always there, smelling of blood and leather. She believed she was the only one he favoured.

When the drive was over, the cab door would swing open and she would climb out, always at exactly the same place, King's Cross Station. She would get out and no one would notice. She would stumble home. During the day her body ached with longing; at night she fell asleep with the sound of the diesel-powered engines in her ears.

Shelagh stopped performing well at work. She began coming in late and then later still, not caring what anyone thought. Eventually, she was sacked. On that day she put on her coat and walked to King's Cross Station where she stood and waited. He did not come. She stood and waited all night, fending off other men in other, inferior, cars.

The streets grew very dark and then light again, until it was so light that she knew he would not appear. She slept on the concourse of the station all day, and stood on Pentonville Road as night fell. He did not come then either. In the middle of the night she grew tired and hailed a taxi on her own. When the driver asked her where she wanted to go she said she did not know. He made her get out and she watched as he drove around the back of the station. That was how she found the black cab hotel and that was when she settled down to wait.

Now Shelagh waits to be driven away. She would accept an empty cab but prefers one with him in it, one reeking of him, redolent of his grave-dirt perfume. He is everything she has ever wanted in a man, more than a man and somehow less, both heart-beating with life and long dead. Without him her life is drained of meaning, as drained as she becomes once she has been with him. He arrives by taxi, leaves by taxi, and does not exist for her otherwise.

A Kind of Desired Invasion

STARTING WITH THE Belgian chocolates, desire seemed a potent and dynamic force, like a nuclear engine,
high-powered and probably lethal. The chocolates
made her melt, sticky, gooey, and desire made her
harden, glass blown by fire. She flexed her muscles
and felt strong and American, like an airforce base in
a foreign country. Strength, however, was not part of
the problem.

He, of course, was a married man, a married
Englishman, like Trevor Howard or James Mason in
an early role. Beneath his pale exterior something
burnt and melted, hardened then softened. She could
tell this by looking at his back as he stood at the bar ordering more drinks. His long neck was tinged a bright
pink as though reflecting some internal glow. He had
just given her the chocolates and she had kissed him.
After their lips parted, he sank into the tatty, beer-
stained seat, then suddenly stood, knocking his knees
on the edge of the table. She felt she had shocked him
and his response was to wing slightly out of control.

The colour of his neck faded as he returned to
the table with the drinks. They were colleagues at the
university. She was not married. She was new to the

country and did not have many friends. It was not like her to flirt with married Englishmen. Her sexual habits had changed with the times and, besides, in England all the signifiers were different. Here the semiotics of sexuality were not her own.

Like celibacy, chocolates seemed an old-fashioned gesture from another time although perfectly appropriate somehow. Perhaps romance had snuck back into vogue, she thought, along with sexual caution. Chocolates, especially European ones, were decadent and luxurious, like love letters and long kisses, something one's parents had before they married. Soft-centred milk chocolates that came as one bit them were almost as exciting with dancing with someone you knew you were about to sleep with used to be.

His marriage to another woman, an immutable fact, posed even greater restrictions on their fledgling nuclear romance. Infidelity had become freshly dangerous, potentially much more lethal to a marriage than previously. Restraint carried with it nobility, safety, a new kind of self-respect.

'Would you like another chocolate?' she asked, leaning against his shoulder. His leather jacket smelt raw, his jeans felt soft and worn. He was dressed like an American, it was she who looked English in her patched tweed jacket and jodhpurs. She looked horsy as well as strong, like a kind of repellent 'Country Living' housewife. But her clothes were not literal, as clothes rarely are; she was as much a bloodsports-woman as he was a baseball fan. Still, he was married, even if he didn't look it. What do married people look like?

'Let's go away for the weekend,' he said.

'What about your wife?'

'She can stay home. I'll say it's work.'

'She won't believe you. It's such a cliché.' They paused and gulped their drinks, anticipating courage from the alcohol. 'Anyway, what would we do?' she asked. 'Play chess?'

'No. We'd go for long walks and eat hot meals and watch the sunset. We'd kiss with the wind in our faces. I'd hold you close and feel your heartbeat.' He placed a chocolate under his tongue and waited for it to melt down.

She looked at him longingly, wondering if he really did want to have an affair with her. She had a theory that Englishmen enjoyed sex even less than her male compatriots. She was allowed to like it, wasn't she? Maybe this new restraint appealed to most people, perhaps everyone felt more comfortable with prudishness.

'I want to look at you without any clothes on,' she said suddenly as she watched him suck his chocolate. His neck began to glow again. He moaned softly. 'I want to see you naked.' The people at the next table moved their chairs forward imperceptibly. He closed his eyes and leaned back. 'I want to run my hands down the length of your legs. Both of them. One at a time.' He moaned more loudly and the people at the next table held their drinks in mid-air. She pressed against the seat, her hands between her own legs. The lights in the pub flickered like a fluttering heart, a clenching and rumbling nervous gut.

After a while he stopped shaking and bit into another chocolate. Its softness covered his teeth, coating his tongue. In a voice thick with sugar and lust he said, 'You are driving me wild. I don't understand you.'

'What?' she said.

'You are so foreign and yet so familiar. Like sex itself, I guess, a kind of desired invasion.'

THEY FUCKED LIKE chickens, their feathers ruffled, pecking and scratching at nothing, everything. She grappled with him as he pushed against her, shoving him away and urging him on. He tried to be controlled, even a bit leisurely but as he pulled back he could not help but rush forward again. He felt the condom tear inside her. It was all he could do to stop.

'It broke,' he said.

'Shit.'

'Is there another?'

'Over here somewhere.' She crawled away and scrabbled through the junk on the bedside table, returning with another foil-wrapped package. 'Let's try again.'

They had been fucking like this for a few months, slyly, without letting on to the outside world. They would meet in her flat – the weekend away was still talked about although not realized. He would arrive at her door and they would begin right away, sometimes before he took his coat off. They did not talk much, what was there to say? She saw more than enough in the guilt and pleasure on his face to make questions redundant.

It would not go anywhere; there was nowhere for it to go. She could not take him back to America with her, he could not take her home. They had sex protected from each other, the little slip of rubber a true barrier made of caution and sensibility. Because of it they simply could not plunder on ahead without thinking. They always had to pause and reflect.

'In my country,' she began like a student from abroad, 'the English are often thought of as fey.'

'Humph. In my country,' he mocked her slightly, 'Americans are often thought of as vulgar.'

'How fey.'

He pushed harder today, knowing he would not hurt her. When he came he pulled away quickly so as not to spill his bodily fluids, like the instructions on the box of condoms said.

She reminded him of somebody from a movie, maybe it was Kathleen Turner in *Body Heat*, sometimes Sharon Stone in *Basic Instinct*. Not an old movie star but someone contemporary and less defined, whose face resembled that of a dozen different actresses. He, too, relied on clichés for guidance, for cross-cultural understanding. He thought he would like to be more like her; when she spoke, people listened. The twang in her vowels commanded attention. And he watched as she capitalized on this, she saw where it could be to her advantage to be perceived as a celluloid creation.

Some afternoons they talked at cross-purposes; it was not just their vocabularies that differed. He would appear cold and withdrawn, tormented with guilt over his wife. She would become overly effusive in response, feeling hopelessly alone. 'Are you mad?' she would ask abruptly, meaning 'Are you angry?'

'No,' he would reply, thinking she was implying he

was mad – insane – with desire for her (which, in a way, he was). Then they would thrash out their anxieties in bed, moaning and coming to false understandings.

Two cultures rarely comprehend each other, especially when one is waxing and the other waning. The weaker needs to copy the stronger – for every one of her foreign bombing campaigns conducted with supreme arrogance and ruthless certainty he had his own dirty little war on distant barren islands, his own vicious murder on the Rock. Were they playing out these scenarios in sex? Did he want to be dominated?

One night he put a Belgian chocolate inside her and as it melted he licked away the cream. 'Do they have Marmite in America yet?' he asked.

She broke off mid-moan to reply, 'We'll never have Marmite over there. It's you who'll get peanut butter over here. That's the way it works.' She was coated with chocolate as he pushed inside her once again.

His marriage seemed like the Atlantic Ocean to her, something vast and unknowable which she could not attempt to bridge but only fly over at a terrible speed. It kept them apart, kept them foreign to each other, him unhaveable, her unhad.

AFTER A YEAR his wife still appeared not to have noticed the smell of another woman on her husband's face. He was always careful to wash his chiselled visage, of course, but in a year of passion one would think some small scent would have escaped, a tracking odour that would put her senses on alert. It was time for the Other Woman to go back to America. Her academic job had run its course. She had found England a cold place. The rooms where she lived were damp, even while the brief summer had flickered. Her career beckoned, the Atlantic Ocean dimmed and became crossable. And yet, there was the problem of her married Englishman. Would she simply leave him behind? Would she just move away and forget?

One afternoon in bed in her flat she said, 'I will be leaving soon, you know.'

He sat up, surprised. 'I thought you had the afternoon free.'

'I do. It's the rest of the time I'm talking about. I have to go home.'

'I thought you liked it here, I thought you thought it was fun living in England and sleeping with me.'

'I do. But I can't be a tourist forever.'

They argued about it for the rest of the afternoon he becoming sullen and sorry, she remaining dispassionate, untouched. She was impressed by his sudden remorse. She had always felt insulated from pain with him, as if the condom served to forever prevent them from getting unhealthily close. Now he was filling their relationship with a seriousness she had always assumed it could not possibly contain.

'Don't you think,' he began to plead, 'that sleeping together automatically provides us with a kind of contract?'

'A legal document? Fucking gives us certain rights over each other? I fuck you therefore I owe you?'

'You can be so crude sometimes,' he said as though wounded.

'It's in my blood,' she replied.

'I think your blood runs a bit cold,' he said.

'You are the one who is married,' she said, 'not me. I know what that means. I know what married people look like.'

'Huh?' he said, like an American. 'What do married people look like?'

She paused and then smiled and said, 'They wear rings on their fingers. They have ties around their hearts. They love their wives and will never leave them.'

'Oh,' he said sadly, and they both knew she was right. They would exchange chocolates and sex for sweet memories. And that would be the end of it.

My Life as a Girl in a Men's Prison

I can feel myself changing at night. Alone, in my cell – it's such a cliché, but it's true, it is my actual situation. I live in a cell in a closed unit, in a prison within a prison; but at night I feel the changes taking place and this is something that no one – not even me – can control. And they are letting me get away with it, they are letting me do it, which is the astounding thing. They, the authorities – another cliché, I know – can't stop me now, it's too late.

LIKE ESMERELDA THE English teacher, Kelsey lives in London; that is, he lived in London before *it* happened. *It* is what Kelsey calls the accident, the event, the thing that happened that got Kelsey locked away. Another queer-bashing gone wrong – Kelsey ended up the murderer instead of the murderee – in old London Town, under the shadow of the gleaming, phallic Canary Bird building. 'The Canary's stopped singing,' Kelsey used to say to John in the kitchen after those Canadian business brothers went bankrupt. 'Oh,' he would continue, looking out the window of their flat,

'I hate that fucking thing.' Secretly this was not true; Kelsey and John rather admired the colossus. It made them think about what it might be like to live in New York, far away from the grimiest end – the grimy east end – of a filthy old city.

Now Kelsey lives in prison, but Esmerelda the English teacher lives in the city. She works in the prison and for her it is part of London; she travels there on a bus down the long, bereft, empty-shop-window high street. But Kelsey and the other inmates on his wing are not in the city any longer, not in the world any longer in fact. They are in the closed wing, the segregation unit, on Rule 43: they are the nonces, the sex beasts, the scum.

Esmerelda teaches English in the prison; she was made redundant when the Putney secondary school where she worked was amalgamated with a secondary school in Tooting. Tooting – nothing to toot about there as far as she could see. Esmerelda misses teaching teenage girls, she misses the single-sex environment of the secondary girls' school. The prison is, of course, a single-sex environment also, but the other sex, the opposite one, men. And yet there is Kelsey, Kelsey who is neither here nor there, neither one nor the other; perhaps Esmerelda's nostalgia for girls is part of the reason why she finds herself drawn to Kelsey now.

London is full of prisons; Esmerelda discovered this when she began working in one. They are part of the unseen, unnoticed structure of the city like underground ventilation shafts and sewers. Spot one and you start seeing them everywhere. Wormwood Scrubs – oh, the very name makes Esmerelda shudder. Holloway. Pentonville. Wandsworth. Brixton. Brrr.

The masculinity of the place is palpable; the air is thick with maleness. Esmerelda thinks she can actually feel it on her skin. The prison smells like a huge locker room that somehow ended up inside an even larger greasy spoon, sweat and socks mixed with custard and frying mince. And tobacco – a dense fogbank of cigarette smoke builds up during the course of the day. They all smoke, all the men, every single one of them, except Kelsey. Kelsey somehow manages to remain nicotine-free, sweetened.

There are twenty of us in this unit, twenty of us lowest of the low, a layer of scum twenty men thick. They're not so bad, the others. I don't mind them. We're just a little misunderstood. Well, actually, we're massively misunderstood, in fact, none of us understands it ourselves really. But we get on okay, we watch each other's backs to a certain extent; it's all right so long as no one from out there can get to us with their home-made weapons, 'shanks' – bent nails, metal chair legs, etc. They're all so butch out there in the open wings, it's frightening; but butch is the wrong word, those kinds of words don't work in here.

ESMERELDA GOES DOWN to the segregation unit once a week to teach an English class. Kelsey doesn't come to her class yet, but Esmerelda has been told about him by an officer and by a governor grade as well. 'He likes to iron, does our Kelsey,' said the Governor. 'He irons everything down there in the seg unit. Ironed shirts, ironed socks, they even have bloody ironed sheets down there. And it's weird,' he continued while Esmerelda smiled and nodded, 'Kelsey is changing. Right before our very eyes, he is changing. His hair is different now and, well,' the Governor paused, his eyes looking beyond the bars for the right word, 'it's uncanny, really, it is.'

The other men in the seg unit did not discuss Kelsey, and Esmerelda did not ask questions about him. The other men – mostly rapists, child abusers, and pae-dophiles – were reading Thomas Hardy and the class held long discussions about fate that Esmerelda found fascinating. Fate seemed to be something they knew about; fate and coming to a bad end. They engaged with Hardy on a completely different level than teen-aged school girls, and this made Esmerelda read Hardy differently as well. When she was in prison Esmerelda found the rest of her life faded away, as though life started and finished at the prison gates. London was not really out there at all, the prison floated some-where in outer space.

Outside the closed unit, in the Education block and on the open wings, things were not quite so ex-treme. One of her students, a man who could recite Coleridge's 'The Ancient Mariner' in its entirety – a lifetime's work – described his cell to her as part of an oral exam one day. 'And I have a view,' he concluded.

'What?' said Esmerelda.

'From the top of B-Wing, where my cell is, I have a view. I can see London from up there. I can see some council flats, some garages, and the back of the high street.'

Esmerelda smiled appreciatively. 'That's London all right,' she said.

'You don't know what a relief it is,' he continued, 'to know that while I'm stuck in here, out there people are hanging up their laundry.'

'Ahh, London,' said another man, 'I miss it. I miss the dirty old town. Brilliant, isn't it? Where do you live, miss?'

'Archway,' replied Esmerelda.

'Ahh, the big old arch over Highgate Road. What I wouldn't do for a ride in a taxi under that just now,' the prisoner sighed. 'Highgate Cemetery – I've got my plot sorted already.'

'Oh?' said Esmerelda. 'Speaking of plots –' and she brought Thomas Hardy back into the conversation.

When Kelsey came to Esmerelda's seg unit English class for the first time he walked in smelling of roses St James's Park summer roses, Esmerelda thought. He took a seat alongside the other men. He had very curly, blond long hair, blue blue eyes, full pouting lips, and bad skin. 'I'm sorry I've missed the first few classes, miss,' he said politely. 'I had prior engagements.'

The other men smirked. 'Oh, so you're engaged now are you, Kelsey?' one of them asked.

'No,' said Kelsey, a kind of Princess Diana at a charity dinner smile across his face, 'but I am terribly, awfully busy.'

Esmerelda needed a few moments to recover from the impact of Kelsey's entrance. Her silence was filled by the other prisoners; they always had plenty to say. Kelsey gazed at Esmerelda, she could feel his steady eyes upon her. 'Where'd you get your shoes, miss?' he asked eventually, as though they were the only people in the room.

'Covent Garden.'

'Oh that dump,' he replied, smiling.

The class went on, Esmerelda's composure returned. Kelsey had done all the reading, and he was smart; she could see he would be a good student. They finished on time and the other men got up to leave, the sound of banging trays and officers shouting. Kelsey walked up to where Esmerelda was sitting on the edge of a table. He leaned over and whispered, 'I've got an English degree.' His breath smelt of mint.

Esmerelda turned towards him. 'What are you doing studying for a GCSE?'

'Boredom, you see. I'd rather talk about Thomas Hardy than mop floors all day. And besides, I heard you were nice. There's not a lot of women around here, you might have noticed. It's important to make the most of every opportunity.'

Esmerelda left the prison at 4:30 that afternoon. Outside workers, education people, probation, psychology left at the same time every day. After that the prison fell silent for a moment before the evening racket began. As she left Esmerelda imagined Kelsey in his cell; as she left Kelsey imagined Esmerelda on her way home. He stood on his bed and looked out his cell window into the tiny seg exercise yard. It was raining and the London sky was very low. Kelsey had a theory, one he used to expound upon with his lover John, that the reason there were so few skyscrapers in London was that in the winter the sky was too low. 'There's hardly room for a five-storey block of flats,' he'd say looking out the kitchen window as he did the washing-up, 'let alone a skyscraper. The Canary Bird has completely disappeared today.'

Esmerelda took the bus home. That evening she stayed in by herself and watched TV. The milk had gone sour so she ate her bowl of cereal dry. The phone did not ring. As she cleaned her face to get ready for bed she remembered Kelsey's skin; it must be the hormones, she thought, although she didn't know why, no one had said anything about hormones.

Which am I: a nonce, a sex beast, or scum? Hmm. Nonce maybe, that seems the most likely. Perhaps I should change my name to Nancy when the time comes. Nance, I'll be used to that. In here I'm just Kelsey, of course, number LV0125 – yet another cliché. I'll have to write a book when I get out: My Life as a Girl in a Men's Prison.

I'LL HAVE TO write a book, thought Esmerelda before she went to sleep: *My Life as a Girl in a Men's Prison.*

Later that week when Esmerelda was getting ready to go teach her seg unit English class, she found herself staring in the bathroom mirror. A new haircut, she thought, that's what I need. A new face. A complete new body. She ran her fingers through her hair and put on more make-up than usual.

In class the men were noisy and reluctant to work. Kelsey came in late, wearing a neck-scarf that appeared to have been torn from a prison sheet. When

Esmerelda glanced from his neck to his face she found he was looking at her. Kelsey shrugged and smiled apologetically, 'A girl's got to make some attempt, doesn't she?' The other men hissed and jeered half-heartedly. Esmerelda blushed. The class continued.

The weeks went by. The season changed in its oblique London way. In prison time passes like water in the Thames, slow, murky, inevitable, taking forever to get to the sea. Kelsey missed his lover John. John missed Kelsey. Kelsey felt he had been wrongly convicted and sentenced. These are things suitable for understatement only.

Esmerelda continued to teach English. She gave assignments. Her classes worked towards taking their exams. Kelsey continued to change. One day Esmerelda thought she could see a hint of breasts beneath his carefully pressed prison shirt. Kelsey came up to her after class, in the few moments before the officers came to shoo everyone away. 'I'm worried,' he said.

'What about?'

'My orals. I'm not very strong on oral exams.'

'You speak perfectly well, Kelsey.'

'Not in exams. I want to practise. When can I see you?'

Esmerelda was a little surprised. No one in the seg unit had ever asked her for extra help. Men on the open wings asked for extra help all the time, but they didn't down here. She was accustomed to coming into the closed unit and then being able to leave.

'Can you come tomorrow?' Kelsey could see Esmerelda hesitating. 'Please?'

Esmerelda consulted her diary. 'I have half an hour tomorrow morning before lock-up.'

'Good,' said Kelsey. 'I'll see you then.'

The next morning while Esmerelda was getting ready to go to work, she went into the bathroom to pick up her lipstick. She put some on, and put the tube into her purse. In the mirror, her make-up looked fine, she was wearing enough. Still, she picked up her mascara, her eye-liner, her eyebrow pencil. She rummaged through the make-up bag she kept beside the sink. She found some eye-shadow, other shades of lipstick, an old pair of fake eyelashes. She picked up the entire bag and put it in her briefcase.

Esmerelda got down to the seg unit a little early; Kelsey was waiting for her. They walked past the cells on the way to the interview room, where it's a bit more quiet, Kelsey said. They embarked on a practice exam; Esmerelda opened her case to find her notes. She brought out the make-up bag instead.

Cleanser, moisturiser, foundation, toner, powder, blush: Kelsey looked best with a dark brown eye-liner, black mascara, his eyebrows darkened and made thick. Esmerelda found it easy to touch him. He tilted his face back and let himself be touched. They consulted the mirror in her compact. Kelsey knew more about make-up than Esmerelda: this did not surprise either of them. 'But your skin . . .' said Esmerelda.

'I know. It's all the drugs I've been taking. For the change – as though I'm bloody menopausal already,' he laughed. 'My skin's gone all funny. But apparently it will clear up again.'

'What's going to happen?' asked Esmerelda.

'Well, I suppose I'll have to be moved to a women's prison sometime soon. Maybe after the surgery.'

Esmerelda held her breath.

Kelsey smiled and said, 'That will be weird. In all of London I'll bet I'm the only girl in a men's prison.'

'You're not a girl yet,' said Esmerelda.

'Well,' said Kelsey, 'nearly.'

Forcibly Bewitched

LOIS STOOD BEHIND a woman whose grey-blonde hair was cut in a perfect line across her neck, like a bleached Louise Brooks. They were both attempting to look at a painting on the wall, but were stuck behind a woman pushing an elderly man in a wheelchair. The family resemblance between the pusher and the pushed was remarkable; Lois had noticed the pair earlier when someone else behind whom she had been standing whispered, 'Isn't that Sir Harold Arnold?' The gallery was very crowded. In a moment the wheelchair would roll on to the next painting, the blonde Louise Brooks (it was dyed, it had to be – now that Lois had started dyeing her hair she took pleasure in assuming that everyone else did too) would have a look and then Lois could take her turn to gaze at the painting, at the two-hundred-year-old blobs of oil and egg-wash or whatever it was that painters used to fix the canvas back then.

There was a man following Lois, she was almost sure of it, although he might be following Louise Brooks; in fact, come to think of it, Lois was following Louise, everybody was following everybody else around the concourse of the gallery. Lois looked forward to the day she could view the paintings on CD-ROM Internet e-mail and would no longer have to visit museums and galleries in person. But then, she liked the crush of popular shows. Her mother had always seen picture-viewing as a chance for 'a bit of a stroll'; she was an eternal dieter and relished the opportunity to do two things at once: culture and exercise, hence a brisk walk around a large museum before tea and cakes. Lois saw the inside of a lot of museums when she was a child, but she had never been allowed to linger over the antiquities, so now when she went to exhibitions she proceeded very slowly and sat a lot, gazing at the paintings, stepping up close to peer at the brush work. Francisco Goya painted that with his own hands, she found herself thinking today, he himself stepped up to the easel on his short legs and applied his brush to the canvas. Painting seemed a physical art; Lois wished she was an artist instead of working in an office, but she knew that was like wishing she had been an astronaut.

Sir Harold Arnold's daughter pushed her father's wheelchair onward and Louise Brooks shuffled ahead and Lois took a step too, then stopped, and the person behind trod on the back of her heel. Lois hated when that happened. She turned to see who had done it. It was him, the man who had been following her. He was short, he had longish, curly black hair, and he smiled up at her rather uncertainly after murmuring an apology. 'Let's get out of here,' he said, taking a step backward into the middle of the room, the space suddenly, miraculously, clear. He reached out and took her hand and took another step backward, drawing her with him, and for a moment Lois thought he was going to burst into song. She held her breath. Was this how it felt to be in a musical? She waited.

But he did not sing. He dropped Lois's hand and said. 'Only joking.' Lois frowned and turned to discover she had lost her place in the crowd snaking round the walls of the gallery. She turned back to admonish Mr Friendly but, of course, he was gone.

Lois managed to insert her body into a gap in the queue and she viewed the rest of the exhibition happily. She had slipped away from the office early; if her boss mentioned it tomorrow she had only to tell him where she had been and, impressed by her edification, he would not mention it again. He was like her father that way, easily overawed by culture, ashamed of his own ignorance. Lois's father had never accompanied his wife and daughter on their jogs around museums; just as well, thought Lois now, gives me something to do if he winds up in a wheelchair.

Lois had married at twenty-two, divorced at twenty-eight, and now, at thirty-two, found herself ensconced in a dwarfish spinsterhood which she rather enjoyed. She had a nice flat, a good job, friends, and she lived near Sainsbury's. Movies, books, a little theatre, restaurants, shopping, cooking, the odd holiday – a lot of flavour, but no spice, as her mother was fond of saying. Lois did not care what her mother thought, and her mother knew it, the disapproved-of marriage, then the unheard of, unmentionable, divorce had ensured that. Lois liked the way her life had turned out; being on her own had not made her unhappy. However, she was not altogether sanguine about the lack of spice.

When Lois emerged blinking from the gallery into the summer haze of pollen and pollution, her man sat waiting in the forecourt of the gallery. His little legs were crossed and he grasped one knee with both hands as he watched Lois come down the steps towards him. His hair seemed even curlier in the humidity. Lois sat beside him.

'I thought you were going to sing in there,' she said.

'So did I, but it seemed inappropriate somehow,' he replied.

Lois found herself agreeing to go have coffee and, as they walked in companionable silence – it was too hot to speak – she found herself thinking that she had never done this before, accepted an invitation from a complete stranger. But then she corrected herself – I can be so deluded sometimes – because the truth was she did this kind of thing all the time.

There had been that man she met on a bus, she had gone for a drink with him; his eyes were so blue. He was Polish and once he had told her that he might as well have given up there and then because Lois could not stop thinking about the word Polish and was it really spelt just like polish and how unfortunate. Then there had been that Nigerian man who had turned out to be very rich; Lois had gone out to dinner with him, but they had disagreed about politics. Lois could be shockingly left-wing – she shocked herself sometimes – and he had turned out to be amazingly right-wing. She let him pay for dinner. And there had been that man she met in a bookshop when they both reached for the only copy of *Pride and Prejudice*. But she had married him: never trust a man who reads Jane

Austen was the lesson she learned from that. One of the lessons.

'Do you read Austen?' she asked the short man who walked beside her now.

'Auster?' he asked, but just then they came to a busy road; their destination was on the opposite side. He took her by the hand once again. His hand was smaller than hers, cool and dry, which was commendable given the heat. I like a man with cool, dry hands, she thought, and then they made their dash, his five-foot-six frame sure-footed next to her five foot ten.

Lois's mother had a thing about men and height; the only good men were tall. Lois's father was six foot seven which even now seemed a little extreme. When Lois was young she had fallen for her mother's height fetish and the man she married was a decent six foot three. But it turned out to be a disastrous misconception, one of many of which her mother was fond, like only married women can use tampons and only widowed women wear black. Life was just not like that any more.

The coffee house was busy but they found a table near the back. 'Did you see the painting?' he asked.

'Which one?'

'"Forcibly Bewitched".'

Lois recalled it; a priest with mad, rolling eyes was lighting an oil lamp held by the devil, a grey, horned satyr, while donkeys danced upright on their hind feet in the background. It was one of a group of paintings of flying witches, cannibals, and lunatic asylums, the kind of thing for which she appreciated Goya.

'Yes, I saw it.'

He nodded, he seemed satisfied.

'You are an incredible beauty,' he said.

Now this was something new to Lois. No strange man with whom she had gone off had ever said anything like that to her before. She nodded, but did not reply. What did he mean by 'incredible'? Did he mean strange? Did he mean surprising, as in not to be believed, as in weird? Did using the words incredible and beauty together actually cancel them both out leaving only ugliness in their stead? Lois thought about this while she looked at her short, curly-haired companion.

'I meant incomparable,' he said.

'Oh,' replied Lois, 'well, that's all right then.'

Their courtship took place quickly. Lois found herself entirely enamoured. His name was Beverley and she was enchanted by the idea of having a boyfriend with a girl's name, as if that might mean he would have fewer of the foibles of previous lovers, more of the charms of a good friend. She loved to tower over him in public and he seemed to enjoy it as well; it became a kind of secret joke between them, creating a *frisson* Lois imagined somehow akin to s&m. It felt kinky. She was excited by it.

They began spending all their free time together. They went to every exhibition in the city that summer, the more crowded the better. Bev would follow directly behind Lois and, in the crush of beholding great art, Lois would feel Bev's body pressed to hers, her buttocks level with his abdomen. She would find herself blushing and, when there was room, she would turn to face him and he would smile at her silkily. Once, just once, he actually did sing. It was an aria from an opera they had recently attended; the lover dies and as she dies, she sings. Bev kept his voice low, he held both of Lois's hands, she caught and held his words even though they were Italian. None of the other exhibition-goers seemed to notice what was happening. It was as though Beverley and Lois were in a higher place.

Organized Religion

TRAINS CONTINUED TO shunt up and down the country despite the fact that scarcely no one could afford
to ride them. Departing from King's Cross Station at
1000, 1030, 1100, on and on, over and over, the trains
pulled north, into those great cathedral-stations, York,
Newcastle and, finally, Edinburgh, blowing black
smoke up into the arches.

Jenny travelled by train because somebody else
paid for it. When asked what she did she would always
reply, 'I'm in business.' 'Business' had become one of
those words people use to explain a complex range of
activity from multinational-backward-buyout-take-
over-bids to selling drugs on the street, a word that
made people nod their heads sagely when they heard
it, asking no further questions. A that-explains-it-
all word, like 'illness'. Taking care of business. Easier
than explaining to people that she was an accountant,
crunching numbers on her computer all day long.
Her long-term project was the total realignment of
the company's accounting process. Jenny enjoyed her
work.

Jenny worked for an English company that special-
ized in manufacturing goods with a Scottish theme.

Scotprod had recently had tremendous success with a line of ready-to-wear kilts made from a blue and green tartan which incorporated a tiny block print of a haggis. Jenny thought the haggis looked more like bagpipes, but without the pipes, just a dangly grey bag. No one else seemed to notice. These products were very popular with tourists who visited Scotland to find their roots.

The trains were remarkably punctual. Jenny nearly always got to her Edinburgh meetings on time. She would arrive lugging her big bag full of papers – one shoulder pulled down by the weight, the other forced upwards – to sit amidst the men with their dark suits and slim attaché cases. The men would ask each other's opinion about this or that, get the only other woman present, the secretary, to make coffee, show charts, give demonstrations, and arrange to meet for drinks later, sometimes including Jenny, sometimes not. But Jenny was there and this, she thought, was a victory. This was modernity. She was good at numbers, numbers were her thing. A woman in a man's world. This was business.

Then one day one of the men took Jenny aside and whispered in her ear that it had been decided she was no longer needed at these meetings. In fact, the company no longer needed her at all. 'I expect you'll be glad to hear it, my dear. You must be tired of that endless journey. Those horrible sandwiches. You'll be glad to spend more time at home, I should think. You could have a baby or something nice like that.'

Jenny did not know what to say. 'But, my project,' she stuttered as he turned to walk away, the creases in his trousers bunching up behind his knees. 'My project, it's not finished.'

'Your project?' he said, pausing to give her an avuncular smile. 'This is the world of business, love, not infant school.'

That afternoon, as Jenny stood in the station waiting for the train, she noticed the glass in the roof overhead was broken. Rain dripped slowly down onto the platform; the water looked black and thick, it left a stain on the ironwork as well as the concrete below. The train was on time and empty as usual and Jenny sat next to the window. She took her papers, her laptop computer, her mobile telephone and her portable printer out of her bag and spread the technology across the table so that no lonely fellow travellers would be tempted to join her. Then she opened the novel that she was reading and tried to stop herself from feeling too upset.

Jenny's rise in the world of business has been sudden, like an unexpected fountain in a still pond. She had left teaching depressed by the stream of children, endlessly arriving, making a lot of noise, and then inevitably flowing away, like standing under Niagara Falls, she thought. Business had seemed the only way to go – it was either that or lose the house – and she'd always been good at numbers. She and her mother – they lived together, Jenny had been married twice but she always came home in the end – had been poor before and neither wanted to repeat the experience. Now what would she do? The novel wasn't gripping enough to stop her from panicking. And she had forgotten to get her mother one of those kilts.

As the train cut through the suburbs, past the massive old buildings overhanging the Tyne and into the shelter of Newcastle Station itself, Jenny noticed a group of young men standing on the platform. There were ten or twelve of them, all wearing scruffy anoraks, their woolly hats pulled down low over their brows, sandwiches stuffed in pockets, Thermos flasks poking out of knapsacks. They had their notepads open and were scribbling, examining Jenny's train, and then glancing back down at their notes, at the front and rear of the train, and then back down again. They talked and gestured animatedly, flapping their arms, looking excited. Jenny wondered what they were doing. As her train began to depart and she saw them run to a different platform she realized they were trainspotting.

Trainspotting. What an incredibly useful thing to do, Jenny thought. Almost as useful as what she had spent the last few years doing. At least they do it together, she thought. At least they do it with friends.

Jenny played with her machines for a while but there was no one to fax any more. She could have called her mother to tell her the news, but she could not face that yet. The novel was beginning to annoy her. She went to the buffet car for tea.

Later, Jenny gazed out the dirty window at the passing scenery. Britain seemed so flat from the train, one flat green plateau from north to south. In Britain the train never had to struggle through mountain passes nor cling to cliffsides as she imagined it might in other places, South America for instance. Flat country, flat people, Jenny thought looking down at herself. 'Flat-chested,' she said, almost out loud.

As the train pulled into York, Jenny noticed that here the crowd of trainspotters was much bigger than it had been in Newcastle. There were trainspotters dotted all through the station, ten or more on each platform. She could see them in the station bar and in the newsagents, comparing notes. When the train came to rest Jenny realized they were shouting to each other, one group hailing the next. She walked down to the end of the empty carriage. She leaned out of the window and listened. Boys with high voices, teenagers with the cracking tones of adolescence, men with deep voices, fathers trying to speak with authority; the trainspotters were yodelling to each other, names of trains, a jumble of numbers, times, dates.

'1982 . . .'

'Twelve carriages . . .'

'Quarter past four . . .' Britain is so small, Jenny thought as she listened, the passage of a train is a spectator sport. Everything is a spectator sport. People watch without taking part. Still, Jenny reasoned, at least they had something to do.

The engineer was blowing his whistle so Jenny shut the window and the carriage moved smoothly away, gliding along the platform, speeding up past the men and boys and their expectant, appreciative faces. As she walked back to her seat the train shuddered gently as though with a premonition. Moments later it shuddered again, more forcefully, then wheezed to an abrupt stop, still within the station. Jenny heard a loud clang and the train gave off a sort of moan. She knew she would be in York for a while.

Pulling up her coat like a blanket, Jenny fell asleep.

She dreamed of dancing haggises, chopped down in their prime by the men in suits. When she awoke the station was nearly dark, low-burning yellow lamps throwing off dim light. She yawned and stretched as she looked out the window. The platforms on both sides of the train were crowded. There were hundreds and hundreds of men and boys, more trainspotters than she had ever imagined there could be in the world, let alone York. They were overhead on the walkways. They were corralled onto the next platfonn. Perhaps they were even on the roof of the train itself. The window between her and them vibrated as though with the sound of drums. Jenny got up slowly. She walked through the carriage and opened the window again.

The trainspotters were calling to each other. They had given up discussing trains and moved on to other topics.

'There are so many unexplained things in the world,' she heard one shout.

'There are so many reasons why one thing happens while another doesn't – endless chains of coincidence,' an older man cried out.

'Organized religions can begin and end wars,' shouted a boy with a round face.

'What if there were no trains at all?'

'What's the difference between a Hindu and a Catholic, a Muslim and a Protestant?'

'Would anyone like me to explain the theory of supply and demand?'

'When half the country does not vote, who wins the elections?'

It was as though Jenny's stalled train had caused

a crisis of confidence in these men and boys and trainspotting had dissolved into random abstract pondering. It was as though, beneath the noble glass, iron, and brickwork of the station, thousands of performing trainspotter philosophers had been created spontaneously.

'What is a Mormon?'

'If a house is not a home when no one is in it, is a chair still a chair once it's broken?'

'Why are some persecuted and others not?'

'Why are some prosecuted and others not?'

'Is this the gospel according to Robert?'

'How can taxation be fair?'

'What's the difference between a trainspotter and someone who collects records?' a man yelled. When he could pick out no answer from the cacophony of voices, he shouted – she saw his face screw up with the effort – '*Music*! It heals you like faith,' she could still hear his voice, 'it makes you feel human. Sometimes it's hard to believe in trains.'

Jenny thought that these last comments might be thought of as heretical but none of the other boys and men seemed to notice. She wondered what the married ones had told their wives they were going to do when they left home that evening. They probably said 'business' and left it at that.

Willow

SHE KNEW THERE was a shortage of work everywhere but she thought her own personal shortage must be exceptional. She was getting behind with her share of the mortgage. Departments were slimming all over the country; education had become anorexic. The collage of bits of work she had glued together over the past ten years fell apart. Women's Studies was no longer an area of academic growth.

So when May read the small advert in the local newspaper – 'HMP Willow Education Department seeks Lecturer in Women's Studies for part-time foundation course for prisoners intending to do degrees' – she rang up about it immediately. The man on the other end of the telephone line was friendly, a loud Scottish voice. 'Come on over to meet us,' he said, 'I'm inviting the first ten callers. Like winning a prize.'

The following Monday May drove out into the countryside, wind and rain lashing the car's small metal body along narrow roadways. She'd never been to the prison before despite having lived in its vicinity for years. As she pulled into the parking area, the rain stopped and she saw cars lined up neatly, red postbox, green lawn, flowers. Her eyes lingered on these bright things as she approached the gates. She hadn't expected the prison car park to be so ordinary. When she arrived home afterwards May went into the kitchen and sat down at the table. Clare was cooking, listening to the radio. She turned around and, seeing May's face, said, 'Oh sweetie, you didn't get the job.'

'No,' replied May, 'I did.'

FIRST CLASS OF the term. 'All right,' she cleared her throat. 'Thank you for coming.' Twelve men sat behind twelve tables. Shaved heads, tattoos, a superabundance of biceps: she convinced herself that she was not visibly shaking. As she looked at them she could not stop herself from thinking, *these men have done terrible things.* 'We haven't had much feminism in here,' Ian, head of department and owner of the Scottish voice, had said when briefing May in his office. 'This is a prison for lifers – you only get life for arson or murder. In fact, a lot of these men have killed their wives.' He laughed in his hearty, catching way. 'That's just the kind of place this is.' And she laughed too, although later she clenched her fists and practised reaching for the alarm bell in her classroom.

'All right,' she said again.

The men looked at her politely. Some were smoking tiny thin roll-ups lit with crudely fashioned lighters. She watched, spellbound, as one man flicked his flint over and over. 'We're not allowed real lighters,' he said suddenly, looking up. 'No petroleum or lighter fluid allowed. We might drink it. We might blow someone up, set them on fire.' He stretched out the wick for her to see, 'It's a string from a mop-head jammed into a bit of wood with the flint attached to that. We're allowed to buy flints.' May stared as the man tugged on the mop-string wick. 'They have trouble keeping the floors clean in here.' Everyone laughed loudly.

Summer was not quite over and it was still humid; most of the men were dressed in shorts, some wore little vests instead of shirts. The display of flesh was nearly overwhelming; May kept thinking of her friend Leo and his collection of 1950s weight-lifting magazines. She hadn't been in the midst of so much masculinity for years. The nearest thing had been nights out in mixed gay clubs where the machismo was directed elsewhere and she herself was joined at the hip with Clare.

'All right,' she started again. 'Women's Studies. Over the next term I am going to try to give you an overview of the history of modern feminism, beginning with its roots in previous centuries. I want to start by getting you to tell me what you already know.'

'The best advice,' Ian had said just before she entered the classroom, 'is to teach the class exactly like you would anywhere else.'

'Aphra Behn,' said one man, thick Birmingham accent, leaning back in his seat, his hands on his gym-enhanced thighs. 'I saw a play of hers once with my wife.' Was that before you killed her or after, May did not ask. Ian had also said that the best defence was not knowing what the men had done, not knowing the crime committed, tried and sentenced for. She wasn't good at remembering names from newspapers and she avoided reading about most crime anyway, not interested in the manhunts, in the big, sensational trials. They are like students anywhere, she told herself, their options are just a little more limited.

'Madonna,' said someone else, a Jamaican inflection in his voice, 'ain't she a feminist?'

'Women are okay,' added another, 'it's just those feminazis that I can't stand.'

May took a deep breath.

And so the class began, heading into territory strange and familiar, May's course plan leading backwards into history. Two ninety-minute sessions per week, covering as much material as they could: Mary Wollstonecraft, Jane Austen, Mary Seacole, Simone de Beauvoir. Often men were missing for one reason or another – visits, appointments with probation officers, psychologists, review boards, ill health, 'having a bit of a difficult time,' whatever that meant. She learned things about them and about the rules of prison life, little things, favourite films, favourite books, which prison officers were trusted, which were not. There was not a lot of time for chatting, and May tried to avoid gaps. She found the men intelligent, eager to learn, not at all resistant to what she had to say, though keen to argue, debate. They did not ask personal questions of her and she did not of them. When she walked through the prison gates at 8:30 in the morning, normal life – Clare, shopping trips, walks in the evening, the local swimming pool, the garden – fell away.

Dresses and skirts were out of the question, fine in class but too nerve-racking out in the prison generally where she was likely to turn a corner and come upon a large group of men she had never seen before, lurking, joking, generating that particular prison smell she took home with her class's notebooks, eau de gym, eau de kitchen.

She dressed more butch than she had in years, borrowing Clare's Doc Martens, tailored trousers, jackets and shirts. There were more women working in the prison than she had thought at first, it was reassuring to find she was not a complete one-off, an oddity. But in a life spent for the most part in the company of women it seemed strange to feel so utterly and distinctly female, to be in a place where her gender was such an enormous, defining thing. To be in a place surrounded by men, men, men; on good days it struck her as absurd, and hugely entertaining, like being in a Busby Berkeley production number, or a Mae West movie, just her and the boys.

'Have you cóme out to them yet?' asked a friend, Susan, over dinner one evening. Behind her back she was known as 'O Earnest One'; the importance of being Ernestine.

'What?' May and Clare spoke simultaneously.

'Have you told them you're queer?'

'No, I . . .'

'They'd eat her alive,' said Clare.

'No they wouldn't . . . maybe . . . they'd . . . I don't know,' said May.

'Do you think they fantasize about you?'

'What?' Once again, May was shocked by Susan's question.

'You know, do they imagine that you're their girl-friend? Do they think about you at night?'

'I don't know. Christ. I don't care.' She hadn't

thought about this, or rather, she had, but she pushed it out of her mind. She wanted it to stay out of her mind. Of course they fantasized about her, their contact with women was so limited. She herself spent a lot of time thinking about them. Not that way but, nonetheless.

HER TWELVE MEN got on well, they were accustomed to working, to studying. All of them had ended up in Women's Studies in such a circuitous manner – crime, arrest, remand, court, gaol, education, Women's Studies – that they were like the best of mature students, there for a purpose, wanting to pass. Some mornings as May stood in the classroom waiting for them to be allowed off the wings they would arrive one at a time, shy to begin with, as though they were surprised to see her there yet again, vying with each other to be the most chivalrous, the most studious. They paid attention to her, these men. But then again, May thought, they had no choice.

One day she was half an hour late, held up by security at the gate, a random bag search – the officers were especially concerned with her unopened box of tampons. She arrived, breathless, sweating, to find her men sitting patiently.

'I'm so glad you waited for me,' she said blushing.

'We're accustomed to waiting,' said Alan, the one from Birmingham. 'It's one thing we get to do a lot in here.'

Some days it was difficult to keep their attention, as though their thoughts were being pulled elsewhere. What was out there in the prison, May wondered, beyond the classroom walls, that could make them seem so distracted? May found herself reworking her course plan, trying to make the connections between their own lives and women's history more concrete, obvious. She left out certain sections: Sappho, domestic violence, Vita Sackville-West. She did a session on the history of Tupperware, labour-saving convenience and the women's sales network, the revolution in work from the home. They found this hilarious, and enjoyed it, and could see what she meant, so she gained confidence; a history of contraception and reproduction politics came next. She taught that class without embarrassment until somebody started laughing and Jim told her they would have to pay the rest of Education to stay away once word got out about their course work.

And she was tough with them, as she would have been with any class. As she relaxed, and they relaxed, she stopped letting them get away with certain comments and jokes, firing back her own. She stopped wondering what they had done, she no longer had to try to prevent herself from thinking about the crimes. She found herself wondering who they really were, and what life in HMP Willow was really like. It seemed impossible to imagine a more loveless place. She wondered if they touched each other ever, at all, she wondered what it was like, having no one to touch. None of the men seemed to be actually, actively, admittedly, gay. All those years of abstinence, or 'prison bent' – did they dream of women's bodies as she thought she would if she was ever sent away from Clare, locked up without her lover's body to hold every night? Was this something she had in common with them then, a longing for women's bodies; was this another of the privileges she had over them – not only was she a woman, but at home another woman waited for her, ready to take her, ready to hold her, ready for her touch?

Stories circulated around the staffroom where the teachers gossiped about their students like teachers anywhere. A prisoner had fallen in love with his probation officer; she had resigned, he had been moved to Willow and they were trying to get married but the Home Office was denying permission. Another prisoner, still insisting on his innocence after more than ten years in gaol, married the journalist who was helping him to publicize his appeal. This was an unconsummated nick union, celebrated amongst the inmates by a kind of ribald envy. May felt embarrassed by the gossip, embarrassed for the men.

'I can't understand how anyone could do it,' said one teacher, 'marry these murderers.' The other staff looked at her aghast.

'That's one way to put it,' said Ian.

'Well, that's what they are at the end of the day, murderers, aren't they?' The others muttered this and that but May pursed her lips to keep from speaking, to keep from saying that she could understand what some women might see in these men. They embodied a kind of potent masculinity – criminal, violent, surviving in this all-male environment – but at the same time they were powerless, without rights, vulnerable. A prisoner would write love letters, a prisoner would think about you, only you, a prisoner would long for your visits, long for your touch with an intensity unrivalled by any free man. This might be appealing to some women, May thought. After all, you would never have to iron his shirts.

Terry, another of her students, suggested one day that May come along to the Debating Society which met during evening association once a week. The following Thursday evening she went to the chapel where the meetings took place. Two members of the local university's debating team had come in to debate 'This House Believes that Rehabilitation Doesn't Work'. May sat beside Alan from her class. She liked Alan. Despite the tattoos and the biceps, he had a nice face, a clean, wide face.

The debate and the following discussion were fierce and absorbing. At the end the chaplain served tea. Alan fetched her a cup. 'What did you think?' he asked.

'Wonderful. Is everyone always so articulate?'

'Yes – although sometimes the language degenerates a bit,' he smiled. 'Depends how many women are present.'

'Do you debate?'

'No, I like to listen. I get too caught up, angry, stop making sense. I have trouble with my temper, like, well, you know.' His teacup rattled in its saucer as though a train was passing. 'I killed my wife.'

May did not speak.

'I didn't mean to. But I did.'

Still May did not speak.

'I hit her too hard one day.' He put his cup on the floor and clasped his hands together, firmly. 'I don't really care about being in here. I'd rather be in here than out there without her. It's why I'm taking your course – to try and understand what it's like for women, what it means to . . .' he trailed off. He was looking at May.

She felt sure she was not visibly shaking. 'We never get the chance to talk much in your class.'

'I'm sorry, but I – there's a lot of material to cover.'

'Oh no, don't get me wrong, it's interesting.' He smiled his open smile.

'Good,' she said.

'It's funny, isn't it,' Alan continued, 'Women's Studies with a bunch of men like us. It makes you think.'

'What about?'

'Oh you know, the weaker sex, the war between the sexes.' He gave his shoulders a shake and then smiled. 'I think you should do a session on women who kill men.' He looked at her.

'Maybe,' May replied, 'I . . .'

'Oh don't worry,' said Alan, he was laughing now, 'I'm only pulling your leg.' Some of the others joined them and the conversation went back to the debate. May felt a drop of sweat slip down her spine.

After that it was harder to cut the discussions off in class, more difficult to decide what was appropriate, what was not. The Suffragettes and their hunger strikes led to a discussion about Willow. The men began to tell her things she did not know: more than three thousand people serving life sentences in Britain, in France less than one hundred, in Italy, seventy. Actual time served getting longer and longer. Slopping out. The punishment block. The prison hospital where you get sent when suffering from mental illness. The changing political will of the Home Secretary. 'And the food – my God, it's terrible,' someone said with real outrage.

The effect of these conversations was weird; May felt herself becoming close to these men at the same time as holding something back, remaining cautious, curious about their violence, but reining in her own voyeurism. Apart from Alan she still did not actually know what any of them had done. Their crimes and, hence, they themselves, remained enigmatic, mysterious. She could never know what their lives were really like.

Increasingly May found it difficult to talk about her job. She would come home to Clare and try to speak calmly, but end up blurting out stories in an unedited stream. 'I asked Terry for his essay today. He hadn't done it. I felt so sad, he's bright, he could get a good grade. He said he was having trouble working, he couldn't see his way through. "It's doing my head in," he said, "a life sentence. I've still got no idea when I'll be eligible for parole – five, ten, twenty years. They keep changing the rules, the regulations. It's doing my head in – I can't work, can't read, can't sleep."' Terry had spoken in the few moments before the end of class and the arrival of the prison officers. '"It's like Kafka," he said, "even when you know you are guilty."' May looked at Clare as she spoke, she watched the expression on her lover's face. Clare opened her mouth and then closed it again, as though there was nothing for her to say.

'Well, you can't reform the entire prison service yourself May.'

'I know Clare,' said May, shrugging and smiling. 'But what's to be done with these guys?'

That night when she and Clare got into bed May felt tense as she approached her lover, pushing her face into Clare's neck ferociously. Clare giggled and slid her body under May's, stroking May's back. They moved together and as they did May looked down at Clare's nakedness and found herself wondering if she could kill her, if she could murder the person she loved most. In what circumstances would she do it? What would it take? How would it feel? Would Clare fight back or would she just surrender? May banished these thoughts as she fought back a surge of nausea, shocked to find it coupled with desire.

Fathers

CARLOTTA AND BORIS were childhood sweethearts. They were introduced by their mothers in the playground when they were both three years old. Carlotta had never seen a boy like Boris before; he had red hair. Boris had never met anyone like Carlotta before; she stared at him without blinking. From that first meeting they were hooked.

They continued to meet in the playground where they would sit on the swings together. Soon their mothers stopped feeling they needed to accompany them. Other children arrived and departed, games were won and lost, bodies were scraped and wounded, but always, in the end, Carlotta and Boris were left on the swings until their mothers came to drag them away.

They grew up together like seeds planted in a garden at the same time. When they were eight they played Cowboys and Indians – they took turns invading and avenging, tying each other up. When they were ten they discovered Doctors and Nurses, ordering each other to remove those trousers please, performing exploratory surgery. Somehow these two games got confused – Cowboys and Doctors and Indians and Nurses

– so that by the time they were thirteen Carlotta was insisting that Boris get undressed before she tied him up with the skipping rope, and vice versa. They alternated between victor and vanquished, they gave each other equal opportunities to be bed-ridden or bossy.

Carlotta's father, Alex, was an ugly man whose passions lay hidden by an impossibly grumpy demeanour. He seemed to hate everything and everyone, including his wife. However, somewhere, deep down, he did have a good side, a happy side, and, occasionally, he gave a glimpse of it to Carlotta. As a result, the girl was his puppet, she would do anything for him, fetching newspapers, slippers, presenting him with drawings she made at school. Alex had a secret; the attention paid him by his little girl was his favourite thing in life.

Boris's father, Ramsey, did not have secrets, hidden sides, or favourite things. He was a handsome man, good at sports. It was clear to everyone in his family that the only thing he really cared about was his job as manager of a firm of accountants. Ramsey was not an affectionate man. Yet Boris managed to garner enough love from his mother and, later, Carlotta, to keep him from psychopathology.

Boris did grow up to be a doctor, although not simply for the thrill of asking dozens of women to undress in his office. He found ill health interesting; it was exciting – titillating even – to think he might cure someone of something one day. Carlotta had wanted to be an Indian when she grew up; like most teenage girls she had particularly unrealistic dreams. From ballet dancer to great academic, Carlotta went through a stack of options all of which might have made her famous or rich. Somehow legal secretary did not have the same buzz. But it was a job, it allowed her to marry Boris before he finished medical school. They moved in together, set up a little flat where they could listen to Country & Western music. George Jones and Tammy Wynette made life seem straightforward.

Despite the twenty-year passion of their offspring, Alex and Ramsey met for the first time at the wedding. They were introduced by their wives who both felt more than a little embarrassed – embarrassed that the men had never met and, somehow, embarrassed by the men. They shook hands, sizing each other up. Neither man had expected Carlotta and Boris to take their childhood romance this far. Neither was pleased by the knowledge that having children old enough to marry meant they themselves were no longer young. Perhaps it was this that bound them together; perhaps it was something even more mysterious that made them decide to be friends.

Carlotta's father Alex was not the kind of man who had friends – he was far too grumpy and only really felt comfortable in the presence of family. Ramsey could easily be described as friendless as well – none of the men with whom he still played football every weekend would have attempted to share more than a beer in the pub after the game. These men had wives instead of friends. No one would have suspected that Alex and Ramsey could become pals.

Which was, of course, what they did become: buddies, cohorts, partners, a team. Alex started training so he could go jogging with Ramsey; Ramsey took over the accounts from Alex's firm. They spoke on the telephone often and saw each other several times each week, lunches, squash games, Saturday sport on TV. Alex joined Ramsey's football team. Both wives were annoyed by this development, and annoyed with themselves for feeling slightly suspicious, recognizing their own jealousy. The two men seemed happy, excited, though – at last! – they were having fun. And about their fun, they were serious.

Boris and Carlotta were shocked. They had had a nice honeymoon but somehow getting married had not changed anything. Life remained the same except for this, his dad and her dad, friends. It was as though Alex and Ramsey were the newlyweds, not them.

'What do you think they see in each other?' Carlotta asked breathlessly. She had been chasing her naked husband around the flat and had finally caught him with her lasso. She wore nothing but a pair of cowboy boots.

'Men's stuff, I guess,' Boris said, panting.

'What?'

'Oh, you know, business contacts, that kind of thing. It's like having their own miniature Masonic Lodge maybe.'

'That's sinister.'

'Rotary Club then. Kiwanis. Lions.'

'Do you think they confide in each other?'

'What is there to confide?'

'Our mothers? Their relationships? Sex?' They shivered and said 'Ugh' simultaneously.

Boris was a good doctor, Carlotta was a good legal secretary. Both worked hard and had ambitions – Boris's long hours in the hospital might one day lead to a consultancy; Carlotta was toying with the idea of becoming a lawyer. On the weekends they were exhausted. Boris had to work more often than not, Carlotta did the housework. They bought a house, a car, lots of appliances and gadgets and games, they went on holiday two or three times a year. They began to get older in an invisible way.

From time to time Boris played football for his hospital. One week they played against his father and father-in-law's team. Boris hung back for most of the game, watching the two men as they kicked the ball neatly between themselves. Ramsey, his hair standing up with wind and sweat, streaked in, took a pass from Alex and scored. Boris watched while they embraced and were patted on the backside by the rest of the lads. Ramsey raised a fist in his son's direction. Boris thought him transformed, unrecognizable. His team had been confident they would beat the old guys but, in the end, they lost.

Sometimes Carlotta went shopping with her friends on Saturday; she stockpiled cowboy boots, Western-style shirts, bolo ties, stiff blue jeans. That weekend she came home with a pair of black leather chaps. 'I'm sure,' said Boris disdainfully from his position on the couch, 'I'm sure that cowboys do not wear designer chaps for which they've paid hundreds of pounds in some ladies' boutique. In fact, I'll wager that not even cowgirls do that.'

'I can't help it, Boris,' Carlotta replied. 'I just can't help myself.' Carlotta knew that Boris would change his mind when it came time for him to undo all those buckles so he could get next to her skin. He had bought her spurs for her last birthday; they knew their way into each other's fantasies. They had been together for so long they were practically the same person; they had interfaced with each other's mainframes.

Still, they alternated parents' houses for Sunday lunch. Carlotta saw enough of her father's good side to continue to be devoted. When they were alone together doing the washing-up she tried to charm her father into telling her what he saw in her father-in-law. 'Daddy,' she said, 'how's Ramsey?'

'Oh as right as rain as ever.'

'Do you see much of him these days?'

'Same amount as always.'

'Is he . . . is he, you know, happy?'

'Happy?' Alex lowered his hands into the water. 'Lovey, what are you talking about? Do you kids need a loan or something?'

Carlotta and Boris's mothers were equally curious about what their husbands saw in each other. Jane and Shelagh did not meet often but exchanged information over the telephone. They had tried being friends over the years; it seemed logical alongside the intense relationship of the children. But Jane did not like Shelagh and Ramsey very much – she found Ramsey's coldness intimidating and thought Shelagh a bit of a snob. Shelagh had tried introducing Jane to her bridge club, but she never really fit in. This had not worried the women although at times, especially leading up to the wedding, they both thought it inconvenient they were not closer.

These spells of slight regret happened with greater frequency now that Alex and Ramsey had become such a duo. Double dates were not on the agenda. In fact it was Carlotta who first brought up the possibility. 'Why don't you and Ramsey ever take Mummy and Shelagh along when you go out?' she asked her father one Sunday.

'Mummy and Shelagh? They don't play squash, you know that,' Alex replied. 'Nor football for that matter.'

'You can't always be playing sport, you see each other too often for that.'

'We never do anything that the girls would enjoy.'

'You just like getting away from them.'

Alex huffed. If Carlotta had been nearer, and smaller, he would have cuffed her across the ear like a dog.

Boris broached the subject with his mother one day. 'Oh,' Shelagh said, as if it had never occurred to her before, 'they wouldn't go for that.'

'Why not?'

'Well . . . they have things to discuss. Neither of them are what you could call sociable. I imagine it takes all their concentration just to talk to each other. Your father would not be able to cope with a four-way conversation. And besides, I don't think he likes Jane very much.' She blushed slightly as she said this; she had no idea what Ramsey thought of Jane, they had never discussed her.

'It's not that Carlotta and I think you should all go away on holidays together or anything like that. In fact we don't care whether or not you four get along. We're the important ones.'

His mother frowned.

'It just seems a bit weird, this friendship thing, it's gone on for such a long time. We want to know what it's about.'

'Sweetheart, you make it sound as though you wish I would spy on them.'

'Oh,' he said, 'that's a good idea.'

Shelagh blushed again. She could not say that this thought had never occurred to her.

But spying was not necessary. Ramsey came home from work on Friday night and, before opening the drinks cabinet as was his habit, handed Shelagh an envelope. Inside was a pair of theatre tickets for the following night, not a musical or anything like that, but Shakespeare. 'Dear?'

'I thought we could do with an outing,' he said, pouring her gin.

The next day when Shelagh realized Ramsey had taken his best suit out of the wardrobe she decided to get dressed up as well. He had cleaned the car that afternoon, he dropped her off in front of the theatre before parking. Shelagh glanced around furtively for Alex and Jane but there was no sign of them.

Alex and Jane were having dinner in the best restaurant in town. Candles, wine, linen tablecloth. Alex was ebullient over his asparagus, complaining about work, complaining about all manner of things. He was hardy and grouchy and Jane suddenly remembered why she had married him.

One month later, it happened again. Then the next month, and three weeks after that. Restaurants and theatres, sometimes both. 'They are having Another Saturday Night,' Carlotta would say to Boris after speaking to her mother on the telephone. It was as though their fathers had made a policy decision re: The Wives. Take them out, keep them happy. Carlotta found their behaviour almost indecent. It made Boris feel inadequate. They both felt outdone, out-romanticked as they sat in front of another lousy video, too tired from work to go out anywhere.

'Maybe Alex and Ramsey went to see a movie together or something, maybe they read the same novel and in it the male lead fell in love with his wife again and decided to start all over,' Carlotta speculated.

'They both had affairs is more like it, and then realized the error of their ways and are now making up for their sins.' Carlotta and Boris frowned. This seemed particularly distasteful.

'Or maybe,' said Carlotta before she had time to think, 'they had an affair with each other – they are having an affair with each other – and this is their way of disguising it.'

'Oh Carlotta,' replied Boris, appalled.

'Maybe not,' said Carlotta quietly.

The next Friday night Boris and Carlotta pulled themselves together and decided to go out. They put on their gear and drove to a Country & Western bar on the outskirts of town. At a gingham-covered table they sat trying to keep awake, drooping over their drinks while a local band played. In the middle of a rather good rendition of 'It Ain't Me You Love, It's Your Sister', Boris took his elbows off the table and stretched. That was when he spotted Ramsey and Alex. They were sitting at a table on the far side of the dance floor. They were both wearing Stetsons.

Celia and the Bicycle

CELIA RODE A BICYCLE. She was too impatient to use the public transport system, in too much of a hurry with no time. For her, the bicycle was a symbol of freedom from constraint. It enabled her to overcome traffic jams, avoid potential attackers, keep in trim, and get from A to B quickly. Two wheels and a set of handlebars meant, to Celia, liberation.

Celia also wore short skirts. During the sixties when short was chic, her mother, an accomplished seamstress, had sewn a series of little red, yellow and paisley skirts for Celia. The ripped-up and anarchic fashions of punk had enabled her to continue wearing the mini while a teenager, then the eclecticism of style in the 1980s allowed her to keep her knees bare until the mini-skirt made its re-entry onto the pages of *Vogue*. But Celia was not concerned with being fashionable; she loved the mini-skirt and that was all there was to it.

For Celia, the mini-skirt was a symbol of freedom from constraint. It enabled her to pedal her bicycle without impediment. With her strong legs free from complicated trousers or the volumes of material involved in other skirts or dresses she could speed her way through the city. The tight-fitting mini-skirt made her feel powerful, spare, economical and streamlined. She thought that if her bicycle had been human it would have worn mini-skirts as well.

Unfortunately for Celia, however, the combination of bicycle and mini-skirt produced explosive reactions on the streets of the inner city. Every time she pedalled down the road she was harangued. Men, always men or does that go without saying?, were compelled to pass comment as she sailed by. 'Oi, sit on my face, sweetheart,' was a popular phrase down the Old Kent Road.

'Nice pair of legs,' was particularly common in the West End and it was not unusual for men in Camden Town to offer the wisdom of 'Don't you think your skirt is a bit short?' as if they were moral arbiters, each one. Engines were revved, windows were hurriedly rolled down, construction workers looked up from their toil.

All Celia wanted from life was short skirts, speed, and freedom. She tried to imagine ways she could get these things. If the man on the scaffolding leaned too far to the right whilst attempting to get her attention he might fall from above into the path of an oncoming car, the driver of which would also be trying to catch Celia's eye, or rather, some other part of her body. That car might swerve to miss the construction worker who by now lay crumpled on the road, running over his legs and then crashing into another oncoming car, the driver of which would also be trying to see up Celia's skirt to where the tops of her thighs meet the bicycle seat.

Celia was not a vindictive woman. She simply had a good sense of fun. She also wanted justice. She believed in justice.

Celia and the Bicycle

Like her spirit, mind, and body, Celia's bicycle was fast and adept but fragile and vulnerable as well. Hers was not a particularly good bicycle – fairly old, both tyres were usually slightly soft and one of the lights was broken. Celia was not a Bicycle Snob. In recent years this terrifying group of people dressed in Italian cycling gear had made riding a bicycle a trendy and fashionable activity. Pushing their lean frames against the wind, the Bicycle Snobs tore up and down the streets of London, dodging traffic lights and dashing up one-way streets the wrong way. They carried complicated and expensive mechanisms for securing the dismantled frames of their well-oiled and pampered machines to lampposts and wrought-iron fences. There were also the Bicycle Couriers to contend with, people who delivered messages throughout London. Recalcitrant daredevils, driven by a mysterious death-wish, the Couriers were also Bicycle Snobs at heart. They overtook Celia on the thoroughfares and by-ways, looking down at her inferior bike with distaste. Unlike the men in cars they did not pass verbal comment, but Celia could tell what they were thinking. She did not care. Celia was a bicycle libertarian; she believed everyone should be allowed to do it their own way. To her the bicycle was a modern icon, symbolic of religious rightness and purity. Cheap, pollution-free, silent: for her it was enough simply to ride. And riding in London was an act of faith.

Celia had a recurrent dream. In this dream, which she usually had after cycling home drunk, she and her bicycle could fly. All they needed was a slight hill, like the one down Pentonville Road from the Angel to

King's Cross, or the one that slides around Brockwell Park en route from Herne Hill to Brixton. Late at night with no cars around she would travel down the hill as quickly as her bicycle could take her and just before reaching the bottom, take off. Pedalling at a leisurely pace, Celia and her bicycle would glide over London like Peter Pan and Wendy, like the Wicked Witch of the West. The city sparkled in the night as they flew over the enormous rail stations and circled around Nelson's Column. Celia dreamed she had seen Nelson's face, a vision of pride covered with pigeon shit.

Upon waking the morning after having had a flying bicycle dream, Celia always felt disappointed and flat. Rubbing her eyes on the way to the bathroom she would stop in the corridor and examine her bicycle. It did not look like it could fly. After breakfast she would take it outside the front door, get on it and set off down the road. The first hill was always a terrible strain and she would huff and puff and curse. But later, as she wove between cars, passing through traffic jams with ease, she would remember her dream and take her hands off the handlebars and flap her arms like they were wings. It was the nearest she could get to the real thing.

The traffic in London creates a special form of madness that makes the ordinarily sweet-natured person aggressive and violent. Car, motorcycle, and lorry drivers become psychopaths while only bus drivers seem able to maintain calm. Cyclists are not exempt from this madness; the more lyrical and graceful movement of a bicycle does not necessarily mean its rider is not angry, does not want to kill or maim. Celia herself valued the rush of adrenalin she received when she shouted at cars that cut in front of her. 'Wrap those legs around me, love' would send her off a bit faster at the next green light. 'We've seen your legs, now show us your tits,' gave her an edge on the cyclist behind. And, 'Lucky bicycle seat,' or 'I wish my face was your bicycle seat,' or 'Is that a bicycle seat or are you excited?' would send her shooting up the next hill as though her legs were pistons and her heart a generator. She would yell back 'Fuck off' or 'Asshole' or 'Bastard' and ride like the wind. Pumping her legs up and down, up and down, she felt purified and hardened and sleek. She felt they could not stop her, they could not put reins on her, they could not suppress her energy with their remarks. She ate up their abuse like a horse eats oats and used it to fuel her journey.

ONE WEEKEND CELIA rose early. She was going to visit a friend who was organizing a boatload of bicycles to take to Nicaragua. Apparently in Nicaragua there was a shortage of that kind of thing. Celia opened her closet and surveyed her collection of mini-skirts. To her they looked functional and practical, like gym shorts only not quite so utilitarian. She chose a blue and white stripy one, not too short, not micro-mini, but a mini nonetheless. With that, a shirt and her plimsolls, she was ready. She ate breakfast then got on her bike.

The traffic was heavy with Saturday shopping confusion. Celia was running a bit late. At a set of traffic lights on Clapham High Street one of the stream-lined neo-Italians passed her in a flash of perfectly attired bright light. Toiling against the wind along Clapham Common, she hummed a tune and ignored the comments which were hurled at her every minute or two. She picked up a lot of speed as she reached Clapham South tube station and it was there, just beyond the intersection, that the man in the yellow Cortina chose to ignore her, swung his steering wheel and tried to take his car into a side street, whamming his foot on the accelerator.

Celia's bicycle, her beloved and much adored, upright handlebar with a male cross-bar and battery operated lights bicycle, slid under the heavy bodies of this man and his metal-shelled vehicle. The wheels of the car crunched and twisted the bike's frame, snapping off the seat.

The bicycle was dead. Forever.

On initial impact Celia took off and flew through the air. For a minute that extended into hours she floated above the crowded and busy street. Clapham Common looked green and peaceful away from the road, traffic-free. The wind rushed around her legs and up her miniskirt. The cars stopped honking, their engines stood idle, and the people on top of the buses stared, their mouths open, their noses pressed against the windows.

Then, with a thud, Celia landed on the roof of the yellow Cortina. The driver got out of the car. His face was bloated and red with anger. 'Get off my car, you fucking slag,' he shouted.

Celia felt shocked. She had just been in the air, she had actually flown and it was not a dream. 'What do you mean, you wanker,' she said. 'I'm not a slag. Don't you call me a slag. It's drivers like you who *kill* cyclists.'

'Who the fuck do you think you are, riding around London with your skirt up your arse? If you were my daughter, or my wife for that matter, you wouldn't get out the front door in that thing.'

'You almost killed me just then, you bastard.'

'Serve you right too, you little slut.'

Something inside Celia burst then. Maybe it was her inner tube or perhaps it was only a bulb in her lights, but something exploded. She stood on the roof of the yellow Cortina and shouted, 'You killed my bicycle, you animal. You're going to pay for this.' She leapt off the car and for a moment she felt free again. Then she landed on the shoulders of the driver. With her legs on either side of his head, he had become her beast of burden, her packhorse, her mule, maybe even her bicycle. She kicked him in the ribs with her heels and reached down to slap him on the backside with one hand. 'Giddy-up, come on, let's go. And with her powerful legs like a Vice on his neck she made him carry her to the door of her friend's house through Balham and into Tooting. On the way she decided that men were just as easy to ride as bicycles not as quick, mind you, not as smooth, but much less work on hills.

My Mother, My Father, and Me

WHEN I VISIT my father I take the train. I leave home by eleven and catch the tube, the Northern Line, to King's Cross, walk across the street to St Pancras, and take the Intercity to Market Harborough. If I get the train at noon, I arrive in Market Harborough just after one o'clock. I walk into the centre of the little town – I have got to know it quite well – and wander around. I tell myself I'm going to go into one of the pubs and have some lunch, but somehow I always feel too nervous to eat, too unsettled by the journey to sit anywhere for long. And, of course, I'm afraid that if I go into a pub everyone will look at me. Everyone will be able to tell. They will know where I am going and, in an instant, they will know who I am and what happened.

So, I avoid lingering anywhere too long, and just before two o'clock I go to a phonebox and ring for a taxi. The local firm are usually prompt, they drive up the hill out of the village in the rapid, neat manner of rural taxicabs. They too are accustomed to this journey.

The prison sits on top of a ridge, the highest point in the area. In winter after the sun drops away and the yellow dome lights come on, the prison glows

247

malevolently, casting shadows over the countryside like a ghastly carved pumpkin on Hallowe'en. The ridge catches the worst of the weather, a breeze becomes a squall, drizzle becomes hard, piercing rain.

Once there, I wait with the others, all the parents, lovers, children, and friends, everyone's face taut with the same mixture of apprehension, longing, and shame. Here I have nothing to hide. In the queue for the visits room I can feel that no one will judge me, or my father.

The security procedure for the visits room, which is on the boundary of the prison, not really inside the prison itself, is complex and time-consuming, even though in recent months the authorities have made an effort to make it easier. I thought that the portakabins next to the prison gates were for the builders but it turned out – things do sometimes change between one visit and the next – that these low plywood boxes are the new visitors' facilities, the much-heralded waiting room and advice centre. At least now we can stay warm and dry while we wait.

I don't get searched all that often any more, which is the only sign that the pale-faced and nameless officers have ever seen me before. My father has been in this particular prison for several years, and I see the same officers every time I come, once a month, but they give no indication that they know me, not even the women, the female officers who have actually laid their hands on my body as they rummage through the folds of my clothes looking for contraband.

If I have brought presents for my father I hand them in to Property. I never feel certain that everything

I bring will get to him, but very little has gone missing over the years. My father doesn't ask for much, magazines mostly, paperback novels the library can't get for him. I always try to bring food as well, fruit mainly, some good quality tea-bags. He insists that he can get everything he needs from the prison itself – meals, clothes, shaving gear, underwear. I once tried to replace the rubber prison slippers he wears with a pair of decent shoes. He sent the box back to me, unopened, with a letter demanding that I get my money refunded. He cannot support the idea of being a financial burden to my brother and me.

I've been coming on my own to visit for a couple of years now. Before that I always came with Auntie Ann. Auntie Ann is my legal guardian. My brother, Toby, and I lived with her after our father was sentenced. Uncle Greg lived with us as well, at first, but then they split up. Other relations worried that their divorce was hard on us, but I think by then Toby and I were immune. You could have hammered nails into our hands and we would not have felt them.

Ann is my father's sister and she has always been good to us. We didn't choose each other but, given the circumstances, everything has gone pretty well. I prefer being on my own, of course. But when you are young you can't just strike out on your own like in a children's book, you've got to be in thrall to adults for a while.

Toby used to tell other kids that we were orphans, but I've never had trouble telling people that my father is in prison. I find this information sorts out the meek from the strong.

WHEN I WAS sixteen I met my first boyfriend at a party. I thought he was very fine. He asked me to dance and then we sat in a corner and talked. Turned out we went to neighbouring schools. By that time I had no trace of my old accent – Auntie Ann lived in London which was miles away from Durham, where Toby and I were born. We danced and talked and had some beer, smoked a spliff together – he was seventeen, almost eighteen. I could tell he was looking for a girlfriend and, as I was looking for a boyfriend, we got along well. We liked the same music, which is important. He liked to talk and I liked to listen to him, he liked to swear and boast and, in his way, he was charming. When I told him my father was in prison a certain look came into his eyes, a look I was familiar with. He didn't ask a single question and I guess he invented a father for me then, a bank robber most likely, maybe even a drug smuggler, or – yes – a spy. He found romance in the fact that my father was a prisoner. I didn't particularly care where it came from, any romance was enough for me.

Ann was very good at helping me buy clothes and shoes, she had a quick proficiency with make-up and hair. I don't think my own mother went in for dresses and high heels, at least not that I can remember. Sometimes when I go into department stores and walk through the cosmetics section I come across a perfume that will bring Ann to me immediately, but I have never found a scent that makes me think of my mother. I don't have any photographs of her, I don't have any of her clothes, the police confiscated everything personal and it was never returned to us. Last Christmas Toby told me he could not remember our mother at all.

ONCE I AM allowed through to the visits room I find a table and sit down. I like to try to stay away from the large family gatherings and the young women who have come to visit their boyfriends. I find the smoking and the noise gets to me, the children always cry and end up running in and out of the room. Some afternoons the young couples will spend the whole time sprawled across the table in each other's arms and my father and I find this embarrassing. As I wait for him to arrive, I wonder how I look, hoping I appear healthy and cared for. My father and I both spend a lot of time trying not to worry each other.

Doors bang, keys and keychains clank, officers shout and eventually my father comes through the door. He keeps his prison blues very smart. He irons his prison jeans and shirts and he always wears a blue woollen prison tie for our visits. Every month I think he seems thinner, dimmer somehow, more and more faded, but this must be an illusion, he would have disappeared completely by now. He looks a tidy little old man, shrivelled and ruined.

Our visits go well, the two hours pass too quickly. I buy cups of tea from the canteen. My father drills me, and I attempt to prise information from him, what he needs, how he is coping. Sometimes when I talk to my friends about their fathers the irony catches me up and threatens to trip me – I know my father much better than they know theirs. They don't spend two hours together every month, two hours that always have and always will feel like the last two hours we may ever spend with each other. I try to bring photos or, at least, news of Toby – my brother does not visit our father himself. And my father tries to make himself understand that I am a grown woman now, that I am not a little girl. I am no longer the child witness.

THAT FIRST BOYFRIEND did not last long, first boyfriends rarely do. I was a morbid little soul and he wanted to have a good time. So did I, really, but things got in my way. I used to dream that I was in prison, that it was me, alone in a cell, not my father. This dream got in our way.

My second boyfriend, a year later, was much more serious. Auntie Ann made it clear that if I was going to sleep with boys I had to take precautions, and she made this easy for me. She would not let Dorian stay the night but then, while Toby and I lived with her, she never brought her boyfriends home either. Dorian, well, Dorian was wonderful. He and I had rapport. We shared tastes and desires, our bodies rolled together like we were in the centre of a big, soft bed. When I told him about my father he did not make assumptions. He once asked if I would like him to come on a visit with me, and he understood when I explained that visits were just for my father and me. He didn't ask any more questions. Like most people, he could probably guess what had happened, and he saw it was not something I could discuss.

We went away together, stretching our student grants to trips to Amsterdam and Malaga, once as far as Morocco. After two years we decided to share a flat. Ann was very good, she made us curtains for our bedroom, drank a bottle of wine with us to celebrate the day we moved. Toby had already left – he was younger than me, but always quicker to do things – and I think Ann was not unhappy to be on her own after her years of sudden, unexpected, child-rearing.

Things began to go wrong in our third year. I had become more absorbed by my studies, I was always an earnest student, while Dorian became more and more disenchanted with his. He said he was not happy with the system, with the fact that the progress of his life seemed almost inexorable – college, work, pension, the rest of it. He wanted fresh excitement. I felt the opposite, I expected complete disaster and so was quite happy to be confined by routine.

MY FATHER AND I are very similar. I don't know if this is because of the years we spent together, or the years we've spent apart. We are both easily embarrassed – our cheeks grow ripe and red for no reason. We share moods – when I am low, so is he. We are happiest when our lives are calm and plain. We have an uneasy relationship with the world, we do not trust others lightly.

During the day I mark the time when my father's cell is unlocked. 8:00 a.m., his door is opened, he washes, has breakfast. 8:45 he is locked into the plastic injection moulding workshop where he is employed. 11:45 he picks up lunch and is locked into his cell between 12:30 and 1:45. 2:00 is back to work, 4:30 he gets his tea and is locked up again from 5:00 till 5:45. In the evening he can go down to watch television if he feels sociable. 8:00 is bang-up for the night. Twelve hours he spends alone in his cell with a bucket to piss in.

It is the night-time that I like best. After 8:oo I know where he is, I know my father is safe. I know he is listening to the radio I bought him, quiet music, or a play. Perhaps he is writing to me, or to Ann. Perhaps he is thinking about when Toby and I were small and he worked in an office and stayed home on the weekends. Maybe he falls asleep and dreams of my mother. Or perhaps my mother keeps him awake.

DORIAN BEGAN TO have an affair. He deceived me as though we had been married for fifteen years and had nothing left to our relationship except wedding rings, children and contempt. He was abrupt, and indiscreet as well, perhaps as indiscreet as my mother had been, I don't know. He was always late. He worried about his appearance. He whistled tunes I had never heard.

I was paralysed by his behaviour. I could not speak to, nor move away from, him. I could not confront him. I could not admit to what was taking place. I stood absolutely still, and let rage entomb me.

One night he came home about eleven o'clock. He was a lime drunk. I was standing in the corridor just outside the sitting room as he came through the front door. He greeted me with happy insouciance and put his arms around me, embraced me, kissing me. I loved the feel of his body next to mine. I knew where he had been but, with his touch, I was willing to forget it.

I leaned back against the wall as we kissed. He pressed his palms against my breasts. I slipped my fingers over his belt and undid his flies and reached inside his trousers. His underwear was wet, not just damp, but wet from fucking her. I withdrew my hand sharply, but Dorian caught my wrist and pulled my hand to his groin. It was awkward, he took a step towards me, the rug slipped, we twisted around trying to stay upright and slid roughly towards the floor. I was on top of him. In fact, I had him pinned down. I sat on his legs, undid his trousers and pulled them open. He smelt very strong. I looked at him and he could see that I knew. He began to speak but stopped when I struck him across the face. Not a slap, but a punch, my knuckles stinging. I moved forward and sat on his chest, catching his arms with my legs. I hit him again, as hard as I was able. I thought if I could lift his head and knock it against the floor and . . . I looked around for something to hit him with but he was struggling against me, pounding his knees into my spine, rocking back and forth. I hung on. Then he raised his hips off the floor and threw me over onto my back, landing on top of me, forcing all the breath out of my lungs. He grabbed my hair with his hand, wrenching my head to one side, pulling my neck taut, my cheek scraping hard against the rug, my back curved unnaturally.

From where I lay I could see into the sitting room. I could see the settee where I had been watching television, and I could see myself there, twelve years old. From where I lay everything was sideways and upside-down and this is what my mother must have seen as she lay on the floor that day, my father on top of her. Her head was pulled back just like mine, her gaze wild and afraid. My father did not realize I was there but my mother saw me watching. She looked at me as I watched her die.

I don't remember my mother's character. I don't know how she ended up on that floor. If she had lived perhaps I would not be who I am. There would be more to the equation than just my father and me, our visits, our dreams, our failings. Auntie Ann tried hard, but she was only Auntie Ann. In the end, we are our parents' children.

Dorian did not hit me. He only pulled my hair to stop me from scratching him. Neither of us was very strong, but he was bigger than me. He got up and left me lying there, my head craned around, my mother; my father, and me.

IT IS ALWAYS difficult when the visit ends. The officers start to call the time, they walk up and down between the tables rattling their chains. My father bows his head and thanks me for taking the trouble to come to visit him. I ask how much longer he thinks they'll make him serve and he says he has no idea. He doesn't want to give me false hope.

I think my father would like to die in prison. I don't know if he could survive if they let him out, if they gave him a freedom my mother will never have. But he won't die, and one day he will get out. But not now, and at the end of every visit this bears heavily on me.

A Modern Gothic Morality Tale

MINA LIVES WITH Vladimir in the docklands of London. Vladimir bought an enormous flat there when the area was first being redeveloped. He likes to be by the river; it reminds him of his voyaging days. The flat takes up an entire floor of one of the old warehouses. They have a lot of room to themselves. Vladimir likes it that way, he says he is a modern man and modern men need to stretch out and be expansive.

The flat, however, is the only thing about Vladimir that is expansive. He lives a closely guarded and careful life. He has to stay out of sunshine and prefers to function at night. During the London summer this limits his lifestyle because in June the sun does not go down much before half past ten and then comes back up again very early. In the summer Vladimir and Mina go on holiday to the dark places of the southern hemisphere.

In the winter London is a night city and Vladimir is content and busy, rising in the afternoon as soon as the sun goes down. In December he is up as early as half past three. In the City he defines his own working hours.

Mina works with physically disabled children in an impoverished area of the East End of London. She has always considered herself left-wing and feminist and before she met Vladimir was involved in many different political struggles. She has spent years campaigning for the rights of the handicapped as well as the rights of the poor, the homeless, the powerless, and what she sees as the various victims of British Imperialism. Mina's grandmother was a Victorian lady who devoted her life to charity. Mina is proud of her heritage.

Vladimir claims that his ancestors were British aristocrats with Russian connections, hence his name and his impeccable accent. The night they met he told Mina he was the only child of parents long dead who left him a vast fortune which he had since made vaster. The fact that Vladimir was an orphan drew Mina towards him; it made him seem vulnerable. Never one to ignore an opportunity to comfort the bereaved, Mina insisted that Vladimir tell her his lonely life story. The tale was a bit thin on details but, despite that, Mina was charmed.

'This is the only photograph I have of her,' Vladimir said, producing from his breast pocket a sepia-tinted picture of a tall, slim and high-cheekboned woman dressed in a beaded shift, her hair in a marcel wave. 'She was young in this photo. It was taken years before she had me, her only child.' Mina could have kissed the picture and wept but instead she kissed Vladimir. His lips were very cool as was his skin but Mina assumed that was because of his class.

The next day Mina spoke to Eileen, one of her co-workers. 'You know my friend who works in the City?'

'You mean the one with the incredible car and the enormous salary?'

Mina nodded. 'I went to a party at her house last night and I met the most extraordinary man. I spent the whole evening talking to him. He drove me home. Or rather, his chauffeur did. He didn't make a pass at me though, he showed me a photograph of his mother.'

'Sounds weird to me. Never trust a man who shows you a photo of his mum the first time you meet, that's what I always say,' Eileen tutted.

'He has black hair and long fingers and a very seductive smile. He is incredibly posh. I've never met anyone so posh.'

'Oh yeah, what's his name?'

'Vladimir.'

'Vladimir? That sounds foreign. Where does he come from?'

'Well, he is English . . .' Mina explained. The other woman said she didn't know what to think; the whole episode was very unlike Mina who was usually prone to having affairs with homeless immigrants and refugees who offered themselves to her like political sacrifices, sent from heaven to gratify Mina's curiosity about the barbaric world outside the East End of London.

That night when Mina finished work she stepped out the door of the building. Just as she was turning her collar against the wind she noticed the long black car. The passenger door opened and Vladimir stepped out. He waved at Mina and, after letting a car pass, walked across the street.

'Would you have dinner with me this evening?' he asked, his face pale under the streetlamp. Mina was flattered. She was unaccustomed to such flamboyant elegance and the interest of a rich man. She followed

Vladimir back to his car, immediately worried about what she was wearing.

'I'm not dressed for anywhere smart,' she said covering her embarrassment with a laugh.

'You look wonderful,' he replied. 'I love a woman who has just been working.' Mina felt even more embarrassed. The car glided off through the night to a small Italian trattoria somewhere. They sat at a table in a dark corner and drank large glasses of full-bodied red wine. When the food arrived Mina noticed that Vladimir did not eat but she was so enthralled with the telling of her own life history that she did not think it worth interrupting. Usually men wanted to talk about themselves.

After the meal was finished, Vladimir smiled his handsome smile and said, in a low voice, 'Would you like to come and have coffee at my hotel?'

'Your hotel?' asked Mina, flustered. 'I thought you said you lived in London.'

'I'm looking for somewhere to buy.'

Mina smiled. By now she felt quite drunk. Vladimir's careful questions had made her feel clever and active, as if all the things she did were fascinating. Earlier she had tried to discover exactly what his business was. All he would say was that he took good care of his money.

They left the restaurant and got back into the car which had waited outside while they ate. On the wide black leather seat Vladimir pulled Mina's body close to his. She felt warm and excited and her mouth was dry with nervousness and anticipation. Vladimir kissed her on the neck. His cool lips felt unbearably soft and Mina let herself relax.

In his fifth-floor suite overlooking Hyde Park, Vladimir poured Mina another glass of wine and, as she raised it to her lips, unbuttoned her shirt. She put the glass back on the drinks table and let herself be undressed. He led her into the bedroom and laid her down on the bed. After taking off his own clothes he stretched out beside her, kissing her hair and her face. His lips travelled down her body and when he reached Mina's abdomen she tensed and said, 'I am bleeding.'

'I know,' he replied. Mina sank back into the pillows.

Not long after that Vladimir bought the flat in the docklands and Mina moved in with him. At night while Vladimir is away working Mina sits up and looks out their windows at the Thames which quietly slaps the concrete embankment below. The old refurbished warehouses seem empty and lonely even though Mina knows all the flats have been bought by people like herself and Vladimir. Sometimes when the wind blows it is almost as if the area is derelict again, lifeless and without industry, the canals and wharves corrupt, decaying.

Vladimir's money buys Mina all sorts of things that she never knew she needed. It brings her warmth, freedom from bother, security and lots of space to be liberal in. Vladimir treats Mina well. He is faithful and amorous, especially when she menstruates. Things have always come easily to Vladimir. Mina thinks she might love him. He is tortured and sad and, beside him, all else pales away.

Irises

1

VIOLET

I CAN'T STOP thinking about her.

We met in a pub, not a student place, but somewhere a bit different, where real people go after they finish real jobs. My friends and I wanted an evening away from college, from libraries, from books. Not that we didn't have evenings off, we had lots of evenings off. In fact evenings off were a way of life for us. We trooped down to the pub, our wallets slim, because students are poor; even students who, unlike me, are from wealthy families, get very poor when it comes to a night out at the pub.

She was there, and I watched her for a bit, then Geoff my friend from Birmingham – the longer he stayed in Cambridge, the thicker his Brummy accent became – Geoff went up to her and started talking. Turned out he knew her, he'd met her at some bar or another, student party, or something. She was a little undergraduate, I should have known by looking at her, she had that thin, under-twenty look, but I was too taken in by it all, by her, by her glossy long hair, and her pale blue-veined skin. I went over and joined them, and Geoff took his time about introducing us, but he did eventually. Her name was Iris. I couldn't believe it. Iris. Like the flower. Like the dark purple colour of her eyes, of her . . . irises. It makes me hold my breath to thrink of her eyes. Iris.

And these were her first words to me: 'Bill,' she said, 'do you understand this place?' I looked around. Did she mean the pub?

'Well . . .' I said, hesitating, not wanting to get this, our first exchange, wrong.

'I mean, they told me Cambridge was a famous university, but they didn't tell me Cambridge was famous for being weird.'

Weird. Of course, she was right, it was weird, deeply weird. I knew that, but I had got used to it somehow, used to the colleges and the formal dinners and the academic gowns and the supervisions with the dons who fell asleep while you talked to them. That actually happened to me when I was an undergraduate. Dr Simms, the man who was meant to be imparting great knowledge unto me, Dr Simms, my supervisor, fellow of St Paul's College, recipient of two honorary doctorates, expert in his field, Dr Simms fell asleep while I read my paper. I could have killed him. Perhaps I should have killed him and done countless other hopeful and anxious students a service.

But, instead, I stayed on, intent on getting my doctorate and maybe one day falling asleep in supervisions of my own.

The other thing about her was, of course, that she was foreign, she was American, so she might have meant the pub, that wouldn't have been far-fetched, it is weird to have to get your own drinks from the bar and to stand, to stand all evening, in the midst of the fake sawdust and the cigarette smoke. She was here on a scholarship, a big fucking scholarship, can you believe it? And she was standing next to me. Geoff had disappeared. I will always love him for that.

'Iris,' I said, 'you're absolutely right. It is weird. It is entirely weird.' And I laughed and she laughed with me.

And then three months later I killed her. And a week after that, I chopped her up. I had to get rid of her body somehow. And by then it was no longer her, no longer Iris in any sense that I could recognize.

THINGS WENT WELL in the pub that night. We liked each other. She had been in Cambridge, in England, for only one month, and I suspect that back in the US she'd seen too many Merchant Ivory films, read too much Evelyn Waugh and Graham Greene, paid too much attention to Hugh Grant and Daniel Day-Lewis for her own good. She thought Englishmen were sexy. I was lucky, she'd been here too little time to be disabused of that. And, I admit, I was on good form that night, I had just that day had my hair cut so unfashionably short that I looked like I was on the edge of some new trend, I'd remembered to shave before coming out, I looked clean-cut, trustworthy, honourable, maybe even a bit American. At the time, I would have liked to have been an American. I told jokes, she laughed at them. She confided in me, after another couple of pints. She told me she wasn't overly impressed with the quality of teaching at the university, in fact, she was shocked by the way they did things here. She'd heard one too many academics say that their real work, the important stuff, was their own research, not teaching. I told her my story about Dr Simms.

I didn't make any mistakes, didn't make a fool of myself. We parted ways at half past eleven, she off to her college, me off to the flat I shared with Geoff and Raj and Tim. I slept like a log that night, I always slept well after evenings out, my head full of Iris and beer instead of books, papers, and all the work I should be doing and was not.

In the morning I opened my eyes and realized I had forgotten to ask what college she was at. I got out of bed and caught Geoff before he headed off to the library. Then I spent the morning writing a note, composing a note, writing her a brief letter asking if she would consider going out with me on Thursday. We had met on Monday – Thursday seemed soon, but not too soon, and Friday, well, it was a risk asking a woman out on the weekend. I don't know why I thought that, I can't remember the reasoning behind that particular theory, it was probably something Geoff had told me and I had taken as gospel since Geoff was one year older than me and always had a string of new and glorious girlfriends. The trick seemed to be to restrict first dates to week nights. And I am never one to question received wisdom.

So I asked Iris if she would like to meet me at the pub, the same pub, the same auspicious pub, on Thursday night at nine p.m. Late enough to get some work done beforehand, late enough so that if we hate each other we can say we need to get home and do some more work. Early enough that we'll have time to drink too much so that we can carry on carrying on elsewhere. Sometimes I sound just like my dad.

DISPOSING OF HER body was incredibly difficult. It made sense to do it, I'd killed her and logic dictated that in order to prevent myself from getting caught I had to get rid of the body. At first I thought I could just keep her with me. That way, she would never be found, and without a body, there could be no evidence. When the bedder came round to clean my room, I pretended we were asleep. I told Geoff and Raj and Tim she had a cold and that I was taking care of her. But, of course, I wasn't thinking straight, and after a week, even in Cambridge where my room was so cold that some mornings I'd wake up and find frost on the inside of the windows, she began to smell. We began to smell. So I waited until the weekend, when everyone was going away.

IRIS WAS AT the pub already when I got there on Thursday night, even though I was a good fifteen minutes early. She was alone, she hadn't brought anyone with her, no friends to make things easier. She wasn't a timid girl and I liked that. She bought the first round. We found seats, it seemed like a miracle at the time. One seat, a wooden bench that required us to sit right next to each other, our thighs pushed together like sausages in plastic wrapping. Nobody that we knew came into the pub, another miracle. We were left on our own, with each other.

We talked about America, she told me about the small town where she grew up. New Hampshire, big wooden houses with verandas and lawns that lead to sidewalks that lead to schools and fire stations and the local library. I tried to picture it, she said it was like *Our Town*, which I hadnt't read. 'Think of a movie,' I said, 'think of a movie with a town like your town.'

She laughed. '*Blue Velvet*,' she said, 'only safe and nice and calm.'

We drank quite a lot, quickly. 'I never really drink at home,' she said. 'But here everything seems to revolve around alcohol.'

'We don't have to drink,' I said, and then I wondered what I meant. I had been looking forward to getting drunk with her. 'I mean, next time, next time we meet, we won't drink, we'll do something wholesome and fun. What do healthy Americans do for fun?'

'Have sex,' she said, smiling, and I wasn't shocked. But the plastic around our sausages suddenly felt a little tighter.

I don't know, I think she must have been very lonely. I got lonely, and I'm English, I'd lived in Cambridge for five years, I knew loads of people, someone was always coming around, dropping by, arranging parties and outings and weekends away. She was only eighteen, she'd never been away from home before, and she was very clever, very intelligent, 'smart', as she'd say, smart and sharp. It couldn't have been easy, being new to university and new to the country all at the same time.

And we hit if off. She didn't show me her loneliness, but I could see it. It shone around her like a halo.

I walked her back to her college. The wind was hoary and penetrating and we hurried along the pavement. After a while I realized she was mumbling, almost under her breath – 'St John's, Trinity, Gonville and Caius' – she pronounced Caius incorrectly, like 'cay-us instead of 'keys' – 'Trinity Hall, Clare . . .' As we walked along past the big medieval walls she named the colleges, as if this would help us on our way. I was too drunk to think this odd, and it was too cold to talk. On Clare Bridge she took my hand. She took off her glove and drew my hand out of my pocket, my bare hand, I never wore gloves, I could never keep track of them for more than a day. Her fingers felt strong and long and her palm slid warmly against mine. Then she put our hands into my pocket, both of them, and they remained there, locked together, knocking against my hip as we strode along the dark street.

At her college, I walked her to the door. She looked wonderful as she turned to me.

'Good-night,' she said.

'Good-night,' I replied, and we kissed as though it was perfectly natural. And I wandered home, warm and excited and pleased.

On Sunday we had arranged to walk to Grantchester, but when she arrived at my place to pick me up, it was raining. We debated whether or not we were hardy enough to go anyway, and decided against it. We made mugs of tea and went up to my room. It wasn't too awful – when I saw the weather I had anticipated this and done some tidying – and we sat on the floor in front of the gas fire and talked. I had a fairly large room at the back of a house owned by the college. It was quiet, outside winter birds called, and in the distance, on the green, they were playing rugby and from time to time we could hear that as well. It got dark just after five, and I made more tea, and we ended the afternoon lying on my bed, side by side, our clothes on, touching.

You know, I wasn't a virgin. Of course not, I was twenty-four by then. I was fairly successful with girls, although not as popular as Geoff, but he was a Sex Addict, we used to tell him he needed counselling. I was a nice young man, I liked women, I liked the way they smelt, and talked, and worried, the way they could be just like blokes when they wanted, then like an alien species at other times. Some men at Cambridge, especially the public-school boys who hadn't gone to school with girls, who'd lived away from their mothers and sisters from a tender age, couldn't seem to catch on to how to relate to the opposite sex, but I didn't have that problem. I had two sisters, you see, and they were older and brighter and braver than me, and when I was young I wanted to be more like them. Iris said she found me easy to talk to. She sat up on my bed, and said, 'Hey, you're easy to talk to, for an English guy, I feel relaxed for the first time in ages.' I took this as a great compliment. And I took it as an opportunity to grasp her arm, pull her down close to me, and kiss her on the lips once again.

HER BODY WAS very white, unlined, and lovely, even after she was dead. There was a mole on her left breast, it had become so familiar, like a signpost that told me I was in the right place. She was quite hairy, dark hair on her arms and her legs, but I liked that, I had luxuriated in her pubic hair and what was buried beneath it. I carried her into the bathroom a couple of hours after everyone left the house. I was well prepared, I'd bought a whole roll of black rubbish bags, and I'd stolen a saw from the garden store in the grounds of the college. I climbed over the fence the night before. I was frightened, but it proved easy to get one of the windows of the shed to open, it had been left slightly ajar. Inside there was an array of saws, as well as axes and hammers, and I took a smaller, sharp-toothed one that I thought would do the job. I wasn't expert at this, no way. I didn't even eat meat.

Iris was a vegetarian too, we had that in common. I knew a bit about the US, the guns, the celebrities, a little history. And she knew nothing about England, absolutely nothing. Sometimes it was as if we weren't even speaking the same language. Being with her made Britain seem so insignificant, in a way I hadn't quite fathomed before. And it is insignificant, it's a pissant little country swilling about in its own shit, dreaming of better days. Sometimes I think it's an indication of where we are at that we still think Cambridge is one of our best universities. Half the decent people who were here when I arrived have left for posts in the US. The entire History faculty seems desperate to leave. Except the old guys, of course, except for the old men like Dr Simms. And there are plenty of them, old at heart, if not in years.

When we made love it was a complete revelation. I

don't know, I guess I'd never done it and fallen in love at the same time before. With other girls I had always struggled to get it right the first time, and with her, it simply was right. It couldn't have been more right. And at the end there was a fabulous reward in it for me: the way she came. She kept her eyes open the whole time, her purple eyes looked right into me without glazing over, without losing focus in her reverie. And when she came she grabbed hold of me as though it was me who she wanted, only me, and she would want only me forever. She said my name and gasped, her breath deep and harsh. And my own orgasm was like a swoon. I sank into her and never wanted to resurface.

From then on we were an item, we were a romance, and we fell into habits and ways that were familiar to us from all the other student loves by which we were surrounded. Except with Iris I felt completely different from all the rest, with Iris I felt as though I had been blessed. I am not a religious person, but I felt beatified, deified, sainted. She was the best of me. We spent a lot of time together, although Iris had her friends, and she kept up with them, she was a good friend, a good person. I kept up with Geoff and Raj and Tim, I lived with them, we had no choice. We all had girlfriends at that point, which was highly unusual, and the house had an enticing sex-fug that permeated the very walls between our bedrooms. We were tremendously relaxed and pleased with ourselves. On the nights the girls were out and we were in, we cooked for each other, ribbed each other, drank cans of lager, and went to bed early.

IN THE BATHTUB, Iris's body looked small, deflated and rigid at the same time, I didn't know where to start. I picked up her left foot, the heel cupped in my hand, and her whole body lifted stiffly, like a Barbie Doll. She had clean little feet, and her toenails were evenly clipped, unpainted. I placed the saw just above her ankle, pushed it back and forth once or twice. There was a trickle of blood, not much. Her heart was no longer pumping.

I'D SEEN IRIS's blood before. About two weeks after we'd started sleeping together, she got her period. Some girls are very squeamish about menstruating, it's as if they think men don't know that this is what happens to women. They behave as though we might suddenly go off them when we find out they bleed. But Iris wasn't like that. She was totally matter of fact, complaining. It came in the middle of the night, and in those first few hours it was evident that she was in a fair amount of pain. She said the best cure for it was sex. She got on top of me and moved back and forth very slowly. We weren't using a condom and we got very messy, blood all over the sheets. But I felt that blood was our ritual bonding, as though we were two kids who had sliced our thumbs and pressed them together. It felt like an enormous, mutual exchange.

We had an amazing month together. We both worked really hard. Iris was academically ambitious, and I got more done than I had during the entire previous year. She was reading English Literature and at night sometimes she would read to me, bits of

Chaucer, passages from Milton, Shakespeare. It was funny hearing this stuff in her New England accent, and she would ham it up, to make me laugh. On days when the sun shone we'd go out on the river; she'd lie elegantly back in the punt and I'd stand at the rear with the pole, singing operatic arias that I made up on the spot. Sometimes in the middle of the night, we'd sneak into my college's brand-new library. We'd have sex on a chair, fully dressed, surrounded by books, the blue light from the computer terminals on our backs and faces.

And then term ended and Iris went home for Christmas. At Cambridge terms are very short, eight weeks, and the break stretches for more than six. I went with her to Heathrow, I had to work very hard not to get upset, and she was so light-hearted, looking forward to seeing her family, her dog, her friends. Her life in America was suddenly real to me, and I found it unbearable that she should have something so far beyond my reach. When she went through passport control and passed out of my sight, I sat down on the steps, right there, in front of the tie shop and the book shop and the place for coffee. People moved around me as though I was a turnstile, an empty baggage-trolley.

GETTING THROUGH THE bones was difficult, but I had anticipated that. I had taken off my clothes and covered every surface with plastic carrier bags. We always had so many carrier bags in the kitchen, as though we collected them specially. Very quickly I was coated in blood. Slippery. There was nothing sexual in it, how could there be? Yet I found what I was doing possessed great intimacy. She was small, but she had been strong, and there was the rigor mortis. I had known her body well, and now I knew it better.

CHRISTMAS PASSED WITHOUT drama. I stayed in Cambridge until Christmas Eve, and then went home to Leicester on the train. On Boxing Day my family and I went to Bobby's for a curry. We sat upstairs and the metal tumblers made my teeth sting. They still had the Diwali lights up along the street. Afterwards, in the car on the way back to the house my sister Susan, the eldest, announced that she was getting married.

'Who to?' my mother cried, craning around in the front seat.

'Jeremy,' my sister replied calmly. She was sitting between me and Liz.

'That ponce,' Liz said under her breath. Susan rounded on her.

'What did you call him?' she asked, raising her fist.

Liz started to smile. 'A ponce,' she said, laughing. 'I'm sorry.' Susan punched her on her arm, hard. Liz screamed ouch, ow, ouch, laughing as Susan continued to hit her.

'Girls!' said my mother, and then she looked at my father, and they also began to laugh.

When we got home we had a party, we had been drunk for the better part of two days anyway. That night, when we went to bed, I sneaked into my sisters' room with my blankets and pillow and slept on the floor between them like I used to when I was a kid. In the middle of the night I woke to the sound of their even, measured breathing.

I went back to Cambridge before New Year and settled in to work, and to waiting for Iris's return from the US. It wasn't a bad time. Geoff and Raj and Tim were there, and their girlfriends, and they felt sorry for me and bought me drinks and made me offerings of cakes and biscuits. In the thin-walled house it was not uncommon to overhear these couples having sex, and sometimes at my desk I would look up, out the window at the dark afternoon, and try to figure out who it was I could hear. I didn't mind, it made me look forward to Iris.

During this time I received one letter from her, one only. It came in a scented envelope with matching lavender paper, which seemed childish, but also endearing. She did not say much, just that things were well, there was a lot of snow, she had been to Vermont to ski. She signed the note, 'with love', and I pondered over that for a long while. I think if she had signed it 'Love' I would have been happier. But these are the kinds of things people like me dwell on, people who are young, besotted, and sweaty.

I took the coach from Cambridge to Heathrow to meet her. Her plane was late, but I continued to wait with the crowd by the doors of the arrival lounge, I didn't want to miss her. It was strange watching reunion after reunion take place – families, young couples, elderly men returning home from visiting their children who had emigrated, gone away. It must have been hard to come back to Britain when your kids lived in Florida. Maybe I would emigrate, maybe

I would marry Iris and we would go live in Texas, or New York, or LA. Or perhaps we'd stay in Cambridge, I would give supervisions, and my lover would continue to be very brilliant for all her days.

Finally, it was Iris who emerged from behind the glass partition. She had a lot of baggage, big American suitcases and travel bags. She was wearing a woolly hat, and a backpack, and her face was burnt and tanned from skiing. She looked young, and somehow incomplete, like she had got out of the baking tray before she was finished. I felt hesitant then, after my onanistic excesses of the past six weeks – was it this girl, this Iris, that I loved, or some kind of phantom girl I had conjured up, based on Iris, but not Iris in any substantial way?

She saw me and came forward, put her hand on my cheek, drew my face down to hers, and kissed me. My doubts fled. On the coach we sat at the back and I tried to get Iris to have sex with me, right there and then, but she didn't want it. I was desperate to see that look on her face once again, to show myself I had not imagined it. She wanted to talk, so we talked; she told me about her friends, about what they had done together. She was full of America, full of the way she lived there, as though she wasn't sure what she was doing here, back in England, as though she was suddenly going to be very homesick indeed. Iris didn't come from money, her family was solidly middle class, but her life in the US sounded materially much richer than mine in the UK, outdoor sports, horses, lots of TVs. 'I was sad to leave my car behind,' she said, and I thought I could understand what she meant, if I had a car I'd be sad to leave it too.

WHEN IT CAME down to it, I couldn't carry out what I had planned. It went all right, the saw, the cutting, when I was dealing with arms and legs. They were portable somehow, the shin-bone disconnected from the ankle-bone, etc., like a new kind of Lego. Soon I had a pile of black sacks near the door and, in the bathtub, less and less of Iris. Not that I thought of the body as Iris. As I mentioned before, there were the familiar markings, but by now there was so much blood and gore that she was mostly unrecognizable. Of course, I was left with her torso and her head. I didn't know what to do. I couldn't face sawing it up, her breasts, her ribs, her navel. And I was not able to decapitate her. I know I should have, it was logical, the smaller the pieces, the better. But I couldn't do it. I didn't have it in me. So I put what was left of her, my Iris, in yet another black rubbish bag, and set about cleaning the bathroom.

THE FIRST WEEK that she was back was great. The moment we got off the coach it was as though she came back to life, as though she realized she was in Cambridge, not still in the US or some halfway place in the air between. She rushed around her college, knocking on doors, leaving notes, embracing her friends who had themselves just returned from the holidays. I waited for her in her room, lying on her bed, content to breathe in the smell of her things. I hadn't spent much time in her room before, her college kept an unofficial but watchful eye over its members' nocturnal activities. But this was the afternoon, and no one was going to ask me why I was there.

When Iris came back into the room, her cheeks were flushed, and she was smiling and happy. She closed the door, locked it, and leapt on top of me. Getting back inside her could not have made me happier. Nothing else could make me feel as complete. And she kept her eyes on me, just like in my dreams, her purple eyes, her Iris eyes, looking right at me.

We had a good time. Lots of socializing, lots of sex, a lot of work. We spent most of our day together, and every night. Iris did seem a little different, but I put that down to the weeks we had spent apart, which, I realized, was more time than we had actually spent together. I figured I had mythologized her a little, and I needed to adjust to the real thing.

The second week of term wasn't so good. Iris had an argument with Geoff. We were sitting around in the kitchen, drinking lager. He'd been slagging off the US, slagging off Americans in general, going on about their foreign policy, what they had done and were doing in Cuba and Central America. Iris clearly didn't know anything about Central America, neither did I, but she was angry. I could see he was goading her, that he wanted to show that she was fundamentally ignorant about her own country, implying that the situation down there was somehow her fault, the fault of all Americans like her. I tried to intervene, but that infuriated her even more. Iris stood up, and announced that she was leaving. I couldn't believe it, I wanted to hit Geoff, I wanted Iris to sit down and stay. But instead of doing something manly and convincing, I burst into tears. Everyone turned and looked, shock on their faces. And then they all laughed at me, and the tension dissipated.

Later, Iris and I got into bed. I guess I was fairly demanding as a boyfriend, but I couldn't help myself, being near her made me incredibly horny. Iris pushed me away. She sat up in the darkness and pulled her jumper down over her breasts. 'Look,' she said, I remember her words so clearly, 'while I was home I met someone else.'

I couldn't speak. My eyes still ached a little from earlier, and I felt fresh tears spring to the surface, like blood to an old wound.

'I knew him in high school, but he's been away like me, and he's really different.' She turned to me as though she expected me to be interested.

'He's my age,' she added.

Which made me feel old, and somehow dirty. I managed to speak. 'Yes?' I said. 'That doesn't mean we have to change, does it?'

She was silent, as though she was turning the thought over in her head. 'I guess not,' she said. 'I'm here, after all, and he isn't.' She lay back down. 'And you are here,' she said, 'aren't you?' Iris made love to me then, very carefully.

I HAD DONE a good job with the carrier bags in the bathroom and I found cleaning up relatively easy. I washed down the walls, every crevice and crack, I'd read too many crime novels to be careless. I gave myself a good bath as well, and emerged feeling cleaner than I had in ages. I put all the black rubbish sacks, including the big one, into my carry-all. I carried the bag to my room, got dressed, went out into the street.

By then it was very late. I thought about riding my bicycle, but decided the carry-all would be too unwieldly. I walked across the green to the Cam. The load was very heavy. One by one I dropped the bags into the river. It was like delivering newspapers, a few hundred feet, drop another, the burden lessening. I walked away from the colleges, along the river. Cambridge is incredibly dark, women students are always complaining, and I'd had some pretty scary trips across town at night myself. but tonight I was glad of it. I figured nothing could happen to me that was worse than what I'd done. When I was finished I dumped the carry-all and took the saw back to the college.

SO TERM WENT on, Iris and I kept going, kept seeing each other, as though nothing had changed. I made her tell me the gory details, perhaps that was my mistake. She had slept with this guy, whose name was Joe, and I found that knowledge made me perform with her, sexually, all the better all the more desperately, dramatically. It was as though by penetrating her more deeply, by making her come more frequently, loudly, I would somehow strengthen my claim on her. We drove my housemates crazy, we were always banging away, quite literally, my head, or Iris's foot, drumming against the wall. That's all we did those weeks, studied and fucked, fucked and studied, there wasn't time for much else.

But then Iris's eyes began to glaze over. I was going down on her one afternoon and I looked up, looked at her sweet face, and saw her eyes had gone out of focus. She was gazing at the ceiling, not seeing anything, not seeing me. I knew she was thinking about her other man. But I carried on as though I had noticed nothing.

I DIDN'T SLEEP very well the night after I dropped Iris in the Cam. The next morning I got on my bike and went down to the river. All the sacks had disappeared, except one, the big one. It was bobbing up and down right in front of a college boathouse. I cycled back into the centre of town, and hired a punt. I poled down the river. Some friends of mine were walking along the bank and they called out to me and stood on their tip-toes as though expecting to see Iris lying in the boat. I waved and thought it best not to offer any explanation. I reached the rubbish bag and steered the boat right towards it. There was a horrible smack when it hit the prow. I manoeuvred the boat around the sack, and punctured the plastic with the pole. As the bag filled with water, it sank. I was so relieved I nearly passed out.

IRIS KEPT ON mispronouncing the names of the colleges and streets in Cambridge, names like Caius, Magdalene. First it was a kind of joke, and then we all started doing it, Geoff and Raj and Tim and their girl-friends, and soon it became part of the way we spoke. It was fun, it felt like we'd created our own language. And as the days passed our relationship grew more and more frenetic.

Until suddenly it stopped. It just stopped. Iris looked at me, and I could see she didn't want me. After Christmas she had loved me less, but she had still loved me. But now even that was gone. I couldn't believe it. How could she stop loving me? How could she simply turn around and stop?

I should have retreated immediately. I should have been dignified and restrained and become distant and aloof – stolen the fire from her. But I didn't. I began to follow her, not like a stalker, but like a puppy dog. Every time she moved, I was there, wagging my tail, tongue hanging out. She'd give me a nice smile and walk away.

It was like being a junkie and losing my dealer. It was like being an alcoholic deprived of drink. I knew it was bad for me.

And, can you believe it, the worst thing, the worst thing of all, was doing without sex. Was living without fucking Iris. Surviving without that grace and faith, that generosity and beauty.

OF COURSE I KNEW they would catch me. I reported her missing, and I cried a lot in the police station, but they knew it was me, and I knew they knew. To my horror and – everyone else's – they dredged the river. They found her hands – that was all, her hands, everything else had disappeared. A supermarket clerk made a statement saying I had bought the black rubbish sacks. Geoff told the police about the missing carrier bags.

The trial will soon be over.

SHE FOUGHT HARD. I knew she would. She was small, yet she was strong, but we were not evenly matched.

I found it easy to do. It occurred to me one moment, and the next, it was done. People are quite fragile really, when you think about it. They die very quickly, one minute full of struggle, the next absolutely still.

The thing they are saying about me in the papers is how normal I appear. How perfectly ordinary – rather handsome, in fact, intelligent, from a nice family. Everyone is saying how they would never have thought me capable of such a thing – such an overpowering love, and such violence. But I am capable of it, and not simply because Iris made me so. I am capable of it. We all are.

We just have to find the right person.

2

WHAT WAS IT LIKE?

I READ SOMEWHERE that the long-term girlfriend of the handsome American serial killer, Ted Bundy, once woke up in the middle of the night to find Ted huddled under the sheets with a flashlight, examining her body. She didn't dump him. A little while later she went to the police and told them she thought her boyfriend was the same 'Ted' as the one reputed to have killed thirty-six women, all of whom had hair just like hers, long, brown, and parted in the middle. Even then she couldn't bring herself to show him the door.

I'm not like that. I would have given him the boot. I am not the kind of woman who hangs on just for the sake of hanging on. For instance, I would not tolerate abuse. Whatever its nature – physical, mental

– whatever. If any bloke even threatened to hit me, I'd be gone. I would know if my boyfriend was a murderer.

In fact, my boyfriend is a murderer. This is proven. He admitted his guilt from the start. As soon as they took him into custody, as soon as he could see that they knew, he told the truth. He admitted his guilt and they put him in prison, they gave him a life sentence, because that is what you get for murder in this country, regardless of whom you kill, your girlfriend, your wife, or a complete stranger. And he served his whole sentence – of course, life doesn't mean life, and nor should it. He served thirteen and a half years and in that time he was an ideal prisoner. He finished his doctorate. He wrote his thesis in his cell. It took them a while to get around to it, but eventually he was awarded his degree. It proved too difficult to continue with his research after that – history – so he did another BA, an English Literature degree through the Open University. Things are slow in prison, time moves lethargically. He went to the gym regularly, he kept to himself, and got on well enough with both screws and fellow prisoners. He didn't need to be reformed, he already was reformed, he killed a young American woman named Iris and went to prison, he wasn't about to repeat the performance. And he was more intelligent than most people who work in the prison service. Despite successive government crackdowns on prisons, the average length of a life sentence is still thirteen, going on fourteen, years. And that's what Bill served.

We met because I was looking for something worthwhile to do, so I became a volunteer prison visitor. It's a scheme for prisoners who need befriending; a lot of men lose everything when they get banged up. They've killed their women, and their children are taken away, and their families are too ashamed to visit. Bill wasn't like that, he didn't have children and his family kept in contact, but still, he was lonely. We began to correspond and I started visiting.

I am not like one of those American women. Before the lights dimmed in Tallahassee when they electrocuted Ted Bundy, he had amassed a large and devoted female following. Women were always writing to him, saying they loved him, sending him things – their knickers, for God's sake. He killed more than thirty-six women, and they loved him! Ted got married during his trial, although not to his long-term girlfriend, by that time she had left him. He and his wife conceived a child in prison – not during a conjugal visit, they didn't have such things, but in the toilet after Ted Bundy had bribed the guards to leave them alone for five minutes. What was that woman thinking – did she get off on the fact that her husband was on Death Row? I am not like that – that's ghoulish. There is nothing like that about me.

The first time I went to the prison to meet Bill was fine. I had been in a couple of times before, to see another man I'd befriended, who had since been released. I looked normal, I didn't get dressed up, I didn't want to look like I needed to impress, I wanted to look ordinary. The way some of the women dress, they should put up a sign at the entrance – Don't Tease The Prisoners. I am a schoolteacher, I teach teenage boys, so I know what they are like, and a lot of men in prison are very young. But Bill is not a teenager, and neither am I. When he came into the visits room, I felt a little bad about the fact that I hadn't dressed up. His prison clothes were so carefully pressed. We shook hands, and thanked each other for the letters we'd been writing. I went to the canteen and bought tea and KitKats, and we sat down and started to try to be friends. It is a very artificial situation, prison visiting. It is difficult to behave anything like you would do normally. Bill was nervous, and so was I.

In my social circle it is not unusual that I am thirty-three and not married. I've had long-term boyfriends, but I used to think I wouldn't get married, that marriage as an institution was bad for women. I don't go to church, so I wouldn't get married for religious reasons.

My parents have never got on all that well, so they are not a great advertisement for it either. Cambridge is not a big town, and among the parents and school governors attitudes differ, but generally, people do live in the modern world. Yet I've met plenty of men who think it's strange that I'm not married, that I've never been married, that somehow my great age endows me with a kind of dried-toast spinsterhood. I was glad to see Bill wasn't like that.

And really, he was just like anyone else, except perhaps someone who'd been away for a while. He was up on everything, all the latest TV, books, music, films, even though he hadn't watched, read, heard, or been to anything – he consumed the available newspapers very diligently. That was one thing I began to do right away, give him my old newspapers instead of recycling them. He knew a lot about politics, about current affairs, and that's always been one of my interests too. We were both avid consumers of Radio 4. And yet, like I said, he had this strange distance from the world, as though he spent his days looking at it through binoculars, studying a little bit at a time. I guess that's only natural after a decade inside.

When we met, Bill was coming up to the stage when they begin to let prisoners back into the world. He was going to be eligible for home leave, for the odd day-trip. Every prisoner is different and he wasn't going to be sent to an open prison. For some reason he was still considered Category B, a little dangerous, but not an A-man. He might be allowed breaths of fresh air, maybe once or twice a year. I think getting to know me was a conscious decision he made, a way of easing himself back into the outside. As we got to know and began to trust each other, he told me that one of the reasons he had replied to my letter was that he thought if he could form a friendship with a woman like me the parole board might look on him more favourably. I wasn't shocked by that, I understood that in prison you do what you must to survive. I understood that he wanted to get out.

At first we kept our lives quite separate. He told me a little about his family, I told him a little about mine. I tried to keep it normal, to treat him like I would anyone, not hiding anything, but not being too forward either. Mostly we wrote and talked about books and the radio – we began to co-ordinate our reading and our listening. And after corresponding weekly for more than a year, after we'd had several visits, I began to find Bill in my thoughts at odd moments, at school when I watched the boys running in the playing field, the way they'd shout and jump and stretch. Out in the evening with my friends, around a table in a restaurant, passing the bottle of wine, listening to Elise tell her wild stories about her misspent youth. At Christmas with my parents in Brighton. I found myself thinking how much Bill would enjoy these things. And knowing he couldn't began to spoil my pleasure. This realization came upon me slowly, and was sweet.

I started to visit more often. We confided in each other more deeply. His letters used to arrive in the morning post. I'd pick them up on my way out to work, and it got so that I didn't feel comfortable reading in the staffroom, I'd wait until I got back to the privacy of my flat in the evening. In the spring, eighteen months after we met – I remember the day clearly – I received the letter in which he told me what he had done. What crime he had committed, how he ended up in prison, instead of shored up in some Cambridge college like everyone had expected. The letter came out of the blue, I had never asked him to explain himself. It seemed too private a thing, the way there too dark, for me to ask about it.

The wording of the letter was very concise.

Dear Laura,

I killed my American girlfriend Iris because I was jealous of her, and she no longer loved me. I was angry, I was hurt, I was shaking her, then she was gone. I am guilty of murder. I had a perfect life with my friends and my studies and the pubs and the football, and I dumped Iris and all of that in the river. I do not deserve

*to be forgiven, perhaps I don't deserve to live. But I am
alive, I am here on this planet, and I have to find a way
to be in this world. Your friendship is very important
to me.*

He went on, and I was glad that I was at home, because I found myself shivering.

That night it took me a long time to fall asleep. Of
course I had known that Bill was a murderer, he was
serving a life sentence. It was in the back of my mind
all the time when we first met, but as we had grown
closer, that thought had slipped away. His letter made
me ask myself all kinds of questions – what is the difference between Bill and me? Why is he a murderer,
and I'm not? Could I be? Could he do it again? What
was it like? What was Iris like? What would she be like
now if she were still alive? Those questions kept me
awake for a long time, but when I woke up in the dark
I woke because I had remembered something.

I remembered when they dredged the river. I remembered that an American girl had been murdered
by a graduate student and that, not only had he killed
her, but he had chopped her up into pieces and thrown
her body into the river in black plastic rubbish sacks. I
had not been in Cambridge long – I'd done my teacher
training in London, and the school I'm at now had been
my first job. They lowered the water level in the Cam,
exposing the muddy skeletons of bicycles and shopping
trolleys. The whole town could talk of nothing else.

There were plenty of notable murders in England,
even then. Plenty of young women who went missing
– estate agents, secretaries, teenagers. But at the time

this news story was especially gripping; it was gruesome, it was local, Bill was my own age. For a while my friends and I looked at our boyfriends with new eyes, as if they too might be capable of such a thing.

At the end of his letter, Bill said he would understand if I wanted to end our friendship, now that I knew what he had done. I got out of bed, and read the letter again. I read his confession over and over. *I killed my American girlfriend Iris because I was jealous of her, and she no longer loved me.* At first I felt angry, enraged, at what he had done. He had murdered a girl, a young woman, who had once been as alive as me. I had been tricked into liking him, into getting close. And I was angry that he hadn't told me the full story, that he hadn't added the words *and then I chopped up her body.* I stayed for a long while curled up on my sofa, staring at the letter and the late-night telly.

By morning I knew that he couldn't have written those final words to me. And he would never be able to say them to me either. How could you ever admit something like that? How could you ever tell someone you cared for, someone you hoped would be your friend? I wondered if perhaps Bill knew that I would remember. He knew that I was already living in Cambridge at the time of Iris's death. Maybe this was his way of telling me, *Laura*, he was saying, *and then I chopped her up.* Why does the fact that he dismembered her body make it any worse a crime? Iris was already dead, after all. He could have done anything to her, nothing could have been worse than what he had done already. And getting rid of the body did have a kind of logic to it, he had gone so far beyond anyway.

And that was the point when I could have ended it, I could have let the American girl and her death live for me, I could have pushed Bill away. But I didn't. Something in me empathized with Bill, something in me wanted to absolve him, redeem him, forgive. Perhaps this is what I have in common with all those female fans of Ted Bundy.

After two days I sat down and wrote Bill a letter. I said I appreciated his honesty. I said I wasn't there to sit in judgement, he had already been judged and found guilty. I said I was glad to be his friend, his companion.

From then on, our relationship was changed. The next time I went for a visit, Bill came into the room and we embraced. He was bigger than me, a lot taller, but I could feel his body trembling. He sat down at the table, and his eyes were watery. That day we could hardly speak.

I began to visit once every month. The intimacy of our letters increased.

I had been seeing a man for about six months, another teacher at my school. David was seven years younger than me, and very good-looking, and we'd been sleeping together most weekends. I had told Bill about him from the beginning, there was no reason not to, and I thought it might help ease the natural tension between us, between men and women over this kind of thing. But I began to find that when I was with David I was thinking about Bill. I decided to end it one Friday night; we'd been to a party and were both a little drunk. When I came out of the bathroom David had taken off all his clothes and was displaying himself for me. The first thought that came into my mind was that I wished he was Bill.

I wrote and told Bill I had stopped seeing David. Two days later I received a reply. It began like this:

Dear Laura,

I can't stop thinking about you.

If I was a free man, and you and I were together, this is what I would do. I would lift your dress over your head. I would take down your tights. I would unfasten your bra, and I would push down your knickers. And I would look at you, I would look at your body, and then I would do whatever you asked. Anything at all, anything to give you pleasure. And you could do anything you wanted with me. I want to feel myself inside you, I want to take you while you are sleeping, I want to be with you always.

I had never heard such words from a man, I never had and never thought I might.

From there we took off, we really did, we wrote nearly every day, and I increased my visits to fortnightly, which was the maximum he was allowed. Those two hours on Saturday afternoon were extreme, febrile, and devastating. The visits room, with all its noise and smell and disappointment, would fade away and Bill and I would be together somewhere else, anywhere else. We'd talk and talk and hold hands and look into each other's eyes.

'How was your week?'

'Oh, it was fine. I didn't do much other than go to school, do my preparation.'

'You work too hard.'

'No, I don't. How about you? What did you do?'

He laughed. 'I went to the gym, I washed the floors on all the landings, I read two novels, and I waited.'

In a sense we were both waiting. We didn't paw each other like other couples, I didn't sit in his lap. It was an old-fashioned courtship, stately, restrained, bound by rules and codes. The prison guards were our chaperones and we did not try to evade them. We were proud, and we were waiting for each other, we were waiting for Bill's release.

I don't think I've ever waited for anything before. I grew up in a generation that is accustomed to sexual gratification, to getting it when you want it, with ease. And I do think that is the way it should be. But with Bill it was different, of necessity. I had never been so con-tinuously and completely excited. On Saturdays when I left the prison I would have to pull over to the side of the road and take deep breaths to still my heart, to quieten my body. In bed on my own at night I dreamt of sex and fucking and Bill.

I don't know why I liked him so much, indeed, why I had come to love him. But can we ever say why it is we love someone? I liked the way he looked, I liked the way he talked, I liked the way he carried himself. He had a very happy laugh, and when he laughed I felt I could see right inside him, into his heart which was open and warm. I liked the way that he liked me.

I'll admit it, there is something odd about falling in love with a prisoner. A captive man, a man in chains, a man rendered powerless. I felt he needed me, and I found that seductive. But not the fact that he was a murderer, not the fact that he had taken the life of a young American. Once I got to know him I discovered that he still had, or rather, what he had done still had a certain amount of notoriety in Cambridge. Every once in a while someone would mention the student who had been murdered. After I got to know Bill it happened once at school, and I kept myself from flinching. But that wasn't part of what I wanted in Bill, that was not part of it for me.

There were some weeks when I couldn't visit because Bill was seeing his parents. They lived in Leicester and were retired, his sisters both lived nearby. He said his sister Liz had wept throughout every one of their visits over the past decade. The other, Susan, had never been to visit him. One day, out of the blue, I received a phone call from Mrs Porter, Bill's mum.

'We would like to invite you to come to Leicester for lunch next week,' she said very quickly, her words almost, but not quite, stumbling. 'Bill has told us all about you, and we would very much like to meet you.' I began to speak, but she wouldn't let me. 'My husband and I could drive down to Cambridge and fetch you, it's quite quick these days, it wouldn't be any trouble, none at all.' She seemed to run out of words.

'That would be very nice,' I said, more out of shock than anything else, 'I can drive up myself.'

'Are you sure?'

'Yes.'

'Sunday week? About one o'clock?'

'Don't go to too much bother–'

'It will just be something light.'

She gave me directions, and we said goodbye.

Bill and I had decided against using the telephone

to communicate with each other. Phone cards were expensive for him and the telephone on his wing afforded little privacy. I wasn't allowed to ring in. But at that point I wished I could pick up the phone, that I could call him and we could have a laugh and make this meeting with his parents a little less odd, a little less out of the ordinary.

That week in school was very busy. One of my favourite students was having difficulty. His parents had broken up, and it was as though when they divided their possessions, they had split him as well. He had been caught pissing against a wall in the gymnasium. Teaching was always hectic and stressful, but events like these added to the strain. When Friday came I felt exhausted. Bill and I had no visit that week, and Saturday was empty. By Sunday morning I was wound tight. I drove up to Leicester and found their house rather too easily. I sat in the car for a while, until I began to feel conspicuous on the suburban street, among the gardeners, lawn-mowers, and dog-walkers. I went up the footpath, knocked on the door, and held my breath.

Mrs Porter answered. She gave me a big hug, unable to speak. Mr Porter stood behind her. He wore a cardigan, she wore an apron. You would not have believed their son was a murderer. They were both effusive in their welcoming. We went into the sitting room where I was introduced to Liz. She was tall like Bill and I could see she was someone I could easily have known, someone who was just like me. We sat down – Mrs Porter offered tea, Mr Porter insisted on sherry. 'Put the drive behind yourself,' he said, 'be at ease.'

They were very anxious to know me. 'Bill hasn't had a friend for a long time,' said Mrs Porter, placing special emphasis on the word 'friend'. 'He's such a loving person,' she said, and then she blushed, realizing she might have gone too far, given that we'd just met. His crime filled the air between us. I pushed forward, nodding and smiling. I felt as though we didn't need to speak, that words were awkward, there was such a lot we shared anyway. Liz alternated between being playful and funny, and on the edge of tears – the brother she knew on the one hand, the brother she couldn't know on the other. When we sat down to lunch it was a little uncomfortable. There were empty chairs, and at first I thought they had laid a place for absent Bill. Mr Porter noticed me looking.

'Susan and Jeremy,' he explained.

'They said they'd come,' Mrs Porter said, more to him than me.

'I know love,' he said. 'But I didn't think they would.'

'They said they'd come,' said Mrs Porter.

Liz changed the subject.

Lunch was not light, but proper and elaborate, right down to the trifle and the cheese. Mr Porter – he insisted I call him William, and his wife, Elizabeth, and I found the doubling of names reassuring – was pouring the coffee, when the front door opened and Susan arrived.

She marched up to the table angrily. Liz was like Bill, but Susan was like them both, that strange and beguiling blending of features that you sometimes see between siblings.

'Why did you invite her?' she demanded of her

mother, not looking at me. 'Why are you having her in this house?'

'Susan, calm down, she—'

'Don't tell me to calm down. I am calm. We don't want anything to do with her – with him.'

Liz stood and went towards her sister. 'Susan—'

'He's not our brother any more,' she said, her voice hard and brittle.

'Susan,' Liz said, low, hypnotic, 'Susan.' She took her sister by the shoulders and turned her away from the table. She began to speak in a tone so quiet none of us could hear. They walked towards the front door.

'She'll take her out to the car,' said Elizabeth, reassuringly, as though this happened all the time.

'They'll go out to her car,' William added.

We drank our coffee in the sitting room. At lunch we had begun to talk about Bill, about his childhood, subjects we found fascinating. I could have listened to them all day. As I went to sit down I glanced out the window and saw Liz and Susan seated in the car. Susan was slumped on the steering wheel, and Liz was leaning over, stroking her hair. They looked comfortable somehow, and I wanted to be out there with them, on the back seat, listening.

And then things began to happen. Bill was supposed to start having home leave. He kept getting it set up, they'd agree to one day in Cambridge, I organized with the Porters that we would converge at my place, and then the leave would fall through. Cutbacks on prison staff, continual changes in policy. Bill wrote letter after letter of complaint to the officials. He said he thought the prison's incompetence might help him with his probation application. He had a hearing coming up in June: He had been in prison for twelve and a half years at that time. We worked hard to keep our expectations in perspective; his tariff, recommended by the judge at the time of sentencing, was ten years, so we thought it likely that he would have to serve at least thirteen. He went up before the board on Wednesday, we had arranged that he would ring me at school at lunch time. That morning I paced back and forth in the classroom and let the students do as they pleased. I had expected them to riot, but they seemed intimidated by me suddenly, and they remained in their seats meekly. At lunch I rushed to the staffroom and stood by the phone, scaring off anyone who tried to use it. I hadn't told any of my colleagues about Bill, in fact, I hadn't told any of my friends, nor my parents. It's not the easiest thing to tell people, 'I've got a new boyfriend, he wears a ball and chain.'

The phone rang, I picked it up and almost dropped it. 'Bill?' I said.

There was no reply. I could hear the prison echoing in the background, the sound of doors, men, and keys.

'Bill?' I said. I heard him draw a sharp breath. He was crying. I knew that he had not succeeded. It would be another year until his next parole board hearing.

That year passed amazingly quickly. I spent Christmas with my parents in Brighton, then drove up to Leicester on Boxing Day. Susan and Jeremy were there, as well as Liz, and even Susan was more at ease with me. The next time I went to the prison for a visit, I overheard one woman speaking to another in the queue to get inside. 'I went up to his parents on Boxing

Day, she said, 'it were right nice, they were right good to me.' She was small and pudgy and had dyed blonde hair; she was wearing a distressed denim mini-skirt, a white bomber jacket, bare legs, and cheap, dirty shoes with high heels. I saw with a shock that she was a convict's girlfriend, just like me; we were both convicts' girlfriends queuing up on visits day.

It was a dreamy time, that time before Bill was released. It was like one long extended Valentine's Day. I wrote love letters, I received love letters. We consummated our passion over and over again on the page. If someone else read our letters – and I often wondered if the screws did read them, they still practised a kind of censorship security – they would have found a strange mixture of trivia, romance, and pornography. *I want to feel myself inside you, I want to take you while you are sleeping, I want to be with you always.* We prompted great flights of fantasy in each other. I'd never known anything like it before.

And then it happened. When we least expected it. Another parole board hearing. Bill had been tipped off by his probation officer beforehand – it wouldn't happen. No explanation, it just wasn't his turn. We made the same arrangement nonetheless – he would telephone at lunch time. I worried all morning, but I was able to work. However, in the staffroom I guarded the phone.

It rang. I picked it up.

'Laura,' he said, 'Laura, you're not going to believe this, but they've given me my licence.'

I didn't reply.

'Laura,' he said, 'will you come and get me?'

3
AFTER EIGHT

LAURA'S LITTLE HOUSE near the Cam was two up, two down, big enough for her and her boyfriend. Bill was unused to having so much space. She gave him his own room, next to hers, although they intended to spend every night in her bed. In fact his room was bed-less, having only a little brown settee. But the room also had a door, and a desk, and in this it resembled his cell, and Bill found it a useful retreat.

When he was first released it was summer, long, bright hot days, and soon Laura's school broke up for the holidays. They spent their time cycling in the countryside, going for long walks, afternoons by the outdoor lido on Jesus Green. Laura told people she was going away, and they didn't see anyone but each other.

SHE DROVE OUT to the prison to pick him up and it was just like in a movie. She waited outside the prison gate. After a long while, the gate opened, and there he was, alone, clutching an old suitcase. He took one tentative step, testing the water, and another, and another, and when no one stopped him, he rushed forward and into Laura's arms. They got into her car and pulled out of the car park, and his head was spinning. The trees were too green, the sky too blue, it was as if he'd been blindfolded for thirteen and a half years and once again could see. He was afraid to look at the prison in case someone was there, waiting to drag him back, bang him up in solitary.

He looked at Laura as he held her. 'Hello,' he said, 'hello Laura.' And he began to laugh, his throat open wide, shouting with laughter, gulping the air with joy and fear and the rushing years of longing. He wound down the window of the car and leaned his head out, hoping to slough it off, blow it out, the dirt of the prison, the stain of the years he had spent locked away.

And Laura laughed too, she laughed with him, although for one moment as she looked at him – his hands on his thighs, his new jeans and shirt his mother had sent – she felt a little afraid. Did she know him? Who was he? But he turned to her smiling a smile greater than any she had ever seen, and he surged into her heart and she remembered everything that she loved about him.

His parents and sisters were waiting at her house, waiting for Laura to bring him home. 'They're very excited,' Laura said, 'they are dressed up, as if they're going to a wedding,' and she blushed when she heard what she had said.

'I can hardly wait,' he said, 'I can hardly wait to get there.' And he turned towards her again, he couldn't wait any longer, he had to touch her right away.

She pulled the car off the road, down a private lane. Through the trees they could see a large house. They walked into the woods, away from the house, sure they would find an open meadow of flowers, or a silky patch of grass. But there was only more woods, and brambles, and broken-down fences. Laura stopped and leaned against a tree. Her heart pounded low in her stomach.

'Come here,' she said.

Bill was looking up at an oak, the thick pavilion of leaves. He walked towards her, and soon he leaned into her. He felt large and strong and she could smell the prison lingering beneath his scent. They held each other very tight, squeezing themselves together. Bill thought Laura felt small and strong; she smelled of lemons and perfume. Laura thought they would make love right there, against the tree, but they did not. Bill said he wanted to wait, he wanted to wait until they were alone, in her house, in her bed, in the night. They had waited a long time and a few more hours would only increase their pleasure, not lessen it.

So that first day was a day of love, and upset, and exclamations. Susan and Jeremy were at Laura's house with William and Elizabeth and Liz, and it was the first time Bill had seen his eldest sister since his arrest. He had missed her wedding. When Laura opened the door of her house, there was a thick silence and for a moment she thought they had gone away, they had changed their minds and abandoned the reunion. But then they burst forward, Liz with her usual tears, William and Elizabeth grinning hugely. While they were waiting they had prepared lunch, but in their joy this was forgotten, and the turkey began to smoulder as they raised a glass of wine, Bill's first red wine in thirteen and a half years, and he thought it tasted rich and slow and thick. Elizabeth smelt the bird first and ran into the kitchen.

Bill felt as though he himself might burst into flame, as though all his nerve-endings were on fire. The wine went straight to his head and he turned to Laura and said, 'You mustn't give me any more. I'm like a child who has never had a drink.'

'Have you really not had a drink in all this time, Bill?' Liz asked as if she couldn't fathom such a thing.

'Prison hooch doesn't count,' said Bill, 'it just doesn't count. In prison I sometimes drank because I wanted to drown.' He paused, still smiling and relaxed, while the others teetered, their faces about to collapse, as if they didn't want to be reminded, as if they had thought that now he was released it would be as though it had never happened. He had never gone away, he had never been in prison, he had never murdered Iris.

'That's right,' said William, saving the day, 'we've got to watch out for our new boy. He's been away.' And the family sat down to dinner in Laura's house and toasted Bill and toasted each other and celebrated every Christmas and every birthday they had missed.

Susan was not flushed and giggling like her mother and her sister, she did not have a lot to say. Every now and then Bill looked at her, tried to engage her, but she was giving nothing away. Halfway through the meal, she got up and went into the kitchen to get another bottle of wine. Bill followed her and the others tried not to notice, they upped the volume of their conversation.

'Susan,' Bill said. It was a day of carefully enunciated names. 'Susan, it doesn't matter, you know.'

She would not look at him, she remained stooped in front of the fridge.

'It doesn't matter, I don't care that you never came to visit – I mean I care, but it is all right. I understand. There is no reason for you to forgive me. And you don't have to see me now that I've been released.'

Susan turned. She did not want to see him, it was true. She had hoped he would never be released, she would have been happy if he had disappeared completely. If he asked she would have told him he had ruined her life. Standing there, Bill could see how Susan felt, and something in him was prepared for that.

'I'm here for Mum and Dad,' she said.

Bill drew a breath. 'Okay,' he said, 'that's fine.' He took a step forward, Susan took a step further away. Bill dropped his hands to his sides. 'It's really good to see you. You look exactly the same.' He turned and went back into the other room. Susan leaned against the counter and pressed the cool bottle of wine against her face.

The hours passed and Bill's father William drank too much, got a little maudlin, kissed his wife, and fell asleep. Liz was driving her parents home, Bill helped them out to the car. Susan and Jeremy had left earlier. The summer night was warm and still, and yet they had remained indoors instead of sitting in Laura's garden. They wanted to keep that afternoon completely private, they wanted to shut themselves away.

And then Bill closed the door and the house felt empty and he and Laura were alone there for the first time. She thought him very handsome as he came to her, and he thought her a great beauty. Music was playing in the sitting room and they danced a little in the lamplight, their feet moving smoothly over the carpet. Bill felt as though his brain was malfunctioning a little, flickering back and forth between the thirty-seven years he was aged now, and the twenty-four-year-old he had been last he was free. Laura couldn't get close enough to him as they danced, she couldn't believe he was here, now, and to stay. After a long while they kissed. And then they went upstairs to Laura's bed. What happened there was remarkable and profound; they thought that together they were truer and better than their individual selves had ever been. *I want to feel myself inside you, I want to take you while you are sleeping, I want to be with you always.*

SUMMER ENDED AND Laura went back to work. She and Bill had developed a strategy – she would say they had met on holiday, it was a whirlwind romance, he had moved in as soon as he could, he'd been a student at Cambridge but had been away. In Canada. He'd been working in Canada, in oil exploration up north. If anyone asked, that would be what she would tell them. And they did ask, of course they asked, first day back, and Laura blushed as she told her lies. Her colleagues assumed she blushed with embarrassment and passion and, of course, that was true as well.

The terms of Bill's licence – he had explained to Laura that a life sentence is indeed life; the state keeps track of lifers once they are released and he would be on probation for the rest of his days – were such that he could do pretty much as he pleased, apart from break the law and leave the country. The stated terms – he kept the sheaf of papers in his desk in the room Laura had given him – included a clause that demanded he 'disclose' his crime to any woman with whom he became involved. Probation officers and the police would pay special attention to any relationship he formed. If they had any reason to suspect he was repeating a pattern, that he was in any way replicating his relationship with Iris, they could take him in, whisk him off the street and back into prison, no need for a trial or hearing. But as far as Bill's probation officer was concerned, this was not an issue. Laura knew about Bill's crime, Laura was not an eighteen-year-old girl, Laura and Bill would be all right. The probation officer had a large, unwieldy case-load, most of the ex-cons with whom he worked were a lot worse off than Bill.

Bill knew it would be difficult to find a job; he'd have to disclose his record to any potential employer. And who would want to hire a murderer with a doctorate, for a dishwasher, for a lectureship? He received a tiny income from the state by claiming he was Laura's lodger, and his parents gave him the money they had saved expressly. He and Laura had discussed it thoroughly, he would not have to get work right away. He could take his time, find his civilian feet, figure out the best way to live. He went running, did the shopping, cleaned the house, and cooked Laura dinner.

Laura had never thought it odd that Bill was willing to come back to Cambridge. She was in Cambridge, he'd been in Cambridge, it was a good place to be. Part of her – most of her – was happy to live as though the thing, the horrible thing, had never happened. Iris. They did not talk about it, about her. That was simply the way it felt best, that made it possible to live.

'What did you do today, sweetheart?' she said as she dropped her books on the table one day after school.

Bill was wearing an apron, holding a wooden spoon. 'I went to the city library. I wandered around the town a bit. I went to my old college.'

'You did?'

'I ran into one of my tutors.'

Laura asked a normal question, sometimes she did it just to see what it was like. 'Did he remember you?'

Bill laughed. 'Yes. It took him a few moments to place me, but when he did. . . He tried hard not to be terrified.'

Laura gasped and then smiled.

'That will give them something to talk about at High Table. He told me that Dr Simms died.'

'Dr Simms?'

'My old supervisor. The one who used to sleep through supervisions. In fact, he died during a supervision. His students didn't even realize it. They tiptoed out of the room like usual. It was left to the bedder to find him the next day.'

Laura lifted the lid off the pot Bill was simmering.

'I feel bad about him, Dr Simms,' he said. 'I sort of admired the old guy.'

It was October now and although the days were often sunny, the warmth did not linger in the evening. Laura closed the door to the garden. Bill followed her into the sitting room. She drew the curtains and sat down on the sofa. Bill sat next to her, drawn to her in a way that had become nearly familiar. They folded themselves into each other's arms and slipped off each other's clothes one piece at a time. Bill could not get over the revelation of Laura's body, the way she gave it to him, the way she let him touch her as he desired.

He stroked her stomach, soft and slightly rounded, and further down, he moved his fingers through her pubic hair. He held her shoulders as he penetrated her, and, later, as he moved in her, he gripped her waist and kissed her neck. They took up a rhythm from which he could not and did not want to escape.

Laura had never felt about anyone the way she felt about Bill. When they fucked she moved beyond herself, into him, with him. For him it was as though every day was a kind of unexpected bonus, and Laura was amazed to find herself included in that. Bill gave her rapture. It didn't matter that he couldn't work, that he was, essentially, her dependent, that her social life had disappeared and her friends thought her a stranger. Laura was happy, she had never been so happy, and it was even more complete when Bill was inside her, in her house, in her arms. She cried out when she came, and he laughed and held her.

Christmas approached and they planned to spend Christmas Eve in Brighton with Laura's parents, travelling up to Leicester on Christmas Day. They drove down to the coast and Laura felt a little nervous; her parents had not met Bill. Over the phone she had told them the same story she told everyone else. Laura hadn't lived with a man in years and it had been a long time since she'd brought anyone to meet her mother and father.

The first hours in Brighton passed stiffly. Laura's parents were not like Bill's, they did not open their front door and step into an embrace. They conducted themselves with Bill as though they were interviewing a prospective employee. Laura's father was a retired headmaster, her mother had never worked, and they led a country life of bridge games and fêtes for charity. Her mother had laid out towels for them both – in separate bedrooms. After dinner Bill sat in front of the television, while Laura rounded on her parents in the kitchen.

'I'm thirty-seven years old, Mother! I can sleep with whomever I choose.'

'Don't speak to your mother that way,' warned her father, always his first contribution to any argument.

'How can you invite us here and then treat us like naughty children?'

'I don't know who invited *him*,' her mother said, her voice very tight, 'but it wasn't me.'

'Who is he?' her father demanded.

'What do you mean?' asked Laura.

'Well, who is he? He seems to have appeared from nowhere. What has he been doing for the past fifteen years? I asked him about Canada – about the oil – but he was . . . well, he was terribly vague. He doesn't know a thing about oil exploration, Laura, does he?'

'Have you been lying to us, Laura?' her mother asked.

She attempted to back-track. 'It's all right about the rooms – it's only one night. It won't happen again.' She went towards the door.

'Don't you turn your back on us, Laura! We want to know who he is. What are you hiding from us?'

Laura turned and looked at her mother. She felt tired, perhaps it might be easier to tell them, to get it out in the open, to end the pretence. It was Christmas, after all, maybe they'd be full of Christian charity.

'Has he been in gaol?' asked her father.

Laura gasped. 'How did you know?'

'Oh, it's written all over him,' her father said. 'From the way he rolls his cigarettes to the way he eats . . .'

'The way he eats?' Laura objected.

'. . . as though any moment someone is going to snatch away his plate – to the way he looks at you.' Her father grimaced.

'Why didn't you tell us?' asked her mother.

'I didn't think you'd approve.'

'We don't,' they said simultaneously. Then they all turned to look; Bill was standing in the door. Laura's father took a deep breath. 'You are not welcome here,' he said, his words directed at Bill.

'All right,' said Laura, 'we'll leave.'

NOT WORKING WAS more difficult than Bill expected; in prison he had always had a job, even if it was slopping out shit for an hour a day. He was already heavily overqualified and he didn't want to continue to study. In the autumn he had tried to get a job in the local sandwich bar, but when he disclosed, as he had to, they sent him away, horrified. He no longer went there for sandwiches. His probation officer offered to get him on a government training scheme, but it sounded like make-work to him, and he didn't want to be involved with other ex-cons. He thought about volunteer work, but by then he was gripped by a kind of sloth. He was accustomed to long hours of doing nothing, so he wasn't bored, and he didn't mind not having money. But he was growing restless.

And then it was January and very dark and the sky touched the ground without lifting. Bill told Laura Januarys were very difficult in prison and he was surprised to find that outside they were almost as bad. There were icy winds in Cambridge and he wore layer upon layer of clothes when he went out running. His body had changed a lot in the six months since his release, he had slimmed down, lost the beef he had built up through the gym and prison food. At Christmas he had retrieved his stuff from his parents' house, and found that he could still wear his old clothes. Sometimes when he ran he felt as though he were re-inhabiting his body, regaining something he had lost, catching up with it. He ran down paths familiar from his student days, past young men whom he imagined could be his former self. He began to deviate from his usual route of Laura's house to the river, across the commons, through the town.

One day he found himself outside his old house, the house he had shared with Geoff and Raj and Tim. The house where he had loved Iris. The house where she had died. He stood opposite, on the far side of the road, and he realized with a shock that there were parts of Cambridge he'd been avoiding. Nothing about the house had changed, it looked as though the same roof tiles were still missing. A young man came along the pavement and turned into the footpath, and Bill faced the other direction, to hide the fact that he was watching. The man unlocked the door and went in. For a moment, Bill was back inside that house, back inside the time when he had lived there with his friends, when he had known the American girl.

He stood in the dark. Lights went on and off in different rooms, on different floors, but no one else arrived, or left. Later, a car pulled up and the passenger door opened. Bill watched as a young woman climbed out. She was small, and she had long dark hair. She walked up the footpath. Bill crossed the road as the car pulled away. She was knocking on the door as Bill reached the gate. He raised his hand and said something, he didn't know what, and as the girl turned to look at him, the front door opened, and a harsh light fell on her face. Bill saw she wasn't Iris, and he backed into the darkness. He pulled up his hood and ran down the street.

January was difficult for Laura as well. Having a dependent, even one as accommodating as Bill, was hard to get used to, tougher than she had anticipated. Her teacher's wage went a lot less further for two and she found she was having to think carefully about simple things like going to the cinema, out to eat. She and Bill had spent six months hunkered down together, not wanting to see other people. This anti-social behaviour suited them both, and it meant they avoided having to explain about Bill's life, having to lie. But Laura was beginning to miss her friends. In recent times she and a group of teachers had gone skiing together during the winter-term break and when talk in the staffroom came round to this year's trip, Laura realized with a pang that she wouldn't be going. Bill wasn't allowed to leave the country yet and, besides, it was out of the question.

'Which resort?' she asked Elise one day.

'We're going to go to Courmayeur this year, Italy, it's cheaper than France.'

'Hotel or chalet?'

'We've got a whole chalet to ourselves, so that will be great.' Elise paused and poured extra sugar in her coffee. 'We didn't – I mean – we just assumed you wouldn't be going.'

'You did?'

'Yes, well, you and Bill seem so – well, I know how it is when you fall in love . . .' she sang the last few words and laughed. 'Maybe next year you can both come? Does Bill ski?'

'Yes,' said Laura, 'yes he does,' although she did not know whether or not he did.

The next week Elise asked Laura if she wanted to go out for a drink, as though she had seen a crack in Laura's armour and was determined to widen it. Laura agreed, she said yes, it would be just the two of them.

When she told Bill her plans, his face fell. She watched as he quickly reconciled himself to the news.

'I can't expect to have you to myself all the time, can I?' he said. 'We do live in the world, after all.'

'Yes,' said Laura, sadly, as though she was agreeing with much more than what he had just said.

So she began to go out with her friends from time to time, and soon irregular get-togethers became once a week. She did not ask Bill if he wanted to come, because, truth be told, she enjoyed getting away on her own. Bill had a certain level of engagement with the world, a particular intensity bred by years spent locked away. Eight in the evening until eight in the morning – these were rough hours for him, the hours during which he'd been banged up on his own every night. Some evenings Laura felt him slip away from her after eight, as though he could no longer occupy any realm other than his own. He might go upstairs to his little room where he had his desk and his door and his radio, or he might remain next to her in front of the television, but either way, he wasn't really there. It didn't happen every night but, even when he coped well, he would generally go to bed before her. She would crawl in several hours later, and he would wake up disoriented, a bit confused, and they would make love, and it would go well.

Laura felt terrible about her parents' reaction to Bill; she hadn't had any contact with them since. She had never got on well with them, but she didn't want to have to think about what might happen next, how she would ever patch things up with them. It was yet another area of her life that she would have to keep separate from Bill. She had hoped that Christmas with the Porters would cure any bitterness her lover might feel and on the day he had seemed happy and whole and optimistic. Bill kept his shadow close by him, Laura had always known that, but now the shadow felt darker, colder and closer as well.

One evening she and Elise were out on their own.

'Okay,' said Elise, 'you've got to tell me about Bill. Who is this guy and why are you two so reclusive – I can understand, when you first fall in love, but come on, we'd like to meet him. He's part of you.'

Laura looked at her friend's face, and thought her lovely and candid, without guile. Surely Elise would be sympathetic? 'Well,' she said, suddenly full of resolve, 'I'll tell you. Bill . . .' she paused.

'Yes?' said Elise. 'Come on.'

'Bill got out of prison last June.'

Elise stared at her without speaking.

'He was in for a long time. He –'

Elise interrupted. 'You met him through that scheme, didn't you? That volunteer thing you used to do – writing and visiting prisoners. I always thought that was strange.'

'Elise!'

'Well, you had your pick, Laura. Everybody wanted to go out with you. Even my ex-husband used to ask if you were seeing anyone.'

'George?'

'Yes, George, the dirty old fool.'

'There's nothing wrong with Bill, he just did something wrong, that's all.'

'What?'

Laura looked at Elise.

'What did he do?'

Oh fuck, thought Laura, here we go. 'He killed his girlfriend.'

'What?' Elise shrieked. In the pub heads turned.

'He was young, she was young. . . It was a long time ago.'

'Oh, and that makes it all right?'

'It doesn't make it all right, it's just that . . . he wasn't a criminal.'

'No, not a criminal, only a murderer – what on earth do you mean?'

'He didn't rob banks or deal drugs or anything – he'd never done anything wrong before.'

'Beginner's luck then?'

'Elise—'

'What do you expect me to say? "Oh, that's great Laura, your boyfriend's a cold-blooded killer, cool." No.' She shook her head. 'No, no, no.' She paused and looked at Laura for an explanation that Laura was not able to give. 'How do you know he won't do it again?'

'I know him, I trust him –'

'How do you know he won't do it to you, he won't kill you? Do you know that for sure, Laura? Could you give me a guarantee?'

Laura looked at her drink. It had been the right tactic, avoiding telling anybody about Bill. She wished she had stuck to it. 'I'm sorry I told you,' she said, and she felt an awful thing: ashamed of Bill and, then, ashamed of her shame. 'Don't tell anyone,' she said. 'Please.'

'Oh Laura, I only worry about you. Shit,' Elise rapped the table with her knuckles. 'Damn,' she said, shaking her head.

'I guess this means you won't be inviting us around for dinner,' Laura said.

Elise laughed a little and said, 'Fuck, I don't know.'

AND DURING THE evenings that Laura was out with her friends Bill began to go out too. He started to go running after eight. He'd go up to his little room, close the door and pull on his layers of clothes, the noise of the prison echoing in his head. He'd got rid of everything else, the prison smell, the prison habit of hoarding matches and tobacco and library books, the prison touchiness, always keeping his back against the wall, but whatever he did, he could not get rid of the noise. Some nights it echoed in his brain like his head was a rattle, a gourd with a pebble trapped in it. Every time he moved, he heard it. He thought running might dislodge it, roll it away.

At night Cambridge was as dark as it had been when he was a student. The Backs were not lit, nor were the commons, but where he had feared it before, he loved it now, he parted the darkness and ran on through the black. It was as though he was hidden in the dark, the city was hiding him. He began to trace a new route. He'd head up to the college where Iris had been a student, to the residence where he had lain on her bed and waited for her to finish seeing her friends. He'd run down past the house where he used to live with Geoff and Raj and Tim. He'd run round the back of his old college and climb over the fence and run around the empty garden shed. They'd moved the tools elsewhere, he wondered if that was because of him, because of what he had done, and he hoped he hadn't caused too much trouble. Then he ran down to the river, to the bank where he had dropped the black plastic rubbish sacks with Iris in them. But once he reached the river, he was unable to keep running. He stopped suddenly, dizzy with lack of air. He staggered along for a few paces, trying to get his breath back, his legs to move. He stopped and fell to his knees. Occasionally in the cold night he had witnesses, usually he did not, it didn't matter. Once someone came to his aid, but he shouted at them, 'Fuck off, fuck off,' and they did. He would lie down across the path like a drunk, facing the river. And he'd watch the water flow by. And he'd think of Iris, of the small dark mole on her left breast, of her hands, of her feet, of her face. Her eyes, her iris eyes, violet.

There was no forgetting, there could be no forgetting, not in prison serving his time, not now that he had been released.

AFTER HER CONVERSATION with Elise about Bill, Laura came home to an empty house. It was the first time she had come home to find Bill gone. She called out his name, went upstairs and knocked on the door of his room. She opened it, he wasn't there. She stepped inside. She hadn't spent much time in this room since Bill had moved in. It had once been her study, now his books were mixed up with hers. She looked at the things he had pinned to the wall, postcards mostly, from Liz and William and Elizabeth on their holidays. She hadn't turned on the lamp and light from the corridor filtered in, casting long silhouettes. It smelt of him, the room, musty and cigarettes. She closed the door and went downstairs.

A little while later, after midnight, Bill came in. Laura called out to him from the sitting room. He didn't answer, went straight upstairs. She followed.

'Bill,' she said, 'Bill?'

He wasn't in the bathroom or the bedroom. The door to the study was closed. She knocked, repeating his name. 'Are you there, sweetheart?' She opened the door, it did not have a lock.

The room was dark, so she turned on the overhead light. Bill was curled up on the brown settee, facing inward his hood pulled over his head. His clothes were caked with mud and she could smell the river rising off him. She moved near him and rested her hand on his shoulder. She felt him shrink away.

Laura went to bed. She knew that re-entering the world was fraught with difficulty for ex-prisoners, she knew that all manner of things could be thrown up for them, none of which would be easy to deal with. She had read a pamphlet that Bill's probation officer had recommended; it said that ex-prisoners might need to be left on their own to come to terms with the missing years of their life, the years during which everyone else has got on with things while they've been locked away. The Rip Van Winkle effect – you wake up one day many years later and everything is changed.

In the middle of the night she heard Bill stirring. He was taking a bath. A little while later, he came into the bedroom. He got into bed in a new way, he climbed under the duvet from the bottom end. She felt his lips on her feet, her ankles. He was kissing her calves, her knees, her thighs. It took a long time, and it was delicious, and when his head emerged from under the covers, she could tell he was smiling as he pushed inside her, and she threw back her head and opened her arms and was his, she was his, she was his.

But things did not get better, they got worse. Bill began to go out after eight p.m. on nights when Laura was staying in. The length of time he stayed out got longer and longer. Laura tried to resist asking him what he was doing, she did not want to put unnecessary pressure on him, but eventually, she gave in.

'I run,' he said, 'you know I like to go running.'

'But for hours and hours, no one runs for hours and hours.'

'I do,' he said.

She didn't ask about the mud he carried back on his clothes, she didn't try to continue the conversation.

February and then March, and still he went out, running and running. Laura began to spend more time away from the house, with Elise and her other friends. But she didn't tell anyone about what Bill was doing; she had no one to tell. They made love less often and, when they did, sometimes it was painful.

'Where do you go?' she asked one night.

'To the river.'

'Why?'

'It's where I belong,' he said, turning away. Laura began to panic. Bill was becoming a stranger, he was sinking deeper into himself. They had stopped having their happy evenings, their lovely weekends where they cooked for each other, did things to the house. She arranged for them to go visit the Porters in Leicester; Bill agreed to go, but he was not enthusiastic.

They drove up on Friday evening. The family was there, William and Elizabeth, Liz and Susan, and they had a party. William mixed cocktails, he'd been taking a bartending course, 'for no good reason,' he said to Laura, 'except to drink!' After a few Margaritas, Liz began to tease Susan about Jeremy who had been unable to come.

'What's he doing, playing darts at your local?' Laura could tell Liz intended to sound light-hearted, but her tone was sharp and piercing.

'He doesn't play darts any more,' Susan said uneasily.

'What – too challenging?'

Susan looked at her sister. It was clear she couldn't think of a reply.

'Oh come on Susie, you can do better than that.' Liz reached out to tussle her sister's hair, but Susan took hold of her wrist, and twisted her arm backwards. Liz winced and, with her free hand, whacked Susan across the back of the head.

'Girls!' shouted William. 'Stop it.' He paused, adding, 'You're both nearly forty!' but his daughters ignored him as they grappled on the couch. Bill got up and left the room, followed by his mother. Laura stood up, unsure of what to do. William had turned away and was peering out the window of the sitting room. 'Look at those roses,' he said, shaking his head. Laura went to his side, but it was dark, and she couldn't see what he meant. Susan howled in anger and pain, and William and Laura both turned as she shot out of the room and up the stairs. Liz stayed on the sofa, suddenly calm as a cat, nonchalantly examining her nails. William sighed and went over and sat down next to his daughter, picking up the remote control for the TV.

Laura hovered in the door of the kitchen. The back door was ajar, she wondered if Bill and his mother had gone out into the garden. She went towards it, and she heard Elizabeth's voice, speaking very softly.

'It's all right, son, it's all right,' she was saying. Laura stood by the sink and leaned over to try and see out the window. The light above the door illuminated the patio as though it was a stage. Elizabeth and Bill were sitting at the far end, overlooking the grass. Bill's head was in his mother's lap, Laura could hear that he was weeping. 'I killed, her, I killed her, and then I chopped her up,' he said, 'I killed her and now she will never leave me.' Elizabeth stroked his hair easily, as though

322

his words cost her nothing to absorb. 'I killed her, I killed her, and then I chopped her up, and now she will never leave me.'

Laura turned away and shoved her hands deep into the pockets of her jeans. He could say these things to his mother, but not to her. For the first time ever she wished to God that she had never met him, and then she hated herself for having that thought. More and more, every day, there were things she could not think about, speak about. Every morning she made a huge effort to push it all away. She pushed it away for Bill, she pushed it away for herself. She wished she could push it away completely.

THEY WENT BACK to Cambridge and communication shut down between them even further. They still had sex, they still fucked each other, they couldn't stop that entirely. Bill's time-clock turned upside-down as the nights grew warmer and shorter he began to stay out later, sleeping during the day. He'd slip into the house before dawn and climb into bed. When Laura got up, she'd find a muddy track through the house leading to the bedroom, his trainers, his clothes, his underwear. She'd pick everything up and put it in the washing machine.

One morning Laura woke to find Bill had pulled the duvet off the bed. He was standing in the corner, staring at her body. She sat up and tried to cover herself with her hands.

'Don't do that,' he said, his voice gentle and sweet. 'I want to see you, I want to look at you.' He came forward, he was naked and muddy, his penis erect. He grabbed hold of her ankles and pulled her down the bed towards him. Then he lowered himself onto her, as though in slow-motion. 'I really want this,' he said, 'I really want you.' Laura tried to relax; she tried to embrace him, but his skin felt very cold, clammy. He began to fuck her, he was slow and loving and she moved with him, feeling herself warming up. But suddenly he began to come, and in the midst of that she heard him whisper. 'Iris,' he said. 'Iris. Iris.' The next minute he was asleep.

Laura struggled out from beneath him. She went into the bathroom, feeling numb and dazed. In the mirror she saw there was mud on her breasts, on her shoulders and, to her horror, one clear mud hand-print on her face. Shaking, she ran hot water in the sink and washed hurriedly. Wrapped in her bathrobe, she walked quickly through the house, picking up his things. In the kitchen she found the backpack that he always carried when he ran. She emptied the contents onto the table. She found the letter she had written to Bill in prison, she found a bread knife, she found some string, and she found a thick roll of black plastic rubbish sacks. Her heart stopped as she handled these things.

Desperate not to wake him, she tiptoed upstairs, grabbed her clothes, and went outside and got into her car. She tried to figure out what to do. She couldn't go to Bill's probation officer – if the authorities found out about his behaviour they would be sure to revoke his licence immediately. He'd be back in prison the same day, no questions asked. Whom could she tell? Not

Elise. Elise would march round to the house, pack Bill's bag herself and force him to leave. Elise would call the police. He needed to see someone, he needed to do something Laura thought, he needed her more than ever, even though she was afraid.

She went to school and fumbled through the day.

BILL WOKE UP, in mid-afternoon. The first thing he thought was, I'm going crazy, I am losing my mind. But then that clarity dissipated and he felt paranoia well up in its place. Do the shopping, he thought, do the shopping, clean the house, make everything very very nice. And so that was what he did for the next couple of hours and when Laura got home he was hanging out the washing. She seemed shy, he wondered why she seemed so shy, and he offered to cook her dinner, told her to sit down and get caught up with her work. She obeyed him, she was obedient. And he cooked supper, he cooked a wonderful meal, steak and mashed potatoes and courgettes in garlic, he got it all exactly right. They sat down, he lit candles and opened a bottle of red wine, and they ate and they drank and it was lovely. Afterwards they watched the news on TV. And then it was eight o'clock. He looked at his watch, the watch she had given him, and the little hand was on eight.

So he went upstairs and got changed, pulling on his layers, and he picked up his rucksack before he went out, turning around to go back and kiss Laura. Kiss Laura. Laura, my girlfriend. And he ran up to Iris's college, to the college where the young girl he had known, so long ago, the young woman, the American

325

he had killed, where she lived. 'Oh yeah,' he said out loud to no one, 'my American girlfriend, that's where she lived, my old girlfriend, the one I killed.' No matter how often, how many ways he got himself to admit to it, no matter how loudly or bluntly or with how much careful consideration, that's what it came down to: Iris, I took her life, I did.

AFTER BILL WENT out Laura sat in front of the television and watched soap operas and sitcoms and a police show and a hospital drama. She watched the news again, and it was nearly midnight. Then she went upstairs and hauled on her trainers and she went outside, in the dark, to look for Bill.

DOWN AT THE river the water flows smoothly and in the black night it is hard to see that it moves. It looks solid, almost, still, although you can hear it lapping, hissing: as though the water speaks with a lisp. The things that live on it during the day are gone – the birds, the punts, the tourists. It is impossible to tell what lies beneath the surface, how deep it is, what swims in its depths. Bill lay on the footpath and crept forward over the edge of the concrete embankment. He placed his hand lightly on the water, but even his hand was too heavy; it broke the tension and plunged through. It felt reedy, the water felt reedy between his fingers, even here where he knew it was not. He put his hands in the mud and pulled his body further out from the embankment, so that his face hung over the water.

He looked down, it was too dark to see his reflection but he knew that it was there. He lowered his face into the water, very slowly. He broke the surface first with his forehead, then with his nose, then he pushed his whole face in and he thought it felt like penetrating a woman, Iris, Laura. He moved his head from side to side feeling the pressure from upstream, the downstream flowing away. He let his body relax, and he felt like an otter as he slipped in.

LAURA WAS OUT of breath as she ran along the river, heading upstream against the current. The moon was quite full, and gave the night a silvery light. She climbed up onto the footbridge and paused there, searching for Bill along the embankment. She looked down at the water and saw a dark shape float by. She ran to the bank grabbed a stick, and fished the thing out of the water. It was a black rubbish bag. Empty, flat, and when she retrieved it, dripping. She dropped the stick and hurried along the water's edge. She came to a place opposite a low group of willow trees that swept the water like languid women. From beneath the branches, she watched as Bill's little rucksack emerged and floated away.

She tore off her jacket and leapt into the river in a tangle of her own arms and legs. She went deep under, and came up gagging, struggling as though she had never learned how to swim, Laura thrashed her way across the river, now fighting the current for real. She grabbed hold of the willow, and the tree parted its branches to let her in to where it held Bill. His body lay beneath the surface of the water as if, even in death, he was too heavy to float. Laura seized his shoulders and turned him over and cradled him in her arms. His eyes were closed and she saw once again how fine and dark his long lashes were. His lips looked stung, stung by her kisses, and she wanted to tell him she loved him and would love him always. The water flowed around them and his head moved slowly, it fell against her shoulder as though he was in a deep and captive sleep.

STORIES FROM
TINY LIES

The Wardrobe

AFTER HER SISTER went mad, Josephine couldn't see the point in carrying on behaving normally but she tried not to think about this and went on with her life. She herself had very little propensity towards madness; she had always been the practical one in the family. It was Fin, her sister, who'd been the flighty one. So when Fin went mad, or rather, decided to stop pretending and do what she wanted, it was Josephine who bore the brunt of it. It was she who made all the arrangements, it was she who consoled the rest of the family, and it was she who put on the brave face to the authorities. Everyone, including her brother Arthur, was incapacitated.

What Fin did is something that many people toy with doing, or perhaps are afraid they'll do. She began by leaving her phone off the hook for days on end, claiming that the noise it made when it rang frightened her and she was sure it would bring bad news. She stopped reading newspapers, listening to the radio and watching television. Talking to her became difficult.

One morning Fin wore her pyjamas to work. Her boss sent her home in a taxi. Fin went back to bed but got up again later in the day and, still in her pyjamas, went for a walk along the river. No one is exactly sure what happened next but Fin was spotted on Lambeth Bridge at about 6:00 p.m., walking along in her night-clothes which couldn't have afforded much protection against the elements. Half an hour later she was seen in an inner-tube floating past the Tower of London. When the police boat caught up with her she told them to leave her alone, she had decided to take to the high seas.

'I'm fucking fed up with all this shit,' she said to the police officer who was frightened by the look in her eyes. 'I'm fed up and I'm damn well getting away from this place. Look at that,' she shouted, pointing in the direction of the City. 'It's fucking disgusting, all those goddamn banks, there is no morality anyway, no one gives a damn about anything. I don't trust anyone any more. You're all bloody liars. The whole world is one big fucking Masonic Lodge, I know it.' The police officer held on to Fin's arm, leaning over the edge of the boat. He listened to her carefully so that he could make a report. In the end all he wrote on his notepad was 'She's a nutter'. Fin was condemned but she didn't care one bit.

A little while later after Fin was picked up Josephine received a phone call from the police.

'Are you Josephine Cutler?' a male voice asked.

'Why, who are you?' Josephine replied.

'This is Sergeant Bulk speaking from the Metropolitan River Police. We've got a woman here who claims to be your sister. She identifies herself as Fin Cutler.'

'Yes, Fin is my sister,' said Josephine, feeling she already knew what had happened. 'I'll be right there.'

At the police station an officer led Josephine into the cells. Fin looked thin and tired as she shivered inside her blanket.

'Josephine!' she said. 'Tell them I do this all the time. Make them let me go, Josie. What bastards they are.'

'Fin, sweetheart, what happened?'

'I was trying to escape, babyface. I was trying to get out of this hellhole before it was too late. I know, I know,' she said shaking her head, 'I should have taken you and Arthur with me. But there just wasn't enough room and I had to get away. I wore my pyjamas so that no one could see me.'

'But, Fin, you can't get anywhere in an inner-tube on the Thames.'

'I could have Josie, if they'd given me a chance.'

A police officer cut Josephine's visit short so they could take her sister to the hospital. Over the next couple of weeks Fin told so many different stories that nobody wanted to listen to her any longer except Josephine and Arthur, but they didn't get to see her very often. Soon it was evident that Fin would have to stay in the hospital for quite a while. Whenever Josephine went to visit her she had some new escape plan.

'This time, Josie, I'm going to wait until it's really windy and then ask if I can go outside in the grounds with my kite. I'm light enough. I know I am. I haven't eaten for days.' Josephine shook her head slowly and on the way home on the underground she found herself in tears.

Still, Josephine carried on working and going to the pub and doing the washing-up. On Wednesdays she had dinner with Arthur and on Sundays she visited Fin. When she had a bit of extra money she would buy herself a new dress. Josephine had a closet that was full of clothes she never wore: black tulle, burgundy organza, dresses with hoops, lace. Brightly coloured long kaftans, shiny blue taffeta, a pink satin mini-skirt: Josephine's closet was like a secret garden that an invisible gardener cultivated and no one ever sat in. She would stare down at it from her window, or rather open her closet doors and look at the colours without ever stepping into them.

Josephine had a whole list of shops she frequented during her lunch hour. She found nothing quite so satisfying as spotting a dress that she wanted. After circling around it for days she would finally gather up her courage and take it off the rack. In the fitting room she would stare at herself in the mirror feeling transformed. This was the only time she actually wore these clothes. A paisley frock with a bow at the back, a black cotton shift with slits up the legs, a crêpe-de-chine skirt with a contrasting top: Josephine spent a lot of money on clothes.

One Wednesday when Arthur was over for tea Josephine said to him, 'Arthur, you've been working so hard since Fin went into the hospital. Why don't you go away for a holiday somewhere? Take a break.'

'Me take a holiday?' replied Arthur. 'But you need a holiday just as much as I do. Besides, I can't afford one.'

'Oh that's nonsense. Flights are so cheap these days. You should go away to Spain or somewhere like that. Lie on a beach and go to nightclubs.'

'Josephine, you know I don't like the sun and I hate

dancing. Besides, I'd worry about you and Fin: Who'd be here to make sure you're all right? Who'd visit Fin on Tuesdays?'

'But, Arthur,' said Josephine, 'you're too young to be so serious.'

'You should talk, Josefiend, you should talk. You're younger than both Fin and I. It's you who goes about with a long face. Fin and I are perfectly happy. I think you should go away on holiday.'

On Sunday, when Josephine was at the hospital, Fin said, 'Josephine, you look terrible. Take a holiday. Go away and get some sunshine. You worry too much. I'm fine,' she said, giggling. 'I tricked a nurse the other day. For three days I didn't speak. Not one word. Then just when she was getting really fed up with me I asked her which was the way to the nearest exit out of this place. I think she wanted to kill me. Anyway, Josie, you should take a holiday. I'm tired of seeing your worried face every Sunday. Give me a break.' Fin winked.

So Josephine and Arthur decided to go away together. They bought European train tickets and packed their bags. Before they left Fin told them where she had hidden her money when she ran away, so they took that with them as well. On the day of their departure they met at Victoria Station.

'My God Josefiend,' swore Arthur, 'your suitcase is enormous! What have you got in it?'

'Just a few things,' said Josephine quietly.

In Paris, on the Champs-Elysées, Josephine wore scarlet mousseline with a matching bow in her hair; in Lyons, crimson moire with a black beret. On a gondola in Venice she wore an olive gabardine dress that was doublebreasted at the front and fitted at the back. Every morning, over the brioche and coffee, Arthur said, 'Wow.' Josephine had never been happier.

They travelled across Europe like two migrating birds, coming to rest wherever they pleased. In Vienna Josephine had to buy a second suitcase which Arthur did not mind having to carry; it made him happy to see his sister relaxed. They sat silently, staring out of the windows of the fast European trains, Josephine's hands folded neatly in her gloves. They travelled beside rivers and along coastlines. Josephine's wardrobe expanded.

After three weeks they returned home to their jobs. That Sunday they went to see Fin together.

'But, you've come back!' cried Fin when she saw them. 'You were meant to escape, not return,' she said, her voice full of anguish as she began to sob. 'Why? Why? Did they catch you? You weren't meant to come back. I thought you'd gone for me.'

Arthur and Josephine stood at the foot of Fin's bed. They were speechless. Josephine went up to Fin and attempted to put an arm around her heaving shoulders.

'Don't touch me!' Fin shouted. 'You could have gone! Now they'll get you too. If you can escape, why don't you?'

'But Fin,' stuttered Josephine. 'Fin. We had to come back. We've got responsibilities. We've got you.'

'No you haven't!' shouted Fin. 'They've got me. You've got no responsibilities except for those you've made up! You're mad not to escape. Mad!' Arthur took Josephine by the hand.

'We'd better go home Josephine,' he said.

'Yes, you'd better,' shouted Fin.

On the underground Arthur sat with his arm around Josephine. 'Maybe she's right,' he said.

'Right about what?' snapped Josephine. 'We can't stay on holiday forever.'

'No, but maybe we should leave.'

'Why?'

'I don't know. Maybe Fin knows something we don't.'

'I'm sure she does Arthur. She must do.' When they reached the next stop they said goodbye and Josephine got off the train. She walked up the street to her flat very slowly. Sunday afternoon was dead in London; everyone had bought their newspapers and shut the door. Josephine made herself a cup of tea then went into her bedroom. She opened her closet doors and stood looking at the colour of her clothes. Then she climbed into the wardrobe and closed the doors behind her.

Franz Kafka's Shirt

GENEVIEVE PAID A great deal of attention to her dreams because she believed they revealed important things about her state of mind. Her dream-life was particularly rich; Genevieve could often remember her dreams with a clarity that she rarely found in her actual waking life. Her dreams were like little absurdist plays, one after the other, night after night. It was as if Ionesco had moved into her subconscious.

From time to time Genevieve's dreams were more straightforward, tiny snippets of wish-fulfilment that lasted five seconds, like the night she dreamed she was given a pen, the ink of which would never blot, and the time she dreamed she went back to school and humiliated the boy who once told her she was ugly. But, more often her dreams made little obvious sense and Genevieve had to spend whole mornings figuring out what they meant. She had her own set of dream-analysis tools, and her own ideas about the symbolism within her. Not for her the Freudian, Jungian, Reichian interpretations, nor even the more hippy ideas of dreaming and astrology.

Genevieve's dreams were like theatre, so she interpreted them like theatre. She enjoyed them and queued for ice cream in the interval. She appreciated the art behind their creation, and she admired the design of the sets. Most of all, she was thrilled with the way she almost always knew all the people in the dream. It was like having a fringe theatre company devoted to the interpretation of one's own life. That was how Genevieve saw her dreams: very interesting, often disturbing, but something that didn't actually have much impact upon the everyday occurrences of her diurnal life.

In this waking life, Genevieve was a normalish type of person. She had a job she didn't like, although it didn't annoy her enough to make her look for another one. She had a pleasant social life and spent many happy evenings arguing with her friends in front of the fire. She went to the cinema, the theatre, the odd party, she wore lipstick in the evening, and she smoked too much. She fell in love and had her heart broken. And she had vivid dreams every night. Genevieve didn't feel there was anything particularly lacking from her own life, although many of her friends, with lives just like hers, did.

Occasionally Genevieve and her friends talked about their dreams. When Genevieve told the others about hers everybody laughed and said they wished they had such entertaining, strange, nonsensical dreams. No one thought there could possibly be anything wrong with the way Genevieve was dreaming.

One night Genevieve dreamed she was wearing Franz Kafka's shirt. In this very brief dream all that happened was Genevieve found herself standing on the pavement in front of where she lived. She looked down at what she was wearing and when she saw the shirt she had on, she knew that it was Franz Kafka's shirt. That was it. That was all that happened in the dream.

But the weekend after having that dream, and after Genevieve and her friends had had a good giggle at the absurdity of it, Genevieve went to a jumble sale. As she was looking through a pile of shirts on a table in the church hall she found herself holding a shirt that she felt, against all probability, was Franz Kafka's shirt. It was an ordinary man's shirt of a variety often to be found at jumble sales, cotton-mix, rather soiled around the collar, and worn thin on the left elbow. The only remarkable thing about this shirt, other than the fact that Genevieve was sure it was Franz Kafka's shirt, was that it was printed with a motif of beige cowboys on beige bucking broncos. It was a discreet motif, the sort of print one would not notice unless one really looked at that kind of thing, like someone with a theory about understanding men by examining the patterns on their shirts. Genevieve was not that kind of a person.

Quickly, and not without exhibiting embarrassment, Genevieve bought the shirt from the elderly woman behind the table insisting on paying twenty pence instead of the ten pence for which the woman had asked. She took the shirt home with her and soaked it in the bathtub for the afternoon, hoping to remove the stain around the neck, and also, even if she didn't think of it, hoping to remove whatever it was about the shirt that made her think it was Franz Kafka's. While it soaked Genevieve sat in the kitchen. She told herself that Franz Kafka had been dead for rather a long time, and as far as she knew he had never lived in her neighbourhood, let alone her country, and the chances that a shirt that had been anywhere near Franz Kafka would turn up at a jumble sale in South London were very slim. As well as all that, she felt quite certain having read several of his books that Franz Kafka would not have worn a shirt with a motif of cowboys on bucking broncos adorning it, no matter how discreet.

Still, once she had taken the shirt out of the tub, washed it, wrung it dry, and hung it up, and then looked at it hanging there, rather limp and not even terribly stylish, she knew that it was Franz Kafka's shirt and there was nothing she could do about it.

So, she wore it. She wore it to parties, she wore it to work, she wore it to the cinema. No one ever noticed the shirt, except for a few people who laughed at the cowboys, and although Genevieve lived with the hope that one day someone would say 'Hey! Isn't that Franz Kafka's shirt?' no one ever did. Gradually Genevieve became accustomed to wearing Franz Kafka's shirt and the urge to find someone to talk to about it, an urge that came over her with particular strength when she was drunk, faded. All she was left with was a rather uninteresting-looking piece of clothing, and a faint sense that something, somewhere, was odd.

Genevieve's life went on as it always had done and her dream-life continued as well. More miniature absurdist dramas took place in her mind than at any real theatre. These dreams continued to amuse Genevieve, and her friends.

Then, one night during the wet and bleak London

winter, months after she had dreamed about Franz Kafka's shirt, Genevieve dreamed about swimming. She was swimming with Franz Kafka in a murky, muddy river. Franz Kafka was wearing a swimming costume, modern and brief in style, printed with the same pattern as his shirt, cowboys and bucking broncos. They were swimming the Australian crawl side by side when Franz Kafka suddenly stopped and shouted at Genevieve, 'What makes you think you can wear a dead writer's clothes?' Genevieve also stopped swimming and turned her body in the water so she could face him. 'That was my favourite shirt,' he added indignantly.

'Oh, was it?' said Genevieve. 'Don't you think you've been dead for rather too long to be complaining about this sort of thing?'

'Humph,' said Franz Kafka, cheekily, 'I suppose it will be my shoes next. Or, perhaps, Dostoevsky's underwear, eh?'

'Shut up,' Genevieve shouted, 'you're dead!' And with that, she lunged at Franz Kafka, travelling through the water like a torpedo, and grabbed him around the neck.

With one hand she attempted to throttle him whilst with the other she tried to twist off his head. The expression on Franz Kafka's face was terrible.

Genevieve woke up when she felt hot water on her hands. At first she thought it was Franz Kafka's blood, streaming from his neck, but she realised quickly that she had unscrewed her hot water bottle whilst dreaming. She screwed the top back in and then sat up, dismayed to find a colossal wet patch in the centre of the bed, like the unpleasant leftover of a wild sexual tryst.

Genevieve did not sleep for the remainder of the night and she was not to sleep for the many nights that followed. Early in the morning she would rise, put on Franz Kafka's shirt and go for long walks along the Thames. From Vauxhall Bridge she would stare down into the murky, muddy water of the river. She half expected to one day see the body of Franz Kafka floating there, identifiable by his swimming costume, the faint pattern of beige cowboys on beige bucking broncos.

The First Mistake
or How To Read Marx

SHE TARTED HERSELF up for him. That was Isabel's first mistake.

She agreed with what he said without really thinking about his words and anticipated his jokes with a smile, sparkling with wit, charm, and light. She said what she thought he'd want to hear and she was usually right. Her feminine intuition did not let her down, although it could be argued that that very same intuition was her downfall. Isabel expended a lot of effort in trying to please Archie. That was another mistake.

Their eyes met at a weekend seminar on Marx at the university. Neither of them had read Marx and, in the pub at lunchtime, they both instinctively recognised each other's ignorance. Archie picked up his drink and walked over to Isabel's table. He had thick, black eyebrows and big hands and feet. When he sat down next to her as she sipped her beer coolly, she thought for a moment she might ignore him, afraid she would be forced to confess to not having read Marx.

'I haven't read it,' Archie said, without looking at Isabel. He gazed out across the pub with a faraway look in his eyes, then said, 'I don't have time to actually read it. I know it through my bones anyway. Sometimes I think Marx is just in the air, something I breathe without having to think. He's just there.'

Isabel sat watching Archie as he spoke. He still hadn't looked at her. 'I know what you mean, in fact,' she said. 'I haven't read it either. I haven't read anything, at least, nothing that matters. I never know what anyone is talking about. That's why I came here. I thought it would be a good place to start.' She smiled at Archie but he was not looking at her.

'I read a lot,' Archie said, still gazing across the bar.

'So do I,' she agreed, 'but I never understand any of it.'

'Never?' Archie suddenly turned and looked at Isabel. She was shocked by his eyebrows. They moved wildly when he spoke, as though a sudden wind had come up from a corner of the room. 'I don't believe you never understand any of it, ever.'

'Well, that's how it feels,' Isabel looked at Archie who was now staring at her. She smiled brightly and then began to feel a little nervous, 'I think I preferred it when you weren't looking at me.'

Archie asked Isabel if he could get her another drink. Once they had finished those they went back to the university and sat through the afternoon of workshops together. Isabel watched the blackboard filling up with equations and formulae. Archie sat and stared straight ahead, occasionally taking notes. Isabel tried to see what he was writing but only managed once: Archie had written, in small neat letters, BUY MILK.

On the following day they met again in the pub at lunchtime. Isabel was wearing a short, pink skirt that a lot of the male Marxists had spent the morning trying to look up. Archie did not try to look up Isabel's skirt, in fact, he did not seem to notice it. He either looked ahead in a studiously dreamy manner or stared right into Isabel's eyes. She found both habits equally unnerving, but after her confession about Marx, she trusted him. It would be a crime not to have an affair after such openness Isabel decided.

Three nights after the seminar, Isabel and Archie met to go to the cinema. They went to see a Russian film made in the 1930s. Before the film they talked.

'You go to the cinema often, do you?' Archie asked.

'Yes, I do. I find the cinema relaxing,' Isabel replied.

'Have you seen *Solaris* by Tarkovsky?' Archie asked.

'No,' replied Isabel.

'Neither have I.'

Isabel found the film she and Archie saw extremely moving. During one bit mid-way through, she found herself in tears. Archie sat perfectly expressionless, gazing at the screen in front of him. Afterwards, when they had walked to the underground and were about to leave on separate lines, Archie put his arms around Isabel's waist. He kissed her on the lips and said goodnight. When Isabel stepped into the train she realised they hadn't talked about the film they had just seen.

Four days later, Isabel rang up Archie and asked him to come to a party at a big house where a friend of hers lived. When he finally arrived at midnight with two bottles of wine, he and Isabel sat in a dark corner discussing Margaret Thatcher and books until about 3:00 a.m.

'Have you read *The History of Sexuality: Volume One* by Michel Foucault?'

'No.'

'Neither have I.' Then Archie and Isabel kissed. They danced for a while in between three and four o'clock. Isabel did not introduce Archie to any of her friends. Archie talked about himself. When he went to the toilet at three thirty Isabel wanted to lie down on the dance floor, she was so exhausted.

'Have you read the *Prison Notebooks* by Gramsci?'

'No.'

'Neither have I.'

Just before dawn, when the party began to wind down, Archie said to Isabel, 'I'm getting tired. I think I'd better go home. I'll find a cab or something.' He paused and, without looking at her said, 'Would you like to come home with me?'

'OK,' said Isabel. 'It's not everyday I meet someone who'll admit to being as badly read as I am.' Archie did not reply.

When they got to Archie's flat and were sitting on the sofa drinking cups of tea he said, 'Well, I feel I've told you my life story.'

'Yes,' said Isabel, 'I guess you have.' She blushed, 'Part of it anyway.'

'You haven't told me much about yourself, Issy.'

'No.' Isabel smiled and then Archie kissed her on the mouth. He peeled off her clothes with his big hands and kissed her scar without asking where it had come from.

Maybe that's where it started, maybe that was where Isabel made the first mistake. Not talking about herself seemed to make her somehow less than herself. When she was with Archie both her personality and her past evaporated. They seemed to blow away like dry leaves, perhaps in the same wind that disturbed Archie's eyebrows. All she would confide was how much she did not know, and that very act seemed to have established in her an unbreakable silence.

Since Isabel felt she could not please Archie by regaling him with multifarious stories from her fascinating past lives she sought another way to attract his attention. The only way she could think of was that much dreaded way, through those infamous and self-denying constructs, feminine charms.

Isabel began to wear more make-up. She did her hair attractively, spending time on it. She wore short skirts and an array of clothes that were greeted with shouts from other men whenever she went out without Archie. One day when she was on her bicycle a man leaned out of his car window and said, 'I wish my face was your bicycle seat.' Isabel was left speechless as usual.

Archie didn't seem to notice the way Isabel looked, although occasionally she thought she could detect, somewhere in the depths of his stare, a kind of hunger. When they made love Isabel's body was filled not so much with desire, but with a longing to please. When he ran his big hand from her breast to her thigh it was not so much his touch that thrilled her, but the look on his face. She sometimes felt she would have given him almost anything.

Isabel began to grow faint, gradually becoming more and more transparent. At the end of each day the little strength she had left she devoted to seducing Archie and drawing him to her with his pleasure. Isabel thought that Archie was happy and that she probably seemed mysterious and beautiful to him. When he said, 'You are quiet Issy,' she knew it was not a question but a compliment.

At night, Isabel lay awake, watching Archie sleep. 'You don't know me at all,' she thought, but she didn't wake him up to point this out. That, too, was a mistake. During the day, from time to time, Isabel would catch Archie watching her from behind his great eyebrows but their only real form of communication was sex. They never ever read in bed.

The affair between Isabel and Archie continued for quite some time until one day, standing on an escalator, Isabel saw herself in a big mirror. As the moving staircase progressed upwards, she examined her reflection, staring into her own empty blue eyes. 'I am disappearing,' she said out loud. 'There's been a mistake. I've made a mistake.' The escalator carried her up and, once out on ground level, Isabel ran to the library. She took out a whole pile of books that she had never read, carried them all home and put them on to her bed.

Isabel spent that afternoon reading and in the evening when Archie came home she said, 'Hello Archie. I've been reading.'

'You've been what, Isabel?'

'I said I've started to read again Archie. I went to the library today.'

'Issy,' he said, his eyebrows quivering slightly. 'Your lipstick is smudged.'

'What?' asked Isabel with surprise. Archie had made his first mistake. And nothing was the same ever again.

In Montreal

IN MONTREAL CHRISTINE was foreign for the first time. She had never been outside the enormous and empty western province in which she had grown up. In fact, she had hardly been away from the small, mountain town where her family lived. To Christine, Montreal seemed as romantic and distant as Paris. Ever since she was a small girl and had seen Quebec on the television, watched those gritty politicians with their gravelly voices and thick accents, she had wanted to go and live there. So, when she was seventeen she packed her bags and, with the money she had made car-hopping in the summer at the Drive-In Restaurant, she boarded an aeroplane and began her adult life.

In Montreal Christine could not speak the language. When she arrived in the terminal and asked for directions to the city in her high school French, she knew immediately that she was out of her depth. The woman at the information desk replied to her in English. But that did not stop Christine. She was brave, determined and stubborn, as only seventeen-year-old girls can be.

Christine knew exactly what she was going to do with her new life in Montreal. She had told her parents she was going to get a job, save some money and then go to university, but she had no intention of doing anything as mundane as that. Christine was going to speak French, dress in black, smoke Gauloises, live by herself, and, best of all, become a lapsed Catholic. In the small town where she had grown up most people were either Presbyterians or members of the United Church, a distinctly Canadian mixture of Protestant religions that resembled a sort of extremely low Anglican. Christine was bored with that now. She wanted a religion with some dignity and mystery so that when she rejected it, as she knew she would, she'd have the pleasure of rejecting something particularly rich.

Within a week of her arrival Christine had a job wiping tables and clearing dishes in a cafe in the bottom of Les Terraces, a shopping complex on St Catherine Street in downtown Montreal. It was one of those totally plastic little places that Montreal enterprise is so bad at, a sub-American kind of dive, decorated in orange and lime-green with mushroom-like tables sprouting out of the concrete floor and dingy mirrors on the walls. Les Terraces, like much of downtown Montreal, is indoors and underground. At Le Hamburger the ventilation worked against the heating and the result was a very hot hamburger bar with grease hanging in the air. But, to Christine, the most extraordinary thing about Le Hamburger was that, despite all appearances, everything about it was absolutely Quebecois. 'Un hamburger, s'il vous plait.'

Along with the job, which paid much less than the legal minimum wage, a fact she didn't have enough French to complain about, Christine found somewhere to live. From an advert in the window of a small corner tabac she rented a one-room apartment at the top of four flights of stairs down by the river in East Montreal. The windows were cracked and the small radiator hissed and sighed while it pumped out heat. The hot-plate in the corner was coated with grime, and the mattress was lumpy. The obligatory bare light-bulb hung from the ceiling in the middle of the room. Christine loved it, of course. It was all hers.

Montreal was all hers as well – Christine felt this as she strolled along the city's streets. The churches, the parks, the cafés, the bar-restaurants that stay open all night, even the taverns on the corners that still did not allow women through their doors; in those first months she often felt like embracing it all. But Montreal was much slower to accept Christine. More often than not when she greeted its inhabitants with her very bad but enthusiastic French she would be answered in English or not at all. The Canadian Language War was at its height and Christine frequently became an unwitting casualty of the hostilities. But youth, determination, and zeal protected her as she calmly got on with her life.

During the daytime, from 7:00 a.m. to 5:00 p.m., Christine cleaned up after the boys who hung out at Le Hamburger. While they dealt acid and punched each other on the forearms, she picked up coffee cups and wiped ketchup off the tables. She listened to their raucous conversation, catching the odd word in English: 'car', 'bar', 'pizza', 'acid', and 'hashish'.

From the big bookstore further down St Catherine Street Christine bought herself a book called *How to*

Speak French and in the evenings once home from work she read it diligently, practising out loud in front of the mirror. 'Bonjour, madame. Bonjour, mademoiselle. Comment ça va?' she'd say to herself. 'Ça va bien, et vous? Voulez-vous un hamburger? Non, merci. Je suis fatiguée.'

On Sundays, her one day away from Le Hamburger, Christine went to mass. She was making a tour of all the Catholic churches in Montreal. This project would take her years to complete, but Christine was undaunted by this in the same way that she was undaunted by much about her new life. She started off with the big ones and on her first Catholic Sunday went to Notre-Dame in Vieux Montreal. Its old world splendour pleased her; the stained glass and high arched ceilings made her feel something she imagined might be akin to Faith.

On the second Sunday Christine attended mass in St Joseph's Oratory, one of the biggest Catholic churches in North America. It sits up on the northeast side of Mont Royale, together with the huge, electrically-lit cross that stands further up the mountain. Christine climbed the hundreds of steps that lead up to the church, steps she would later learn to her blatantly Protestant distaste that thousands of pilgrims had climbed, and were still climbing, on their knees every year. Inside the Oratory, Christine was impressed by the grandeur of the building and the extreme religiosity of the ceremony. She lit a candle and then fell asleep during the service. The mystery of Catholicism was a complete enigma to Christine and besides, it was all in French.

Back at Le Hamburger on Monday morning, Christine communicated with her boss, a small and dark Québécois man named Rene, by smiling, nodding and then going back to work without the slightest idea what he had been saying. He, however, seemed pleased enough with her and Christine believed that he must not realise she could not speak French but merely thought she was a bit quiet. When the boys who hung out directed their conversation towards her, she merely smiled and occasionally said 'Oui'. She had learned by that time how to say 'Oui' with the appropriate Montreal accent rendering it completely unlike anything she had learned in high school. The boys were not convinced.

As spring gradually moved into summer the overheating at Les Terraces became over-air-conditioning. Christine continued to work at the hamburger bar and incorporated into her Sunday tour of the churches lengthy diversions into the Parc Mont Royale where she would spend the afternoon lying in the sun reading French grammar books. She was progressing well with the language, warming up to it with the weather. By June she had learned enough to ask for more money from her boss at Le Hamburger.

One day, a boy who hung out, leaning his thin frame against the orange plastic table for most of the afternoon, drinking cups of Rene's foul coffee and, occasionally, dribbling ketchup over the limp fries that were the speciality of the place, looked up at Christine while she was wiping away spilt sugar from the next table. 'Hello', he said, in strongly accented English. 'Where are you from?'

'Quoi?' replied Christine.

'Come on,' he said, 'I know you are not French. I know you are an Anglo. Speak up, eh? Where are you from?'

Christine smiled at him. 'Mais, je suis Française.'

The boy laughed and said, 'You are about as French as Rene's hamburgers.' Christine continued to wipe tables while all around her the boys, No. 7s dangling from their mouths, laughed.

By August, the hottest and stickiest month in Montreal, Christine was reading novels in French and beginning to build up a small collection of books in her room. She was reading Colette and Marie-Claire Blais and had even embarked upon *À la recherche du temps perdu*. During the evening, after she finished work, Christine would leave the cold underground environment of Les Terraces and walk down St Catherine Street, heading east. When she reached St Denis she would turn to the right and find a seat in one of the many cafés that spill out onto the sidewalk. There she would sit sipping a beer and read, ignoring the sweat that ran in rivulets down her back. Usually some jazz would be wafting out of the café and Christine would feel, as the verbs, nouns and adjectives came off the page and told her stories, that she was beginning to understand her adopted language. She would sit and read Proust very happily for several hours until she felt her eyes grow heavy, then, just as the cafés were beginning to fill up with Montrealers out for the evening, she would pick up her book, empty her glass of beer, and walk home to her little room.

At about ten o'clock one evening, the time Christine

usually headed off, a young woman with dark eyes and a mass of curly hair stopped beside her table. 'Bonjour,' she said, and still speaking in French, 'Is anyone sitting here?'

'No,' said Christine, in French, 'please sit down. I was just about to leave.'

'Oh,' said the woman, 'you are not French?'

'No,' said Christine, 'I come from the West.'

'But you speak French? Where do you live, here, in Montreal?'

'Yes, I live down by the river.'

'By yourself?'

'Yes.'

'But that is very brave,' replied the woman, who then introduced herself. Marie-Sylvie was a student at the university nearby. She came from a small town up the St Lawrence River and did not speak one word of English. Christine talked to her in French without pausing to think as she did so. They ordered several beers together and watched while the activity on St Denis grew more frenetic as the night drew on.

'So,' said Marie-Sylvie. 'You live all by yourself in a tiny room by the river and you work every day in a greasy café wiping up after obnoxious boys who treat you badly. You are paid very little. On Sundays you go to church, although you are not Catholic and the rest of the time you spend reading French grammar books. Why?'

'Well,' replied Christine in her young and steady voice. 'It seemed the only way to begin to learn how to think in French.'

Around midnight Christine got up to leave. It was

still very hot and when she stood she suddenly felt quite drunk.

'Au revoir. Will we meet again?' she asked Marie-Sylvie whose dark hair was damp with sweat.

'Au revoir,' said Marie-Sylvie, 'I come here often; I am sure we will.'

Christine wove her way through the tables of the café and began to walk back down St Denis towards St Catherine Street.

Tiny Lies

OCCASIONALLY THERE IS A story told about someone who has disappeared without trace. After a long
search, friends and relatives eventually give the missing person up for dead. They resume their lives, recover from their grief, and may even make a grave on
which to leave flowers. Then one day an acquaintance
who knew the missing person vaguely and is on a vacation in a distant part of the country reports a sighting.
Late at night, in a bar, they meet an apparent stranger
who, after a long conversation, they realise must be
that missing person from all those years ago. They
want to ask, 'Why did you do it? What happened?' but
they also want to avoid embarrassment so dare not,
just in case they are mistaken.

And so it transpires that the missing person may
not be dead. Once again, there is doubt. They could
have simply left their proverbial clothes on the beach
and gone down to Liverpool or London, taken on a
new identity and embarked on a completely new life,
perhaps changing their appearance and even the way
they speak, blow their nose, or laugh. They might have
forgotten their previous life, blanked it. They don't
want to be found out. And, back at home, the friends

and family listen to the description of the holiday encounter and wonder if it could possibly be true. All they can think to ask is 'Why?'

Unusual perhaps, but this happens often enough to be part of that subterranean cave full of stories our culture digs up from time to time. More frequently people make a kind of partial break by remaining where they are but ceasing to ring up old friends. They leave the job they did every day for ten years and start a new one, or become unemployed and lose touch. They move to a new city and tell tiny lies about their previous existence. They break off with a lover and stop being part of the social circle in which the lover moves. They fall out with their family and decide to cut the ties in a final, dramatic kind of way. They change continents, or maybe they just dye their hair. They run away from something they don't like and, in the process, believe that they've recreated themselves.

After Monica had the abortion, the relationship she was in shattered. Somehow there was too much guilt and pain for it to continue. She and Chris attempted to keep it going; after all they did feel bonded together in some strange way, if only in their mutual loss. But Monica was angry and that did not help. She felt she had suffered and that Chris had refused to acknowledge it; he'd been too wrapped up in his own difficulties. They sliced each other up with long and sharp arguments until, finally, their relationship lay in pieces around their feet. It was almost a relief, but not quite.

Monica decided to walk away. She packed her bags and divided up all the possessions which had made their home. She took the teapot and left him the per-colator. He was happy with that, never having enjoyed their domesticity anyway. Rolling up her poster, she looked at him and said, 'Well Chris, I hope you're sat-isfied. Shame about the messy bits though. I have to say, I feel well fucked over.'

'Oh you do, do you Monica? Well, I have to say that I feel a bit fucked over as well. And that poster is mine.'

She considered moving in with one of her friends, but knew that none of them really wanted that de-spite their offers. Monica had this idea that everybody disapproved of her after the abortion. They weren't anti-choice, Monica's friends, they were simply un-comfortable with Monica's fuck-up, Monica's pain, Monica's depression, Monica's deteriorating relation-ship, and the way when they all got drunk on Friday night Monica would always end up in floods of tears babbling about her mother's dreams.

'What do you mean, Monica, when you say your mother's heart would break if she knew what you'd done? Your mother hasn't got anything to do with your relationship with Chris. She is not an invisible force passing judgement on your every action.'

'Oh yes she is,' Monica would reply. 'If she knew what I've done . . . she doesn't even think pre-marital kissing is a good idea, let alone pre-marital sex. Oh my God, what if she was right and I am wrong? She always says it's the woman who is left to suffer. She always says that.'

'Oh yeah? And I bet she also says that sex is a mari-tal duty, doesn't she? Lie back and think of the Falkland Islands?' Monica felt misunderstood. Maybe she was, maybe she wasn't. But she was definitely unhappy and she needed a change.

So Monica decided that she would attempt to make a fresh start. This idea grew bigger and the restart became a clean break, and the clean break became a move, and the move progressed from around the corner to a different town and before she knew what had happened, Monica found herself in London with a new job, a flat, a routine to her week and a new attitude to life. She left Chris and her girlfriends behind and there seemed no point in telling them where she was going.

At the new job when people asked what Monica had done before she gave an elaborately edited account revealing only those bits that were relevant to her new position. When the woman at the next desk asked why she had left her home town, Monica told her that she'd wanted a change. Then when the man at another desk asked her, in a predatory kind of way, if she had a boyfriend, she'd panicked and said that she was married. And when her boss, upon discovering that she was married, asked her if she had any children, Monica winced and shook her head. Hearing the other women sitting around at lunch telling each other their medical tales of woe, Monica refrained from discussing her own. She didn't want to tell anybody anything.

Yet, when Monica went home at night and looked in the mirror she saw herself, her same old self, the face she had grown up with. Same old body, same old scars. So the next move was cosmetic. Monica went to the local hairdressing school and bought a completely new hairstyle. She gave the student free rein and he transformed the straight blondish hair that Chris had run his hands through, the same hair that had gone lanky and dull while she was in the hospital, into a short auburn bob. Then she acquired a new wardrobe. She took up cigarettes and lost weight. Lying in the bath late one night she decided to paint her toenails red. She sold all her jewellery, the tiny stones she wore in her ears, the gold bracelets, the locket which had been given to her by Chris, and bought some big silver hoop earrings and large clunky bracelets. She took to wearing scent. Monica spent her evenings in the big city that she didn't know at all plotting her transformation.

One of the other women at work who sat opposite her and watched these rapid changes was intrigued. 'You get better looking every day, Monica sweetheart,' she said to her one day. 'I'm having a party on Friday night. Would you like to come?' Siobhan had followed Monica into the women's toilets. 'There won't be any people from the office there. Here's an invite. It's got my address on it. Come about ten. Oh yeah,' she said, smiling, 'bring your husband.'

'Oh,' said Monica, blushing, 'he doesn't like parties very much . . . but I'd like to come.' As Siobhan walked toward the door Monica called out, 'Thanks.'

That Friday at lunchtime, Monica went down to the shops and bought a party outfit: a little black dress and some new tights. At five o'clock she rushed home and took a long bath, this time painting her fingernails as well as her toenails. She spent a long time powdering her body and stepping on and off the scales. Drinking beer as she worked, she put on her make-up and then, just before it was time to go, she slipped on the new dress and the black patterned tights. Her mother had always told her not to wear black as it is the colour for mourning. 'Well,' thought Monica, 'I am in mourning. I'm mourning all that time I wasted with Chris. All that spent passion.'

Monica took a cab to the party and, reaching Siobhan's house well before ten, went into the pub on the corner. She drank more beer sitting by herself at a small table. The place was fairly empty and nobody gave her a second look. As Monica sat, she inspected her outfit.

'I'm twenty-five years old. I'm married, no, I'm separated. I've got red hair and I smell of a sort of musky perfume. I smoke long cigarettes and . . . I come from France and my name is really Monique . . . no, no.' Monica sipped her beer and smiled to herself. After a while, she picked up her handbag and walked over to the party.

Siobhan lived in a medium-sized, two-bedroom flat with her best friend Diane. They had worked hard to prepare for the party, all kinds of snacks and a punch were set out on a big table in the kitchen. The sitting room had been cleared out to make room for dancing and the coats went into Siobhan's bedroom, while in Diane's room big cushions were scattered on the floor where people could sit and talk. When Monica walked in there were only about fifteen people there but the hostesses were already fairly drunk. Siobhan got Monica a drink and introduced her to Diane who wanted to know where she had found her dress, a question that pleased Monica immensely. They chatted for a while about shops and clothes, then more people came in and Monica was jostled into the kitchen. Standing beside the refrigerator, she downed a couple of glasses of punch when she thought no one was looking and helped herself to some food. Siobhan kept coming in and out of the kitchen introducing everyone in sight and giggling, nervously. Monica smiled at her calmly. She drank the punch at a steady speed and began to feel quite comfortable. When Siobhan introduced her again to Diane she felt ready for conversation.

'So Diane, where do you work?'

'Oh,' replied Diane, 'at a similar sort of place to you. Boring, dead boring. Don't like it much, I want to do something more interesting. Do you like your job?'

'Uh,' said Monica, hesitating, 'no, well, I mean, uh, no.' In fact, Monica did enjoy her work but it didn't seem appropriate to say so. Everything was still new and exciting to her.

'All I really like about my job is the holidays. Siobhan and I are going to Spain next month. Have you ever been there?'

'Uh,' said Monica hesitating again, 'yes. Yes, I've been to Spain.' She hadn't.

'Oh yeah? Did you like it, was it nice?'

'Yes . . . good food. Lots of sun. Cheap. I went with my husband before we were married. We're separated now.' Monica said, laughing, 'I guess we didn't have enough holidays together!'

'Oh, I know just what you mean,' Diane said in a sympathetic tone. 'You need lots of time to relax together for a relationship to survive these days. My boyfriend and I broke up late last year and I think it's because we never had more than a Sunday morning together for relaxation. I tried to get us away on a holiday, but he didn't even have time for a weekend off. That's what happens when you live in London; it's so hard to get out of it.' Diane paused and downed another glass of punch. 'And then, of course I got pregnant. That didn't help things either.'

'You got pregnant,' Monica said, paling.

'Yes, yes. It was stupid I know, but we all make mistakes. We used to get drunk and forget to use the stuff. You must know what it's like, don't you?' she said, looking at Monica rather helplessly.

'Did you have the child?' Monica asked, barely audible above the general roar of the party.

'Are you kidding? Me, have a baby? I couldn't, I didn't even consider it. We didn't even get on that well. He would have been a lousy father and I would have been a worse mother.'

'Oh,' said Monica, staring into her punch. 'I'm sorry.'

'What's there to be sorry about? Worse things can happen. I'm resilient, or so Siobhan tells me. You're tough, old girl, that's what she says to me. Tough I say, but not that tough. Oh, there's Barry, I'd better go and say hello. See you in a bit Monica.' Diane smiled confidently and walked off towards a good-looking man who had just appeared in the kitchen.

Monica leaned heavily on the fridge. Thinking about the space between her legs, the part of her body that had burned with such pain so recently, she remembered with terrible clarity how it had felt to be overwhelmed by the anaesthetic and what slow agony it had been to wake up on the hospital bed, her body throbbing with loss. Having never described it to anyone, until she spoke to Diane she was convinced that no one else would have felt the same thing. The experience had been pushed way way down inside herself.

Later that night a man who was trying to pick Monica up told her a long and rambling story about how when he was a boy his best friend had disappeared and they had all eventually decided that he'd been kidnapped and was dead. Years later another boy from the same street ran into someone in Edinburgh who seemed too much like Jeff for it to be a coincidence. He'd tried to find out as much as possible about this man, but the stranger was too reticent to give much away, a fact that made the other man all the more suspicious. Convinced that the person in Edinburgh was his long lost friend, he had come to the conclusion that, for some reason, Jeff had run away all those years ago. 'You know,' he said to Monica, 'I'd really like to see him again. Just to ask him why. Why did he run away? And where did he go?'

Monica went home alone that night. The next morning as she lay in the bath she thought about her new life. It looked good; her future was a blank page. Maybe she'd go to Spain with Diane and Siobhan. Diane had survived, so she should be able to as well. She had, she reminded herself, come from somewhere; she could edit her past but not deny it. With the abortion, something had ended. It was a most powerful metaphor for change.

Lois and the Ancients

LOIS'S LIFE HAS been punctuated by Egyptian hieroglyphics. Its various stages have been marked by strange involvements with cryptic designs from the ancient people of the Nile. For Lois, the writing on the wall is literally that of the blue Egyptian beetle, straight out of the Book of the Dead.

There is a photograph of Lois that was taken during her trip to Egypt. She is standing inside a tomb in the Valley of the Kings. The photograph is very dark but the symbols on the wall directly behind her are still visible. The columns of pictographs end halfway up Lois's legs and then, stretching across the wall, a banquet is depicted, complete with naked serving girls ministering to those dark, androgynous beauties who seem to have made up the Egyptian ruling classes. On Lois's right in the photograph stands the boyfriend she was travelling with at the time. He has struck what he considered to be a typical ancient Egyptian pose: his arms and legs are all bent at opposing angles, jutting out in a sort of bony and humorous version of a swastika.

In this photograph Lois herself is peering at the camera. She looks small, young, and like a tourist. She is sunburnt, round and very unlike the ancients who pose in straight lines over her head, or the modern Egyptians who wait patiently outside the tomb for her to pay them. Lois's affinity is with the symbols on the walls but it is not obvious in this or other photographs.

Lois has no Egyptian connections, as far as she knows. She is the granddaughter of farmworkers and history has never been one of her interests. She has no obvious link to the Book of the Dead. Ordinarily, Lois lives her life like most people and she is only very occasionally prone to acts of deviance. On a quiet Wednesday morning in the British Museum she once climbed into an Egyptian sarcophagus. She lay on her back on the cold timeless stone for a few brief moments before climbing back out.

The most serious problem in Lois's relatively problem-free life is that she has terrible trouble trying to find somewhere to live. The rental market dealing in small self-contained flats is out of her reach financially and the local housing bodies all see her as too single, too able, too young, and too uninsistent to house. So Lois has had to be content with the shifting, precarious, and increasingly less legal existence of a squatter. Her clothes, her bed, and her box of photographs and postcards from her one trip out of the country have moved with her from derelict property to boarded-up flat to unserviced nightmare and back again.

This unsettling lifestyle does not suit Lois at all. She is the kind of person who likes to know where she will be in three months' time, a not unusual personality trait, even amongst the young. Lois feels every time she gets her room sorted out, the photos and postcards stuck on the wall and her bed comfortably arranged, she has to pack it all up again and move on. This makes Lois nervous and unhappy.

'Let's move into this house,' Lois said to her friend Clara as they wandered around gazing into other people's warm sitting rooms.

'Why this house?' asks Clara. She, too, is tired of moving.

'It looks nice. We could get in through the back. It probably has electricity and everything.'

'Who do you think owns it? We want to be careful this time. No more moving into empty houses that belong to that Duke, or Lord, or whatever he is. He'll have us out in an instant, just like before.'

'That's right. I don't think he owns anything around here though,' Lois said to Clara, staring up at the house's big windows, her eyes following the unbroken line of the guttering. She was trying to imagine what the house was like inside and what she would look like in it, what it would be like to live there. 'It's kind of posh around here, Clara. The pavements are so clean.'

'Mmm. The neighbours won't be used to squatters. They'll probably form a vigilante group and hound us out in the middle of the night, like the time before last.'

'No,' said Lois, 'that was the time before the time before.'

'Oh,' said Clara, 'well, that's probably what they'll do anyway.'

While Lois and Clara stood outside the house and talked they watched what went on in the quiet street. Eventually they decided to move into the house.

They got in through the back late that night, and

then changed the lock of the front door. That took all night and so it was the next morning when Lois brought all her belongings to the house with the help of a friend with a van. Clara had put a piece of paper on the front door. It said. 'This property is legally occupied'.

Lois said to Clara, 'That sign will bring us to the attention of the neighbours. Let's take it down and hope they don't notice us. We only want to lead quiet lives, after all'.

'All right,' said Clara, and she went outside and took the sign down.

The house was very big and lovely with large, airy rooms and high ceilings. The services were all on and functioning and there were even carpets in one or two of the rooms. Everything about the house was in remarkably good shape, especially considering its age and that it had been empty for several years. Lois and Clara settled down to a springtime of home improvements. They did a bit of work on the garden and tried to dry out the basement which suffered from damp rising from no one knew where.

Without knowing who owned the house or what its fate, together with theirs, might be they worked on becoming more and more at home. Lois felt particularly attached to her bedroom. As the summer warmed up, her room remained cool, and there was always a sepulchral silence in it. The walls were panelled with dark heavy wood and were tremendously thick. Sunlight never fell on the north-facing rooms of the house, but they were well lit artificially. Lois felt happy there. She arranged her postcards of mummies and sphinxes on the wall in a way that pleased her and, as the summer progressed and she spent more time in the garden, she began to take on that round and sunburnt look that she had had in the photograph, which she stuck on to her wall as well.

Late one night, Lois awoke suddenly. She sat up, turned her light on and looked around the room. Getting out of bed and putting on her clothes, she walked to the furthest wall in the room, the one adjacent to the windows where the fireplace must have been. Lois decided that it was time for the heavy wooden panelling to come off the walls. She went downstairs to find the hammer, crow-bar, and wedge, then she set about carefully prizing the panelling off the wall.

The panelling itself was very old; it had probably been on the walls for several hundred years. The nails were thick and square and the plaster of the wall beneath was solid. Lois strained and banged and pulled for a long time before the first panel gave slightly. Just as it was beginning to come away, Clara walked into the room.

'What are you doing Lois?' she asked, rubbing her eyes and yawning. 'It's terribly late. I thought we were still working on the basement. It seems a shame to start something new before we've finished down there.'

'I want to get rid of these panels. They're too dark,' Lois said, although she wasn't really sure why she was taking them down.

'Oh,' said Clara, 'I like those panels. We could have traded rooms; mine doesn't have any panelling.'

'No, I like this room, I want to stay in it. I don't like

these panels though. You can have them after I take them down.' Lois was attempting to be very methodical and careful about removing the panels but, even so, as one came away there were splinters and sawdust.

'All right then,' Clara said walking out of the room. 'I'm going back to bed.'

A few minutes after Clara was gone, Lois succeeded in pulling the first panel off the wall. An enormous cloud of dust came out from underneath it, filling Lois's eyes and nose and smelling powerfully of the past. Lois kept working despite being unable to see properly and the panelling started to come away much more quickly once the first bit was removed. Every time she pulled a piece of the heavy wood away from the wall another large cloud of dust would come whooshing out. Lois got dirtier and dirtier and her eyes became reddened and sore. The smell grew stronger. It was a dry, musty smell that spoke of years of preservation, reminding Lois of something very particular that she could not quite place.

As soon as she got the last panel down Lois went off to have a bath, before the dust had settled. She shook herself out in the garden before getting into the warm water, then scrubbed her skin and shampooed her hair. Her body felt coated in dust and, despite her soaps and flannels, it continued to cling to her. Lois felt it was inside her body as well, filling her lungs and abdominal cavity. She drew the bath a second time and went through the whole process again. Once she had finished she felt marginally cleaner so she got out of the bath and dried herself off. She filled the tub again and dumped her clothes into it, then, clad in her towel, climbed the stairs back up to her bedroom. By then it was after dawn. Lois's entire room was covered in the thick disentombed dust: her bed, her clothes, the carpet. The smell was thick as well.

The panels were stacked in a pile where Lois had laid them, one by one, as she prized them away. The wall itself was there for Lois to gaze upon now. There were the vertical lines of hieroglyphics, scarab, bird, eye, lotus; there were the tall and slender men and women with that impenetrable, passive, and, at the same time, commanding expression on their faces; their sandled feet, their bejewelled ears and necks, their exquisitely long and lean arms stretching out towards the offerings of the naked serving girls or themselves making offerings to the mummies who were encased in gold and surrounded by jackal-headed minions.

Lois stood and looked at the wall for a long time, finally remembering where she had smelled the dust before. It was the same smell that hung in the air of the tombs in the Valley of the Kings. Ancient, dry, and scented ever so faintly with fragrant oils, paint, and gold: the smell of mummies and the wealthy dead. Lois went over to her bed and shook out the bedclothes. She climbed in underneath them and closed her eyes. In her last thoughts before she fell asleep she wondered who owned the house in which she was living and how long it would be before she and Clara were evicted.

The Unbearable Shortness of Holidays

IN PERUGIA ALL sensibility is lost. It floats away on the warm sectarian breeze that drifts up from the South becoming thinner and thinner as it crosses Europe. For the out-of-town, out-of-country visitor this hill-top town, surrounded by rich and fragrant farmland, can seem like nirvana.

'Ah,' sighed the tourist, 'there is no hurly-burly here.'

'Mmm,' sighed the other tourist, 'the only hustle is the evening rounds of the cafés and even then one can always find a seat.'

'Mmm.' The two tourists were in reflective mode, which they termed as the Italian mode. 'Somewhere someone must be working,' said one tourist to the other as she opened her lazy eyes and took a languid look around. 'But I can't see who.'

'Well,' the other replied, 'it's not me.' They both sighed again and went back to sleep over their Cinzano in the mid-day sun.

In Perugia the tourist need not be intrepid to discover the joys of the local environs. The cafés, bars and restaurants are easy to find; the atmosphere lulls without any effort. The wine is in the shops, the smell of flowers in the air, the doors of the churches open, and the lanes and byways are to be walked through. There is even a Roman aqueduct, conveniently placed across the fuchsia-laden slope. You don't have to look for anything – an indolent tourist's dream come true.

The day began like this: six o'clock, it was sunny, Elena woke up. The pigeons were cooing loudly, a cool breeze came through the shutters on the window. 'My God,' Elena thought, 'another day here. Another day away from my job. Another day to drink Campari and wear dark glasses and smile. My God.' She lay still in her narrow bed listening to the morning sounds that drifted through her window.

In the next bed Lucia lay sleeping. The two women had adopted Italian names for the duration of the holiday. In fact, Lucia was dreaming that she was an Italian running through a field of mimosa. At one end of the field a small village fair was taking place. There was only one table at the fair. It was draped with a banner that read, 'The Revolutionary Communist Party of Italy'. The table was laden with food. The Italian communists were selling Gnocchi alla Gorgonzola – little balls of heaven smothered in blue, briny delight. Lucia smiled in her sleep.

After another hour the two women had risen and were making their way through the morning rituals of showering and dressing. Elena kept collapsing on to the bed with her copy of *L'Uomo*, a men's fashion magazine. Lucia was trying to read Shelley but found she could not concentrate whatever the time of day, the lazy morning, the quiet afternoon, nor the peaceful evening. Every day in the café she would bring out her book and begin to read. 'Many a green isle needs must be/In the deep wide sea of Misery,' and every day she yawned and stretched and looked up from her book at the people passing by.

'Elena,' she said, 'I can't concentrate on anything, not even a poem.'

'No,' said Elena, who didn't attempt to read, 'there's too much to look at, smell and drink.'

After dressing, the two women floated out of their pensione and wandered over to the coffee bar where they ate custard-filled pastries and drank cappuccino, weak tea and juice for breakfast. They stood inside the coffee bar while they ate, alongside the older men, cloth-capped and short, and the younger women who were smartly dressed for business. The tourists' eyes were steamed open by the coffee machine which hissed and puffed as they stood without speaking, listening to the morning conversation around them. What did the words these Italians used mean as they flew back and forth over the sleepy heads of Elena and Lucia? The elderly man in the felt vest – was he talking about the weather which was perfect, or the coffee which was aromatic, or the day ahead which to Elena and Lucia seemed magical? Or was he talking about politics and the strength of the Italian economy, 'Il Sorpasso,' the money in the North and the poverty in the South? And what did he do during the war?

Elena was nodding off over her coffee so Lucia suggested they get another cup from the busy man behind the coffee bar and move to one of the rickety tables outside. There they sat in the morning sun, Elena napping behind her dark glasses, Lucia examining an English newspaper.

'Home has never looked so bleak,' Lucia said to Elena. 'I can't imagine why I live there.' Elena, looking up, let her dark glasses slide to the tip of her nose so she could peer over them at Lucia.

'You live there, Lucia, because it is home,' she replied, pushing her dark glasses back up on to the bridge of her nose.

'Yes, of course, it is home. But it does seem terrible from here. Look at this weather report. It has been raining all week and will continue to rain all next week. The government is introducing austerity to the poor – isn't that a bit like introducing the Pope to God? Look at this Elena, look at this,' Lucia said, holding up the newspaper and pointing at the headline, mass suicide on london bridge: twenty brokers dead. Can you explain that?'

'They'd probably been caught fiddling or something,' Elena replied. 'I wonder how high the suicide rate is here?'

'Suicide?' she laughed. 'In heaven?' She shook her head.

'Lucia,' Elena said firmly, lowering her dark glasses once more. 'One tourist's heaven can be a resident's hell.'

'Hmm,' muttered Lucia folding up her newspaper and resolving not to buy another. After sipping her coffee she cleared her throat and, simultaneously, cleared her mind of unemployment, racism, and decline.

Elena and Lucia spent their days repeating a

seemingly endless cycle of enormously pleasurable activities. They would rise, breakfast, and then spend the morning wandering around Perugia with their mouths open. They looked in the shops, toured the churches, wandered along the hillside spotting remnants of the Etruscan city from a time before. They sniffed the scented breeze and followed their noses to a shop where they bought food for a picnic lunch: olives, artichokes, marinated tomatoes, bread, Gorgonzola and Orvieto vino bianco secco. Then they'd find a park or a piece of grass in a churchyard where they would sit in the sun and eat and drink and maybe chat to other tourists while quietly and slowly falling asleep. The mid-day zephyr would play along the hem of Elena's skirt, sliding up her leg like a warm hand. Lucia dreamed of Mario Lanza; she could hear 'Ave Maria' in her sleep.

After a while they gathered their things and walked back up to the town centre, climbing the narrow steps that wind up through the buildings, past medieval churches and under Etruscan arches. Perugia is like that, all up and down, steps instead of streets; there is a lift that travels from one part of town up on the hill to another part down below. The tourist stumbles upon sudden views; rounding a corner you are greeted by the valley and surrounding hills. They call out to you like a dream of Italy, too lovely to be real. The poplars stand straight like boy soldiers; the tourist can lead an enchanted life, not like home at all.

Back in the huge cobbled square that forms the town centre Lucia and Elena would spend the rest of the afternoon sitting in one of the six or seven outdoor cafés that line the square. They'd nibble on bar snacks and drink Cinzano and Campari and aqua minerale and coffee whilst attempting to read or write on postcards. They'd speak in broken English to the people at the next table, foreigners studying at the University for Strangers, one of the city's institutes of learning. Elena felt that she wanted to move to Perugia and be a stranger at the university herself.

The afternoon sun shone down on the town square. Lucia hiked her dress up, exposing her brown legs. 'Elena,' she said, 'I don't want to go home.'

'Neither do I, neither do I.'

'Maybe we could ring up our bosses and tell them we're not coming back. We could ring our banks and have them transfer our accounts to the Bank of Perugia. We could find someone to move into our flats. Then we could stay here forever. Growing old in Perugia, Elena, we won't get rheumatism here! We won't end up starving on tiny pensions. Oh, oh, we can be Italians and wear dark glasses and study Gramsci and discuss Fellini and eat fettucini Alfredo until we die!'

Elena opened her eyes. 'Lucia,' she said, 'this is a holiday. We are tourists. Life isn't like this, Italy isn't like this. How would we live, we'd have to get jobs, who'd be our friends, what about our responsibilities?' Elena sighed and shook her head slowly in the afternoon sun. 'We're tourists here.' Lucia sighed then as well, feeling great sadness as she stared into her Martini bianco. Life seemed so perfect.

The afternoon became early evening and the two women left the café and walked back to the pensione. Once again, they showered and dressed with the windows wide open on to the sunset. The smell of cooking floated up from a kitchen nearby as they headed off to find a restaurant for dinner. Lucia and Elena would spend a good hour examining menus and debating about where they should eat.

'Bruschetta,' said Elena. '1 demand bruschetta. It's bruschetta or nothing, I swear!'

'Mmm,' said Lucia, '1 want zucchini. I want tortellini. I want it all!' Eventually, they settled on somewhere and had a long and drawn-out meal, arguing with the people at the next table while being either charmed or ignored by the waiters. Around midnight they made their way home, giggling as they tripped on the cobblestones, stopping for gelati on the way. The next day they woke up early and everything began again.

Eventually, the day came when the return flight was scheduled to take off and no matter how much they objected, swearing to the skies and cursing the great God of Work, they were on it, like dutiful daughters.

The next year Elena and Lucia met in a London pub to plan their forthcoming holiday. It was a dark and raining February night.

'Well, where shall we go this year my dear?' Elena asked Lucia.

'To Italy, of course!' replied Lucia, shocked by Elena's question which she felt implied there was an alternative.

'We'll go to Perugia.'

'Again?' said Elena.

'What do you mean, "again"?' said Lucia, her voice full of surprise and hurt.

'Well, we could go to Greece and sun ourselves

amongst the ruins, or we could go to Spain and eat paella, or even Portugal, I hear it's nice and not crowded.'

'But what about the cafés in the town square? What about our walks on the hills? Our day trips to Lago Trasimere?' Lucia stared into her pint of beer moodily.

Two months later she and Elena were on the plane, heading for, ultimately, Perugia.

When they arrived they found the very same little pensione where they'd stayed the previous year. The first evening they went back to their favourite restaurant where the head waiter recognised them, greeting them by name. Lucia smiled broadly at Elena once they were seated.

'Ah, it is paradise. Aren't you pleased that I was so keen to come back? We'll have a wonderful fortnight, I know it.'

'Yes,' replied Elena. 'We will.' They spent the evening lingering over a tremendous meal and then stopped for gelati as they stumbled home.

In the morning, they awoke early as the birds began to sing and the first rays of sun broke through. The sounds of the town filtered up into their room. Lucia stretched her limbs out on the bed. Elena was already up, getting ready for a shower.

'I think,' said Lucia, 'I think I'll have a gelato for breakfast.'

'A what?' replied Elena, aghast.

'A gelato, Elena. I want a gelato for breakfast. A pink one. Then we can go and have the brioche and coffee like we always do.'

'A gelato,' said Elena thoughtfully. 'Well, why not? You're on holiday, you can have whatever you want!'

So the two women set off to find Lucia ice cream for breakfast. Luckily, one eager entrepreneur had anticipated this foreigner's early morning urge for sweetness and had opened his gelato counter at dawn. Lucia asked him for a pink one, a triple, and they sat on the steps of the medieval town hall while she ate it. The sun grew steadily stronger while the two women made their way to a coffee bar where they stood in the steam of the espresso machine and drank cups of hot coffee and ate brioche. They spent the morning reacquainting themselves with Perugia and then, as before, bought themselves the ingredients of a picnic for lunch. Taking a bus out of town, they disembarked at the first poppy-covered hill they saw and, sitting in the shade of a Lombardy poplar, ate.

'The air is so soft,' Lucia said, 'it's like ice cream. Soft and smooth and delicious.'

'Ice cream?' said Elena, slightly annoyed. 'But ice cream is cold and here the air is so warm.'

'Like warm ice cream then,' replied Lucia, her head tilted back and her face in the sun. 'Melted.'

They spent the afternoon dozing on the hillside, listening to the sounds of the country. In the distance a farmer was toiling. He glanced their way from time to time.

At about half-past four they arose and began to walk back into Perugia. Three-quarters of the way there Lucia said, 'When we get back into town, do you know what I'd like?'

'A Cinzano,' said Elena greedily. 'Or maybe a Campari. Vino bianco. Vino rosso . . . vino . . .'

'A gelato,' interrupted Lucia. 'A green one.' Then

she smiled to herself, a large benevolent grin, the fat smile of a happy woman.

'And you shall have it, I decree,' replied Elena. When they reached the town they wandered towards the centre through the cobblestone byways and up the narrow staircases. Then they found a table at a café in the town square. When the waiter came over to them, Elena asked for a Martini bianco secco and Lucia asked for gelato, the green kind, in a dish with whipped cream. They sat in the late-afternoon sun and laughed at each other.

The next morning after they'd showered and dressed and were on their way to breakfast, Lucia made a slight detour into the corner shop where she persuaded the proprietor, with broken Italian and much gesticulating, to sell her a gelato. Elena had assumed that Lucia had gone into the shop for something much more basic, like tampons or tissues, but tried not to show her surprise. Lucia ate the ice cream like a starved person as they walked in the direction of the coffee bars.

The same thing happened on the way to their lunchtime picnic and then, as they were making a tour of the restaurant menus trying to decide where to have their evening meal, Lucia slipped away while Elena was musing over the tortellini and came back licking a gelato. A blue one this time.

'Lucia!' exclaimed Elena, alarmed. 'Another gelato?'

'So?' she replied defensively. 'Another gelato, so what? I like them. Do you mind?'

'Not at all, my dear, but it would spoil my appetite.'

'Well, it doesn't spoil mine,' answered Lucia. 'Not one bit.'

Over the course of the next couple of days Lucia ate more Italian ice cream than most Italians would eat in a month, maybe even a year. She ate all the flavours of gelati she could find then she began to comb the city for more. Pistachio, lemon, orange, fruit, coffee, rum, chocolate, amaretto, strawberry, peach, chocolate-chip, blueberry, blackberry; and all the alcoholic varieties: Lucia was compiling a mental list. On the occasions she was unable to find a new flavour she was not put off, but would take the opportunity to reassess what she'd thought of it the first time.

Elena watched with increasing dismay. She tried to curb her friend's new habit with subtlety at first.

'Too much sugar is not good for your skin,' she said gently.

To which Lucia replied, 'So what?'

'Too many dairy products are not good for your blood or your digestion.'

To which Lucia replied, 'Bollocks.'

'You'll get ice-cream gag,' she tried one afternoon mid-gelato, 'and then you'll never want to eat it again.'

'No way,' replied Lucia. 'That will never happen to me. I love it too much.'

'You're telling me,' whispered Elena under her breath.

In the early evening of the fourth day when Lucia was about to embark on her sixth gelato of the day, Elena could stand it no longer. 'YOU'LL GET FAT!' she shouted as loudly as she could.

'I DON'T CARE!' shouted Lucia back.

The next morning Elena packed up her belongings and moved to another room in the pensione. She began to tour Perugia and the environs on her own. She took a day-trip to Florence and stood and stared at Michelangelo's David for several hours. She travelled around the countryside swimming in the gentle lakes and walking over the quiet hills. One day she went to Assisi to see the frescoes of Giotto. There she met an Englishman who offered to buy her a gelato. She thanked him but said no and took the bus back to Perugia. Then she went looking for her friend.

Lucia was seated at a café in the square. She'd grown quite brown in the days since Elena had seen her last. In front of her on the table was a large silver bowl full of ice cream, fruit and whipped cream. When Elena spotted her she was poised to dive into it with a big silver spoon.

'Hello there,' said Elena. 'How are you?'

Lucia dropped her spoon. It fell into the whipped cream and disappeared like a plane flying into a cloud. She looked up at Elena and then back down at the ice cream. 'Hello,' she said without looking back up. 'Where did it go?'

'Look,' said Elena assertively. 'I've got something to say to you.'

'Oh don't bother. I know what it is already. Well, I'm not going home this time. I'm not going back to that dark mucky place. The ice cream is lousy there.'

'I'm not asking you to come back,' said Elena. 'What I'm asking is why. Why are you doing it this way? You could have found a quicker way.'

'A quicker way to what?' asked Lucia, looking up. 'A quicker way to eat ice cream?'

'No, a quicker way to freeze time,' she replied. Lucia

looked back down at her ice cream. The swirls of colour, cheerful bits of fruit, and mountains of whipped cream looked heavenly to her. In the ice cream she could see a better world, one that would fit her, that she could eat up and feel happy in. In gelato there is certainty, a priceless commodity in a post-modern world. 'I don't want it to melt away,' she said to Elena who remained impassive behind her dark glasses.

'Neither do I, Lucia, neither do I.'

The Fact-Finding Mission

DORA CAME HOME and found the note on the kitchen table. It said, in large bold letters, **THE ENGLISH ARE REPRESSED BECAUSE THEY HAVE NO LAKES.** Dora sighed when she read this and wondered if it was true. There are a few lakes, somewhere, but they are all kept in the Lake District, as if one can't allow lakes just anywhere. If lakes are not kept where they belong everyone might start throwing off their clothes and jumping in and we all know where that would lead.

Dora sighed and sat down. She was very tired. She had been out on one of her fact-finding missions. As usual, she had found there were no facts to find. 'One day,' thought Dora, 'one day I'll give up my search and then where will we all be?' She sighed again, then picked up the note and turned it over. On the other side it said, **THE ENGLISH ARE REPRESSED BECAUSE THEY HAVE NO MOUNTAINS.** 'No mountains and no lakes,' thought Dora. 'How true.' She slumped off to bed.

In the morning Dora got up, not at all refreshed, and set off on one of her fact-finding missions again. Dora strove to find facts nearly every day now. She felt she was being driven mad by misinformation. 'There are so many lies everywhere,' she often said. 'They are lying about everything these days. Wars, identities, deaths. I can't believe anything. I must seek out the facts. I must find out the truth.'

Dora knew she was being a bit ridiculous, but she was unemployed so that kind of thing didn't matter to her. Besides, when she set out on her fact-finding missions she felt really terrific, like Simone de Beauvoir, or Mrs Emma Peel, or Isabelle Bird. She'd put on her favourite clothes and pretend the No. 77 bus was a Bat-bus and that her umbrella had a gun in it. Not that Dora would ever actually try to shoot anyone. Well, no one, except of course, The Liars, if she could find them, wherever and whoever they are.

Dora took the No. 77 bus up the Strand and got out in front of the High Court. She already knew there were no truths, or facts, there but she went anyway, from time to time, just in case. As she was about to head through the doors, she spotted a note on the wall. It said, YOU HATE THE NEW TELECOM PHONE KIOSKS MERELY BECAUSE YOU ARE RESISTANT TO CHANGE. On reading this Dora knew she would not find any facts that day, so she gave up before she had started and walked down the Strand towards Waterloo Bridge, where there are no facts, only sandwich bars and shops selling briefcases.

Dora had been unemployed for a rather long time. She was very poor and her activities were restricted for the most part to listening to the radio, fact-finding missions, talking to friends and other free or very cheap things, like walking in the rain, making up theories about her compatriots, and worrying. She did a lot of the latter. Her friends in work found her increasingly difficult. No one could understand these fact-finding missions.

'Except the person or persons who keep leaving me those notes,' said Dora aloud in the kitchen. She sighed heavily. 'When will I find the place where the facts are? When will I discover where the truth is kept? In the same place as they keep the jobs, I'll bet.' She decided to go and see one of her friends.

Dora went to visit Nora, who lived just around the corner. Nora had also been unemployed for a very long time and she had recently decided to give up applying for jobs and devote her life to the pursuit of complete happiness. This did not involve happiness-finding missions, but it did involve a lot of soul-searching and some heavy-duty reading. Nora was slowly realising that she could not actually afford anything that she thought would give her complete happiness, like a trip to the Soviet Union, for example.

'Oh Nora,' said Dora, 'you're so materialistic. Happiness is one of the free things.'

'Shut up Dora,' screamed Nora, 'it, is not! Happiness costs lots and lots of money, and besides, wanting to fly to Rio isn't materialistic. Don't try to tell me that your fact-finding missions make you happy. I have the ease in life, but none of the good things to enjoy in that ease. I have the leisure, but none of the leisurables. I can't even afford to play squash!'

'Oh Nora,' said Dora, 'Don't be so miserable. I didn't know you were so miserable. If only I could tell you the facts. If only I could explain things.'

'Dora,' said Nora, 'you're a real dreamer. Even more

of a dreamer than I am. At least I'm trying to pursue something that will get me somewhere.'

'Oh,' said Dora. She felt rather depressed. She got up and kissed Nora on the cheek and then left. As she was unlocking her bicycle, she saw the note taped to the cross-bar. It said, **THE ARISTOCRACY IS EXPANDING AT THE SPEED OF LIGHT.** Dora got on her bicycle and rode home.

When Dora got home, she took a bath. As she lay there in the hot water, she thought about Nora and what she had said that morning. Dora didn't think Nora was being very realistic.

'How can you find complete happiness if you don't know the facts? How could you ever be sure that what it was that gave you complete happiness wasn't, in fact, something horrible and monstrous? Factually unsubstantiated happiness would be so risky: any day you might find out the facts and bang your happiness would be gone.' Dora submerged herself in the bath water. She wished she understood things better.

When Dora got out of the bath she found a note pinned to her towel. It said, **ALL HISTORY IS THE SAME: RUTHLESS, BITTER, AND MEANINGLESS.** 'Ha!' thought Dora, 'is that a fact?' She dried herself off and went into her room and tried to plan the next day's fact-finding missions. But she was running low on ideas and decided to get back into the bath. When she got out of the bath again, quite a while later, there was another note pinned to her towel. It said, **THE UNEMPLOYED WRINKLE MORE EASILY THAN THE EMPLOYED.**

Dora got up the next day and thought about what she should do. So far that month she'd been to The City,

Highgate Cemetery, The Granville Arcade, Southwark Town Hall, The British Library, Hyper-Hyper, the Centrale Café, 'Cats', several branches of W.H. Smith, Kennington Police Station, the Polytechnic of Central London, and many, many other places, each of which had seemed potential and, in some cases, promising fact-sources until Dora actually investigated them. At the end of each mission she was always forced to conclude the same thing: that facts are, indeed, elusive little items.

So, Dora decided she would ride the Circle Line until she found the truth. She got on at Victoria and began to circle central London hoping to pick up some facts rather like a vulture circles its prey. At Paddington she noticed the note stuck on the window behind her. It said, **THERE IS NO SUCH THING AS A FACT; ALL THAT EXISTS IS ABSOLUTE FICTION.**

Dora read this note and then read it again. She sat on her seat on the Circle Line train and wondered if the note was true. If it was true it meant that she would now have nothing to do every day, no mission in life, no reason to get up. So, Dora chose to ignore it, as people ignore even the most obvious of messages. The Circle Line carried Dora away from Paddington Station. And then, eventually, it brought her back again.

The Moose

SHE ARRIVED BY aeroplane on a sunny January day
at lunchtime. They flew in over British Columbia, a
province which consists of endless mountain ranges,
logging developments, and small towns nestled in the
valleys. As the plane flew further north distances between the increasingly tiny towns became greater and
the landscape grew more vast and impressive. Irene
felt glad to be leaving the South behind. She had been
up to the North before and imagined she knew what
it was like: empty and mysterious, more legends and
myths than people. The North is the last frontier in
Canada, consistently unconquerable.

The plane landed on the small Whitehorse runway.
As everyone stood stretching, yawning, and reaching
for their parkas and sheepskin coats, Irene shivered.
The doors of the plane were opened and they piled
on to the tarmac. Once out in the sharp, clean air she
breathed in slowly and, with a shock, felt the hair and
skin in her nose and throat freeze. She breathed out
again quickly and, with relief, felt them thaw.

The sunlight was brilliant and blinding as it reflected on the windows of the terminal. The air itself was
prickly, as if full of ice crystals, and very dry in contrast

to the bog-like climate of Vancouver. She followed the crowd, none of whom seemed to be alarmed by respiration problems as they were herded into the building.

Irene was able to recognise the man who had come to meet her as he was holding a sign bearing her name, 'Irene Jacobs'. The man was very large and wore a huge grey parka that reached his knees.

'Hello,' said Irene.

'Hello,' he said. 'I'm Harry. Do you want some coffee? Was your flight all right? We'll need to wait a bit for the bags.'

'Yes,' Irene replied. 'I'd like some coffee. The flight was fine.' She paused and then asked, 'What's the temperature here today?'

'Oh, it's not very cold, only −20°C or so. It's warmed up a bit since last week. We had a fortnight's stretch of −40°C. Haven't you ever been here before?'

'No,' replied Irene.

'You're in for a shock,' replied Harry, laughing. Irene felt stupid, new, and uninitiated.

'When was the last time you were in the South?' Irene asked Harry as she sipped her coffee.

'Well, my wife and I went to Edmonton last year and we're going Outside again next month. We try to get Outside once a year. Mind you, we're always glad to come home. It gets weirder and weirder out there, I swear.' If the rest of the world is 'Outside', thought Irene, then it follows that the Yukon must be the 'Inside' making it sound like an exclusive club, or perhaps, a prison.

By the time Irene's bags arrived in the terminal and she and Harry were heading towards the truck, it was almost 1:30 p.m. and the sun was going down. 'The days are short here,' Irene commented.

'No,' Harry said, 'the sun just goes down early and comes up late. Still have to be at work at 7:00 a.m.' They drove out of the airport and along the ridge, then took the road down into town.

Whitehorse lies in a valley on the banks of the Yukon River. On the colder winter days when the rest of the Yukon sky is clear this valley fills with ice-fog, frozen exhaust mingled with wood smoke from the town's cars and houses. As Harry and Irene headed into town it became increasingly difficult to see but Harry seemed to know where to go.

'We'll just pick up the kids and head out to the house,' he said. 'I've got to get back down here for a meeting.'

'OK,' said Irene as they drove past houses that looked warm and friendly, nestled close together in the snow. 'Why is it so hard to see?'

'Ice-fog.'

'Oh. What's that?'

'It's what people get lost in,' said Harry looking at Irene out of the corner of his eye. After a couple of minutes they pulled into a driveway. Getting out of the car, Irene followed Harry through a door in the side of the house. Inside they met a woman who pointed towards two small boys and said, 'These are Barry and Bobby. Barry doesn't like to eat much and Bobby, well, he's very sweet.' The woman shook Irene's hand firmly and said, 'Good luck.'

Barry and Bobby were already bundled into their parkas, gloves, hats, scarves and boots so Harry and

Irene carried them out to the truck. The children sat in between the adults on the big, wide seat, so heavily dressed they could hardly move. Irene envied them, it wasn't just the little hairs inside her nose that were freezing. Harry backed the truck down the drive and began to head out of town.

'Hello,' she said to Barry and Bobby. 'How old are you Barry?'

'Four,' he said. Irene smiled.

'How old are you Bobby?'

'Baby doesn't talk,' said Barry. 'He's only one.'

'Oh,' she replied, unable to think of what to say next.

Harry was watching her.

They sat in silence for about ten miles. The truck climbed back up the hill and turned on to the highway that ran along the ridge. Irene stared out the window into the darkness. Occasionally they'd pass some form of life on the side of the road, a garage and café, a rather well-lit junkyard, the odd house. The road was fairly straight, slightly hilly, and unpaved but so frozen it was smooth.

'I wish we were doing this in the daytime so I could see where we are going,' Irene said to Harry who was absorbed by the driving.

'There's not much to see,' he answered. 'Just skinny trees and big dogs and dead animals on the side of the road.'

'Oh,' said Irene. Barry and Bobby seemed to be asleep.

Wondering if they had suffocated under their bulky wrappings, she leant over to have a better look at them. But both boys were breathing and Bobby was actually awake. He looked at her silently with large brown eyes.

'Hello,' she said. He smiled.

After another ten miles or so of the same untenanted landscape, they turned off the main road and headed into the trees. 'This is Wolf Creek,' said Harry. 'This is where the house is. I'll take you in and show you how everything works. Then I'll have to go back into town.'

'OK by me,' Irene said cheerfully. 'This is going to be fun.' She stared out of the window at the moonlit trees. Irene could hear Harry's beard scrape against his parka as he turned his head to look at her.

The drive up to the house was long and narrow, a badly cared for road full of holes and paved with ice. Harry drove up it confidently and when they reached the dark house swung the truck around.

'Here we are kids,' she said, opening the door. Irene unbuckled Bobby's seat belt, lifted him out and carried him up an icy set of wooden steps that led to the door of the house while Harry followed behind with the keys. Irene went inside and fumbled to find the light, but before she could, it was on and there stood Barry saying, 'It's over here. This is my house.' Smiling sourly Irene went back outside to get her bags.

Once everything had been brought inside Harry led Irene around showing her all the switches and taps and giving instructions on how to work the appliances. They went down into the basement and Harry stopped in front of the furnace.

'This is your lifeline,' he said. 'Without it you and

those boys will freeze. It's a wood-burning furnace: you see these logs?' He pointed to a large and neat pile of trees, denuded of branches and bark, that sat in the corner. 'The furnace requires one of these every few hours or several of them a couple of times a day. You open this door', he said, opening it and giving her a brief glimpse of hell, 'and shove them in head first. Don't forget.'

After a few more brief explanations Harry said, 'Well, I'm off. My number is beside the phone in case you need any help. There's a note from Barry and Bobby's mum there too. They'll be back in the afternoon a week from tomorrow. Good luck.' He smiled and was gone, leaving Irene alone with the boys.

The house was based on the A-frame design but with extra bits attached so it was more like an M-frame. The bedrooms were up in the peaks of the roof with small triple-glazed windows and thick carpet. The kitchen was well-equipped and stocked with enough food for a month. The back room, the one they had come in through, was full of boots, skis, a sled, a toboggan and other winter necessities. The freezer was also in this room and Irene opened it to find what looked like an entire moose hacked up and frozen in small packages. On the wall above the freezer hung several rifles.

Wandering through the house, Irene went into the sitting room and found Barry and Bobby sitting in front of the television. They were watching a rerun of 'The Munsters', thumbs set firmly in their mouths. The sitting room had several comfy chairs, a sofa, a dining-table and a piano. The room took up most of the front of the M: the walls sloped up to a high point and the huge, curtainless windows looked out onto the trees making the house feel very exposed. Reflected in the window were Barry and Bobby, their faces made blue by the light of the television. Beyond them there was nothing.

Irene turned around and surveyed the rest of the room. On the wall above the entrance to the kitchen hung the head of a moose, its great set of antlers still intact. He stared down with huge, limpid, brown, moose eyes set into a big, rounded, moose head. Irene thought he looked sad and slightly dopey. She could imagine him standing in the wild outside the window, his enormous warm bulk held up by skinny legs and knobbly knees.

'Bullwinkle,' she said out loud. 'You'll keep me company.'

'What?' said Barry with his thumb still in his mouth.

'Nothing,' she replied. 'Are you hungry?'

'No,' said Barry.

'Oh. Well maybe Bobby is.'

'Yep. Baby's always hungry.' On hearing that Bobby took his thumb out of his mouth and, pulling his eyes away from Herman Munster, smiled at Irene. She walked back into the kitchen.

In the Yukon, there are two seasons: summer, which is light and windy with 24-hour daylight, and winter, which is long, dark, and formidable. In between there are very brief and violent intervals when everything either freezes or thaws overnight. The time elsewhere known as 'spring' is particularly shocking. The thaw sets in and, suddenly, the rock-hard ground becomes thick with disgusting muck, capable of swamping a four-wheel drive. The frost recedes and the permafrost is prone to the heaves, accomplishing Herculean feats like picking up a large stretch of hitherto straight road and throwing it thirty-five feet to the left. The most extraordinary spectacle by far is when the rivers break up. The ice, which may be many feet thick, begins to crack and move downriver producing a terrifying cacophony of noise; groaning, screeching, and crashing. To newcomers it may appear that Armageddon has arrived.

But when Irene landed in the Yukon it was mid-January and spring was far away. Like most good Canadians, she knew all about the North, but had never seen it. She came to the Yukon to make money and thought of baby-sitting Barry and Bobby as the first step. To her the North was a foreign land where if she couldn't get rich by mining gold, she could at least make a good living by serving beer to those who were.

On her first day, daylight had come and gone in the space of a few hours. There was no wind and no snow and the temperature could drop at any moment to well below −40°C where it might stay for days on end. Whitehorse itself remains quite lively in January, the bars are busy until late at night and people go about business undeterred. But to Irene, twenty miles out of town, in a big house with two small children, surrounded by trees and perpetual darkness, it seemed as though the world had stopped and there was no one else left alive. It was definitely more than she'd bargained for. And so unbelievably quiet as well.

That first evening Barry wouldn't eat anything so she fed Bobby and read them both a long story.

'That's dumb,' Barry said, 'things just don't happen that way. Can I watch television?'

'No,' said Irene, 'read a book.'

'No,' replied Barry. 'When's my mummy coming back? I don't like you.' Bobby tugged at Irene's sweater. When she looked down at him, he smiled.

After putting them to bed and stoking the furnace, a task she was not about to forget, Irene turned the television back on. Being so far from anywhere meant that the only channel available was the CBC and whatever was on looked dull, so she turned it off. She sat with the lights on and stared at the window, wishing there were curtains to pull. In the reflection she could see the head of the moose. He was staring at her staring at him in the window. Beyond that was the dark night.

They spent the next morning colouring and when the sun came up Irene announced to the children that they were going for a walk. Barry became impatient while she was putting on Bobby's coat, boots, and all the other clothes that he needed in order to survive the elements. She carried the small boy outside, down the stairs, and then went back to fetch the sled.

The sun was shining and the air was crisp and cold. Irene became used to it quickly as the inside of her nose froze and thawed with reassuring regularity. They walked past the big windows of the sitting room and headed out through the trees. It was tough going as there was little snow, lots of broken branches and stubby sawn-off stumps blocking the path of the sled.

'I'm cold,' said Barry.

'We'll warm up as we walk,' Irene replied.

'No we won't,' he retorted, 'it's too cold to warm up just like that.'

'Look at that tree Barry, isn't it a strange shape? What does it remind you of?' She pointed to an oddly bent tree on the left.

'Nothing,' said Barry. They struggled on through the woods. The sun shone weakly as they passed skinny tree after skinny tree. They seemed to go on forever.

'Where are we going?' asked Barry. 'I'm bored.'

'OK,' said Irene, 'we'll go back.' She felt relieved; she was beginning to think they'd get lost. Her feet were cold, her cheeks were smarting, and the landscape was a little too empty. They made a swoop around a couple of trees and headed back the way they had come, which was, in fact, hardly any distance at all. The house was less than one hundred yards away. As they struggled back towards it Irene heard a quiet thud behind her. Turning around she saw that Bobby had fallen off the sled. He was lying on his back with his arms and legs spread out around him, too heavily dressed to move. He smiled sweetly and attempted to raise his arms when Irene reached down to pick him up.

Back inside, she tried to persuade Barry to eat lunch but nothing tempted him.

'Peanut butter sandwiches?' Nope.

'Toasted sandwiches?' Nope.

'Macaroni?' Nope.

'Eggs?' Nope.

'Soup?' Definitely not. In the end he agreed to eat some cheese. Irene left him sitting at the table mutilating a piece of bright orange Cheddar and took Bobby upstairs for his nap. He'd eaten all his lunch and was sleepy.

They passed that afternoon quietly, ploughing through book after book, colouring, drawing pictures, and, eventually, building a fort. After yet another unsuccessful meal that Barry refused to eat and Bobby accepted gracefully, Irene let them watch television while she had a go at the piano. Bobby wanted to sit near Barry on the sofa and, when Barry would not let him, demonstrating his lack of enthusiasm by bashing Bobby on the head, the baby began to holler. She continued to play 'Summertime' while Bobby screamed. Stopping, Irene tried to console him. Bobby sobbed and looked at Barry who was watching 'Animal Kingdom', unrepentant. None of her efforts to soothe the baby succeeded, including a promise of sweeties, so Irene went back to the piano and played Cole Porter and Irving Berlin, drowning out Bobby's wails.

Later that night, after she had turned off the television and was sitting on the sofa with a book, Irene looked up at the black window. The moose now appeared to be smiling at her. ' Asshole,' she mumbled.

That was the shape her days took; arguments with Barry over food, unsuccessful outings, and Bobby made inconsolable by cruel brotherly acts of Barry's. Irene spent every evening alone with the moose. His eyes looked progressively more moist and alive at the end of each day and, one evening, as she tried to avoid his gaze, she thought she saw him blink. Without looking back at the window she got up and turned off the light. In the dark there was no reflection in the excessively large windows. She sat back down on the settee and stared out at the absolute darkness of the cold Yukon night, wondering what had happened to the aurora borealis.

Once she had sat long enough for her eyes to adjust she discovered that the darkness was not so complete. The moon shone, and in the partial light the landscape was eerily fraught with shadow and movement. Irene thought she could see hundreds of moose moving through the trees, big, angry animals in the frozen peopleless night. She turned the light back on and there he was again, staring at her balefully with just a hint of reproach in his eyes.

Irene did not know a single person within a 1,700 mile radius of where she was staying. She felt trapped in the incomprehensively vast wilderness with two children whom she could not abandon, let alone keep amused. Evading boredom became increasingly difficult. She played the piano more often and louder, cooked elaborate meals that Barry would not eat, and began retiring to bed very early to avoid the eyes of the moose who hung over her life so omnisciently.

On the fourth day Irene decided to take the children and drive into town. As soon as the sun rose she bundled them up and into the truck that had sat in the drive since she arrived. Managing to get it started, she drove into town without any problems. In the shopping centre she felt as if she was seeing adult people for the first time in months. She wanted to sit in one of Whitehorse's many bars, drink herself stupid, and then tell somebody about the moose. But instead, she bought chocolates for the children and headed home.

Irene found the truck large and unwieldy. The front of it stuck out a long way, as did the twelve-foot bed, and the gears tick was almost half her height. As she turned off the main road she began to worry and by the time she was actually at the beginning of the drive to the house she was trembling with fear. Both Barry and Bobby were asleep, satiated with the excitement of their trip into town.

Cautiously, Irene began to drive up the icy, rutted road. Three-quarters of the way there she felt the wheels slip on the frozen troughs and before she knew what was happening the truck escaped her control. It slid violently from left to right and everything she did to stop it made matters worse. After a moment, the duration of an ice age, the truck ceased moving. It was wrapped around a tree next to the house and would not go forward, nor backwards. The children woke up and began to wail. Irene got out of the truck, cursed it, kicked it and the tree, then wept, but the vehicle would not budge.

That night Irene dreamed that the moose spoke to her from his position of honour overhead. 'Are you dumb!' he said gleefully. 'And you thought I looked dumb! I'm going to get you, you know. Just like they got me. There's nobody around for miles. The darkness muffles noise. You're all alone up here, all alone. Nature, and that includes me, is not benevolent up here. It's too big to be kind: too cold.'

Irene backed away from the moose, away from his stare and his threats. But as she moved towards the window the moose came towards her, his disembodied head floating free of the wall. Her back was

413

against the cold glass – she could feel it through her shirt – and then, suddenly, she crashed through it and out on to the snow. When she picked herself up and looked around the house had disappeared. Irene was alone in the Yukon at last, just her and the ghosts of the goldrush.

She woke up in a sweat convinced that the moose in the sitting room was possessed by some kind of demon. The same evil spirit inhabited the truck as well – it sat there in the drive waiting for her to put the key back into the ignition so it could take off on another self-destructive run with Irene flailing in front of the dashboard. She lay awake and considered her options. She couldn't live with 1,700 miles of wilderness, not even as an abstract fact. Perhaps, she thought, she should make some kind of offering to appease the moose. Maybe it liked children.

Fingers in the Cookie Jar

WHEN BRENDA WAS a little girl she got into trouble with her best friend's mother once.

'I saw you reach for the biggest bun,' Mrs Benson said to Brenda when she and Debbie came inside and were sitting at the kitchen table.

'What?' asked Brenda, confused.

'I said that I know you reached across the table and took the biggest bun.' Brenda blushed and said nothing. She felt so embarrassed that she couldn't eat or drink and sat in silence while Debbie begged her mother to let her go back outside again. But permission was denied so Brenda went home, mortified.

Still a little girl, Brenda saw her best friend Debbie steal several pennies off the mantelpiece in the sitting room of a third friend. When Debbie and Brenda left the house Brenda said to Debbie, 'I saw you take those pennies.'

'What pennies?' said Debbie. 'I don't have any pennies. My mum doesn't let me have money. She says I'll spend it on sweets.' Brenda knew that this was probably true. Debbie often had sweets that came from unexplained sources.

When Brenda became a big girl, she left home

and moved to the city where she worked in a chain of American restaurants. It was her responsibility to make sure there was a constant supply of thin and over-priced chips which were sold by the ounce. Brenda worked at this job for over two months then one day she was late, the next day she was later, and the next day she got the sack. When she returned home her eldest sister said to her, 'You useless thing you. Can't even hold down a moron's job. Well, I'm tired of having you hang around. You'd better find somewhere else to stay, Brenda. This is the real world you know. You're not a little girl any more.'

So Brenda decided she had to move out of her sister's flat, although she did not have the slightest idea where to go. At the restaurant she had made friends with one other girl who had been sacked about a week before. Brenda remembered where she had put the address and the next day went around to visit Spike.

From the outside, the house was obviously a squat. There were no net curtains at street level and the place had that unmistakable air of dereliction that comes to houses abused and then left to rot by their owners. The guttering along the front eaves hung off at an alarming angle and there were several holes in the roof. Brenda walked up the crumbling staircase to the front door. The bell was broken so she banged as hard as she could. Within a few minutes, the door was pulled open and there, to Brenda's relief, stood Spike.

'Brenda! Hello, how are you? What brings you up this way?' Spike exclaimed, smiling broadly.

'Well . . .' said Brenda, shyly.

'Don't tell me you're still in that hellhole they call a restaurant, are you?'

'No,' replied Brenda, 'I got the sack the other day.'

'Great! You're better off without it. I don't know what I was doing in that dive. All that meat! Yuck!!!'

'I know what you mean,' Brenda said, smiling. 'It was enough to make me a vegetarian.'

'I already was one!' shouted Spike. 'Oh, the horror, the horror! Come in, Brenda, and have a cup of tea.' Brenda followed Spike inside. A few days later she arrived on the doorstep again, this time with all her worldly goods which consisted of an overnight bag and two copies of *La Nausée* by Jean-Paul Sartre. When Spike saw those she said, 'I figure that guy worked in a hamburger bar while he wrote that.' Brenda agreed and was shown to her room.

The house was large with six usable rooms, a kitchen and a bathroom. The toilet was outside in the back garden. The three rooms on the top floor of the house were totally out of bounds due to the holes in the roof. Rain came straight through the ceiling of one room. If you stood in the place where the bucket usually sat and looked up, you could see the sky. In winter the house was heated by several electric bar-fires that were transported from room to room, depending where heat was needed most. There was no gas and no hot water, so meals were cooked and bathwater was heated on the hotplate that sat on top of the disconnected cooker in the kitchen.

When Brenda moved in Spike was living with two other women, one named Vanessa and the other, Martie. None of the young women had jobs.

'Well,' said Spike, 'I've had more shit jobs than a human can stand to have and I'm not going to take it any more.'

Vanessa nodded her head and said, 'When I left school I went on a school leavers' scheme. They put me in an office as a junior. When I realised that I was being paid less than half the wage of the lowest paid person there I left. Nobody is going to make me get them coffee and straighten their ties for money that a dog couldn't live on.'

Martie nodded her head as well and said, 'Since I left school I haven't been able to get a job full stop.' The next day, with instructions from her three friends, Brenda went down to the unemployment office and signed on.

Spike, Martie and Vanessa were all extremely proficient at making a home on less money than a mouse, let alone a dog, could survive on. They drank very little, ate very little, went out very infrequently, and never bought clothes, records, or books. At the end of the day they'd go around to the local market and pick potatoes and leeks and half-rotten carrots up off the ground and out of the bins. They were very adept at sorting through rubbish and salvaging anything usable; the house was furnished with an eclectic mixture of odd chairs, broken settees, and pieces of mirror.

Spike had developed a sixth sense when it came to skips. She could always spot the good ones and her geographical knowledge of London was defined by what one could find and where. Covent Garden? Very lucrative for discarded office equipment, such as files, paper, and even desks. Pens, paperclips, notebooks: this was where Spike had found the electric typewriter that she gave Martie for her birthday, its only fault being a hole where the '£' key should have been. Soho?

Very good for restaurant rubbish such as mildly damaged chairs, large empty tins (useful for catching rain as it comes through the roof), and sometimes even food. Vanessa had once found an entire box of perfectly good avocados in Soho. They had eaten guacamole until they were ill. Hampstead? Now that's the place for furniture, especially beds and settees and dressers and even wardrobes – the only problem being, of course, that of transportation.

All of this, and more, Brenda learned from her three companions and before long, with their help, she had furnished her bedroom.

'The only problem', said Spike one afternoon when it was raining, 'is jewellery. We can get clothes and even shoes from the skips and jumble sales, but where can a girl find a decent pair of earrings to wear?'

'Yeah,' said Vanessa, 'I may be on the dole but I don't want to look like it.'

'That's right,' said Martie, 'ugly. No one should have to look ugly.'

'Of course,' Spike said, smiling, 'make-up is a problem as well.'

'Mmm,' said the others, nodding.

The next day the four women rose early, got on to their bikes and rode to Oxford Street. They entered one of the many large and undemanding department stores and splitting up, wandered in different directions. Martie tried on hats, Vanessa, shoes, Spike, dresses. Brenda watched from a distance, not quite sure of what to do. Looking at stuff she knew she couldn't possibly buy made her nervous: she felt an economic failure, without the power to buy herself a dress.

The three other girls all slowly made their way through the shop, each pausing at different times in front of the make-up and jewellery counters. Brenda watched as they joked with the sales assistants and sprayed themselves with 'J'Accuse' and other perfumes. Then, one by one, they all left by the rear door.

Back at the bikes, Brenda said, 'So, what was that all about?'

They smiled slyly and said, 'Wait and see,' then got on their bikes and rode home. After making a big pot of tea, they sat around the kitchen table emptying their pockets.

'Three lovely pairs of earrings. I especially like these large, gold, dangling ones. A bracelet, a pink plastic necklace, and some eyeliner,' said Vanessa.

'A scarf ("ooh, that's nice"), some dark glasses! And a bottle of perfume, worth £35!' announced Martie.

'A matching set of earrings, necklace, and bracelet. Toilet water. Lipstick, eyeshadow, *blusher*! Make-up remover. Bright red nail polish of the non-chip variety. A bow for my hair,' Spike proclaimed.

'Oh!' squealed Martie. 'We'll all be so beautiful! I can't bear it! Let's go again tomorrow!'

'But,' said Brenda, feeling foolish, 'did you steal all of that?'

'Of course,' said Spike, 'or do you think it all just fell into our pockets?'

'But what if you get caught?'

'We don't. We never do. They're too daft.'

That night Brenda lay awake in bed thinking about new clothes and matching accessories. She dreamed about perfume, skirts, hats, and drooled into her pillow. When she woke up the next morning she felt disappointed that her designer dreams weren't true. She walked over to her wardrobe and pulled it open. Her clothes all looked drab, dated and boring. She didn't have any jewellery to speak of, nor any make-up. Life looked dull.

Brenda went downstairs. Vanessa was sitting in the kitchen eating her breakfast and reading a book. 'Where are Spike and Martie?' asked Brenda.

'Oh, they've gone down to the market to get some food. They'll be back very soon I should think.'

'Great,' said Brenda. 'I hope they find some fruit. I'm dying for an orange.'

'Fruit's not so easy to get,' remarked Vanessa. 'It's often bruised or mushy. But sometimes they're lucky, especially Spike. Would you like some tea?'

About an hour later the front door slammed and Martie came running into the kitchen, breathless.

'They've got Spike!' she shouted. 'They picked her up when we weren't watching. They've arrested her and taken her down to the police station! They said it was illegal to take stuff from the bins. They said that even though it was in the bins it was still somebody else's property. The property of the borough rubbish men.'

'Do you mean the police got her?' asked Vanessa, shocked. 'The filth?'

'Yes, that's what I said! They just came along and stopped us. We were going through a big box of peaches that somebody had thrown away. A whole box. It was hardly damaged at all. We tried to talk them out of it, we were polite to them and everything, but it was two female cops and I think they're meaner than the rest of them, they have to be.'

'Well, what are we going to do?' Brenda shouted. 'They've got Spike! We've got to get her out of there!'

'It's no use panicking,' Vanessa said calmly. 'We'll ring Release and get a solicitor. I've got a plan. Martie, you go to the police station and ask to see Spike. I'll go to the phone kiosk and try to get a solicitor to go down to the station. Brenda, you wait here in case Spike gets let out and comes home.'

'All right,' said Brenda, 'I guess there isn't much else that we can do.'

Vanessa and Martie headed off out of the door in a mad rush and suddenly Brenda was left in silence. She sat in the kitchen and wondered what she should do. She put the kettle on to the hotplate and cleaned the teapot of tea leaves. When the kettle boiled, she made tea. Then she sat next to the kitchen window. The sun was streaming in. Everything seemed quite unreal.

A couple of hours later nothing had happened and no one had come home. Brenda was beginning to feel bored and also a little useless. She'd tidied the kitchen, sitting room, her room, and written a letter to her mum, not mentioning the events of the day. Then she paced about a bit and stood looking out of the sitting room windows at the street to see if she could spot anyone coming towards the house. But the street was empty. She decided to get on her bike and go and look for the others.

Once outside Brenda felt a little better. She rode around the streets near the house, past where the telephone kiosk stood, but there was no sign of Vanessa.

She rode along the High Street and looked in the news-agent's but nobody was in there either. It occurred to her to go to the police station, but then she realised that she didn't know where it was. So she decided to go for a bicycle ride and return home after that.

Before she knew it, Brenda found herself down in Oxford Street along with the buses and taxis and millions of shoppers. She rode up and down between Marble Arch and Tottenham Court Road several times before tying her bike up outside Selfridges. Entering the large department store through the side doors, she walked up and down the aisles gazing at the perfume, tights and the menswear. She thought to herself, 'I wonder if they've let Spike go yet. I wonder if she'll have to go to jail. Can they really do you for stealing rubbish? I hope she's OK.' Brenda strolled around the ground floor of the store and found herself at the foot of the escalators which carried her up to the first floor, then the second, and then the third: Ladies' Wear and Home Furnishings.

Wandering through the settees and kitchen sets, Brenda began to think about her wardrobe. She need-ed some new clothes. 'What I need', thought Brenda, 'is a nice dress. That will cheer me up.' She wandered through the racks of clothes and spotted, in amongst the cocktail dresses and the office wear, a lovely red party dress with a wide, round skirt. She went over to the dress and stood looking at it. The price tag said £110.00.

'Hello,' said a woman who had suddenly appeared beside Brenda. 'Can I be of any assistance?'

'This is a nice dress,' Brenda said, 'I'd like to have it.'

'Oh, yes, it's a new style, only been in the shop since yesterday. I think it will be very popular. It comes in other colours, would you prefer it in green or brown?'

'Oh, green I should think, a colour that will give me control.'

'Right, well I'll just go and see if I can find you one. I'll be five minutes.' The woman began to walk away and then paused, turned and said, 'Will that be cash?'

Brenda nodded and smiled. Then she bent over to have a closer look at the dress. It was covered with intricate stitching and looked well made. She took it off the rack and pinned it against her body. It felt cool and light on her skin. She held the dress in her arms carefully and looked down at it tenderly, as if it was a sleeping baby.

'Spike,' she said to the mirror, 'This dress is for you.'

Brenda walked towards the escalator and travelled down the series of moving staircases until she came to the ground floor. Walking past the perfume and the tights, she stopped in front of the electronic anti-shoplifting devices with a vague idea that if the alarm went off she might see Spike sooner than she would otherwise. But nothing happened and Brenda went out of the exit to Oxford Street. She tied the dress on to the back of her bicycle and rode home.

There was still no one there when Brenda arrived back. She carried the dress through the house and into her bedroom then laid it on her bed. It looked lovely and Brenda felt pleased with herself. She sat down to wait for the others to return.

Revolutions Past and Gone

MANY YEARS LATER, Agnes was sorting through her collection of tapes. She had a stack of ancient cassettes with nothing written on them to indicate what they recorded. Agnes picked up a dirty old cassette and plugged it in, expecting to hear some badly muffled Pink Floyd or maybe even the Doors. Instead, when she pushed 'Play' she heard the voice of an old boyfriend, Michel. She'd forgotten that he'd ever made her this tape. He must have been drunk, or on drugs or something, at the time because his thin and reedy young Québécois voice was singing her David Bowie songs, complete with a British accent. A little bit out of tune, a little bit slow, but with a great deal of conviction. Agnes listened while Michel's voice rose out of the tape-machine. It was like hearing the voice of a dead person.

They'd been together back in the heady days, before Quebec felt secure and comfortable, lost the Separatist Movement and elected a Liberal premier. Agnes had lived in Montreal when late at night in the bars in the east of the city everybody was in love with that big romantic idea of Quebec dropping the bossy and boring Anglais and going out on its own. Sceptics said they'd be swallowed immediately by the US but the romantics – the majority – said that it would be wonderful, Quebec would be a French-Catholic-Socialist State with both divorce and abortion and without censorship laws. The liberating and the sordid all rolled into one.

Those were the days when you could get into a punchup in Montreal Vieux for being from the wrong province and an inappropriate degree of waspishness could make you a complete social pariah. But even 'les maudits' – the damned – the Anglophones who hadn't left with the exodus of the 1970s, thought that Separatism was sexy, at least as an idea, before one considered the economics of the whole thing.

'We are not to be another Louisiana,' Michel said to Agnes when they first met in a downtown bar. He was trying his best to ignore her; her French was appalling and she was obviously from Alberta or somewhere else similarly Western. But he couldn't simply disregard her like that. She had the most extraordinary eyes and such a nice smile and she obviously wanted to talk to him.

'No, you are not going to be another Louisiana,' Agnes had answered. 'Louisiana is in the US. This is Canada you are talking about. We are far too polite to do to you what the Americans did to their French. Besides there are too many of you. And you've got Trudeau. You can't lose now.'

'Trudeau, pah!' snorted Michel. 'He'll sell us down the St Laurent.' Michel decided he really should be ignoring this woman. Who was she anyway, what did she know about Quebec? 'I bet,' said Michel looking at Agnes, 'I bet you are a student at McGill University.'

'How did you know that?' asked Agnes.

'The last frontier of Anglo-Protestant supremacy.'

'That's right. And proud of it.'

At that, Michel got up and took his beer from the table where he'd somehow managed to end up sitting with Agnes. He walked through the smoky bar shaking his head.

Agnes sat at the table watching Michel stomp off. She looked back down at her beer. She was on her own, attempting to have a good time away from McGill. The university was a big disappointment. It was, as Michel had said, implying it was her fault, a little island of anglo-culture right in the middle of Montreal, a big, steamy Québécois city.

But Agnes had come to Quebec because she too had romantic notions about Separatism. In 1970 when she was fourteen years old, she was thrilled by Le Front de la Libération du Québec and their revolutionary antics. She watched everything on the television; it had seemed so extreme when Trudeau had brought in the army. He was French, what was he doing? By the time Agnes got to Quebec Canada's miniature civil war was in the rapidly receding past and Separatism had become a more acceptable political issue, fit for the ballot box, not bombs and guns.

Ten years later, when Agnes heard Michel's voice on tape it was as though she had pushed a button marked 'Play' in her memory. They had such a good time, eventually, when Michel got over trying to despise Agnes and Agnes stopped thinking he was the greatest thing since Che Guevara. He'd taught her a lot of French and taken her to places in Montreal that someone so obviously Western and, well, 'McGill', would never have known about, let alone ended up in late at night. Agnes met all kinds of people through Michel, the Greek-Québécois intellectuals, the Jewish-Québécois intellectuals, the Portuguese-Québécois intellectuals: everybody was an intellectual in those days. They were all making films and writing poetry, novels and plays, having parties, doing performances, publishing magazines and splitting and resplitting into different political factions. She'd even met Leonard Cohen once, but everybody who lived in Montreal had met him and no one was allowed to be the slightest bit impressed.

That first night, in the bar, Agnes had sat by herself for several hours. She fended off drunks by speaking to them in her bad French, repelling them with her Englishness. She didn't even have to say 'Go away'; they left as soon as they heard her accent. Agnes just sat at her table smoking Gauloises and taking it all in.

Michel had gone off and found his friends who were engaged in a lively argument about, what else, Separatism. They were all shouting and gesticulating and making sweeping generalisations and damning the English in ever more inventive ways. Michel joined in, downing his beer. But he kept finding himself looking across the room at Agnes, sitting there at her table. To him she looked both serene and determined. He could tell she was not about to give up; she wanted to fit in. Eventually Michel surrendered his cool and wandered back over to her table.

'You're still here,' he said.

'Been here for three hundred years,' Agnes answered. 'Ever since we won the war. Don't intend to leave either.' She smiled and Michel was lost.

Agnes continued going to classes at McGill, despite her disillusionment with the institution. She kept thinking maybe she'd run into Marshall McLuhan or Charles Taylor or Hugh McLennan, but of course, that's not the way universities work. She continued struggling with Kant in the library and having arguments with her professors in the Philosophy Department, most of whom were Anglophone, male, middle-aged and pompous, just as Michel imagined them.

'I met the head of department today,' Agnes said one evening when she and Michel had met on Rue St Denis to go drinking with Michel's friends.

'Oh yeah, what was he like?'

'Well, he's a Kierkegaardean Christian Existentialist.'

'Aren't they all?'

'He has devoted his philosophic career to programming a computer that can read all of Kierkegaard and, hopefully, one day when the programme is complete, finish Kierkegaard's "Unfinished Postscript".'

'No.'

'Yes. He even knows Danish. He and Søren, they're like that,' she said holding up crossed fingers.

'Jesus,' said Michel. 'What a place.'

'You should go there with me one day, Michel. Even if it's just to the bar. An insider's view, you know. It would be good for the revolution I'm sure. You can't storm the Bastille without knowing what it's like inside.' Agnes smiled when Michel stuck his tongue out at her.

With each successive school term Agnes moved farther and farther east, away from the university and the student 'ghetto', as the area right next to McGill was called, until eventually she was living with Michel out on East Ontario Est, as the street sign said. They became quite domesticated, speaking French in the evening and English at breakfast, when Agnes couldn't cope with saying 'cornflakes' with a Québécois pronunciation. Michel was a student at the Université de Montreal, a whirling pool of radicalism.

As she sat in her sitting room listening to Michel sing David Bowie songs from ancient history, Agnes asked herself, 'Where is Michel now?'

In the fourth and final year of her degree Agnes had to leave Montreal. Her father died suddenly and her mother was taken ill. She hadn't minded leaving her degree unfinished, from the very beginning it had only been a means for her to stay in Montreal. But she had minded leaving Montreal, of course, and Michel. She felt she had finally penetrated the impenetrable and people were beginning to forget, occasionally, that she was one of the damned.

Neither Michel nor Agnes had expected that Agnes's abrupt departure would end their relationship. That spring they spoke on the telephone regularly, Agnes's voice cracking in French. Michel came to Calgary in the summer to work for a Canadian oil company that needed bilingual employees for negotiations with Quebec. It wasn't his chosen area of interest, but he'd never been West before and was longing to see Agnes. The second day after he arrived they were downtown shopping – Michel needed shirts and ties, items he had never acquired. They stopped in at the liquor store on the way home and Michel bumped into a man who dropped and smashed a bottle of wine. When the enormous Albertan with a red face and a cowboy hat heard Michel's accent as he apologised, the man called him a 'frog-kike-wop' and attempted to punch him in the face. Michel decided he hated cowboys and the West.

A few weeks later the annual Calgary Stampede took place. During the week of festivities, rodeos, fun fairs, parties, horse-races, cattle-roping, and other pseudo-American Wild West antics, Michel and Agnes went to a party. Everybody was shouting 'Yee-hah' and slapping each other on the back and he decided it wasn't such a bad place after all. They spent every weekend camping on the bald prairie. Standing in the middle of a wheat field that seemed to stretch three hundred miles to the endless ridge of the Rockies, he felt he knew Agnes a little better.

The summer ended, Michel went back to Montreal and Agnes's mother's health worsened. When he finished his degree, he found a good job. The referendum took place and the people of Quebec said no to Separatism. Trudeau went in and out, and then in and out again, of retirement. The French language became firmly institutionalised in Quebec through strict legislation. Without warning, years had gone by and Michel was married to somebody else. 'A Québécois girl, no doubt,' Agnes thought as she sat in her sitting room. 'But I wonder what happened to Michel? I wonder what happened to all the Montreal intellectuals? And what do they argue about now that the urgency of

Separatism has faded? Have they stopped making films and writing poetry? Do they still think I'm damned?'

The tape ended and Agnes thought in silence. 'I must go back to Montreal. I must go back and find Michel. I'll go back for La Fête de St Jean-Baptiste. We'll get drunk in the sweaty Montreal night and wander through the streets shouting "Vive Le Québec!"'

Agnes got up, turned the tape-machine off, and went to bed where her husband was already asleep.

The Battersea Power Station

SHE SAID OUT LOUD to the man conducting the job interview,

'I had to give up my black leather jacket when I realised it had once been animate. I gave it back to its rightful owner, some cow I never met.' And then she said,

'Yeah. We met on the underground. We spent the night snorting cocaine and fucking in the Battersea Power Station.' She continued with, 'No, I don't eat much any more. I kept wondering if it's really fair to eat vegetables. Maybe they have a right to live too. Right now I'm trying hard to work out some way for me to live by photosynthesis. But the sun never seems to shine any more.' Then she smiled and told him her best joke,

'What do you call a man standing in a pot of ratatouille? Basil.' She laughed away to herself. Then, she collected her things and said she had to go home and scare the rats out of the kitchen. She put on her jacket, tearing the lining again, and walked off. She walked through Covent Garden oblivious. She hated it there so she pretended she wasn't there at all. She smiled at the bags of shopping as if they were people and looked at the people as if they were bags of shopping, which some of them actually were. On the Strand she got on a bus. A man sat next to her; it was the man she had met on the underground. He said,

'I quit my job today. My boss underpays me, he fiddles the books, gives people dead turkeys at Christmas, and expects them to be happy. Dead turkeys. I can't believe it. Most people need money.'

'Jobs don't matter anyway,' she said. 'It's a bad thing, doing what you're told to do. You can go on the dole and eat chocolate.'

They got off the bus at the Battersea Power Station and snorted cocaine and fucked all night. When dawn crept through the grimy windows of the control room, he said to her,

'We mustn't snort this stuff, you know. It probably comes from South America or Asia or somewhere and they probably force people to grow it when they should be growing vegetables to eat.'

'Vegetables,' she said. 'Dead turkeys, vegetables, my black leather jacket.'

'You'd look good in a black leather jacket,' he said. 'What do you call a man with a car on his head? Jack.' She said this and sighed and touched the boy from the underground with the back of her hand. 'Maybe photosynthesis is a bad idea, maybe I can survive on sex alone.' So, in the name of scientific experiment, they started to fuck again, while in the boiler room some slime grew, the pigeons cooed, and the girders rusted.

The next day was sunny, so she stretched out on the roof garden and smiled at the sun. With her legs spreadeagled, her arms fully extended, her fingers and toes spread and stretching, her eyes closed, and her gums exposed, she tried very hard to photosynthesise. Just in case she could not live by fucking alone. The sun felt great, all over her body.

After a while one of her flatmates came up on to the garden and said, 'Hey. What are you doing?' She just smiled, exposing her gums a little more. The flatmate said, 'Do you want something to eat?' She shook her head. The flatmate went away. Soon she could smell cooking. She wondered what her flatmate had killed. She got up off the roof, looking hopefully at her arm for a tinge of green, then went down to her room. She fumbled around in the closet for a dress and pulled out a suede jacket instead. Oh no. She sighed to herself, then took it into the sitting room where her flatmates were devouring things and said,

'Look at this. I'd forgotten all about it. What am I going to do with it, whose is it, does it come from Jersey, Hereford, or Loseley? Some cow I never met.' She smiled at her flatmates and did a brief tap dance. 'What do you call a girl with two eggs, chips, beans, toast, and tea on her head? Caf.' Then she danced away before they could catch her. She walked to the National Film Theatre and watched a Fred Astaire movie. When the lights came on she discovered she was sitting next to the man from the underground. They got on his push-bike, she sat on the seat, he stood and pedalled, and they rode to the Battersea Power Station. From Nine Elms Lane it looms like eternity. Even at night it casts a gothic shadow. He called to her as they rode along, turning his head so the wind would catch his words and carry them to her.

'Being unemployed is like waiting for a train. The train never comes so you amuse yourself by reading the posters backwards. You get to know the posters very well. Soon these posters start to excite you. You are sure they are trying to tell you something, not just about the product, but something about the meaning of life. I'm glad I'm unemployed. It gives me a greater understanding of things.'

'Being unemployed makes me worry about eating,' she said.

Then they were inside the Battersea Power Station, up in the control room, fucking on the parquet floor, reading the dials on the walls when they paused. He said,

'Why do we fuck on the parquet floor?'

'Because the boiler room is too scary,' she replied. Then she giggled and said, 'Oh, my suede jacket,' as if those words had meaning, and he said,

'You'd look good in a suede jacket.' Later, when they leaned against the cut-glass windows overlooking the boiler room she said,

'What do you call a man with a pigeon on his head? Cliff. Or Nelson.'

The next day was rainy so she sat in the kitchen and cut up the newspaper and put it back together but with the sentences, paragraphs, articles all mixed up so there was an article on how to holiday in Israel on the overseas news page and an article about the ANC on the entertainment page. One of her flatmates came in and offered to cook her breakfast but she said,

'No, thank you. I am trying to survive on sex alone. Not just ordinary sex, of course, but sex with the man from the underground in the Battersea Power Station.

You must understand the connection there. Sex – energy – power – fuel – electricity – you know, all those things. Sex in the Battersea Power Station, that should be enough, don't you think?' Then she put on her favourite dress and walked to the British Museum. Peering into a mummy case she saw the face of the boy from the underground. She turned around and he was there. He took her in his arms and they did a slow waltz through the room full of large, wonderful, Egyptian things, past the art deco porcelain and into the room with the sixteenth-century religious icons. They zigzagged through history like a sewing machine and came to rest in front of Oscar Wilde's handwritten manuscript of *The Importance of Being Earnest* and she cried to the museum guard who stood watching,

'We will go down in histrionics,' then she laughed and they salsaed all the way to the Battersea Power Station and fucked on the floor of the boiler room. They looked up at the decaying girders and columns, they listened to the pigeons cooing, and the water that ran along the floor collected in a pool around them. His voice echoed through the enormous chamber when he said,

'Being with you is like being with a spirit. Being with you is like just catching a train. Being with you is like riding downhill,' and she said,

'Thanks, I like you too. You always show up at the right time.' They kissed for a while and the Battersea Power Station groaned from disuse. Then she said,

'What do you call a man with a bog on his head? Pete.' They laughed and then after a while he said,

'That's my name.'

So We Swing

A GREAT MANY physically astounding feats can be performed on a set of playground swings. You can rock from side to side slowly, jerk back and forth quickly or even smash into the person on the next swing. We used to have swing wars when we were very young, screaming out of the sky as we pushed ourselves off, braced for the crash. We'd twist the seat around and around until the chains were wound up tight and high, lifting us far off the ground. Then we'd let go and the chains would unwind, spinning our bodies so quickly that once it was over we'd have to get off and stamp our feet on the firm and, thankfully, solid earth.

One favourite game was to stand up on the seat and swing at such an angle that the playground would disappear completely, leaving only the sky. It was almost as if we could fly. The daredevils could jump off mid-swing, hurtling to the ground like giggling bombs, but I would always end up dragging my feet in order to slow down.

As I walked by the swings tonight I heard a small girl chanting at a small boy, 'I'm not your friend, I'm not your friend.'

'I don't care,' replied the boy.

'Neither do I . . .' said the small girl, pausing, 'I'm going to die soon anyway.'

I walked on and left them to quarrel, wondering how the notion of death had reached such a small girl so young. Perhaps she was making childish threats or maybe she had foreseen something that we, the big people, had missed. The question I asked myself then was this: how will she die? There are so many ways, like the junkies next door, or the homeless alcoholics on the corner, or those who make their suicide more sudden and real, off a block of flats or a bridge. Or perhaps this small girl will die a daredevil's death and leap as the swing reaches the highest point in its arc. She will throw her feet out first, her body following after, and she will smash herself into a small girl pile of death on the very pavement we all at one point have feared smashing our own heads on.

I had a friend in school who conducted the preliminary stages of all her major adolescent romances on the set of swings behind the primary school. On warm summer evenings this friend of mine would lead her prospective boyfriend to the swings and there they would sit talking and showing off to each other. There is something remarkably sensual about flying through the warm soft night air with your legs stretched out in front. Swinging in counter-rhythm you swish by the boy you like: behind, in front, behind, never quite touching.

It always worked, this swing business. The boys my friend took to the swings always fell in love with her. Sometimes even now I long to get on the swings myself, just to fly through the air like a child.

But my friend is gone now, she probably married one of those boys, and the childhood swinging sessions have been replaced by other, more adult, thrills and chills. Now when I walk past the playground on my way to the bar I rarely glance over at the wooden seats or notice their slightly macabre chains hanging in the moonlight.

Last night I was disappointed to see Lisa kissing the pushy boy who hangs out in the speakeasy. Every weekend I watch as he gets drunk and falls over. When I left the bar early this morning, they were asleep in a pile on the floor. Nick wasn't there so I assume that in her boredom she let that pushy boy prey upon her. Lisa has been chasing Nick for over half a year now. His expression when he greets her always seems to be saying, 'Go ahead, get on with it,' and Lisa does, full force. She turns her whole body on to Nick, her face saying, 'I want you, I want you,' her hands saying, 'I want you, I want you,' she herself probably saying, 'I want you, I want you,' into his ear, her lips touching his neck. He lets her do it, he leans back in his chair as she throws herself at him, recklessly hurling her body across the room.

The rooms in the speakeasy are dark, lit only by fire or candlelight but when Lisa walks into a room she can sense immediately if Nick is there. She told me this, but if you watch it's obvious. She walks into the room with her shoulders held very high, as if she is sniffing the air. She always looks tense and when she spots Nick her body tightens; if he isn't around her body crumples with disappointment.

Most nights, Lisa stands at the bar and talks to

someone else. When Nick is sitting at a table with his friends Lisa keeps a smile on her face but every few minutes she loses track of the conversation. Her head turns Nick's way and she has a quick look, just to see if he's still there, or better yet, to catch him looking at her. Then she turns back to whichever pushy boy is occupying her and smiles and nods.

I sit in the corner in the dark room, drinking the cheap red wine that they sell there, and watch as every few moments Lisa looks at Nick. To me, her eyes are singing that refrain of 'I want you, I want you' and I know she feels desperate, her body is full of desire, she is making herself feel dizzy. The openness of her hunger startles me and seems wonderful.

One night, several months ago, Lisa walked in and found neither Nick nor any of those pushy boys that she is always falling back on. She looked a little tired, as do most of us who frequent the speakeasy. She asked the bloke behind the counter for a bottle of wine, then came and sat at my table. We knew each other through continual sightings at the bar; we probably wouldn't have spoken had we passed in the street. But there was nobody else for her to talk to on that night. Besides, she must have seen me talking to Nick on previous nights and this formed a connection in her mind.

'Do you mind if I sit here?' she asked. I replied by pulling a chair over for her. 'None of my friends seem to be here tonight. That's unusual,' she said, looking around. 'I almost always know somebody. I wonder where they all are? Have you got any ideas?' I decided to be blunt and told her that Nick had gone away for the weekend.

'Oh?' she replied, blushing. 'He didn't say anything about that. Although I suppose that shouldn't surprise me.' She paused and drained her glass. 'We haven't been on the best of terms lately.' I had heard from friends Nick and I had in common that they'd never been on particularly good terms. Nick had a girlfriend somewhere, Indonesia, I think. She was an artist and they didn't see each other often but that was where Nick's attentions were directed, as far as I knew.

'He's a wonderful person really, Nick, don't you think?' Lisa said, expecting me to agree. I smiled and nodded without saying that I thought he was just all right.

'Don't you think he's incredibly good-looking?' Thinking about all lanky six feet four inches of Nick and his cheekbones I had to admit she had a point, but I didn't tell her that the most interesting thing about him was her obsession with him.

Lisa drained another glass of wine. She was drinking quickly and mercilessly, as usual. 'We had an affair, did you know that?' I shook my head. 'Yeah, well we did. I think he is so beautiful. We had an affair, but he doesn't seem to want to see me all that much any more. I still want to see him though. That's why I come to this place, to see him. I don't really like places like this, no offence. But it doesn't always work out the way I want.' I was surprised by her frankness. I poured her another glass of wine.

'I feel pretty bad about it. I thought he was beautiful the first time I met him, but that was almost a year ago. He's a friend of some friends. We met here. Doesn't everybody?' she said, giggling. 'I shouldn't say that he's handsome too often because he is charming and intelligent and interesting as well but for some reason when I think of him it is his looks that I think of first. We talked to each other a bit, he winked at me a few times. Then one night it was very late. Everyone was going home and somehow I managed to talk myself into asking him to come home with me and he did. He did.' Lisa smiled broadly at me. 'It was great. I didn't believe that he would actually stay until he had all his clothes off and was kissing me in my bed, under my blankets. But he did. And the next night as well. And then the next weekend . . . well, it was too good to be true. Beautiful men don't just fall from the sky like that.'

Lisa stopped talking for a moment and poured herself another glass of wine, offering me some which I accepted. There was more than one drunkard in this place. Then she spoke again. 'I have this problem. I fall in love with men I think are beautiful and they always turn out to be unobtainable. Oh, sometimes they let you get them into bed but that doesn't mean very much somehow. There's something in the beauty that is unobtainable.' Lisa paused and I thought to myself that it was more likely to be the other way around – there is something about the unobtainable that is beautiful – a well-known principle of consumer culture.

'Sometimes I think I took advantage of him by seizing him at a moment when he didn't particularly care what he did. Or maybe he took advantage of me, letting me do all the hard work, make the decisions. I asked him one day why he'd slept with me, since he didn't seem so keen to do it again. He said that it seemed like a good idea at the time and there wasn't anything else to do, so why not? I don't think that's very nice. It meant such a lot to me. I told him so.'

'You know what he told me then?' she asked, looking at me without waiting for me to reply. 'That he doesn't find me sexually attractive. That he likes me but he's not attracted to me. Then he said that it had nothing to do with me, it was all his problem, but I don't know what he meant by that. If I was thinner and darker he'd probably change his mind. Other men think I'm sexually attractive. He made it sound like he only fucked girls who look like they stepped out of adverts. At first I thought how it must be awful to be so shallow and physical but then I realised that I always think of Nick's looks first. He must be pretty arrogant to imagine that I like him for something that includes his mind and his heart as well as his body when, really, I don't know him at all. He's just this friend of some friends.'

Lisa didn't look at me when she finished but looked out across the room, as if she thought Nick might have walked in and overheard her. 'That's not it as far as I'm concerned though,' she said shaking her head. 'I think he'll change his mind if I persist for long enough. I'll beat him down with my devotion. It can be done, you know,' she said, looking at me angrily. 'I've seen it done. We're friends now. I swallow my lust, drown it with lager and wine and won't sit too near to him. If I do there's always the chance that I'll stand up and beat my breast and shout at him, "I am sexually attractive you fool, the most sexually attractive person around and you are really stupid if you don't see that." She paused, 'I wish he wasn't so handsome.'

Well, as I said, that was several months ago and when I saw Lisa in the speakeasy the next weekend she was there at the bar still stealing looks at Nick. He ignored her but she didn't speak to me again. Either she'd forgotten our conversation or I was incidental to her thought processes. I continued to watch her.

There was a night not very long ago when I was coming home late. As I walked past the playground I could see Lisa there with a few of her pushy boyfriends. She was on the swings laughing and swinging up into the warm night air, flying very high, her legs stretched out ahead of her. Each time she reached the highest point in her arc she would turn her head quickly and look at Nick's window across the playground. Is he there, can he hear me, does he know I'm here? Will he come and swing with me? In those quick glances before the swing came down once again, in that brief flash of Lisa's eyes, there seemed a greater declaration of love than any words or endless paeans could express. She looked, at once, desperately unhappy and full of passion and, somehow, to me that seemed wonderful.

I walked by and Lisa kept on swinging. Sometimes she must think she is flying. It's almost as though she is keeping herself up in the air with will-power alone. If Nick had come out to the playground to see her right then I'm sure she would have leapt off mid-swing and flown through the air into his arms. And I'd admire her for it, even if he dropped her or she missed him and smashed her head open on the solid earth below.

The Flat-Sitter

ONE DAY THE hitherto benevolent local authority, particularly vulnerable to squatters with its massive surplus of derelict property and lack of funds, suddenly awoke and, with a roar, swiped Stella's house off the face of the earth. It was as though a slumbering bear had been aroused by a bumble bee. Stella had buzzed happily and innocently in her little house for too long.

Since then, chance, luck, or the rising salaries of her friends had enabled Stella to avoid homelessness through serial flat-sitting. Her friends felt more secure, as they lay in the sun in Ibiza or Sri Lanka, knowing that someone responsible was keeping the burglars away.

Stella's first engagement had come about when Sally and Zoë went off to Greece for ten days; Stella moved in with explicit instructions on which plants liked water and which did not. For the first few days alone in Sally and Zoë's flat, Stella was cautious and polite, behaving as though she were a house guest whose hosts were only momentarily absent. She slept in the spare room, keeping her toothbrush in her make-up bag which in turn she kept in her suitcase. She watered the to-be-watered plants and washed the

447

dishes immediately after every meal. When Sally and Zoë returned they pronounced her a model flat-sitter and took her out to dinner in a posh restaurant. It was on the success of those first ten days that Stella's reputation as dependable was founded.

Shortly after that, Stella moved into Stan and Matthew's flat for a fortnight. Stan and Matthew were going to Barcelona and they left Stella on her own in their big old house that stood just across the road from a park. Once they'd explained the cooker and left, Stella began to feel a bit more expansive than she had in the previous flat. She moved into Stan and Matthew's own bedroom, began leaving the breakfast dishes in the sink all day, read a letter from Stan's mother that she found on top of the television late one night and towards the end of the fortnight went out in the evening wearing Matthew's aftershave cologne.

'You smell great tonight Stel,' her friend had said lecherously. Stella smiled.

Still, she refrained from dipping into Stan and Matthew's collection of twelve-year-old whisky and did not scratch any of their records. Her reputation remained intact.

Stella's life went on and she moved from one flat-sitting engagement to the next. During the daytime she worked in a sandwich bar doing everything from the accounts to making egg mayonnaise. The job was rather poorly paid but Stella liked it. She had a certain amount of control. Conquering the lunchtime queue made her feel happy. In the evenings she went out with those of her friends who were not on holiday and after that she went home to someone else's flat. She became quite accustomed to a lifestyle of shifting and strangeness.

Still, when Bev and Joe asked Stella to stay in their flat while they were in India she felt relieved.

'Two months!' she shouted at Bev. 'Two whole months! You don't know how happy this makes me!'

'Oh,' said Bev, 'well if I knew how badly you wanted to get rid of us we would have gone sooner.'

'Please, don't get the wrong idea!' said Stella, still shouting. 'I love you both dearly and if you don't come back I'll miss you terribly, but, two months, it's too good to be true.'

So Stella ensconced herself at Bev and Joe's. By this time her flat-sitting technique had advanced to a record level of casualness. Simply by taking a quick stroll around a new flat Stella found she became intimate with it immediately. She had been to Bev and Joe's before, for dinner and parties, but there are always certain aspects to a home that the infrequent visitor misses. For example, until the evening after Bev and Joe's departure, Stella had not known about their large collection of Bruce Lee videos. Nor had she suspected that when they were not cooking lobster bisque and bulghar wheat salads for their dinner guests, they dined on enormous quantities of frozen potato chips and fish fingers. And, if asked prior to moving in, Stella would never have guessed that behind the Miles Davis records Bev and Joe had Tammy Wynette and Loretta Lynn, and that underneath the biographies of Rosa Luxembourg they kept Jackie Collins and Barbara Cartland.

But Stella took all these revelations in her by now professionally adaptable stride and only blushed slightly when she discovered the oddly textured and shaped sex toys in the drawer beside the bed.

'I am here for the duration,' Stella said out loud, dropping an unusual green object back into the drawer. Other people's intimacies did not affect her.

Bev and Joe's flat was simple – two bedrooms, one of which was used as a study/guest room, a kitchen with a table in it, a sitting room, and a decent-sized bathroom. Although fairly cluttered, it was comfortable and posed no problems to Stella in her role as flat-sitter. Not even the plants were complicated. At night a bright street-lamp shone orange through the bedroom window but Stella quickly grew to appreciate it. When she was watching television in bed she did not have to get up and turn on the light in order to find out what the newspaper said was on next.

Stella had never before watched television in bed – it seemed a strangely American habit to her – but while she was staying at Bev and Joe's she suddenly took to it like a duck to water. On the third night that she was at home on her own she sat up with a huge plateful of thawed and fried potato chips and watched her first ever Bruce Lee video. Stella imagined that this was exactly what Bev and Joe did on their nights in together. She fell asleep with a can of beer in her hand just as Bruce was about to make his three hundredth kill.

Watching Kung-Fu in bed while eating lovely greasy chips was not the only habit that Stella unintentionally adopted when she moved into Bev and Joe's flat. She continually found herself doing things that she felt sure the occupiers did themselves. In the mornings she got up and ate cornflakes in her underwear. She began drinking her coffee black and did not pick the dirty clothes up off the floor for days. During the second week in the flat she left unsigned cheques for both the milkman and the paper-boy and the following Sunday morning she found herself playing a Johnny Cash album at the wrong speed with the vague hope of annoying someone although she was not sure who.

During the day Stella went to work and behaved as she had done for several years. Nothing unusual, new or different took her fancy there.

By the third week when Stella came home from work she found herself feeling inexplicably cross as soon as she stepped inside the door of the flat. On Thursday evening when she opened the front door and stepped inside she felt an absolute fury burst forth. Slamming the door shut, she stomped into the sitting room, dumped her things in a pile, turned on both the radio and the television as loudly as possible and threw herself down on the couch. After several minutes she realised she was waiting for someone to come into the room and start fighting with her. Looking down at her hands she saw she was clenching her fists and her knuckles had turned white. Stella stood up and shook herself violently, once, and then again. She walked around the sitting room, turned the television off and the radio down. Then she went into the kitchen and poured herself a drink.

The next morning she got up and, after the now familiar cornflakes and underwear routine, went off to work. She felt perfectly normal all day and had an enjoyable evening out with friends. Having had quite a lot to drink, she was extremely sleepy on the underground on the way home. But as soon as she got through the front door of the flat she felt an uncontrollable rage well up inside her again. She hurled her coat to the floor and, quite without planning it, shouted, 'I hate you! I hate you when you come home like this! You make me want to crawl with disgust. Why do you do it? Why?'

'Because,' Stella replied to herself, 'because you're so bloody boring and self-righteous and proper, that's why! You and your godforsaken family.' She walked over to the record-player and put the Johnny Cash LP on at 45 RPM again.

'Don't do that to my Johnny Cash records! You are so mean and horrible! You know that record means a lot to me. Christ, take it off!!' Stella marched around the room a bit and found herself struggling near the stereo. 'Leave it,' she shouted, 'I like it better this way.'

'You only do it because you know I hate it!' Stella shouted, then she ran down the hallway and locked herself in the bathroom and turned on the shower full blast. When she got out and dried herself off the music had stopped and shortly after that she was in bed with a plate of chips watching Bruce Lee.

The next morning Stella ran into the occupant of the flat downstairs on the pavement outside the door of the building. Bev had introduced them prior to her departure.

'So,' said the neighbour, 'Bev and Joe back early, are they?'

'Umm,' said Stella slowly, puzzled. 'No, they're not due back for another six weeks or so.'

'Oh,' said the neighbour, frowning, 'that's odd. I could have sworn I heard them last night.' The neighbour then blushed.

'That must have been me,' replied Stella quickly. 'I have a difficult time with the record-player. It's a bit more technologically advanced than I am.'

'Oh,' said the neighbour, still looking confused.

'Bye,' Stella said walking away. She went home to stay with her parents for the weekend and did not return to the flat until late Monday night. She managed to get into bed without any incidents and just before she went to sleep wondered if she had dreamed the whole thing.

The week passed uneventfully and Stella went out to a party on Friday evening. At the party she drank rather a lot of beer and smoked a fair amount of dope. A friend dropped her back at Bev and Joe's in his car and by the time she got through the front door of the flat she was speeding with anger.

'You are so fucking late, where the fuck have you been?' she shouted.

'None of your goddamned business!' she shouted back.

'You've been out with that person again, haven't you? Ugh, I can smell it, I can smell it on you. You are disgusting,' Stella said very slowly, her lip curling. 'You make me feel sick.'

'I make you sick? Well you make me fucking well feel like goddamned dying, that's how you make me feel. Every night on my way here I realise how much I hate you. You and this godforsaken filthy flat.' Stella stormed over to the record-player, snatched Johnny

Cash off the turntable, held it up above her head and then quickly brought it down across her raised knee. The record broke cleanly in half. 'Take that, you bastard!' she shouted.

'You broke it, you fucking broke it, goddamn you!' Clutching her hair and gritting her teeth she muttered, 'I'll teach you to break my records,' then she marched out of the sitting room and into the bedroom and over to the bedside table. She pulled the top drawer all the way out of the table on to the bed.

'No, no,' she shouted, standing back away from the bed a bit. 'Not the sex toys,' she said deploringly, 'not my collection.'

'Your collection makes me feel ill, you pervert.'

'You never said that before, hypocrite!'

'I never realised what a pig you are before.'

Stella picked up the drawer full of strange little gadgets and went to the window. After a brief struggle she opened it, and, before she could shout anything else, emptied the drawer into the street below. Without saying another word, she picked up her keys and her coat and her cheque book and walked out of the flat, slamming the door.

Outside on the pavement Stella stood waiting for a cab to go by. She examined the things that lay strewn across the ground. It was an odd assortment of what looked like over-sized rubber jumping jacks, tiny plastic dildoes, and things that resembled mutant rubber ducks. She kicked one of them across the street just as she saw a cab approaching.

When she arrived at Sally and Zoë's, they were about to go to bed having also been at the party.

'Stella!' said Sally looking surprised. 'What are you doing here this time of night? Have you locked yourself out of Bev and Joe's?'

'No,' said Stella. 'Listen, Sal, do you know if Bev and Joe argue a lot?'

A Mother's Advice

BEFORE GRAHAM DIED Lucille had not thought it possible that she would find herself turning into her mother. She always knew that there might be little things she could not avoid, like the lines around her eyes and the slight propensity towards cuddliness that made her start when she looked at herself in the mirror after a particularly heavy night. Lucille thought she could gauge her judgement by measuring her own responses against what she guessed would be her mother's. This parent curled her lip at bad house-keeping so Lucille embraced filth; her mother was warm and comforting so Lucille tried to stay hard and unyielding. As she grew older these uncompromising stands sometimes made her feel tired but one look at the mirror in the morning, the time she resembled her mother most obviously, never failed to smarten her up.

Before Graham died Lucille felt steadfast in her absolute hatred of couples. Since discovering sex at the tender age of fourteen, she had made it clear to her multitude of lovers that not one of them was allowed to lay any claim on her. Not only did she shun marriage and all common-law arrangements, she assiduously avoided seeing less than two men at a time. She would rather be celibate than 'in a relationship' and would throw any poor fool out of her bed if he whispered words vaguely related to fidelity. Lucille never bothered about missing any of the men she chucked out – there were always at least two replacements.

That was before Graham died.

When Graham fell ill Lucille felt ill in sympathy. They were friends, the two of them. After meeting in an exercise class, they spent many an evening sodden with drink and caked with dried sweat, gloating over their latest conquests. If Lucille liked lots of men, so did Graham, and they had a kind of sexual empathy not uncommon between gay men and heterosexual women. Her mother would never have understood.

When the first warning signals came Lucille ignored them and when Graham worsened she ignored that as well. It was as though she gave him the odd evening's respite. Graham seemed to appreciate it; Lucille knew he had other friends who were there to help with the reality. When their visits began to take place in the hospital she and Graham pretended they were elsewhere and Lucille became religiously jolly. She would have been incapable of behaving any other way, even if he'd requested it.

On her last visit Graham was not quite capable of jolliness and Lucille fled in tears. Then he died and she was left on her own wondering what he expected her to do now. In an attempt to recover, she took a fortnight off from work and flew to Spain for a holiday. As she had booked into a cheap package deal for single people, something that, despite her predilection for bed-hopping, she'd never done before, she took off expecting to spend the time 'fucking herself silly'.

But in her bikini on the Costa Brava beach Lucille found herself fending off advances. The first couple of nights she sat alone in her hotel room, explaining to herself that she needed a few days to think about Graham and relax. So she worked on her tan and said no to the many offers of drinks.

On the third day she came off the beach in the late afternoon and sat in the shade of a bar.

'Now look here,' she said to herself, 'stop being such a stick-in-the-mud. Graham wouldn't have wanted this. What's slowing me down? I don't want to spend this fortnight alone, do I?'

That was when she spotted him, across the road on the miniature golf course. He seemed to be practising putting on his own. Lucille watched as he swung his club carefully and then gave a small jump of victory when the ball went into the hole. His concentration was admirable, as was his tan. After seeing him putt an endless string of holes-in-one, Lucille picked up her towel and walked across the street to the fence beyond which he played.

'Hello,' she called out, assuming he was English. 'Not bad, for an amateur.'

He straightened his back and looked up at her, smiling. 'Hello,' he said, 'do you want to play?'

'No,' said Lucille, 'I don't do things in miniature. I prefer them big, you know, life-size,' then she smiled at her own suggestiveness. She found it was a tactic that always disarmed and sometimes charmed. 'Want to have a drink?'

'OK,' he said, 'I'll just finish this round.' Moments

later Lucille found herself confronted with the product of her wiles.

'Well,' she said, 'what are you doing in Spain?'

'Escaping Britain, I think. How about you?'

'Escaping Britain, my job, my friends, my family, you know, the works.'

'That sounds rather extreme. What prompted that?'

'A death,' Lucille answered, regretting it immediately.

'Oh, I'm sorry to hear that. Was it someone close?'

'Unbearably,' said Lucille, then she smiled and changed the subject. Within an hour they were in her hotel room and she heard herself saying, 'Just a moment, I'd like to have a quick shower, I'm very oily from the beach.' She left him lying on the bed, his baggy shorts pulled taut in anticipation.

Under a stream of hot water Lucille lathered her body which glistened with health and sunshine. She surveyed her flat stomach, her strong legs, her brown hands, and she found herself thinking of Graham. He had become unimaginably wasted and grey while he died, utterly unlike the person who had shared her obsession with looks. Lucille thought about the man in the other room and how Graham would have hooted in appreciation of his body when she described it. Then she realised that she could not remember, or perhaps did not know, the man's name. She stuck her wet head between the shower curtains and shouted, 'Hey, what did you say your name was?'

'Graham,' came the reply.

'Oh Jesus,' thought Lucille, 'I wish I'd never asked.' She stuck her head back under the shower and scrubbed her body with renewed vigour.

A Mother's Advice

Lucille's mother had married young and expected her daughter to do the same. Throughout her girlhood Lucille had had advice dispensed to her from the kitchen sink. The washing-up seemed to make her mother philosophical.

'Lucille,' she would say, 'men like their wives fresh and neat and pure. Young women seem so quick to hop into bed with every dumb sod who comes along these days – it can only be bad news. You lose your self-esteem as well as your reputation Lucille, they love you and then leave you with nothing. What you want is a good man who'll take care of you.'

Lucille would continue drying the dishes. At the age of eight she listened closely to her mother; she listened quite carefully at nine as well. At ten she half-listened, just in case anything new was said. She tried to get her mum to talk about sex when she was eleven but all she heard was some mumbo-jumbo about marriage and babies, and so by the time she was twelve she stopped listening altogether. By the age of sixteen she was more sexually experienced than her mother would ever be. Promiscuity brought Lucille release from a life she thought was otherwise mundane.

Eventually she came out of the shower wrapped in towels and went back into the bedroom where Graham was lying in the same position, as handsome, available and excited as ever.

'Sorry I took so long but baby oil makes dirt really stick to my body,' she said, by way of an excuse.

'That's OK,' he said, 'I don't mind waiting.' He smiled and asked, 'Where do you keep that baby oil?' and Lucille felt herself melting back into her old routine.

'Keep sinning,' was what she used to say to Graham when they parted, 'Keep sinning and keep your pecker up.' It never failed to make him laugh.

Lucille dropped her towels and lay down on the bed beside Graham and, although she could not bring herself to call him by name, she proceeded to become intimate with his body. He seemed to want to lick every conceivable part of her so she lay on her back and stared into space.

He had not asked about birth control – but they never did. The assumption was that a woman so intent on having sex with complete strangers would have taken care of that. They were, of course, correct. As always, her body responded famously but her mind wandered far away from the slightly seedy Costa Brava hotel room. She stared out of the window at the neon sign. 'Octopussy Disco' flashed over and over again.

Lucille remembered how before Graham had become seriously ill he had spent a couple of months being angry. Once when they met he said to her, 'I never thought it would happen to me, I mean, I'm just too much of a golden boy for this. Too brassy, too fast, too strong. I always thought it was just another part of the great right-wing conspiracy, you know, like the weather and unemployment. They wanted us to give up and come home, to stop having so much fun. I thought it was just a threat, the kind my mother would have used to make me behave.' At the time Lucille had nodded and poured Graham another drink. They had both taken great pleasure in such defiance of the doctor's advice. Until Graham realised he was going to die he had gone out of his way to be naughty, although he had managed to give up sex pretty quickly. 'I'm not that thick-skinned,' he'd said to Lucille during one of his weaker moments.

Lucille's thoughts were interrupted by the other Graham.

'Do you mind if I pour some more of this oil on your body?' he asked.

'No,' said Lucille absently, as if he'd requested another slice of cake. 'Go right ahead.'

Graham had never offered Lucille any advice or become at all sentimental during his decline. He had never said, 'If this can happen to me it can happen to you,' although from time to time when she had tried to entertain him with stories about her social life she thought that she spotted a shadow of admonishment in his eyes. The fact was that while Graham was dying Lucille started seeing even more men. She felt as though she had to do it for Graham as well as herself, to prove to them both that it was not the sex that was killing him, it was something else. Having always thought of herself as way ahead of the crowd, she could not quite believe that promiscuity had so quickly become a thing of the past. 'Still plenty of victims around to be had,' she said to him with bleak irony.

But Graham did not say anything to Lucille; it would have broken their unspoken pact, although she now found herself wishing he had. He had probably thought that she would accuse him of turning into her mother, but she would not. Her mother had told her, repeatedly, that pre-marital sex would lead to grief, but the threat it held for her mother was very different from that now threatening Lucille.

'I always thought my greatest fear was the nuclear bomb,' Graham had said. 'I never thought I'd become a sort of nuclear bomb of my own.' Lucille had laughed loudly when he'd said that, and a nurse had popped her head through the door disapprovingly. Graham had laughed as well but when they stopped their expressions were grim.

'You're not a nuclear bomb,' said Lucille. 'You're just ill.'

Once again, the stranger forced Lucille away from her thoughts. He had climbed on top of her and was sliding around in the oil spread all over her body, attempting to push his way between her legs. Lucille held them clamped together, almost instinctively.

'Hey,' said Graham, 'What are you doing?'

'Oh nothing,' said Lucille, relaxing. 'I was just thinking about my mother.'

'Your mother?' he said, breathing heavily.

'Yes,' she said slowly, 'my mother thinks it's the wrath of God and that we had it coming to us. A girl's got to keep her reputation intact or God only knows what will become of her. Mother will be able to say that she told us so, she knew it would happen all along. But mother,' said Lucille, pausing, 'she got it all wrong.'

'What are you talking about?' Graham whispered in Lucille's ear.

'Morality,' replied Lucille, 'my mother's ill advice.'

The Micro-Political Party

I REMEMBER WHEN politics were real, when men were men and women were feminists, and everybody read semiotics and understood what it meant. Times are different now: none of the old ways exist any longer. Nothing ever happens these days and no one searches for meaning any more. No more leaping naked through the frangipani of rhetoric. Life has become very dull.

I remember when, before politics were made illegal, life was rich with contradiction and dilemma. Everybody had something to be cross about. Now, no one is angry. We are all happy consumers. We all have lots of clothes and get new haircuts as often as we want. If I am feeling unhappy I can go out and buy myself some new shoes, anytime I so desire. We have Style and the authorities say that is enough for anyone. We have more Style than any other nation in the entire world and, the authorities say, that is something of which to be truly proud. Looking good can solve any kind of problem. The economy chugs along, the people are satisfied. We all have plenty of Style and Style is plenty for us.

I remember the old days though, before the Style Party took over in a bloodless designer coup, when everything meant something different to what it does today. In fact I remember, for I am very old, when Roland Barthes was not the brand name of an extremely popular type of bluejean. I cannot, however, remember who or what Roland Barthes actually was. Still, it is enough for now to know that Roland Barthes bluejeans are not what they seem.

I have my doubts though. Perhaps my memory is tricking me into investing more faith than is due to foggy notions of meaning. I was a child at the time of the coup and no one ever speaks of that distant past. I have flashes of memory and it is these that disturb me and lead my thoughts away from Style and on to meaning, even though I know it is quite futile. I remember my mother before she disappeared. She would stand in the kitchen weeping into the washing-up, and singing to herself,

'Where, oh where, have my politics gone? Oh where is my Party today, today?' I would hide beneath her skirt, holding on to her legs, and feel her tremble with frustration and sadness. She would mumble and mutter for hours. 'Politics are gone. The Party is over. Everything is meaningless. Nothing is permitted.' I did not understand this as a child and I do not understand it now. All I know is that there is something about Roland Barthes bluejeans that makes me very uncomfortable and it is not the way that they are cut.

But now I am not so alone. I have met others like me. None as old or with such definite memories but others who have a vague feeling that all is not as it appears. We meet in secret, late on Friday nights, in a derelict warehouse near the river. We sit around and drink wine out of the bottle and make disparaging comments about Life. Sometimes we dance and sometimes, after several bottles, we sing the songs from my childhood, tunes I can remember that were played on the radio before the coup. We sing, 'Ooo-ooo, ooo-yeah, Holiday', and we feel like true revolutionaries, although the supposed religious connotations of this song are beyond us.

We know that we are doing something illegal, outlawed and Unstylish, the ultimate in anti-social crimes. We know that what we do on Friday nights, from late until much, much later, is form a Party. We know that drinking from late until later is somehow political. I know, because my mother went to the Party, and spoke of the Party. She adorned herself with jewels and smeared bright red lipstick across her lips and went to the Party. I know the Party welcomed her because I remember how she sang and spoke of politics and what the Party meant to her. When we gather together on Friday night, wearing our most Stylish clothes, and drinking ourselves into oblivion, we have made a Party and no one can take that away from us. Except the authorities, of course.

So, we continue dodging our *Face* reading seminars, to meet, drink, dance, and attempt to talk about all sorts of things. We find conversation extremely difficult. Our lives are so narrow and so completely concerned with Style that we are virtually incapable of general discussion and only barely able to manage small talk. But we try, and on a tiny level, we succeed. We are engaging in micro-politics. Ours is the Micro-Political Party. Our motto is 'Revolution is Chic'. We know one day we will be able to throw off the chains of Style and burn our Roland Barthes bluejeans. In the meantime, Friday nights will help us stay calm.

A Brief But Electrical Storm

FOR NO APPARENT reason whatsoever Clare Smith suffered from intermittent, but chronic, depression. Every once in a while she would feel tempted to cut short her days with some self-destructive act – not suicide or anything as dramatic as that but something that would lose her her job or, worse yet, her friends. She would wake up, very suddenly, and feel a desperate need to cry, wail and maybe even moan. And that is what she would do, without hesitation, all the while wondering why.

'I am a happy woman,' she would say to her friends, 'I lead a happy life. I have a good job where I work with good people. My social life is rewarding and I feel involved with the community in which I live. I like my life and my friends. I am,' she'd conclude heartily, 'a happy woman.'

But every couple of months Clare woke up in the middle of the night and felt full of despair, anger, and grief. Often she spent several days feeling this way. Unable to work she cancelled all social engagements and sat at home in her room, drinking endless cups of tea and weeping. Or she continued with her usual routine but at work and socially she was, generally speaking, a misery.

'Oh Clare!' her friends would say, exasperated. 'Whatever is wrong with you today?'

'I don't know,' she wailed. 'If I knew I probably wouldn't feel like this.'

'Here,' they would say patiently, 'have another drink.'

'Haven't you ever been struck down with grief in the middle of an ordinary week for no apparent reason?' Clare asked hopefully.

'No,' they replied in unison. 'Not me.' And Clare would wander home by herself, wiping her nose and eyes and marvelling at the extraordinary equilibrium her friends all seemed so adept at maintaining. A few days later all of this had passed and she would feel happy and healthy again, having almost forgotten her previous mood. And yet, while Clare forgot, her friends did not and there remained in the backs of their minds a small bit of worry left over from Clare's last bout. 'Will she or won't she?' they thought to themselves.

In between these dark moods Clare sailed through her life like a ship in smooth and sparkling water on a clear day. In fact, there was a time when she went for almost a year without encountering a single storm. Her life was so even-keeled that she had almost completely forgotten what it was like to feel even a tiny bit depressed. She became the most solidly happy person that anybody knew. Some people found it alarming, she was so perpetually cheerful and lively. In fact most people like a bit of darkness here or there and are unnerved by too much happiness. Almost all personalities have a *memento mori* embedded somewhere within.

And then late one night after having been the life

and soul of a party, Clare woke up suddenly. She sat up with a start. At the foot of her bed stood The Reaper. Clare blinked and when she opened her eyes, it was gone. Her window was open and the curtain billowed out into the room. It was raining heavily outside, a hot summer rain, heavy and portentous. The air was thick and a moment later Clare's room was lit up as lightning flashed nearby. In that flash Clare saw that her room was empty. Darkness fell again and Clare sank back on to her pillows, overwhelmed with sadness. She felt as though her heart had just been broken. She felt as though someone very near to her had just died.

Clare lay on her bed feeling numb and unable to think clearly. She looked up at her ceiling while the ills of the world washed over her as the sea washes over a shipwreck. As she stared up at the plaster swirls and cobwebs the ceiling began to change shape. Soon she thought she could make out a relief map of the world and a moment later the countries all began to glow brightly, half of them red, half of them green. The sea shone an intense blue as if it was about to boil. She stared up with horror until lightning flashed again and, in an instant, the ceiling was covered with familiar and ordinary plaster swirls. Her room fell dark, all that was left was the sound of the rain splashing down, and the rustling noise of her curtain as it fluttered and undulated in the wind.

Clare's heart was beating at a frantic pace. 'What is happening to me?' she thought to herself. She lay on her bed, on top of the covers, as the breeze sent her papers skittering around the room and opened and closed the books she had beside her bed. She stayed like that all night. When the sky began to lighten near dawn, the wind died down, the rain slowed to a shower, and the air no longer felt full of electricity. As the sun came up Clare dozed off to sleep, waking an hour or so later when her alarm went off. At the sound of the bell, she opened her eyes, looking first to the foot of the bed and then up at the ceiling. She felt slightly calmer although very tired. As the smell of the coffee brewing in her automatic coffee machine wafted into the room she sniffed and, with a shock, felt tears run down her face. Turning over, she buried her head in the pillow and began to cry. She cried and cried while the coffee burbled cheerfully in the next room and when she heard its alarm go she wiped her face on the back of her pyjama sleeve and went into the kitchen.

Everything looked just as it had the night before. Clare poured herself a cup of coffee and sat at the kitchen table and wept. Tears rolled off her face and on to her pyjamas while she sipped the coffee. In the shower her tears mixed with the hot stream of water. After drying herself and getting dressed, she went down the stairs and out on to the street which had that after-rain freshness which usually made her feel so clean and light-headed. Dragging herself to work, Clare sat at her desk feeling weak and miserable. Her colleagues settled in around her, shuffling their papers and blowing their noses. Gerry, the office jerk, said out loud to no one in particular, 'That was quite a storm we had last night. Was anyone awake for it? I sat up and watched. It seemed right over the city.' Everyone in the office nodded without looking up from their papers and cups of tea. 'My mother says that storms like that, electrical storms, are God's reckoning, um, God's way of expressing his displeasure with the way we are running our lives. She thinks it has something to do with the decline of law and order in our society. God doesn't like it.'

'Do you mean, Gerry,' said Greg, the office smart-ass, 'that God thinks there should be a greater police presence on the streets?' Greg snickered cynically, looking back down at his work.

'Well, yes, I guess so,' Gerry said nodding and smiling.

'I always thought that if God was a human he'd be Metropolitan Chief of Police,' Greg replied without looking up again. Everyone else in the office shifted uncomfortably in their seats.

Clare could feel her face blushing red. She stood and walked quickly to the ladies' room, where she went into a cubicle, locked the door, sat on the seat and began to cry. She cried so hard that by the time ten minutes had passed she had made herself sick. Despite not having eaten she threw up several times. She knelt on the floor in front of the toilet and watched the tears fall from her face into the basin. She felt unbearably desolate.

After about half an hour one of her co-workers came into the ladies' room and, hearing Clare in a cubicle, banged on the door.

'Clare, is that you? I thought maybe you'd gone off to do some shopping or something. Are you all right?'

'No,' Clare sobbed. That was all she could manage.

'Jesus,' said Susan, 'you sound ill. What's wrong?' Clare moaned. 'Just a minute,' Susan said with concern,

'Just wait while I pee and then I'll get you out of here. We'll put you in a cab and send you home.' A few minutes later Susan's face appeared under the locked door of the cubicle. 'OK sweetie, will you unlock the door?' Clare attempted to lift her hand to the lock but couldn't do it, so Susan crawled under the door.

'Jesus Christ, Clare, you look awful!' she exclaimed. Standing up and pulling Clare with her, she unlocked the door and dragged Clare over to the sink. She splashed her face with cool water and then dried her with a paper hand-towel. It felt rough on Clare's tear-streaked skin and that made her want to cry even harder. 'Come on baby,' Susan said patiently, 'I'll take you home.'

Within an hour Clare was tucked up in her bed with a hot water bottle, a box of tissues, a coldpack on her forehead and the radio on. Susan had made Clare a cup of tea and some toast which she watched her eat before going back to work. Clare listened to Susan's footsteps recede down the stairs outside her flat. She watched the steam from the cup of tea curl up into the air. And then she fell asleep, a deep and dreamless sleep that carried her without emotion into the next day.

When Clare woke up in the morning to the sound of her ever faithful alarm she felt groggy and her eyes were swollen. She could smell the coffee as she went into the bathroom. Shocked by the way her face looked in the mirror she got into the shower and let the hot water massage her body, washing the salt away from her skin. When she had dried herself she combed her hair slowly and thought about the previous two nights and the day wedged between them. Clare felt puzzled. She couldn't quite remember what had happened. She went into her bedroom and put on a dress, thinking hard all the while. Speaking out loud to herself in the mirror she said,

'I went to work, didn't I? There'd been a storm. A nightmare? I was ill. I felt a bit depressed, energyless, anxious. Living in the city is bad for my health.' As hard as she tried, she could not recall much about that night but she felt more relieved than worried. It was as though something was preventing her from remembering; her mind went a certain distance back in time and then stopped, as if facing a wall.

Clare went to work and when Susan asked her about the previous day's drama she found herself saying,

'I saw the Apocalypse late that night and it made me feel ill,' but before those words had time to register with Susan, Clare corrected herself and said,

'It must have been something I ate.' But no one, including Susan, believed her.

Acknowledgements

Stories in this collection were previously published in *Tiny Lies* (Picador 1988) and *My Life as a Girl in a Men's Prison* (Phoenix 1997). Versions of the following stories have appeared in anthologies:

'A Serious Arteriopath', *Body Parts*, Brindle and Glass, forthcoming in 2012

'Public Image Ltd', *Punk Fiction*, Anova Books, 2009

'Heaven Knows I'm Miserable Now', *Paint a Vulgar Picture: Fiction Inspired by The Smiths*, Serpent's Tail, 2009

'In Lieu of Parenting', *Is This What You Want?: The Asham Award Short-Story Collection*, Bloomsbury, 2007

'At Home with George Clooney and Jodie Foster', *The Mechanic's Institute Review*, no. 3, Birkbeck College, 2006

'Fur Coats', *Harlot Red: Prize Winning Stories by Women*, Serpent's Tail, 2002

'Forcibly Bewitched' and 'Charlie', *Forcibly Bewitched*, 1996

'My Mother, My Father, and Me', *How Maxine Learned to Love Her Legs*, Aurora, Metro, 1995

'Dear All', *Bad Sex*, Serpent's Tail, 1993

Acknowledgements

'A Kind of Desired Invasion', *So Very English*, Serpent's Tail, 1993

'My Life as a Girl in a Men's Prison', *Smoke Signals*, Serpent's Tail, 1993

'A Modern Gothic Morality Tale', *Sex and the City*, Serpent's Tail, 1990

'Celia and the Bicycle', *Storia 1*, Pandora, 1988

'The First Mistake', *The Fiction Magazine*, 1987

'Franz Kafka's Shirt', *New Statesman*, 1986

'The Fact-Finding Mission', *Emergency*, 1986

'The Micro-Political Party', *City Limits*, 1986

'The Battersea Power Station', *Emergency*, 1985